Published by Acoustical Books, LLC

KenLozito.com

Cover design by Tom Edwards

IF YOU WOULD LIKE TO BE NOTIFIED WHEN MY NEXT BOOK IS RELEASED VISIT

WWW.KENLOZITO.COM

Paperback ISBN: 978-1-945223-71-6

Hardback ISBN: 978-1-945223-70-9

FALLEN EARTH

KEN LOZITO

ACOUSTICAL BOOKS LLC

1

ETHAN SAT in a small transport shuttle that had just left Earth's atmosphere. A message chimed on his wrist computer, and he glanced at it.

Do what you must—Cynergy.

The cold words appeared in amber lettering amid a small text bubble on his personal holoscreen. He began to enter a reply but kept deleting the words. Nothing he could write was going to console her. After three months of waiting, his recall orders had come, and they hadn't given him much time to report in.

A video comlink appeared on his holoscreen, and he acknowledged it.

Lieutenant Anton Stone smiled at him and let out a hearty grin. "My man! Tell me you're finally getting off your sorry ass and back in the pilot's seat where you belong."

Ethan winced a little and nearly rolled his eyes. "I am, but not with the 7th. Not yet."

He and Anton had gone through elite fighter training together to pilot the Talon V Stinger Class space fighters. They were the tip of the spear, and they'd been assigned to the 7th A-Wing that had been attached to the expeditionary force from New Earth. The Colonial Defense Force had sent a powerful battle group to Earth, using FTL for the first time and traveling sixty light years to investigate what had happened to Old Earth.

Anton frowned, looking confused, and leaned toward the camera. "Come again?"

Ethan glanced around, not wanting the other people on the transport shuttle to hear his conversation. "I'm not active on the 7th. My orders are for me to report to the lunar staging area for combat shuttle duty."

Anton blinked. "Combat shuttle duty," he repeated with a frown.

Ethan heaved a sigh. "I know. Believe me, I know. After three months sitting on the bench, they assigned me to something any rookie pilot straight out of flight school can handle."

Anton regarded him for a moment, raking his teeth over his bottom lip for a second. He looked as if he was reconciling two diametrically opposed ideas. Then he shrugged. "They're easing you back in, that's all."

A flash of annoyance made him grit his teeth for a second. "There's easing you back in, and then there's the obvious thing that says they don't know what to do with you."

His friend arched an eyebrow. "Well, you've changed a lot."

Ethan blinked.

Ever since Cynergy had changed him into a Vemus hybrid, he'd been poked and prodded like some kind of lab rat. He thought he'd be sidelined for a few weeks while he was monitored, enduring all manner of evaluations to ensure he was still the same. Physically he wasn't. He was stronger and had superior recovery capabilities. He could also think quicker. He'd always been able to think on his feet, but his abilities had increased. Becoming a hybrid had been a blessing, with the exception of a few minor incidents.

Anton cleared his throat and Ethan looked at him. "You brood more now. You're kinda whiny, and you've got a rather large chip on your shoulder, Lieutenant Gates. That kind of conduct is unbecoming in an officer of the CDF. We're to uphold a higher standard in our soldiers."

Ethan smiled with half his mouth and chuckled. "Are you quoting directly from the recruitment memos now?"

"I have them memorized."

"I bet you do."

"So, you're flying combat shuttles now. I guess they're not ready to take the training wheels off just yet."

Ethan shook his head a little. "It doesn't make any sense. I've passed every psych eval they've thrown at me. They have no reason to keep me on standby for so damn long."

Anton cocked his head to the side. "Except the obvious one."

Ethan stared at his friend, and they regarded each other for a long moment. "Yeah," he sighed.

Anton smiled a little. "It could always be worse. You could be stuck on a shuttle with Massey."

Ethan snorted. "Still a talker?"

"Never shuts up. I've had to mute his comlink a half dozen times since you've been gone."

Ethan's eyebrows raised. "You've got to stop him at the beginning before he builds up momentum. That's how I used to manage him."

Anton rolled his eyes. "It makes for some entertainment."

"Is that so? Where do they have you now?"

"Recon and escort duty throughout the star system. They've been keeping us busy. We've got a long deployment near Neptune."

Ethan pinched his lips together for a second. "It's almost as if they want you as far from Earth as possible."

Anton shook his head, chuckling. "You're not that important. Now don't get all high and mighty, thinking that the brass deploys us just so they can keep you away from us. You're important, but you're not that important. I mean, they've got me after all."

Despite evidence to the contrary, because Ethan's father was a general in the CDF there were some who expected that his family connections would give him preferential treatment. The people who believed that had absolutely no idea who his father really was. Ethan would rather walk away from the CDF altogether than suffer the humiliation of asking his father to make things easier for him. He'd rise through the ranks based on his own merit or not at all. But he'd always know the truth in his heart—that his father would never compromise his own integrity in such a way.

Ethan narrowed his gaze playfully. "And Massey?"

Anton frowned in surprise and then laughed uproariously. He quickly lowered his voice after several people off-screen were heard asking him to quiet down.

"Nothing wrong with that wit of yours."

Ethan tipped his head to the side. "You should see me with a rifle these days."

Anton raised his eyebrows. "Oh yeah?"

He nodded. "I'd qualify for sniper school now if I wanted to," he said, thinking of his Uncle Sean, who held quite a few achievements with a sniper rifle, and that was before becoming the foremost expert in space combat.

"So that's how you're spending your time? At the range?" Anton asked.

"That and running a few obstacle courses. Training with Clip and the other hybrids. Mostly PT," Ethan said.

He was downplaying it. The training had been rigorous. Clip was determined to get him to push his limits, which was nothing new to Ethan.

Anton gave him an appraising look and Ethan frowned.

"What?" he asked.

Anton shook his head quickly. "It's nothing. Just…nothing. I bet that went over well."

"Well, they couldn't lock me up."

"No, they wouldn't. So, when did you get recalled?"

"About two hours ago."

Anton blinked and tipped his head to the side. "Did you say two hours?"

Ethan nodded. "Barely enough time to make it to the departing transport."

Anton pursed his lips. "You know how it goes. Hurry up and wait, which then becomes go, go, go!"

Ethan smiled. "Yeah, it's got all the hallmarks of something put together at the last minute."

He shrugged. "We go where they order us to go. It's gotta beat being grounded."

Ethan hesitated and Anton gave him a knowing look. "You haven't been gone long enough to miss her yet. How'd she take the news?"

The text message he'd gotten from Cynergy came to his mind. "She's surprised."

Anton snorted. "Heh, she took it *that* well, did she?"

Cynergy had certain ideas about their future. "She'll be fine."

Anton nodded slowly, and there was something irritating about it.

"She will," Ethan insisted.

He held up his hands. "Look, you don't need to explain anything to me."

Anton knew about his relationship with Cynergy and how she'd saved his life by making him into a hybrid. She'd risked dying herself to save him, and in doing so had forged a bond between them. What had started out as mere attraction had become something more, and he sometimes wasn't sure what he was supposed to do. When his recall orders came, he didn't hesitate. It had felt right at the time—barely a few hours ago—but now he hesitated, wondering if he'd done the right thing.

The lull in the conversation dragged on for a few moments, and Ethan scratched his forehead.

"Look Ethan, I'm speaking as your friend here, okay?" Ethan nodded, and Anton continued. "You're in uncharted territory with what's happened to you. It's going to take time, and you have to face the possibility that you might never get back to the 7th."

"Is this your version of a pep talk?"

Anton shrugged. "I could just lie to you, tell you some crap like, 'Yeah, you'll be back here.' Just do this mission and don't give them an excuse to ground you."

"But you decided to be my friend," Ethan said.

Anton nodded.

"What if I don't want to be friends anymore?"

He chuckled and waved away the comment.

Ethan grinned. "I appreciate it."

Anton became serious. "You know I'll always have your back no matter what happens. Even if you start sprouting tentacles or any of that other crazy stuff people think hybrids are."

"Thanks for that, Anton. Appreciate it," Ethan replied dryly.

He leaned toward the camera. "Do you have any?"

Ethan frowned. "Huh?"

"Tentacles, man. Spikes, horns, anything like that?"

"Oh yeah. Do you want to see them? It's crazy. I just gotta do this," Ethan said and gave his friend the royal salute.

Anton laughed, slapping the table, and a small chorus of shushing came from around him. He quickly mumbled a few apologies and turned back to the camera.

"My time is just about up, and I need to report to preflight," Anton said and eyed him for a moment. "You remember those?"

Ethan considered it for a second. "Let me guess, it's Vijura doing the briefing."

Anton nodded. "The one and only. He hasn't lost his knack for a dry and no-nonsense briefing."

"Could be worse. Imagine if Massey was running the briefing. You might never get out of there."

Anton laughed as he stood up and crouched toward the camera. "They're kicking me out. Take care of yourself, Ethan."

He smiled. "You too, Anton. Say hello to the others for me."

"I will. Expect Massey to contact you soon."

The comlink severed and Ethan lowered his arm as whispers of a grin appeared on his face. He missed his old squad. They'd trained and served together for almost two years. He'd known that eventually they'd separate and be reassigned, but they would always share a bond. They'd fought together, and they'd watched pilots they knew die in battle. It was one thing to train for combat, but it was quite another to come face-to-face with it. Nothing could prepare you, and he knew he'd never be the same. None of them would.

Ethan returned his attention to the shuttle as it approached the landing zone inside a somewhat newly constructed operating base on the lunar surface—a hollowed-out crater wall near the bottom. Ethan saw evidence of a previous installation nearby, but it had to have been hundreds of years old.

Sometimes it was better to remove and rebuild rather than reuse.

As he exited the shuttle, a warning flashed on his internal heads-up display. He quickened his pace, making his way across the hangar, and entered an automated tram.

After using his implants to send his credentials and military identification, he was then able to input his destination. The tram quickly sped away from the hangar and brought him to another part of the base. Ethan used the time to acknowledge receipt of the message, but as soon as he did, another warning message flashed on his HUD.

The message was from Captain Chip Waller, and it contained updated coordinates. He'd only received his orders a few hours ago, and they kept changing his destination. He was going to be late.

The tram doors opened, and Ethan sprinted out of it, his kit bobbing against his back as he ran. More than a few people looked over at him as he hurried past them, so he eased his pace a little. When he exerted himself, his hybrid markings appeared on his skin. His flight suit covered most of him, but the markings also appeared on his face. It made people stare at him, so he concealed it as much as he could. Cynergy assured him that he could eventually do it without thinking about it, and she'd been right. It had become easier, but sometimes he lapsed, and people began to stare at him again.

Ethan spotted Captain Waller near a row of combat shuttles. There were several CDF platoons nearby, and Ethan looked at the operation. He didn't know anything about what he was going to be doing, other than flying one of the shuttles.

Captain Waller's beady eyes focused on the holoscreen in front of his square-jawed face with its small round nose. The man on the holoscreen was older, and scowling. Ethan stood a short distance behind and waited.

"Understood, Major. We'll be able to make up the time en route," Captain Waller said.

A name appeared on Ethan's HUD that identified the man on the holoscreen as Major James Racine.

"Last-minute changes are happening all the time, but this one is something I tried to offload. I was overruled. Now *you* get to deal with it."

"Understood. Is there anything else I need to know, Major?"

Major Racine looked right at Ethan, recognizing him. "Your new pilot has arrived, Captain. Get him briefed and I'll expect a mission eval when finished."

Captain Waller saluted his superior officer and the holoscreen shut off. He turned toward Ethan and gave him a once-over.

They'd been talking about him, and Waller was as enthusiastic about Ethan's assignment as he was.

"Lieutenant Ethan Gates, reporting for duty, Captain," he said and saluted.

Captain Waller returned the salute. "At ease, Lieutenant," he said and just looked at him for a moment. "You're a long way from a Talon V jockey. When was the last time you've flown one of these?" he asked, gesturing toward the combat shuttle.

"I've maintained my flight status on the Eagle, but it's been over eight months since I've flown one, sir."

Captain Waller gave Ethan another once-over, looking as if he was searching for something to warrant his disapproval. Ethan calmly waited, not seeking to fill up the time by speaking out of turn. Waller must know about him and was trying to decide whether he was going to clear him for duty.

"You're late, Lieutenant."

"I apologize, sir. I just received my orders less than three hours ago and came on the next available transport shuttle."

Captain Waller considered this for a moment, as if going through some mental checklist. Nothing like a warm welcome.

"I can fly that shuttle anywhere you need me to, Captain."

He sighed. "Your record indicates as much, but that was before… Well, you know."

"Sir, I've passed every kind of evaluation that's been sent my way. I can assure you it won't be a problem."

He'd almost said "his condition" and silently chided himself. He didn't have a condition, and since he was setting the status quo, he didn't want to establish his being a Vemus hybrid as detrimental to being able to perform his duty.

"This isn't a permanent assignment, Lieutenant Gates. It's temporary. I want to be clear on that."

"Yes, sir."

Captain Waller's gaze hardened. "I'm going to lay my cards out on the table, just so there's no misunderstanding. If I get the sense that your new…" He looked at Ethan as if he wanted him to supply the word. Ethan remained quiet. "Whatever. If you do anything to compromise the safety of anyone under my command, I will throw the book at you. I will not hesitate. Is that understood?"

"Crystal clear, sir."

Waller eyed him for a moment. He might have been hoping to exact some kind of response from him, and Ethan wasn't about to give him any ammunition.

He heaved a sigh and gestured for Ethan to walk with him.

"Mission brief is that you'll be flying a shuttle with a CDF recon platoon. You'll be transporting them to evaluate the salvageability of key assets necessary for rebuilding efforts on Mars."

Ethan frowned a little. "I thought the Martian colonies were among the first to fall during the Vemus Wars, sir."

He'd done more than a little bit of research on the Vemus Wars while the expeditionary force was journeying to Earth, and he knew the history backwards and forwards.

Captain Waller's eyebrow twitched in what might have been acknowledgement. "That's what we thought, but recent surveys have found key installations that might be worth salvaging. However, there is a strong indication that there are remnant Vemus forces in those areas. You'll be part of the recon mission to evaluate whether any of those sites are worth trying to salvage." He stopped and gestured ahead. "Report to Lieutenant Hayman. You'll be piloting for him."

"Yes, sir," Ethan said and began walking ahead. He stopped and turned around. Captain Waller watched him. "Sir, I just wanted to thank you for the opportunity to serve."

Ethan didn't wait for a reply and wasn't sure if he'd have gotten one if he had. It was better to just make the statement and then move on. Waller didn't want him here, but he was following orders just like they all had to.

Ethan found Lieutenant Dexter Hayman overseeing the loading of equipment onto the combat shuttle. Hayman had dark skin, a pronounced brow, and a thick mustache.

"My pilot is finally here," Hayman said.

Ethan stopped in front of him and gave him a salute. They were of equal rank, but Hayman was the mission commander.

Hayman regarded him for a second. "What'd you do to get assigned to me?"

Ethan smiled. "Just lucky, I guess."

Hayman chuckled. "Or you drew the short straw." He scratched his eyebrow and waved away the comment. "Yeah, I don't care about any of that stuff. All I need from you is to ensure that this lovely piece of fine CDF machinery is flightworthy enough for the mission. Take care of that and we'll get along fine. I'm transferring authorization for the shuttle's systems now."

Ethan's wrist computer vibrated upon receipt of his new authorization. "Received, sir."

Hayman nodded. "Good, now get to work. We leave in thirty."

Thirty minutes was cutting it close to perform preflight checks and an inspection on a bird he'd never flown before, but he'd get the job done. He brought up his checklist and started making his way through it, one at a time.

2

THE CALM WATERS of the lake shimmered under the midmorning sun. A warm breeze lifted Lauren's hair, and she closed her eyes, raising her face to the sky. She cracked open one eye and spotted Amelia mimicking her.

The little girl had just celebrated her ninth birthday. She had long, dark hair and pale skin. Faint patterns were slightly visible on her skin. They became darker as Amelia inhaled a deep breath, holding it for a few seconds, then releasing it in a long, calming exhale.

Amelia, like her mother, was a Vemus hybrid whose ancestors had somehow survived the Vemus contagion. Hybrids could be found on Earth and among the space stations of the solar system. Now that the ancient orbital platforms that had once quarantined Earth had been destroyed, the planet was open for refugees to return. No longer would they need to survive on space stations, asteroids, or any number of repurposed ships that had long since passed their expiration date. All were getting a much-needed fresh start. Lauren just wished they hadn't brought some of their biases with them.

Amelia glanced up at Lauren and smiled. An adorable little dimple appeared as if by magic on her cheek.

Lauren grinned. "What do you say, peanut? Are you ready to learn how to swim?"

She lifted her chin, leaned toward Lauren, and whispered. "I already know how to swim."

"Is that so?"

She nodded. "My papa taught me last night. I can swim across the lake and back."

Lauren's eyes widened a little, though she shouldn't be surprised. Hybrids had unique capabilities that presented as adaptations. Some of the hybrids had an affinity toward things like swimming, but it wasn't long ago that Amelia's hybrid nature had almost killed her. She's been covered with dense skin patches and had severe scoliosis that couldn't be cured with the medical treatment available on the space station where she'd lived. Lauren had treated Amelia's symptoms, which in essence both cured her and helped train her system to keep her healthy. Her rate of recovery, especially with the curvature of her spine, had been remarkable. Amelia was now a young, vibrant girl bursting with life, and her hybrid nature was something she embraced instead of endured.

"I'm not supposed to tell anyone," Amelia whispered.

Other children began running into the lake. Both human and hybrid alike frolicked in the warm waters, splashing and playing.

Hybrids, when they invoked their abilities, caused their appearance to change. The intricate patterns on their skin darkened, as did their skin tone, becoming almost black with a purplish hue. Several hybrids dove off a floating platform and disappeared under the water, only to resurface a full five minutes later, hundreds of meters away. They waved back toward shore.

Many people from the nearby settlement visited the lake, and several schools had taken it upon themselves to give swimming lessons to the refugees. Earthers were much more tolerant of hybrids than spacers had been. A bloody history existed between the spacers and their struggle for survival among the solar system that had been ravaged by the Vemus. Hybrids had been viewed as a threat to humans and were exiled or killed. Spacers believed that hybrids were somehow stuck, pausing the process that prevented them from becoming a full Vemus. There were historical records that indicated that these things did happen, and lives had been lost. However, it had been so long since those events that Lauren didn't think the risk of it repeating was likely. The hybrids of today were descendants. None of them had become an actual Vemus, but the old prejudices endured. She tried to remain objective, but her brother becoming a hybrid made her more than a little concerned. Many hybrids had serious health issues that seemingly developed without cause. The only way to be prepared and save lives was to study the survivors, both the humans and the hybrids.

One of the instructors began calling the children over for lessons.

Amelia looked longingly toward the lake.

"You better get moving," Lauren said. Amelia stared up at her. "You never know what you'll learn, and never assume you already know everything. You got it, peanut?"

Amelia smiled and gave Lauren a sideways hug before running over to the other children.

Braun walked over and nodded in greeting.

"I heard you've been giving swim lessons."

He nodded. "It was necessary."

Lauren frowned. "Necessary?"

"Yes, she was having a growth spurt. When they happen, it's better to explore them so the adaptations that are presenting can be mastered."

"And Amelia's had to do with swimming?"

Braun glanced toward his daughter. She sat on the ground with the other kids while the instructor was speaking to them.

"Evidently. She's able to expand the skin between her fingers and toes, and I'm convinced that her hands and feet are larger than they were yesterday. She can swim extremely fast," Braun said and lifted his chin toward the water. Several of the older hybrid youths were swimming toward the shore. "She can swim circles around them."

Lauren frowned in thought, and Braun eyed her. "What's the matter?"

"I'm just concerned that the onset of changes happened so quickly. What would have happened if you hadn't brought her to the lake last night?"

Braun considered it for a few moments. "I'm not sure. Possibly nothing or maybe a lot of pain." He pressed his lips together and gave her a long look. "Before you came along, our days with Amelia were numbered. We'd seen it before with other families."

Lauren's eyes tightened. She's treated many patients over her short career, but there were always those who wound their way into her heart. Amelia was like that. She was very attached to her.

"I'm just glad I could help, but the sudden changes worry me."

Braun nodded. "Me, too. It's like that with us, though."

"Now that there are more of you together, we can record

others' experiences and come up with better information and treatment plans."

Braun's expression became guarded. "Be careful who you say that to."

Lauren frowned. "You have to know I'd never do anything to hurt you or any other hybrid."

Braun smiled a little. "Of course, I do, but you know the history. The experiments. The distrust. We won't go back to that."

"Nor should you, but that doesn't mean we simply do nothing. There has to be a middle ground where we're able to study exactly what's happening to you so we can help you in the future."

Braun drew himself up and sighed. "*You* I trust, Lauren. It's others I don't trust. There're even rumors of things being forced on us."

"Biochips help monitor the overall health of the individual. We all have them."

"And if we choose not to get them?"

"We're not going to force it on you. I know you're worried about it. I hope one day you'll change your mind."

He smiled. "That's what I like about you. You know when to push and when not to. One of the things that worries me is what will happen to us when your fleet leaves."

Lauren frowned. "We're not leaving anytime soon."

"Granted, but right now, you're acting as peacekeepers. Eventually, that role needs to be ours," Braun said, making a circular motion.

Hybrids would never have a majority population on Earth.

"You're right, Braun. I don't know anything about when we'll return home or what the future holds. What I choose to focus on is today. Right now, I'm concerned that sudden changes that are so prevalent among hybrids occur virtually unchecked. For all the advantages afforded being a hybrid, there are significant risks —things that happen so quickly that we can't even react." Braun began to interrupt, but Lauren held up her hand. "Let me finish, Braun. I know this is how it's always been done. You were in exile, and resources were scarce, but that's not how it is anymore. I hope that one day all of you will come to accept that."

Braun regarded her thoughtfully. "You're still worried about Ethan."

"He's my little brother. I'm always going to worry about him."

A colonial rover drove toward them, and Isaac stepped out. His thick, dark hair had a perfect wave to it, and the edges of his mustache lifted when he smiled.

He tossed them a wave as he strode toward them. "I just heard about Ethan."

Lauren frowned. "What about him?"

"He's finally been reactivated," Isaac said.

"He's back with his squadron?"

Isaac shook his head. "Not yet. He's at the lunar base and is heading to Mars for a reconnaissance mission. He's flying a shuttle," he said, looking amused.

Braun frowned. "I don't get it. Why is this amusing?"

"It's because my brother is trained to fly a Talon V space fighter. Having to pilot a shuttle on a recon mission is a bit of a step down," Lauren said.

Isaac nodded. "This is probably a test run for him. He must hate it."

"You see," Braun said. "Even your CDF has concerns about hybrids."

"Well, of course they're concerned," Isaac said. "He's been

fundamentally changed in ways we're still learning about. It'll take time for him to build up his credibility."

Braun looked at her. "Has Ethan changed?"

"A little. He's still my little brother, but this has changed him —his experiences, I mean—and being a hybrid is going to change him further. I know it was necessary, but I just want to prevent him from being hurt."

Braun smiled and gave Isaac a nod. "Your loyalty to your family is commendable. I hope he has an easy time with it."

Lauren sighed. "He'd have an easier time of it if we knew more about what happens to a person who's been turned into a hybrid." She shook her head. "That doesn't sound right, but I can't think of a better way to put it."

Isaac nodded and looked at Braun. "She's right. It would help if there wasn't so much secrecy about it."

"We have good reason to be secretive. Spacers are hostile enough about us."

Lauren shrugged. "They know it's possible."

"It *is* possible, but there aren't many who can actually do it," Braun replied.

"And those who can are just as likely to keep their ability a secret so as not to draw unwanted attention," Isaac said.

Braun looked away from them for a moment. "People have a right to their privacy."

"Another strike against getting a biochip," Lauren said, and Braun nodded.

"Another way to classify us and perhaps make targets of us."

"You're leaping, my friend," Isaac said.

He shrugged. "I'm just being honest. You asked me to help you understand hybrids. I'm just doing my job," he said and eyed Lauren. "Like you said, maybe one day it'll be different."

They were quiet for a few minutes, watching the children run into the water.

"Does Amelia know you're coming with us?" Isaac asked.

Braun nodded. "Of course. I told her I'll be back in a few days." His gaze narrowed. "It'll only be a few days, right?"

Isaac smiled innocently. "That's the plan," he said and looked at Lauren. "I grabbed your things."

"I'll be sure to point out anything you missed," Lauren replied.

Isaac grinned. "I'm sure you will."

She doubted he'd missed anything. Isaac was quite adept at picking out the details of things, but sometimes he omitted certain things as well. She brought up her wrist computer and checked the list of registered teams scheduled to travel to the smaller settlements.

"I put us on the schedule," Isaac said.

She spotted their names and closed the holoscreen. "I was just checking."

"Don't you trust me?"

Lauren smiled sweetly. "I do. That's why I was checking."

Isaac's shoulders moved as he grinned. "No underlying mission. Just setting up the mobile clinics like we talked about."

Braun eyed the rover. "We're driving there?"

Isaac shook his head. "Are you kidding? No way. I thought you said you only wanted to be away for a few days. It would take us a few days just to get there."

He frowned and looked at Lauren. "Where are we going?"

"First stop on the list is a place call Providence," Lauren replied.

"I don't know whether to be reassured or concerned," Braun said.

"Just go with it and it'll all work out. Everything else is just opportunity masking itself as a problem," Isaac said.

Lauren eyed him for a second. "Did you just make that up?"

He smiled and didn't reply. Instead, he began walking toward the rover.

He'd made it up.

3

CONNOR STOOD in an office building at what had once been the heart of the North American Alliance. It was nine o'clock in the morning. He glanced at the wall of tall windows to the expanse of clouds that whispered of breaking to allow the sun through. The residents called the city "New Hope," and it was located near a vast river. The air outside was humid and warm, hinting at what was likely to be a hot day as spring gave way to summer.

The office building was of newer construction, having been completed within the last fifty years. The vast cities of the old NA Alliance were gone. All of them had been lost in the old wars. The colonists referred to them as the Vemus Wars because the conflict had stemmed from the Vemus, but the survivors had different names for them. Some of the continents had changed so much that they were remnants of their former selves. He still had to suppress a thoughtful frown when he looked at a global map of the region. The wars had triggered terrible seismic activity that changed the very landscape of the planet. Huge bodies of water dominated regions where cities had once dwelt, and the source of the water hadn't been melting polar icecaps. If anything, the icecaps were larger than they'd been hundreds of years before and were attributed to the huge amounts of water that resided beneath the Earth's crust having been released. Powerful weapons had been targeted along fault lines where the crust was weakest, triggering earthquakes and tsunamis and savage death and destruction to stop the Vemus. Connor suspected, based on the evidence, that what may have started as a war on the Vemus had slid into a wholesale power grab that unleashed havoc on the planet and the colonies of the solar system.

Since they'd first learned of the destruction of Earth and the reason the destination of the Ark had been changed, Connor had tried to imagine what had happened to cause such devastation. He'd witnessed wide-scale destruction before, wrought on the Ovarrow by the Krake. There had been hundreds of variations of New Earth where the Krake prevailed over the Ovarrow, with one exception. However, returning to Earth—a place he'd once known well—to find it irrevocably changed, and knowing that family and friends had been left behind to endure it, made him feel somber. It was something he'd noticed among the colonists who had been born on Earth.

A chime came from a pair of wallscreens and a video comlink became active. Brigadier General Sean Quinn was on one holoscreen and Colonel Oliver Martinez on the other. They commanded the two voyager class heavy cruisers that formed the heart of the expeditionary force.

Both men gave a salute, as this was a formal meeting among the three of them.

Connor returned the salute. "Good morning, gentlemen."

"Good morning, General Gates," Sean said.

Martinez said the same.

Sean narrowed his gaze thoughtfully. "If I were a betting

man, I'd wager you'd rather be back on the *Douglass's* bridge than on Earth."

Connor flicked his eyebrows and grinned a little. "Sometimes, but our workload won't let up if we spend all our time wishing we were somewhere other than where we are. Let's get started. Martinez, why don't you go first."

"Yes, General," Martinez said. "We've been deploying recon drones throughout the outer star system, but we haven't detected anything that's of alien origin. It's taking longer to sweep the entire system, but it's what we expected based on the sheer amount of debris left over from the Vemus Wars."

Connor knew the task he'd given to Martinez was the equivalent of searching for the proverbial needle in a haystack, but it needed to be done. "It might've been easier if they'd left us something to find, but I'm thinking they didn't want to do that."

Sean cleared his throat. "Nothing has been reported from COMCENT back home, either. I don't understand why they'd transport the probe swarms all the way to Earth and even go so far as to place them throughout the star system, and then disappear."

Connor smiled a little. "They could be monitoring us, seeing what we're doing somehow. Or maybe they intend to come back. The other thing it could be is that they've moved on. They've done this part and then washed their hands of it."

"And that leaves us wondering why. I don't believe it."

"Neither do I," Connor said. "We still need to look for them as best we can."

"Understood," Martinez said.

Connor looked at Sean. They'd been friends for a long time.

"We're still discovering people who had effectively cut themselves off from other space stations and are reluctant to believe that Earth is open to them," Sean said.

"We've been encountering them as well," Martinez said. "We've found many who set up small colonies on asteroids. They had protocols in place to hide themselves from passive scanning capabilities available to places like Magnus Station."

"Understood. Transfer a means for them to communicate with Earth, and they can contact us for help with relocation," Connor said.

"They have concerns about adjusting to Earth's gravity," Sean said. "They've been living in environments with 0.5 G to reduce energy consumption for their artificial gravity emitters. I've assured them that we have the means to help them transition to withstand 1 G as they're transported back to Earth."

"How'd they react to that?" Connor asked.

"They wanted details on how our protocols work. Some of these places are quite rustic. I'd offer to figure out a way to just transport their homes toward Earth, but I'm not sure they'd survive the journey."

"Are the spacers able to help take on some of the load with relocation services?" Martinez asked.

Connor smiled. "It's on our agenda today. I know we've been doing the bulk of the work, but until we've got a solid tech-base setup they won't be producing ships anytime soon."

Martinez smiled. "Understood, General. I'll inform my team."

Sean chuckled. "Coordinate with me and we'll prioritize the relocation of the refugees."

Connor considered it for a few moments. "I'd suggest as a part of first contact with these people that they be informed that their place in queue to return to Earth will be affected by how quickly they accept that we're there to help. Long waits cannot be avoided if they decide to change their minds after your task forces have moved on to other regions of the star system."

"It might even work," Sean said.

Connor wasn't averse to applying pressure when the situation called for it, and he also knew that if expectations weren't set, people quickly became unreasonable.

"Just so we're clear," Connor said, "the priority is getting refugees back to Earth and identifying places that could be used for salvaging materials. That doesn't mean we salvage it for them. Those places just need to be marked for future reference."

"What about searching for the aliens, sir?" Martinez asked.

"Let the recon drones do their job. Monitor them for the time being. If something is detected or they actually show up here, we'll reprioritize," Connor said.

He quickly wrapped up the meeting and left his office. Lenora met him in the corridor and smiled as she came toward him.

"You left early this morning," Lenora said.

They headed back down the corridor.

"I had a few things I needed to take care of before we meet with others today."

"Why does it feel like we're always in meetings these days?"

Connor shrugged. "That's because we have been. Shouldn't last much longer."

Lenora arched an eyebrow toward him and smiled. "I'm usually the one who looks on the bright side of things."

"What can I say? I've evolved. Your work is complete."

She grinned and he joined her.

The buildings in this sector of the city were all connected and accessible by large, covered walkways.

"Fabian has requested that this building become a colonial embassy here in New Hope," Lenora said.

Fabian Dumont was the head of colonial diplomatic relations and was quite capable of running an effective meeting.

"It is, unofficially, but until they have some kind of global government, I'm not sure how long it will be," Connor said.

"It reminds me of the early days of the colony—bringing people out of stasis and setting everything up."

Connor eyed her, amused. "I recall you spending most of your time scouting Ovarrow ruins well away from the actual building going on."

She smiled, her eyes becoming distant. "Good times."

They shared a look. They'd first met during those early days of the colony. It seemed like a lifetime ago, and so much had changed.

She narrowed her gaze and pursed her full lips. "Stop luring me in with that smoldering gaze of yours."

"What can I say? You bring it out in me."

If he had to spend days in long and important meetings, having Lenora at his side made them a lot more bearable.

They entered a conference room. The high ceilings were constructed from angled windows that were so high he could hardly see the frames used to keep it all together. It was an engineering feat that he appreciated. So much of the city he'd seen had been built with reclaimed materials, but there were a few buildings that had been constructed with a nod toward aesthetic beauty as well as function. Lenora was right, this was like the early days of the colony.

They made their way toward their designated seating area. The conference table was large and oval-shaped. There were areas where holoscreens had been set up so representatives from remote locations could attend these meetings.

New Hope's mayor, an older man named Richard Peabody, began the meeting.

Connor and Lenora sat with the rest of the colonial diplomatic envoy, which consisted of Fabian Dumont, Samantha

Orthon, and Qenirian. The people of Earth weren't used to Qenirian, who was the only Ovarrow that was part of the envoy. Both spacers and Earthers alike couldn't help but stare at Qenirian. He didn't mind. It wasn't so long ago that the Ovarrow had become part of the colony on New Earth, and the people who'd lived there had to get used to Ovarrow living among them.

Qenirian had several other Ovarrow that were part of his staff.

Connor looked at the other people at the meeting, noting some of the familiar faces. This was the second day of the official summit among the leaders of the former spacers and cities of Earth.

"Now that we're all here, we'll officially get started," Richard Peabody said. "My role will be as the facilitator of the meeting, and I will be representing the city of New Hope." He went on to describe the agenda for the meeting and what they hoped to accomplish.

"Before we go any further," Peabody said and turned his attention toward Connor and the others, "your help has been invaluable these past few months, and I know I represent the majority of people here in saying that your sacrifice in disabling the quarantine around Earth and bringing people who for generations were stranded out in the solar system can never be fully repaid."

Fabian Dumont leaned forward. "We appreciate your kind words, Mayor Peabody, and as I've already reiterated to you and the other leaders we've met, Governor Preston and the rest of the colony would like you to know that we're committed to helping you rebuild."

Connor eyed an older man with silver hair and piercing blue eyes. Colonel Elias Cooper oversaw a peacekeeping and field operations group that was supported by New Hope and some of the surrounding cities. It was as close to a military as the people of Earth had. Elias glanced at Connor and gave him a nod. Connor liked the man. His son had encountered him shortly after he'd crash-landed on Earth. Elias Cooper was patient and firm, both of which were good qualities in a leader.

The meeting went on, with various leaders bringing forth issues that were important to them. Communications among the Earth's survivors had been spotty until the CDF had destroyed the orbital platforms that enforced the quarantine of the planet. With that removed and the use of new communication satellites, the people of Earth were able to communicate freely in a way that had been closed off to them for hundreds of years.

"Mayor Peabody, I have an item I'd like to bring up for consideration."

Connor turned toward the man who'd spoken and recognized him. Pandu Mukhtar had been a labor party leader on Magnus Station. He had dark skin, narrow shoulders, and angular facial features.

Peabody considered it for a few seconds, and it looked as if something unspoken had passed between the two. Then Peabody sighed. "I recognize Alliance of Spacers representative Pandu Mukhtar, formerly of Magnus Station."

Pandu Mukhtar stood. "Thank you," he said and turned to address Connor and the others. "As Mayor Peabody indicated at the start of this meeting, progress made toward humanity's rebuilding would not be possible without your help and sacrifice." He paused for a few moments. "Representative Dumont, you've advised that we, the people of Earth, should cooperate to become a better global society than we were before the Vemus War. I also believe a step toward the future involves the unification of the people of Earth, an alliance that stands on democratic principles. However, does the Colonial Government require a seat in this future government in return for all your assistance?"

Fabian Dumont frowned for a few seconds. "To be honest, we haven't considered what our future role would be, or even if a direct role would be appropriate."

Pandu Mukhtar looked as if he'd taken a bite of his favorite food and was relishing the taste. Dumont shook his head and began to speak, but Pandu Mukhtar cut him off. "Interesting. That statement would leave one to wonder whether your commitment to our rebuilding efforts is as reliable as we might assume."

Dumont glanced at Peabody and the other representatives for a moment.

Mukhtar looked at Connor. "General Gates, I'm sure you have strong opinions on this matter."

Connor glanced at Dumont, who gave him a small nod, so he stood and regarded Mukhtar. Instead of directing his comment toward him, Connor decided to address the other attendees. "If you're wondering what the price of our help is, then don't. The help we offer is freely given to you without strings—"

"That's good to know," Mukhtar said.

Connor narrowed his gaze, and Mukhtar's eyes widened a little in mock surprise.

"I apologize, General Gates. I was overjoyed that there wouldn't be yet another burden placed on us during this vulnerable time in our history."

Connor stared at his opponent as one sizes up a target. "Forgiven," he said and looked at Peabody. "Something that you all should remember is that we've had to rebuild our colony almost from the ground up several times since its inception.

We've fought wars and suffered hardships. It's for this reason that, upon realizing there were survivors here, so many volunteered to help the people of Earth."

Peabody nodded enthusiastically and looked worried at the same time. "Please do not be offended, General Gates."

Connor frowned a little and glanced at Lenora and the rest of the envoy. Peabody and many others looked afraid that the colonial expeditionary force would just leave them at the slightest provocation. Connor didn't like the perception or the implications that were conveyed in this line of thinking.

"If I may continue," Mukhtar said. "General Gates, will colonial assistance include the sharing of your impressive technological advances, including faster-than-light travel?"

The edges of Connor's lips lifted, recognizing the opportunistic finagling to get to what he'd wanted to bring up all along. Connor considered his answer for a few moments. Silence was a powerful weapon. It compelled some to fill in the gap by giving away their true intentions.

"I think you're getting ahead of yourself," Connor said and held up his hand when Mukhtar began to interrupt. "You asked a question. Now you will allow me the opportunity to answer it."

Connor stared at him, his gaze unwavering. Mukhtar regarded him for a few moments, then sat down. Connor knew the man wasn't cowed; he was simply affecting a strategic withdrawal.

"I'm going to reiterate what's already been agreed to. Our highest priority is helping people and refugees get established here on Earth by improving living conditions and getting people access to basic needs that includes medical treatment and education. This will also include access to prolonging treatments. No longer will your generations be limited to one century. Average colonial lifespans are two hundred and fifty years. Be assured that we're not simply going to up and leave tomorrow. We intend to help the people rise beyond what has come before."

Many of the representatives smiled. Pandu Mukhtar wasn't among them. While the others voiced their affirmations, Pandu Mukhtar regarded Connor thoughtfully before tipping his head to the side once.

Connor hadn't answered Mukhtar's question about giving advance technology that included FTL to the people of Earth. He wasn't authorized to. It was neither his decision nor anyone's from the diplomatic envoy. Not even Governor Preston could authorize the sharing of their technology without consensus from the Colonial Security Council.

Connor sat down and Lenora leaned toward him.

"I'm almost surprised he didn't ask for some of our ships while he was at it," she said.

He leaned toward her ear, catching a whiff of floral scent from her perfume. "This was just the first meeting. He'll get to it—either him or someone else. Mukhtar has supporters in this room."

Lenora pursed her lips in thought for a moment and then nodded.

4

THE GUARDIAN CLASS combat shuttle was designed for midrange armored deployments that included transporting soldiers, vehicles, and supplies. They had point-defense capabilities, along with a flak cannon mounted below the nose. The shuttle's powerful communications array bolstered comms between platoons but could also stretch communications capabilities between ships. These included standard comms broadcast signals capabilities, as well as a subspace transceiver with limited range.

Ethan sat in the pilot's seat and glanced at the nav interface on the main holoscreen. The combat shuttle wasn't meant to be flown across an entire star system, although he'd heard of some pilots having to do that in the past. The inner planets of the star system were much closer than the outer planets, and the flight from Earth to Mars had taken them eleven hours. Speedy, combat shuttles weren't. In a Talon V Stinger class, he'd have covered the distance much quicker but at the cost of fuel and time in a combat engagement. However, an actual carrier could cover the distance quicker and had much more fuel capacity than the Talon Vs.

He was alone in the cockpit, staring at the main holoscreen that showed eight shuttles flying with them to Mars. The CDF was making the best use of their resources, spreading them as thin as possible but without compromising combat capabilities. He'd reviewed the data from the survey probes sent to Mars. The Martian colony had once supported a population of over a billion people across multiple cities on the planet. Through the use of plasma reactors, they'd been able to convert carbon dioxide to provide oxygen supplies to the dome-covered cities. Before the Venus Wars, the Martian colony had made great strides toward terraforming the atmosphere to support life. Remnants of that effort were apparent by the limited cloud cover of the planet. Huge pale-colored fields that were once part of the terraforming project had become dormant. The atmosphere was thicker from the buildup of greenhouse gas, but the samples from the recon probes indicated that the atmosphere had lost some of its viability with the collapse of the colony. If it weren't for the abundantly rich mineral deposits on the planet, Ethan doubted there would be an inclination for people to return to Mars. The human population had been decimated and now numbered only in the millions here in the solar system. Going back to Earth was their best option for survival, but Earth's mineral reserves had been largely depleted. Salvaging refined materials would greatly assist the rebuilding efforts, but they also needed raw materials, and Mars could provide that.

Major James Racine authorized the final approach to their designated search areas. Ethan made the announcement, and the platoon readied themselves for deployment.

Ethan angled the combat shuttle's descent into the Martian atmosphere, flying through minimal cloud cover and the ruins of Martian cities below. Fractured remnants of domes framed a massive debris field with huge craters among them. There were impact craters surrounding the area as well. The Vemus Wars must have been unimaginable. They'd infiltrated cities and outposts. What Ethan hadn't seen was any exoskeletal material, which was a good indication of whether there were any remnant Vemus forces still present.

Ethan flew the shuttle past the city, heading toward an underground mining facility. The facility wasn't covered by any domes. There were large landing pads over top, but they didn't have any power. The recon drones had shown a smaller landing pad near deep canyons.

Ethan opened a comlink to the rest of the shuttle. "Stand by for final approach to the LZ."

He set the shuttle down on the landing pad near a personnel entrance to the mining facility. They kept it separate from the high-traffic offloading of materials extracted from the mine. Ethan had spotted maglev tracks leading away from the city. Mars had had extensive railways to transfer raw materials for processing. It was more efficient to process raw materials on the planet than to bring the materials off-world for processing.

Once the shuttle was down, he powered down the flight systems, and then he stood up. Ethan palmed the door controls and went back to the others. The CDF soldiers were gathered at the staging area where they donned their combat suits.

A few looked over at him, lifting their chins a little in Ethan's direction. One of the men turned toward him. He wore a combat suit, but his helmet wasn't engaged. His blond hair was high and tight, and he frowned toward Ethan in shock.

"What happened to Peneti? I thought she was flying the shuttle." he asked, then shook his head. "Sorry, Lieutenant…" he said and blinked a few times.

"Gates," Ethan replied. Furtive glances were shared by the others, and Ethan waited for the young man to reply.

He swallowed and then stood straighter. "Sorry, Lieutenant Gates. I'm Private Braxton Armstrong, sir."

Ethan gave him a once-over. "That's quite the name to live up to."

Armstrong frowned and glanced at the others for a second. "I don't understand, sir."

Ethan noticed the other soldiers regarding each other, and he suspected they were figuring out who he was. "Never mind. Look it up sometime after you're done here. Your family name is actually quite famous."

Armstrong grinned a little. "Oh, that. Five hundred years ago, the first man to walk on Earth's moon. I get that a lot. No family relation to mine."

Ethan spotted Lieutenant Hayman at the rear of the shuttle.

"Lieutenant Gates," Armstrong said, "are you related to—"

Ethan began walking. "Next time, Private. You better get your kit in order."

He quickened his pace but still heard one of the other soldiers assert that Ethan had to be *that* Gates. He understood, but he wanted to speak to Hayman.

Ethan walked toward the back of the shuttle where Lieutenant Hayman was speaking to his squad leaders.

"We'll begin our sweep here. Burk, get your squad out there first and get the recon drones deployed so we can see what we're dealing with. The best intelligence we have, which is pretty thin, is that every city here fell to the Vemus. It infiltrated every part of the colony, but their penetration might not have included mining facilities."

"Yeah right, Lieutenant," Sergeant Burk said. "That's what we thought about the outposts near Midway Station."

The other squad leaders agreed.

Hayman lifted an armored fist. "I get it. Nothing is supposed to be alive here. There has been no response to communication attempts, so if we encounter anything like those damn outposts, we'll bug out and they'll nuke the site. Now, get to it."

The squad leaders left him, and Lieutenant Hayman looked over at Ethan. "What can I do for you, Gates?"

"Sir, I was hoping you could use an extra pair of hands for the scouting mission," Ethan said. Hayman gave him a once-over. "It's all this sitting around. It makes my feet go to sleep."

Hayman chuckled and gave him a knowing nod. "Appreciate the offer, but I need you to stay with the ship."

Ethan glanced toward the other squads for a second. "You look a little shorthanded. You sure you don't want some help? I wasn't always a pilot. I've led scout forces before."

Hayman's eyebrows raised. "Oh yeah? You were in infantry before going to OCS?" Ethan nodded. "Look, I need you to stay here with the shuttle in case we need an extraction."

"Understood. What happened at Midway Station?"

Hayman's expression became grim. "We were coordinating with some of those salvager groups, the ones with those hybrids. They're supposed to be able to detect active Vemus soldiers, so we decided to check out one of the asteroid outposts. We'd done a few missions with them, and I thought they were more reliable. Stumbled onto a Vemus nest and lost an entire squad to them. They won't admit it, but something happened with the hybrids on that team. Not sure what, but I think they were compromised. We had no warning, and the salvagers wouldn't talk about it. They locked themselves on their ship.

Ethan stared at him, trying to think of what could've happened with the hybrids. Cynergy had told him repeatedly that they weren't vulnerable to the control signal. "What happened with the mission reports?"

"Filed them as normal and then they pulled us out of rotation until we got assigned to this scout mission. They can't afford to keep us sidelined for long."

Ethan almost sighed. He'd certainly been sidelined for a while.

"What happened to Peneti? A couple of people thought she was flying the shuttle."

Hayman grimaced and shook his head. "With all the hurry up and wait, I didn't even mention you to the others. Yeah, Peneti was injured defending the ship. I'll tell you this, though, none of us will ever work with hybrids again. It's not worth the risk. They're unstable and not reliable, as far as I'm concerned."

Ethan clamped his mouth shut before he could utter a rebuke. He felt like he should zip up his flight suit to cover up his neck and the hybrid lines in his skin. Hayman didn't know he was a hybrid, that was for sure. He knew there were serious divides among spacers regarding Human-Vemus hybrids, but he hadn't expected the attitude to spread to the CDF. The fact that it had to this platoon in particular made him wonder what other soldiers thought of hybrids elsewhere.

He hated the thought of sitting around waiting for the recon team to come back. It was going to take them hours to make a sweep of the facility, and then they'd have to do it all over again at their next set of coordinates.

After the CDF platoon headed inside the facility, Ethan turned back to the cockpit. There was a man sitting at the auxiliary workstation, peering at a wide holoscreen filled with combat suit video feeds. He wore a pale blue uniform, indicative of a science officer.

He turned toward Ethan. "Hey, Jared Andrews."

His eyes were set deep, overshadowed by severe dark eyebrows and a glinting dark intelligence. His hair was neatly cut, and the short beard he wore emphasized the long lines of his face, the grim slash of his mouth, and the angular strength of his jaw.

Ethan didn't recognize him. He thought he'd seen the entire platoon during the flight here. "Ethan Gates, where did they hide you?"

"I've been around."

Ethan lifted his chin toward the holoscreen behind Jared. "What are you doing?"

"I'm to monitor the platoon from here," Jared said, and Ethan frowned, noticing the medical insignia of his uniform. "Yeah, I had another year to go to get my medical qualification, but I was able to put that on hold to join the expedition."

Ethan pursed his lips, impressed. "You were a year away from becoming a doctor and you put all that on hold to join the expedition?"

Jared's thin lips formed a grim line. He swallowed hard and looked away for a second. "My fiancé volunteered, and I wasn't about to stay behind while she came here."

Ethan bobbed his head once. "A lot of people volunteered like that," he said, remembering his father's reluctance to join the expedition.

Jared sighed. "Yeah, but...she didn't make it."

Ethan blinked, not knowing what to say. "I'm sorry."

Jared nodded a little in acknowledgement.

"What happened to her?" he asked.

"She was with the spacers, and a few of them were hurt. She was determined to build bridges, learn all she could about them. Then the attack happened, and…" Jared's voice trailed off and he gritted his teeth.

"It's okay. You don't have to say any more," Ethan said.

A comlink registered on Jared's workstation, and he acknowledged it.

"Hey, Doc," Hayman said. "Are you receiving?"

Jared sat and checked the sub-windows. "All except for Sergeant Burk and his squad, sir."

"I'll get it sorted. Let the squad leaders know if you see anything we should be concerned about," Hayman said.

"Understood, sir," Jared replied, and Hayman severed the comlink.

"What does he want you to monitor for?" Ethan asked.

"Anything that could be a threat. I'm not going to let them get taken by surprise again," Jared replied without turning around.

Ethan turned toward his own workstation and brought up the feeds from the reconnaissance drones that had been deployed earlier. He hadn't realized that this platoon had recently suffered any casualties. It had been months since the attacks before they'd reached Earth. He'd lost friends too, but Hayman and the others seemed determined to believe that their loss had something to do with the hybrids that had been part of the salvage crews.

Ethan exhaled a long sigh, his gaze narrowing a little. There was no way Captain Waller wasn't aware of this. He'd assigned Ethan to this platoon knowing how they felt about hybrids. He felt like he was being set up to fail right from the start. The trouble was that he wasn't sure what to do about it. Should he hide the fact that he was a hybrid? That might work for a while, perhaps even long enough for him to be reassigned. It was as good a plan as he could come up with. He didn't like having to conceal his identity like that, but what choice did he have? It wasn't as if he could disobey orders. He wasn't sure how long he'd be at this post, but he was going to request a transfer after the mission was over.

5

ETHAN SPENT the next hour reviewing the recon drone feeds that had made a sweep of the surrounding area, though it wasn't nearly as thorough as he would've liked. There was only so much an automated search could accomplish.

Jared focused on the video feeds from the platoon, occasionally speaking with the different squad leaders as they requested his input on things they saw. There were areas with exoskeletal material. The dark-brown, hardened substances looked like something that had been alive, their surfaces like some kind of fossilized muscle, but they appeared at random places—in rooms or the dark corner of a corridor.

The CDF platoon had split up to explore the facility and was almost a kilometer away from the landing pad.

Ethan brought up the shuttle's flight systems and ran a quick check.

Jared turned toward him. "What are you doing?"

"I'm going to do my own sweep of the surrounding area. There are some gaps in the data collected by the recon drones."

Jared regarded him with a disapproving frown. "Hayman wants us to stay here."

Ethan turned back toward his holoscreen. "I'll clear it with him," he said and opened a comlink to Lieutenant Hayman. "Sir, I'd like permission to take the shuttle and do a sweep of the area. There are some gaps in the recon drones' search grid that warrant closer inspection."

"Understood, permission granted. Hayman out."

The comlink severed, and Ethan engaged the shuttle's engines.

Satisfied, Jared turned back toward his own holoscreen.

The combat shuttle ascended into the air and Ethan began a patrol of the area. He used the shuttle's scanner array to begin sweeping but kept them within comlink range of the platoon.

They flew toward the nearby canyons that the recon drones had ignored. The canyons were more than wide enough to accommodate several shuttles in some places but narrowed in others. They were also deeper than he expected, and he flew down into them. Parts of the mining facility could be seen from the canyon walls. They looked like exhaust ports of some kind, and then there were occasional exterior walkways that led out of sight.

Jared swung his seat to face the main holoscreen and rubbed his eyes. Then he stood up and stretched, gesturing toward the holoscreen. "The facility extends all the way out here? How far away are we?"

"Just over five kilometers."

The canyons narrowed, and Ethan flew lower to clear the rocky outcroppings jutting from the sides.

"It's odd. I didn't think mining facilities extended this far away."

Ethan frowned in thought. "I don't think it's the same facility

—" An automated comms request appeared. He blinked, then peered at it for a second. The comms systems checked the request, comparing it with what they had on file about pre-colonial communication protocols.

"What is it?" Jared asked.

It wasn't a challenge protocol; it was a status check. When Ethan acknowledged the request, a waypoint appeared on the nav system and a beacon was detected.

"Whatever it is, it still has power," Ethan said and flew toward the waypoint.

He took them along the canyon and found a steep overhang. Underneath was an open hangar bay. Ethan glanced at the blinking red lights near the edges of the hangar bay doors. They looked as if they'd just been opened.

A few aircars sat to the far side of the hangar and looked as if they'd been there for a very long time. He flew inside and set the shuttle down.

"Wait, what are you doing?" Jared asked.

Ethan stood. "I'm going to take a look around. See that door over there? It's active. This place still has power."

"Yeah, but you don't know what this place is."

Ethan palmed the door controls and stepped through while Jared watched him from inside the cockpit. "I know. There's no indication that the Vemus are here. I'm going to have a quick look around."

Jared narrowed his gaze, upset that Ethan wasn't following some predetermined protocol he thought should be followed. "You should report this to Lieutenant Hayman."

Ethan almost rolled his eyes and shook his head. "Loosen up a little, okay? If it makes you feel better, you can report in to Hayman. I'm going to take a quick look around. The recon drones missed this place. Who knows what we'll find?"

Jared glanced back at the camera feeds showing the outside of the shuttle. The hangar was dimly lit.

"Okay, just be careful. I don't like this. We shouldn't even be here."

Ethan eyed him for a moment. "We're explorers, Jared. It's at the heart of what we're doing. Look, I'll check in with you. I'll take a quick look around and then come right back so a real team can be assigned to check it out further. I just want to make sure it's worth their time."

Jared considered that for a few seconds and then nodded.

The door to the cockpit closed and Ethan quickly slipped into an EVA suit. He went to the arms locker and grabbed an AR-74, then selected an ammunition block. The rifle powered on, and the new nanorobotic ammunition registered with the weapon's system. A subtle pitched whine rose higher until it was barely audible. Ethan focused on the sound, and after a couple of seconds, he heard the whine with stunning clarity, as if the speakers in his helmet were beyond the maximum. In addition, he felt faint vibrations coming from the central core of the rifle. His fingers glided over the stock in a gentle caress. Exhaling through his nose, he willed his heightened senses back to normal. Both the vibrations and the high-pitched whine were instantly gone, as if he'd suddenly snapped back to consciousness.

"Lieutenant Gates, are you all right?" Jared's voice came over the shuttle's speakers.

Ethan cleared his throat. "Yeah, I'm fine. Just thinking of something. Heading out now."

He walked toward the airlock and stepped inside. The airlock pressurized to match the Martian atmosphere and then he opened the hatch.

Sometimes the abilities that came from being a hybrid just occurred as if something had flipped a switch inside of him. It had surprised him more than a few times, but he'd learned to control it.

He walked down the ramp and into the hangar, glancing out the hangar bay doors at the reddish canyon walls. Multiple layers of rock showed the geological history of the planet. Years of traveling New Earth with his mother on archeological expeditions had taught him how to spot the different layers that gave insight into how the strata had been formed, and he could see that Mars had once had vast oceans.

He turned away from the doors and walked across the hangar. A data comlink registered with his EVA suit, and Ethan acknowledged it. He then shared his suit's camera feeds so Jared could monitor what he saw.

"How's the image?" Ethan asked.

"Clear."

Ethan walked toward the personnel entrance and wiped away the decades' worth of dust that covered the control panel. Some of the sediment crumbled, but there were stubborn bits caked onto the main panel. Ethan banged it lightly with his fist, breaking it away. Then he aimed the jet that was built into the forearm of his suit, using controlled bursts to blast away the rest.

"Clever," Jared said. "Where'd you learn that trick?"

Ethan grinned. "My mother has a knack for getting into ancient ruins on New Earth."

Jared sounded as if he was going to respond but muted the comlink at the last second. He had probably been contacted by one of the squad leaders.

The control panel glowed as it powered on for the first time in what had to be hundreds of years. A prompt appeared on the small, protected screen requesting that he transfer his credentials.

He brought up the authenticator program on his wrist computer and opened a connection to the door. The authenticator went through a series of protocols to test the level of security that controlled the door. More secure systems would only allow a few attempts before a lockout was initiated, which would make him have to force his way through the door, and he didn't want to do that. Other security protocols would initiate a data purge, but this hangar was located near the mining facility and there really shouldn't have been a need for that kind of security.

Ethan looked at the number of virtual sessions his authenticator application had opened. It must have been able to mimic the interface, and it began going through various attempts to open the door.

A flash of green came from the control panel and Ethan locked in the security protocol that gained him entry. The metallic door opened toward the inside and Ethan pushed it the rest of the way.

He stepped inside the airlock and closed the door, hearing the life support system equalize the pressure with the interior atmosphere. Then a failure message appeared on the control panel for the interior door.

Ethan initiated an override of safety protocols. He hadn't expected the facility to still have life support systems after all this time had passed. However, according to his suit sensors, there was a remnant atmosphere well below minimum.

He opened the interior door and heard a faint gasp from inside. The atmosphere was definitely toxic, not that he had any intention of removing his helmet.

A dark corridor lay beyond, and a reddish glow came from emergency lighting near the ceiling. Ethan engaged his EVA suit lights, and his helmet did the rest. The suit's sensors enabled him to see far down the corridor, making the best use of the light inside.

Ethan walked down the corridor and came to a turn. Around the corner was a room that reminded him of a security checkpoint.

"Looks like overkill for a mining facility," Jared said.

"I don't think this is part of that mining facility. This is something else," Ethan replied.

Jared was quiet for a few moments. "Well, why don't you just mark the location and then a full team will come investigate it? Come on back to the ship."

Ethan shook his head and walked toward the security desk. "Where is your sense of adventure? There is no indication of danger here at all. I'm going farther inside."

Jared started to reply and stopped himself. Then he muted the commlink, which was just as well. Ethan was getting a little tired of Jared's attitude. He understood following protocol, but leaving without any understanding as to the purpose of this place would be a mistake.

Ethan walked inside the small room and used the credentials his authenticator program had found earlier to open the door to the inside of the facility.

The main door opened, and Ethan quickly went through it. There was a series of workstations over to his right, and even though no one had been there in a long time, everything was in place. The chairs and desks along the walls were pristine, and a soft glow came from inactive holoscreens, indicating that they still had power.

Ethan walked by a couch and spotted several offices farther inside. He came to a metallic staircase and walked down, glancing above him at the high metallic ceiling. The offices looked like temporary HAB units, but they were open, and the walls facing the walkway were semi-transparent. He walked toward the nearest one and peeked in. There was a small bed and desk inside, along with a storage container. People must've sometimes slept there, though the bed looked as if it hadn't ever been slept in.

Ethan checked the other HAB units, and they were all the same. He followed the walkway and came to a ramp that led toward a series of field laboratories. They reminded him of the kinds of remote labs the colony used while studying various parts of New Earth.

"Are those…" Jared began and paused.

Ethan walked down the ramp. "They look like remote labs. Maybe they were researching something here."

"You might be right. See the tanks on the outside of that unit on the left? There, near the top."

Ethan searched for the tanks. "I see them."

"They're for purging samples."

He peered at the tanks and frowned, sighing. Old abandoned labs were spooky, and it didn't matter whether they were on New Earth or here. He'd seen Ovarrow bunker sites with the stasis pods. At least here on Mars, there wouldn't be any dangerous animals trying to kill him.

Ethan turned and began heading away from the lab.

"Wait. Go into the lab. See if those systems are still working," Jared said.

"In a second. There's a control center here. If there's a computer system that can tell us what they were working on, it will be there."

Ethan walked toward an open space and spotted a phalanx of workstations past transparent double doors. The doors opened as he walked toward them. Whatever security protocols had been placed at the entrance didn't extend here.

"That's convenient," Jared said.

"I'll take it," Ethan replied. "At least we know now that only people who were authorized to get inside had the run of the place."

Jared sighed. "Why is that important?"

"Think of it this way: it's like being allowed on a warship and you can suddenly go anywhere you want. Not secure at all. Either this place wasn't that important, or it was so well hidden or temporary that they weren't worried about discovery. I'm leaning toward it being temporary."

"Good point, but why would anyone want to hide something here?"

"That's what I want to find out."

Ethan walked toward a trio of workstations. There were cordoned-off work areas nearby. He sent his acquired credentials to the workstation and a holoscreen came online.

"I've got to go offline for a minute. The team needs me," Jared said.

Ethan watched as a data window appeared on the holoscreen. The system startup screen appeared and went through a series of checks.

"Better Research, Better Tomorrow" appeared at the top of the holoscreen. Ethan brought up the log entries and read the dates, and his pulse quickened. They were during the Vemus Wars. There were several messages referencing data that indicated other facilities going offline. Operations had been moved from Earth.

Ethan scanned the data and stopped.

He blinked, leaning toward the holoscreen.

Source located. Attempted extraction is in motion. Prep lab for receiving samples. Authorization to begin testing at the designated targets.

Ethan tapped the reference for the targets, and it showed a high-level view of the mining facility.

Source located? Source of what?

He began downloading the data to his suit.

Jared reactivated the comlink. "Gates, get back here. We're being recalled. ASAP!"

Ethan looked at the screen and then blew out a breath. The data downloading to his suit stopped, and a warning flashed on his HUD about unauthorized access.

"Darn it. I'm locked out of the system."

"Gates, can you hear me? Hayman has recalled us. They need us ASAP. Do you copy?"

Ethan had been backing toward the door, frowning in frustration at the holoscreen and lockout message. He just needed a few more minutes to reestablish connection and override the security protocols. But Jared became impatient, and Ethan shook his head, turning around.

"Copy that. I'm on my way back," Ethan said, and started jogging back the way he'd come.

The Source? The source of the Vemus? Could they really have found it? He pressed his lips together and shook his head. He shouldn't rush to conclusions.

"Jared, mark this site for another team to come back to. It's important. Really important."

"Understood. What did you find?"

"Looks like there was data transferred here right around the time Earth was being quarantined. I found references to the mining facility, and I think someone was performing some kind of operation here. Plus..." He hesitated, uncertain whether he should share what he thought. It could be nothing. "They just need to get back here as quickly as they can. I think this place is important."

"All right, got it. Now hurry up and get back here."

6

ETHAN DOUBLE-TIMED it back through the research facility, wishing he'd brought more equipment. Hindsight was kicking him in the posterior, and he shook his head more than once. All he needed was a remote power unit and a data exfiltration unit to pull all the available data from the old computer systems here. He'd used systems like that before. They'd been specially designed for old Ovarrow computer systems that were barely operational.

He should've known better, but he hadn't expected to find anything. He thought it would've been easier to extract the data, since these were computer systems similar to what the colony used, and he wondered what had triggered the lockout. It must've been some kind of latent security check that periodically checked system usage. He'd warn the team that came back here to bring the right equipment.

He ran through the lobby and headed toward the corridor, looking around with regret. He wanted to come back to find what had been stored here. What kind of experiments had they been doing, and why were they targeting the mining facility?

The logs indicated that they'd been cleared to proceed. There wasn't anyone left in the research lab, so did that mean they'd executed their orders? *Were* there orders? The language used in the communications he'd read were similar to that used in the CDF, but not quite. There was definitely the tone of authority in the messages, so whoever was here must've carried out the request, but being locked out of the system meant he couldn't trace it.

He went through the airlock and entered the hangar bay. The small holoscreen on his wrist computer was still active. He slowed down as he looked at it but kept walking toward the shuttle. Jared had said Hayman wanted them ASAP, so he didn't want to delay.

While he waited for the shuttle's airlock to cycle, he looked at his wrist computer. He'd been able to get a partial data dump from the system before he'd been cut off. He suspected the system had detected him copying the data, which had initiated the lockdown. Still, there might be something useful in what he'd retrieved.

He entered the shuttle and retracted his helmet but kept his EVA suit on as he headed to the cockpit.

Jared looked over at him as he entered. "Good, we've got to go."

Ethan sat in the pilot's seat. "What happened?"

"We've been ordered to meet one of the squads and transport them to another part of the facility. Hayman and the rest are going to investigate farther."

Ethan frowned. "You said ASAP. Are they in trouble?"

"He didn't say, and besides, we're overdue," Jared said and then received another comlink request from the away team. He turned away from Ethan and began speaking to someone else.

Ethan brought the flight systems out of standby and engaged

the shuttle's engines. The combat shuttle lifted, and he used the maneuvering thrusters to push them back out of the hangar bay.

As the shuttle rose above the canyon, Ethan entered the coordinates, and a waypoint appeared on the main holoscreen. He glanced at Jared, who was busy speaking while peering at a sub window.

The edges of Ethan's lips lifted as he engaged the shuttle's main engines, and they sped toward the waypoint. The sudden burst of speed momentarily overwhelmed the shuttle's inertia dampeners and Jared shifted in his seat, his voice rising as he struggled to steady himself.

Jared had said they needed to get there ASAP, and that was exactly what he was going to get.

They quickly closed the distance to the CDF squad, and Ethan sent a broadcast to the team with their ETA.

The squad was waiting for them near a small maintenance shack. Ethan set the shuttle down on the Martian surface and opened the rear hatch. The CDF squad quickly climbed aboard, and the squad leader came to the cockpit.

The doors opened and a man leaned in. "Sir, thanks for getting here so quickly. We were told it might be longer."

Ethan resisted the urge to glance at Jared and instead smiled at the soldier. "I was told it was urgent," he said and glanced at the soldier's name, "Sergeant Burk."

He frowned toward Ethan. "Lieutenant Gates?" he asked.

Ethan nodded.

Sergeant Burk's eyes glinted with recognition. "Do you have a sister named Lauren?"

"Yes," Ethan replied, and then his gaze widened. "Were you on the shuttle with her and Isaac?"

Burk nodded. "Yeah, me and Corporal Nance."

Jared watched the exchange, bewildered.

Burk lifted his chin toward Ethan while looking at Jared. "This is General Gates's son."

Jared's gaze darted toward him in surprise. "Oh, I hadn't realized."

"I don't advertise it," Ethan said and shrugged, "but I don't deny it either."

Burk chuckled. "I hadn't realized you'd been assigned to us—"

Ethan saw where this was heading and cut Burk off. "It's just a temporary assignment. I was recently cleared for duty. This is likely a shakedown assignment for me."

Burk's mouth was partially agape. His eyebrows pushed forward but then he quickly recovered, sensing that Ethan wanted a little discretion. Since he'd been with Lauren, he likely knew that Ethan had been turned into a hybrid.

"Okay, tell me where Hayman wants me to take you," Ethan said.

Burk nodded and gave him the coordinates.

Ethan set a course and they began flying toward the new waypoint.

"What's there?" he asked.

Someone handed Burk some water and he quickly drank it before answering. "We've found exoskeletal material inside the facility, and Lieutenant Hayman wants us to confirm whether it's farther away from the other teams," he said and then tipped his head behind him. "I've got to get set up."

After Burk left, Ethan sensed Jared glancing over at him a few times, and he sighed. "What?"

Jared shook his head. "It's nothing. I'm just surprised."

Ethan arched an eyebrow. "In general? Or is it something specific that surprises you?"

He rolled his eyes a little. "Come on, you have to expect it."

"Actually, no, I don't. The only thing I expect is professionalism, even from a science officer."

Jared held up his hands in a placating gesture. "Fine. I apologize for being shocked that you're General Gates's son."

"I can let it go, just this once," Ethan replied while flying the shuttle to the new LZ.

Jared shook his head and turned back toward his workstation.

Less than fifteen minutes later, Ethan set the shuttle down at the new landing area. He'd spent the time reviewing the data he'd managed to take from the research facility and discovered that one of the targets was located nearby. He double checked the nav points and then stood up.

Jared looked up at him, his eyebrows raised. "Where are you going?"

"I need to stretch my legs a bit," Ethan said and left the cockpit.

The CDF squad had gone through the airlock and were heading down the shuttle's loading ramp. Ethan engaged his suit's helmet and grabbed his rifle. He palmed the door controls and followed the squad.

He quickly caught up with them, and Burk turned toward him.

"Mind if I ask what you're doing, Lieutenant Gates?"

"I thought I'd tag along. I found a reference to this area on the computer systems from a nearby research facility," Ethan replied.

The squad looked at him and then at Burk.

"I wasn't aware of any research lab nearby, sir."

Ethan nodded. "Neither was I until I found it. Go on, Sergeant. I'm not going to interfere with your orders from Lieutenant Hayman."

Sergeant Burk considered it for a few moments and then turned toward the maintenance hatch on the ground. "Braxton, get that hatch open," he said, and walked toward Ethan. "Sir, I can't stop you from coming, but we can't be divided down there. Are you sure this can't wait?"

Ethan smiled a little, appreciating the position Burk was in. He'd had to manage superior officers a few times himself. "Our objectives overlap, Sergeant. Let's do this."

Braxton got the hatch open and a couple of soldiers went down first. They checked the area and cleared the others to come down. Ethan went last.

They went through an interior airlock and Ethan was surprised to learn there was also a minimal atmosphere here.

"Just like before," Corporal Nance said. "An atmosphere just like the other areas. No toxins detected, but I doubt breathing it would be healthy for any of us."

"Understood," Burk said. "Let's go."

They walked down a dimly lit maintenance corridor, which connected to one of the mains. Ethan looked around and saw that they were moving toward an entertainment section. A staircase led down to a recreation area. There was a food court and the nearby tables had trays on them, covered in some kind of dark substance.

"Sergeant," Private Braxton said from ahead, "there are human remains here. Skeletons." He gestured behind a holotank.

There were three skeletons, looking as if the victims and fallen dead in their tracks. One of them had a hole through his chest bone, and the hand of another skeleton reached toward the first. By the fit of the uniforms, Ethan thought they might have been a man and a woman. The woman's skeleton lay on its stomach. Someone had shot them.

Braxton squatted down near the third skeleton a short distance away. "Looks like this one shot them. He's got holes in his clothes. Dark stains. Yeah, he was definitely shot or stabbed. I don't see the weapon, though."

Ethan searched the area, looking for more clues. "Is there any way to tell if they worked here?"

Burk looked at him and frowned. "What do you mean? Why wouldn't they have worked here?"

"Have you found bodies elsewhere?"

He nodded. "Yeah, but not many."

Ethan took another look around.

"Sir, is there something I should know?" Burk asked.

The rest of the squad regarded Ethan as they waited for him to answer.

"I found data indicating that people from a research facility were coming here. I'm not sure what they were going to do, but the logs indicate that they were running some kind of experiment."

Burk was about to reply, but one of the soldiers called out to him.

"Sergeant, I've found an active console here."

Ethan and Burk went to the soldier.

"What have you got, Gutierrez?" Burk asked.

Specialist Gutierrez had attached a hardline from his combat suit to the console.

"I've got systems access."

"Can you bring up the log entries? What was last recorded?" Ethan asked.

Gutierrez glanced at Burk, who gave him a nod, and he brought up the log entries. "Looks like there was some kind of emergency," he said. "The Vemus were here."

Braxton shook his head. "We already knew that, Gutierrez.

How about telling us something we don't know?"

Gutierrez's gaze narrowed. "Don't you have something better to do?"

Braxton backed away without offering a reply.

"Can you access the logistics system?" Ethan asked.

Gutierrez frowned and then brought it up.

Burk looked at Ethan. "You think they delivered something?"

Ethan nodded.

Gutierrez made the holoscreen bigger and ran a search. "There was a nonscheduled delivery here. Looks like basic maintenance equipment for the life support systems."

"That could be it. Where did they take the delivery?" Ethan asked.

Gutierrez ran another search and found the location.

Burk looked at Ethan. "What are you thinking, sir?"

Ethan looked at the location and inhaled a breath. "I'm thinking that whoever was at the research base brought something over with them. They'd been cleared to start an experiment. Delivering equipment for the life support systems seems innocuous enough to get in with little fuss, especially if they're already running in short supply."

Burk blinked and then licked his lips. "How do you know they were running short?"

Gutierrez nodded.

"That's easy. The Vemus Wars were already starting. Earth was being quarantined. Other wars were breaking out. First things to get impacted are supply chains. Come on, let's go check out that location," Ethan said.

Burk ordered the squad to move out and then walked next to Ethan. "You seem certain that we'll find something."

"I'm just following the evidence."

Burk frowned. "Your sister said you were a pilot. I'm also a pilot." Burk snorted a little and Ethan frowned.

"What?"

"I was just noting a family resemblance...similar behavior."

"You've met my father?"

Burk shook his head. "No way. Are you kidding me? I meant your sister. She gave Agent Diaz a few things to think about while we were checking out all those outposts."

Corporal Nance looked over her shoulder at them. "That's because she's tenacious."

Burk grinned. "Careful now. You're about to impress me with those fancy words of yours."

She shook her head and chuckled.

Burk looked at Ethan. "We've been partnered up for a while."

They made their way through the recreation center, heading toward a receiving area. The designers of the mining facility had placed the life support systems near the residential area.

Following the signs on the walls that were pointing to the facility's life support systems, they eventually entered a large hangar-bay-size area where the different systems were located. Large empty cisterns stood nearby. The water reclaimers had long since run dry.

Burk looked at Ethan. "It could be anywhere. Do you have any suggestions for where we should start looking?"

Ethan looked around and then shook his head.

"Excuse me, sirs?" Specialist Gutierrez asked. They looked at him. "Are you sure about the experiment? The Vemus contagion spread by coming into contact with actual Vemus. If that's true, then there isn't anything here that would do that."

Burk's eyes widened as if a sudden idea had come to him. "All right, listen up. We need to search for a portable biocontainment system. Could be as small as a stasis pod or as big as one of these cisterns. Pair up and begin searching the area."

Ethan nodded and Burk stayed at his side. A few minutes later, Braxton called them over.

"I found it," he said.

They found him between two rows of storage equipment in some kind of holding area. There were several open white containers.

"Looks like they didn't know what to do with these," he said.

Ethan glanced at them and turned to Burk. "Anyone got a sample kit?"

Burk nodded. "Murrey, get over there and collect a sample to look at…" He paused, looking at Ethan.

He swallowed. "Anything to do with the Vemus."

Ethan walked toward the container and stood by Murrey. The soldier peered inside the container and hesitated.

Ethan leaned forward and saw Vemus exoskeletal material on the bottom, but it wasn't brittle and dead like it had been elsewhere. He grabbed the soldier and pulled him back out of the way with a shout.

The soldiers brought their weapons up and aimed them at the container.

"Lieutenant?" Burk asked.

Ethan peered at the container and saw a shadow stir just out of sight. "Torch it!"

"Braxton!" Burk shouted.

Private Braxton lobbed a grenade inside, and they quickly moved back. There was a bright red flash and both containers were destroyed.

Burk titled his head to the side. "Say again, doc?" he asked, and gestured for Ethan to come over to him.

The soldiers checked that there was nothing left of the Vemus exoskeletal material.

"What the heck, man! This should've been dead!" Braxton turned toward Ethan. "Lieutenant, you said someone shipped those containers here?"

Ethan nodded.

"Why would they do that?"

The squad of soldiers stared at him, except Sergeant Burk, who had his back toward them while he spoke with Jared.

Ethan inhaled a deep breath and looked at where the containers had been. The ancient grav pallet they'd been carried on lay on its side. He lifted his gaze toward the soldiers. "Because they were testing the Vemus. They brought it here to experiment on the people who lived here."

The soldiers regarded each other in shock. Ethan looked away from them, recalling the things his father had told both Lauren and him about what he suspected happened with the Vemus.

Braxton shook his head. "I don't understand. Why would they do this? It doesn't make any sense. Hadn't they witnessed what happened on Earth?"

Sergeant Burk had his hand pressed to the side of his helmet, and he glanced at Ethan.

"There was a group who were trying to control the Vemus," Ethan said. "There could be more containers like this. We've got to warn the others."

"Lieutenant," Burk said, "doc has an update."

Ethan connected to the team comlink channel. "Jared, what have you got?"

"The other squads have encountered the Vemus. There's more than they thought were here. It's like they suddenly woke up. You've got to pull out and get to safety," Jared said.

Ethan shared a look with Burk. "Are they in trouble?"

"Unknown," he replied.

"I'll keep you posted," Jared said.

The comlink severed and Ethan looked at Burk. "Are you able to reach Lieutenant Hayman?"

Sergeant Burk frowned. "Why?"

"Because he needs to know why this place is important," Ethan replied.

"I don't know why this place is important," Burk said, and then gestured to where the containers had been. "I don't know how that stuff is still active after all this time, and you—" He stopped himself.

Ethan stepped toward him. "We've got to focus now, okay?"

Burk blew out a long breath. "You don't understand. They're going to destroy this place. Doc told me before you joined us."

Ethan's eyes widened. "What? Why?"

"Because of the damn Vemus. There are other teams encountering them," Burk said.

A high-pitched squeal sounded over the facility's speakers. It was ear-piercing, as if there was something interfering with the speakers. The soldiers quickly lowered the volume inside their helmets and Ethan moved to do the same, at least until he heard something else. There was a pattern within the squealing, and something inside him responded to it.

Sometimes his hybrid nature manifested itself in unexpected ways, but this was the first time it had reacted to something beyond himself. Ethan squeezed his eyes shut and tried to focus his mind to calm down.

"Lieutenant!" Burk shouted.

"What's wrong with him?" Braxton said. "Look at his skin. It's dark. How the heck could it just change like that?"

Ethan gritted his teeth. "Wait," he said, his voice sounding deep and strained. "Just wait."

7

"HE'S ONE OF THEM!" Braxton said, lifting his weapon.

Ethan heard several of the others hiss as they brought up their weapons.

"He's a hybrid, a damn hybrid!" Braxton shouted.

Burk moved to stand in front of Ethan. "Lower your weapon, Private!"

The signal sounded like alarms blaring in Ethan's head. He gritted his teeth and tried to shut it out of his mind, focusing on his breathing and putting all his attention to it.

"What's wrong with him?" Corporal Nance asked.

"I don't know," Burk replied. "Lieutenant, are you okay?"

Ethan heard Nance order the others to lower their weapons and keep an eye out for the Vemus.

"I can hear it," Ethan said.

"What can you hear?"

Ethan swallowed hard. "Them. The Vemus. It's coming through the speakers."

Burk stared at him for a few seconds and aimed his weapon

at the nearby speaker on the ceiling. He took it out and ordered the team to shoot the others in their vicinity.

The reprieve from the signal was enough for Ethan to reassert control of his hybrid nature. His breathing steadied, and he made himself return to normal.

"Thanks," Ethan sighed.

"What did it do to you? Has this happened before?" Burk asked.

Ethan shook his head. "No, it hasn't happened before. I knew that the other hybrids could sense the Vemus, but that was it."

Burk narrowed his gaze doubtfully. "This is more than detecting the Vemus, Lieutenant."

Ethan heard the alarm and uncertainty in Burk's voice. "It's my first time. Sometimes when something new happens, it's more intense until I learn to control it. It's just a learning curve."

Burk blinked a few times. "But you started to change."

"I know. It's fine. I'm fine." He glanced at the others. "I'm not going to suddenly change into a Vemus. That's not how it works. None of the hybrids turn into Vemus."

Some of them didn't look as if they believed him.

Burk nodded slowly and then scowled at Braxton as he started to speak. "Lieutenant Gates says he's fine, then he's fine. Now secure whatever gripes you've got about it. We need to head back to the shuttle and retrieve the others."

Ethan could still hear the Vemus cries coming through the speakers from farther away. It was a rallying cry or a summons. Something was mobilizing them. The Vemus his father had fought to protect New Earth from were part of a hive controlled by an Alpha. Were these the same? Was there an Alpha here?

The squad began going back the way they'd come.

"Wait," Ethan said.

"Hold up," Burk shouted and turned toward him.

"Gutierrez," Ethan said. "Can you bring up the other squads' locations based on their last check-in?"

The tech specialist paused for a second and then brought up his wrist computer. A map of the structure appeared on his holoscreen, and it showed the other two squads' last check-in had them near a central mining area.

Ethan peered at the map for a few seconds and then looked at Burk. "We can't go back to the shuttle and wait for the other squads. They're going to be cut off."

Burk frowned and looked at the map. It was three-dimensional and showed the multiple floors of the facility that connected to the actual mine. Lieutenant Hayman had to see if the mine itself was intact so its resources could be put to use.

"How do you know that?" Burk asked.

"It's a subsonic capability that the Vemus have. It's how they communicate."

"You speak their language?"

"I don't speak it, but I can understand some of it. It's strange, but they're converging right where the other teams are."

Burk stared at the map for a few moments. Technically, Ethan wasn't in command of this squad. His role in this mission was as a pilot. Unless Lieutenant Hayman ordered his platoon to follow Ethan's orders or Hayman became incapacitated, Sergeant Burk didn't have to follow any orders that Ethan gave.

"Check with Jared," Ethan said, and then shook his head. "Negate that. Gutierrez, try to reach the other squads. See if they're in trouble."

Specialist Gutierrez looked at Sergeant Burk. "Sergeant?"

Burk exhaled forcefully through his nostrils. "Do as he says, Specialist."

Gutierrez tried to contact the other squads.

Ethan peered at the holoscreen with the map of the facility.

Gutierrez's voice rose as he spoke to some of the other squads through comlink. "Say again? Not like normal Vemus fighters? Repeat the last?"

He shook his head and looked at Burk. "Comms are down, sir. Some kind of interference."

"Try to raise them through the shuttle," Burk replied and turned toward Ethan.

He'd snatched away the map and brought it to his own personal holoscreen. They still had recon drones mapping the inside of the facility.

"What are you looking for?" Burk asked.

"A way to reach the other team. They're getting boxed in. They just don't know it."

Burk glanced at the map and then at Ethan. "Lieutenant, I have my orders."

Ethan had had about enough of dwelling in this gray area where orders were concerned. "I'm taking command." The others looked at Burk. They'd take their orders from him, but not all of them. He thought Corporal Nance would back him if it came down to it. "Listen up," Ethan said. "Communications are spotty at best. Lieutenant Hayman doesn't have the big picture. He's getting boxed in by whatever Vemus remnant forces are still crawling around this mine. If you go back to the shuttle, you'll never see the rest of your platoon again." He paused for a few seconds. "It's a fact. They're moving in from these areas, backing the other squads into the primary mine."

"How could you possibly know that, sir?" Sergeant Burk asked.

Ethan pointed at Specialist Gutierrez. "Did the other team report finding an increase in exoskeletal material?"

Gutierrez blinked a few times and then his eyes widened. "Yes, Lieutenant."

"What's that got to do with it?" Burk asked.

The edges of Ethan's lips lifted a little and he gestured toward Gutierrez. "Tell him, Specialist."

"Fabian said he thought it was coming in places they'd just scouted, sir."

"They're being boxed in. Do you understand now?"

Burk blinked. "I understand that you believe it, Lieutenant, but what can we do about it?"

Ethan blinked and leveled his gaze at the others. "We go in there and snatch them away from the Vemus. That's what we do. I'm not going to let them all die without trying to do everything I can to save those soldiers."

A couple of them nodded, even if they looked uncertain about him.

"I'm a hybrid. A Vemus hybrid. It was either that or die. See this?" Ethan asked, showing his Colonial Medal of Honor for valor. "I got this for stopping the orbital defense platforms and the maser mines from taking out our ships. But in doing so, I was going to die. My ship was slipping toward Earth's atmosphere, and I was wounded. More than half of my body was burned, and my flight suit was fused to my skin. I had a spacer with me, a hybrid. She'd been exiled from Magnus Station, and she had the ability to change others. She changed me into one of them to save my life," he said, remembering those moments on an ancient space fighter, his final moments of being human. "I'm different, but I'm still one of you. I'm a CDF soldier. We're the line between those who do and those who can't." Ethan's gaze leveled at Burk. "Which one are you?"

Sergeant Burk lowered his chin once. "We're with you, Lieutenant Gates." He saluted Ethan, and the others followed his example.

Ethan felt a swell of pride fill his chest. He looked at all of them and bobbed his head once. "Okay," he said. "Gutierrez, get as much data from the recon drones as you can. Update the map with the known locations of the exoskeletal material. I want to know where it's gathering."

"Yes, Lieutenant."

Burk stepped toward him. "What's the plan, sir?"

"It looks like the Vemus are gathered in these areas," Ethan said gesturing toward the map.

"Do we know if there are any of them in these empty areas here?"

The holoscreen refreshed and the map updated. The areas that Burk pointed at were still clear. Gutierrez informed them that this data was part of the drone's data feed sent to the shuttle.

"I thought there would've been more of them," Burk said.

"This was an experimental site, and we don't know how many Vemus were here. We could be dealing with a much smaller force, but they still outnumber us, and they can use the exoskeletal material," Ethan replied.

Burk slowly nodded. "Okay, so how do you want to do this?"

8

ONE OF THE first things Ethan had learned about reconciling what the map showed and the actual path they encountered was that sometimes the differences could be startling. Recon drones recorded blockages in corridors with a rating that could use some improvement.

Corporal Linette Nance squatted and peered through a blockage that looked as if several floors above it had collapsed. She couldn't have been a couple of inches over five feet, but the combat suit gave her additional height. "There's a gap that'll get us through some of this, but I can't be sure if it goes clear to the other side."

This was the fifth corridor that had been blocked. None of them looked recently destroyed. Ethan thought they might've been defensive measures taken by the residents who'd died there hundreds of years ago.

"I wouldn't recommend cutting through this. At least not here," Corporal Nance said.

Making their way toward the other squads had proven to be

much more difficult than Ethan anticipated. Main corridors were blocked in the same manner as one of the smaller maintenance corridors, and some of the squad began muttering their frustrations. The only clear path was the way back to the shuttle.

Ethan looked at Gutierrez. "Are there computer systems online?"

He shook his head. "Negative, Lieutenant. I've been scanning for them, and none of the recon drones have detected anything."

Ethan frowned in thought. "We passed a data console a short way back. Go back there and see if you can pull a schematic of the area."

Gutierrez frowned. "Without power, I'm not going to be able to pull any data from the console."

"You can. Use the power from your combat suit. You should be able to pull maintenance data from the console. I need to know what's in the area," Ethan said and brought up his wrist computer. "Here, I'm sending a program suite for you to use. It'll be able to regulate the power from your combat suit to the console."

Gutierrez's wrist computer chimed, and he nodded. "Understood, sir. I'm on it."

He jogged down the hall and Burk ordered Braxton to go with him.

"Nice trick," Burk said.

"It will be if it works."

Old data consoles had stability issues when they were brought back online. The program suite would attempt to extract data from the console while regulating power.

"I'm not sure what data that console could have that would be worth anything."

Ethan was about to reply when he received a message from

Gutierrez. He glanced at Burk. "Here we go," he said, bringing up the data attached to the message.

An engineering schematic appeared on his holoscreen, and Burk peered at it. The schematic contained data hardlines, as well as various life support systems that connected throughout the entire facility.

"There it is. Got it," Ethan said.

Burk arched an eyebrow. "Are you going to make me ask?"

Ethan smiled and shook his head. "No. See this dark area over here? It's beneath us. We should be able to get above it in one of these adjacent rooms nearby. We can use it to get past the blockages. Got any thermite charges? We need to cut through the floor."

"Where?"

Ethan led them into a nearby storage area. There was a wall of lockers along one side and racks of supply crates. "Help me pull this out of the way."

"Murrey and Logan, clear this away," Burk said.

The two soldiers quickly pulled the racks out of the way. Gutierrez and Braxton returned and began helping them.

Ethan checked the schematic and then pointed toward the corner. "There."

Burk nodded. "All right, Logan. You're up. Make a hole big enough for us to use."

Logan handed his rifle to Braxton and began setting thermite charges.

Burk looked at Ethan. "What's underneath there?"

"It's part of the supply tram network. They're reinforced and should be intact for us to use. We should be able to make our way down it and get back into the main facility using a maintenance hatch."

Burk frowned. "How do we know there aren't any Vemus in there?"

Ethan shrugged. "We don't."

There was a bright flash as the thermite charge quickly burned through the floor. A loud thud sounded as part of the floor sank down out of sight.

Logan retrieved his heavy rifle and looked at them.

"Down you go," Burk ordered.

Braxton and Logan dropped down through the hole.

"Clear," Braxton said.

Ethan and the others dropped in. They were inside a long, dark tram tunnel, and stood in the middle of the tracks used for the maglev supply tram. The tunnel was carved out of the Martian rock with just enough clearance for a tram to use. They could walk down the tracks in pairs.

"I didn't even know they had anything like this here," Braxton said to Logan.

They made their way down the tunnel. The only light penetrating the unending darkness came from their combat suits. Even with vision enhancements, they could only see so far. The CDF squad didn't fill the time with idle chitchat. They focused on staying as quiet as possible while moving as quickly as they dared.

Ethan remained at the back. He wore an EVA suit that didn't provide him with any protection against weapons, something Burk had pointed out to him.

They found a maintenance hatch and Logan had to use another thermite charge to melt a hole large enough so they could force the door open.

They entered a short corridor and saw emergency lighting overhead.

"Lieutenant, I've got the other team on the line," Specialist Gutierrez said.

"What's their status?" Ethan asked.

"They're under attack, sir."

"Patch me through to Lieutenant Hayman."

A few seconds later, a new comlink registered with Ethan. "Gates, is that you?"

"That's right. We're making our way to you right now," Ethan said.

"I hope you brought enough explosives to take out a small army because that's what it's going to take," Hayman said.

"Sergeant," Braxton said, "there's something you need to see."

Burk walked ahead.

"They're pinning us down," Hayman continued.

Ethan brought up the map of the area. With the active comlink to Hayman, he could pinpoint their location.

"Are you able to hold that position?" Ethan asked.

"Negative, we've had to move. They're slow but strong, and they keep coming."

"Sending a set of coordinates to you. Can you reach it?"

Hayman was silent for a few moments. "That'll leave us boxed in. They'll grind us down."

"Not if we open the way up for you. Then we can escape out of the shaft and take it all the way to the surface."

"Okay, I see it now. We'll do this your way, Gates."

The comlink severed and Burk walked toward him, grim-faced.

"What's wrong?" Ethan asked as he walked toward him.

"The way is blocked with exoskeletal material," Burk said.

Ethan frowned and looked down the corridor. Then he started walking ahead.

"I told you, the way ahead is blocked."

"I want to see it."

Ethan strode ahead, and the rest of the squad hastened to keep up with him.

"Sergeant, I thought you said he was just wearing an EVA suit," Braxton said.

"He is," Burk replied.

Combat suits could assist the wearers to move at rapid speeds, while ordinary EVA suits couldn't. He hadn't realized it, but he'd embraced his hybrid nature. A video feed of his face appeared on his HUD, and he saw that his skin had darkened with a near purplish reflective glint. Knowing it would unsettle the others to see him this way, he blocked the transparency of his faceplate.

The corridor opened to some kind of annex, and Vemus exoskeletal material was blocking the entrance to the corridor they needed. He stared at it for a few seconds. The material was dark and lifeless. He walked over to it and reached out with his hand.

"I don't think that's a good idea, Lieutenant," Burk said.

Ethan placed his hand on the folded material and closed his eyes, trying to feel if there were any vibrations coming through it. It would've been easier without his suit but that wasn't an option.

There was nothing—no vibrations or any other indication that the exoskeletal material was alive.

He shook his head and removed his hand. Then, using the butt of his rifle, he smashed a hole through it. The exoskeletal material crumpled and disintegrated into a pile of dust on the ground.

"It's dead. No way it can harm us," Ethan said, then looked at Braxton. "Fire an explosive round right in the middle of it."

Braxton glanced at the hole Ethan had made and nodded with approval. "Yes, sir."

He brought up his rifle and updated his ammunition configuration, then fired his weapon. A glowing bolt slammed into the middle of the dead material, penetrating deep inside. A few seconds later there was a bright flash and the exoskeletal material collapsed to the ground in waves of dust. A large, gaping hole the width of the corridor opened the way to the other side.

Burk gestured for his two scouts to go on ahead and then turned toward Ethan. "How could you tell it was dead?"

"There were no vibrations inside. It wasn't warm, and the outside was brittle. Even a Vemus will die, eventually. The scientists studying the fleet that attacked the colony had theorized that they'd survived the journey by going into some kind of hibernation, but it required that they cannibalized a portion of the population to sustain the rest."

Burk sneered. "That's disgusting."

Ethan nodded. "That's a hive. No individuals. They'd lived only to serve."

"What about the ones here?"

He shrugged. "Remnants? I don't know. They know to attack, so that leaves us with very little choice. We need to wipe them out."

Burk nodded.

Braxton looked over his shoulder. "Now you're speaking my language, sir."

They quickly made their way through the corridor, heading toward one of the main mining shafts that led up to the surface. The other squads would be approaching at a higher level on the other side.

Along the way, Ethan spotted brownish residue along the grating near the ceiling. That must've been how the Vemus used the exoskeletal material to infiltrate the facility. They weren't limited by the blocked corridors. The residue was remnants of the material and looked as if it had recently moved.

"Stay out from under those grates," Ethan said, gesturing above.

He couldn't tell if there was anything up there, but they needed to move quickly. The squad scattered to both sides of the corridor, weapons aimed at the vent.

"Keep going," Ethan said.

Braxton and Logan began moving and the rest followed.

Burk glanced up worriedly at the vent. "Are you sure about the vents?"

"It was in some of the mission reports from their fleet that attacked us on New Earth," Ethan replied.

Burk considered that for a few moments as they went and then said. "How many of those reports did you read anyway?"

"All of them," Ethan replied.

Burk stared at him, pressing his lips together. "Yeah, right. There were thousands of them. You're telling me you read and know the details of all those reports?"

Ethan leveled his gaze at him. "Know thy enemy."

Burk blinked. "You're serious, aren't you?"

He nodded.

"So that's what you did with your free time."

Ethan grinned a little. "I didn't get much rack time either. Actually fell asleep in the simulator once."

One of the foundations of the CDF was the level of training they did to prepare for combat. Drills and training programs were nothing to scoff at, and anyone who lacked the focus and dedication required didn't last long in the CDF.

"I bet that went over well," Burk said.

He nodded. "Nearly got me kicked out of my flight group."

Gutierrez looked back at them. "We're due to check in with the other squads."

Ethan shook his head. "Don't. Maintain comms blackout until we're closer."

Gutierrez frowned and then he winced. "It'll draw their attention to us."

Ethan nodded.

The Vemus could detect short-range comms—at least the ones the CDF had fought during the war could. He didn't know if these could do the same, but they needed to be stealthy.

Logan and Braxton opened a maintenance hatch to the ventilation shaft, and the rest of the squad quickly followed them out onto the walkway.

Ethan moved next to Gutierrez. "Are there any drones in the area?"

"Negative, Lieutenant. I've been trying to get some routed to the shaft to scout for us, but they keep running into the blockage."

"Understood," Ethan said.

They climbed up a ladder to the next level, preserving the power core of each of their suits for the battle ahead. They heard distant sounds of weapons fire, along with concussive blasts.

Ethan glanced up toward the exhaust vents, and they were all closed between the levels they'd climbed. At every other level there was a main vent, and all had a dark residue left over from the Vemus exoskeleton.

They reached an area between ladders where a rock wall separated them from the CDF squads fighting for their lives. Burk ordered Logan and Braxton to set explosive charges. They attached the devices, configuring the blast to focus toward the rock wall of the shaft.

"Any idea how thick these walls are?" Logan asked.

None of them did. The schematics they had didn't show that kind of information. If Logan set the explosive power of the charges too high, it could hurt the other team, but if they were too weak, they wouldn't penetrate enough to open the way for them.

"Use standard breach protocol," Ethan said.

"Yes, sir," Logan replied.

There were multiple vents all around the area, as if this was some kind of convergence point.

"Cover those vents," Ethan said, gesturing toward the others.

Some of the vents appeared large enough for them to crawl through but would be a tight fit with combat suits. It would be too easy for a soldier to get pinned down in there.

Ethan heard a loud clicking sound wobbling through the area. It reminded him of someone banging on a taut steel cable, and it sounded like hundreds of cables. It echoed through the space, and each wave made him tighten his gut. He'd heard recordings of the Vemus fighters the CDF had encountered, but they couldn't convey how powerful the sounds actually were. Waves of dust swirled through the air above.

Ethan looked at Gutierrez and gave him a nod.

The specialist sent a broadcast comms to the other team, giving them a five-second lead time to anticipate the blast.

The explosion shook the entire shaft, and rocky debris blew away from the wall, falling down the long shaft. Clouds of pulverized rock billowed into the air, and Ethan tried to peer through the gloom. The sounds of fighting shrieked closer to them but were still muffled at the same time.

"Dammit!" Logan shouted. "It didn't penetrate deep enough, and I've only got a couple of charges left. I don't know if it's enough to break through."

Ethan looked at the others. "Is anyone carrying more charges?"

Burk shook his head. "Negative. Logan is our heavy hitter, Lieutenant.

Ethan looked at Gutierrez. "Specialist, see if they've got explosives on the other side."

As he tried to reach the others, Burk looked at Ethan. "We've got explosive rounds. Might be worth a shot."

Ethan shook his head. "Save it. We'd go through too much ammunition, and we still need to make it out of this shaft."

"They've only got one or two charges on their end, Lieutenant," Gutierrez said.

Burk scowled. "Which is it, Specialist? One or two?"

"He wasn't sure, sir."

Ethan blew out a breath and raised his gaze, peering at the wall above them.

"What are you thinking?" Burk asked.

He kept looking above them at one of the larger vents, considering. "I can get through there."

Burk followed his gaze and shook his head. "And do what?"

"I can reach the others and bring the rest of our explosives to them," Ethan said, quickly examining the area, trying to think of something else he could do.

"You'll get yourself killed. We can just set out a charge on this side and coordinate with them," Burk said and looked at Logan. "Get on a comlink with the other team and figure out where the best place to set the charge is."

Logan frowned for a second, glancing at Ethan. "That's not going to work, sir."

"Why the hell not?" Burk barked.

He held his rifle up with one hand and circled his fist toward it. "Because the explosive yields opposing each other might not be enough to penetrate what's left. But a combined yield going in a single direction might be just enough to open the way."

Ethan nodded. "He's right."

"Okay," Burk said. "But you're not going, sir. Braxton, take Logan's last charge and bring it to the other team. You're a vent rat. Get going."

Logan handed Braxton the charges, and he stared up at the shaft. Then he turned toward them.

"I don't think I'm going to fit, sir," Braxton said.

"Make it work," Burk said.

Ethan shook his head and gestured for Braxton to give him the explosives. "He's right. None of you are going to fit through that vent, but I can."

Burk gritted his teeth in frustration and looked at the rest of the squad.

Ethan made the face of his helmet transparent. His skin had darkened, and his visual spectrum expanded beyond what his normal eyes could accomplish.

Burk sneered a little and leaned away on reflex. They'd conducted operations with hybrids before and knew some of their capabilities.

"Hold this position. I'm going in," Ethan ordered and ran toward the wall.

He leapt into the air and slammed his fists through the vent cover, then grabbed the ledge and pulled himself up, squirming inside.

Ethan scrambled along the vent, noting that a buildup of exoskeletal residue slickened the walls. Using his momentum to slide forward, he pushed on the sides of the vent walls, building up speed. Less than a minute later, he spotted a vent cover along the bottom and tried to slow down. Cursing, he slid past it. The ventilation shaft sank into a slope, and he slid helplessly down it.

The shaft widened and he tried jerking to the side. The area ahead of him darkened and he saw some kind of gap ahead. He stopped flailing his arms and locked them at his side, angling his body right at the hole. Ethan shoved his hands in front of him, hoping that his speed would carry him to the other side of the hole. He might be able to catch himself.

He was wrong.

When he'd gone into the ventilation shaft, he thought he'd climb a short distance and punch through a grate to help the other team.

Instead, he slid toward a large hole, seemingly in slow motion. As he cleared the edge, he reached for the other side, scrambling to get a handhold, but there was a buildup of the exoskeletal reside left on his gloves. He slipped off the edge, causing the metallic shaft to hum as he plunged into the darkness.

The breath caught in his throat, and he tensed into a ball, cradling his rifle to his chest. Then Ethan slammed onto the ground. Something sloshed away from him as if he'd landed in a small, shallow pool.

He pushed up with his elbow and stood, bringing his weapon up. Brownish liquid covered the camera on his helmet, and he quickly wiped his faceplate, clearing it away.

He stood in a dark room. Vemus exoskeletal material covered the nearby walls in a gruel. His pulse quickened, and he backed away from it. There were deep puddles of it on the ground and he hastened away, searching for a door. He remembered reading reports of his father's experience on the Vemus Alpha ship, and how there was so much exoskeletal material that it had sucked in the CDF soldiers aboard. It had somehow infiltrated their combat suits, getting at the soldier inside. His father had almost died. Ethan had never asked him about it. He knew his father had lost close friends during the Vemus Wars, but he'd read the reports and knew he was in serious danger. The thick, mucus-like sludge moved slowly toward him, as if sensing his presence.

He blew out a harsh breath and spotted a door. The sludge thickened around his feet as he ran, so he elongated his slides, trying to make as little contact with it as possible. Leaning his right shoulder forward, he shoved his way through the door and into an empty corridor. The Vemus clicking sound reverberated through the walls like taut steel cables. He heard weapons fire coming from nearby so he couldn't be far from the other squads. The ground along the corridor was free of the sludge, and Ethan ran down it.

He reached a corner and slowed down. Glancing behind him, he saw the sludge moving along the walls toward him. He peeked around the corner and saw hulking, dark figures lumbering down the corridor. He frowned, watching their movements. Moving slowly at times and then with a sudden burst of energy, they charged forward, matching what he knew they were capable of. Then, as if their energy were immediately depleted, they slowed down to a crawl.

Ethan crept around the corner, sneaking behind the Vemus fighters. There were eight of them in the corridor.

A comlink attempted to reach him and he scrambled to disable it, but it was too late. The closest Vemus fighters spun toward him, letting out a screech-like moan, but they didn't attack. They just stared at him, hesitating.

Ethan brought his rifle up and fired, aiming center mass. High velocity darts punched through the nearest fighter, knocking it off-balance. Ethan attacked, moving toward them, firing his weapon in controlled bursts. The Vemus seemed reluctant to attack him, as if they were confused. He was close enough to aim for their large, dome-shaped heads. The fighters sank slowly to the ground as if reluctant to do even that.

He ran past the rest, firing his weapon and felling them as he went. He didn't know why the Vemus hesitated, but he'd take whatever advantage he could get.

He ran to the end of the corridor and slowed to a halt. Bright flashes came from around the corner. He didn't want to risk a comlink, so he flashed the lights on his helmet. He had to repeat the sequence a few times before he noticed a green laser point appear on the wall across from him. It flickered on and off several times. The CDF squads knew he was there.

Ethan poked his head around the corner and peered down the corridor. Through the haze and smoke, he saw that the corridor opened fifty meters from him. Low flames flickered despite the extremely low oxygen in the atmosphere.

He began making his way down the corridor. Hopefully, Gutierrez had told them he was coming. The ground crunched beneath his feet. Parts of the wall had collapsed during the fight, exposing an open area to what must have been a processing plant. He hovered in the shadows, peering at where the CDF squads were holding the Vemus at bay. They'd managed to use old machinery as choke points, forcing the Vemus fighters to funnel toward them. The only problem was that there were hundreds of Vemus fighters between Ethan and the squad.

He chewed on his bottom lip while he tried to think of a way to get past them. Some of them had fallen, their ragged bodies being torn apart, but the others only fell for a short time before they stood and rejoined the fight.

The Vemus fighters didn't have any weapons that he could see. They threw themselves toward the CDF soldiers as if they were running on autopilot. Their hands were gigantic, and their webbed palms showed long, thick fingers and viscous-looking claws. They propelled themselves forward in a burst of energy, but like the others, they quickly slowed down.

Ethan heard a sharp, fleshy, cracking sound and saw a large group of Vemus hunched over to the side about thirty meters from him. By the way their heads bobbed up and down, they looked like scavengers devouring a meal. Breathy, screeching noises came from them, gaining in intensity.

His eyes widened as he realized the Vemus were feeding from their dead, and the contents in his stomach heaved upward as he fought not to vomit into his helmet.

One of the Vemus broke away from the huddle, racing toward the CDF soldiers. It didn't slow down. Multiple soldiers concentrated their fire on it, only bringing it down when it was on top of them.

Most of the Vemus must be starving, and they were cannibalizing some of their own to regain their strength.

He was running out of time. If enough Vemus fighters held back and waited for a large group of them to regain their strength, they'd overwhelm the CDF soldiers. He needed to get to them so they could blow a hole in the wall to escape.

He crept out from cover, and killing the helmet lights he no longer needed, started making his way toward the CDF. Several soldiers popped out from one of the barricades farther away, drawing the attention of the Vemus.

A comlink registered with his suit.

"No time for sneaking. Get your ass over here now!" Hayman said.

Ethan ran.

A scathing howl came from the Vemus behind him, and Ethan glanced toward them. A huge, dark mass of hulking forms sped toward him like a nightmare come to life. Ethan fired his weapon at them, not really aiming, just to give himself some covering fire. He didn't know if he hit anything. Several soldiers also provided covering fire and he ran toward a gap in the barricade. As soon as he was through, a soldier gestured for him away from the barricade. The soldiers pushed the barricade closed and backed away, firing their weapons at the Vemus as they hurled themselves over the barricade.

Hayman gestured emphatically toward the far wall where another soldier waited. Ethan put on a burst of speed, flying by the other soldiers while moving at speeds that shouldn't be possible in a standard EVA suit, and if he'd been only human, he wouldn't have made it.

Ethan reached inside his storage compartment and pulled out the explosive charges. He quickly handed them to the waiting soldier, who then added them to the others on the wall. It looked as if they'd rigged something up beyond the explosives they'd brought with them.

Hayman pulled Ethan away, and the soldiers moved to a safe distance.

Bright, blazing light flooded the darkness, and Ethan felt the impact of the explosion press him into something hard. The sound of it drowned out the Vemus. Ethan felt someone pull him back and he saw a large hole through the wall where Sergeant Burk and the other squad waited.

Ethan got his feet under him and began running. He was through the hole and the soldiers began climbing up the shaft. A soldier grabbed Ethan, and using his suit jets, they rose to the level above. Something hit them hard, and Ethan slipped from the soldier's grasp, crashing onto the walkway.

He glanced through the walkway and saw the Vemus bursting from the new entrance into the mining shaft, looking like giant bats erupting from a hollow.

He pushed himself to his feet and started running.

Several CDF soldiers paused in their ascent to fire their weapons at the Vemus, slowing their pursuit.

He hastened toward a ladder and pulled himself up in heaves, skipping groups of rungs as he quickly ascended and catching up to the soldiers that had halted for some reason.

"There's a huge cluster of them above us. We're going to be pinned between them!" Sergeant Burk said.

Ethan quickly scanned the area and saw the cluster of nightmarish figures in the gloom above. It looked as if there was a dark wave of death gathering above them.

The shaft was a hundred meters across, and there were several open areas where the soldiers could flank the Vemus if they moved quickly.

Ethan spotted Lieutenant Hayman staring at him. He knew what Hayman was thinking. Ethan, being the only one of them in an EVA suit, was a liability. It was time for him to change that assumption.

Embracing his hybrid nature sometimes made him feel like his body was flooded with adrenaline, and he was sure the doctors accurately described it based on the data from his biochip.

He leaped onto the railing. Balancing on it like a cat on a perch, he looked down at Hayman and said, "Don't slow down on my account. See if you can keep up!"

Ethan ran along the railing, racing toward the end, and leaped high into the air, easily reaching the walkway above. It shouldn't have been possible for him in an EVA suit, but being a hybrid pushed the boundaries of human performance beyond anything he'd been capable of before.

Ethan ascended several levels and provided covering fire for the CDF soldiers, quickly closing the distance to him.

Hundreds of Vemus fighters flooded the shaft and raced along the walkways, trying to intercept the fleeing soldiers.

Ethan paused and fired his weapon at the walkway supports. The structure jerked away from the wall, tilting toward the inner shaft and causing dozens of Vemus fighters to plunge over the side. Their screeches sailed out of earshot.

Several of the CDF soldiers copied what Ethan had done, causing the metallic walkways to drop onto the other Vemus fighters that were climbing upward.

Ethan reached the rim of the shaft first and had to slow down so he didn't get too far ahead of the CDF soldiers.

He quickly found a maintenance door that led to the surface and broadcast a waypoint to the rest of the squad. Soon the other soldiers joined him on the surface of Mars, and they secured the door by fusing the locking mechanism.

As they began making their way toward the shuttle, Ethan noticed more than a few of the soldiers watching him, muttering toward the others. As they went, it was as if there was some kind of invisible barrier between Ethan and the rest of the platoon. They didn't trust him. He'd just saved their lives and they were wary of him, as if he was going to suddenly turn into a Vemus fighter and attack them.

He ignored it and kept going. He was still one of them, still part of the CDF. Even as he thought it and believed it in his heart, a small part of him thought the argument was a little shallow, and he began to wonder whether he was fooling himself. Was this how he would be regarded by other soldiers outside of this platoon from now on?

9

Ethan spotted the combat shuttle ahead and looked for Hayman. The CDF lieutenant had been speaking with Sergeant Burk, probably getting a report of Ethan's behavior. Ethan gritted his teeth and chided himself. It was Burk's duty to report to his direct superiors. Ethan decided to walk toward them.

Hayman waved him over as he came. "Burk was just filling me in. I guess we owe you one."

Ethan shook his head. "It was nothing that any one of you wouldn't have done in my place."

Hayman regarded him for a second, considering. Then he looked at Burk and tipped his head to the side.

Dismissed, Burk quickened his pace, leaving them.

Hayman looked at Ethan and sighed, his face a stoic mask. "You're a hybrid, huh?"

"You saw it for yourself," Ethan replied.

"You should've told me."

Ethan considered his reply for a few seconds. "Doesn't fall under a need to know."

Hayman blew out a harsh breath and several soldiers turned toward them, eyeing them from afar. "Are you serious, Gates? Do you know what we've been through?"

"Not until after I'd gotten here," Ethan said and paused for a second. "Although I suspect Captain Waller knew."

The rest of the implication went unsaid, but Ethan was sure Hayman could figure it out. Waller had put them together, knowing the history of Hayman's platoon.

Hayman shook his head, looking toward the shuttle for a few seconds. "Yeah," he said in resignation.

When they reached the shuttle, Gutierrez met them at the shuttle's loading ramp.

"Sirs, I have Captain Waller waiting for you on comlink."

"Understood," Hayman said. "Sergeant Burk, get some eyes on that mining shaft. We secured the door as best we could, but I don't think it's going to hold for long."

He raised his wrist and a holoscreen became active. Hayman glanced at Ethan for a second, and then Captain Waller appeared on vidcom.

"What's your status, Lieutenant?" Captain Waller asked.

Hayman gave him a brief rundown of what had transpired. He stuck to the facts but didn't go into the details of Ethan's part in their escape.

Captain Waller nodded. "We've been getting reports of Vemus activity at the other sites in the area. They're going to nuke the site."

Ethan's eyes widened. "Nuke the site? Captain, I sent a report in earlier about a research lab with critical intel found nearby."

Captain Waller narrowed his gaze as he recognized Ethan. He looked away from the camera and his eyes appeared to be scanning something off screen. "I see the report. It's been flagged for revisiting, Lieutenant."

Ethan blinked. "But, sir, if the site is nuked, you'll lose all evidence of what happened here."

Waller sneered and leaned toward the camera. "I thought you of all people knew who the enemy was, Gates. We've suffered losses here. You do remember whose side you're on, don't you?"

"I know who the enemy is, sir, but the research site could have data from the early days of the Vemus Wars."

Waller rolled his eyes. "Ancient history, Gates. Now stop wasting my time. Hayman—"

"You're missing the point, Captain," Ethan snapped. Waller's gaze swooped toward him. "There is evidence that points to this site being part of an experiment by a group called the Syndicate. They modified the Vemus pathogen to target humans. Data such as this is designated a high priority by CDF Intelligence. Destroying this site—"

"It's already done, Lieutenant Gates. You're being recalled. Now get on that shuttle and fly that platoon back to the operational waypoint, at which time you'll be sent back to CDF command at the lunar base," Waller said. "Lieutenant Hayman, if Gates does not comply, you're ordered to take him into custody. Also, I'm going to bring your performance under review for allowing a pilot to abandon his station."

The video comlink severed and Ethan clenched his fists, staring at the blank holoscreen.

Hayman swore. "Sergeant Burk, escort Lieutenant Gates back to the cockpit of the shuttle. Lieutenant Gates, surrender your weapon to Sergeant Burk."

Ethan glanced down at the AR-74 in his hands and then thrust it toward Burk, scowling.

Several soldiers nearby lifted their weapons a little—not enough to point them at him but enough that he got the message. If Hayman gave the order, Ethan would be taken into custody. The only thing he could do was follow his orders.

Ethan turned toward Hayman. "You know this is wrong. This site has strategic enemy intelligence that could give us insight into how the Vemus spread throughout the solar system."

Hayman narrowed his gaze for a second, and a message chimed from his wrist computer. He quickly read it and ignored Ethan. He turned to address the rest of his platoon. "We're clearing out of here. Nukes are inbound. This site is being sanitized."

The soldiers headed up the shuttle's loading ramp and Hayman turned toward Ethan with a hardened glint in his eyes. "Don't you have a shuttle to fly?"

Ethan stared at him for a few seconds and then walked up the loading ramp. He kept his eyes forward, ignoring the other soldiers as he passed them. He'd saved their lives, but all they could see was that he was a hybrid, some kind of Vemus half-breed that wasn't to be trusted.

Corporal Nance walked in front of him and turned around when they reached the cockpit door. She leaned toward him and whispered, "Thank you, Lieutenant."

Ethan gave her a small nod and went inside the cockpit.

10

LAUREN HEARD Isaac speaking to a young boy, reassuring him that the medical scanner wouldn't harm him.

"See here now, David," Isaac said, "I'll let you hold my spare scanner if you let me have a look at you. How's that sound?"

Lauren barely heard the boy's response.

"What? I can't hear you. Would you speak into my good ear?" Isaac asked.

She'd seen him do this before. He pretended to be deaf in one of his ears to get more cooperation from kids. They loved it, and so did she.

"Yes!" the boy exclaimed, and his father grinned.

Lauren looked over at them and Isaac winked while he scanned the boy with his palm scanner. "I thought we fixed your ear this morning. What did you do to yourself?"

Isaac closed his eyes and pretended he was blind. "David, I can't see anything. Is that lady doctor here again?" he asked, extending his hand out and grasping at the air.

David made a sweet uh-huh sound amid a gale of giggles.

"Oh good. Tell her that if she kisses my eyes, I'll be healed. Would you tell her for me, please? I'm blind and she might not hear me."

David laughed. "He wants you to kiss him."

Lauren smiled. "Oh, I know he does, but I'm not going to."

Isaac moaned in mock exaggerated pain. "The sting of rejection is killing me."

Lauren squatted down so she was eye level with David, then leaned toward his ear conspiratorially. She glanced at a rash on the back of his neck and noted it. "Tell him if he wants to see, he just needs to open his eyes."

"Open your eyes!" David shouted.

Isaac blinked several times and shook his head. "I can see." His eyes widened and he touched his ear. "I can hear, too! David, you're a miracle worker. I think you could be a better doctor than I ever could."

David's eyes became round with excitement, and he beamed at his father, who gave him an encouraging nod.

"Really?"

Isaac nodded. "Absolutely. You can be whatever you want, kiddo. Just you wait." He stood up and ruffled David's head. "Go ahead and put your shirt back on."

Lauren looked at David's father. "Hello, I'm Lauren Gates."

"Dr. Gates, it's nice to finally meet you. The whole town has had nothing but good things to say about you both. I'm Brian Remington."

They'd been traveling to different settlements for the past few days and decided to make a few extra stops.

"The skin irritation looks like a contact rash. Has he been anywhere new recently?" Lauren asked.

Brian thought about it for a few seconds. "He went camping with his cousins the other day."

Lauren looked at David. "Is that right, David? Did you go camping?"

David nodded. "Yes, at the sleeping giant."

Lauren frowned and looked at Brian.

"It's the name of the small hills nearby. They resemble a sleeping giant when you see them from the southwest."

Lauren nodded and smiled at the boy. "Did you find anything?"

David's eyebrows raised and he glanced at his father, then nodded a little.

Brian frowned and said, "It's all right. Just tell the doctor what you saw."

"It was something Benjamin had. He said he got it from New Hope."

Lauren looked at Brian. "What's New Hope?"

"It's one of the larger cities not far from here. My brother Trav lives there with his family," Brian replied and then pressed his lips together for a moment.

Lauren frowned but didn't say anything, deciding it was best if she waited for Brian to continue.

Brian stepped away from the table where David sat, and Lauren went over to him.

"This has become more of a sensitive topic recently with all the new people in the area. My brother and his family are all hybrids."

"Have they had any trouble with anyone?" Lauren asked. It was best if she kept questions about hybrids as general as possible so as not to add to the growing tensions among people in the larger settlements.

Brian's shoulders slumped a little and he glanced at his son. Isaac was distracting the boy with a few questions.

"Trav just said that they were considering moving away.

There are a lot of rumors about certain groups becoming territorial about their neighborhoods. Things like that. I'm really not sure what to think about it."

Lauren nodded a little. "Are you a hybrid?"

Brian shook his head. "If I am, it's never done anything to me. I've never had any symptoms that people sometimes get. As far as I know, David hasn't either."

Lauren considered Brian's response for a few seconds. She thought about Ethan and then Amelia, whose hybrid nature had almost killed her, and Ethan's had been a struggle from time to time.

Brian stared at her for a few moments. "Should I be concerned...about David?" he asked quietly.

"Not now. He's healthy and doesn't show any signs of being a hybrid."

"Can you test him? Is there a test you can do for him, just to be sure?"

There was, but Lauren hesitated for a moment. "Brian, your son is fine. It's not going to be like it was before. We're helping to establish clinics in the cities. There will be a place for you to get help if David becomes sick."

"But will you test him?"

Lauren shook her head. "It will do you no good to test him. He's barely seven years old. According to other hybrids I've met, some don't present symptoms until they reach puberty. My opinion, based on helping other hybrids, is that if David were at serious risk of adverse reactions stemming from being a Vemus hybrid, the symptoms would've presented by now. Keep doing what you have been doing—watch over him, love him—and you'll both be fine."

Brian's gaze sank to the ground, and he nodded a little. Lauren hadn't realized how worried he'd been about this and wondered how many other people carried the fear of being a hybrid in their hearts.

Brian walked over to his son and picked him up. "Time for us to go. Say goodbye."

David waved. "Thank you!"

They left, and Isaac smiled.

"Cute kid."

Lauren nodded. "Yeah."

He looked at her and frowned. "What's wrong?"

"Brian is worried that his son is a hybrid. That it'll make him ill, and he'll suffer."

Isaac shrugged. "It's an understandable concern to have."

"I don't like it, Isaac. How many people are living in fear of this?"

He blinked. "They've been living with it for a very long time now."

"Maybe that's the problem."

"What do you mean?"

She shook her head. Her emotions were getting the better of her. "Nothing. I don't know if convincing people to relocate to one of the nearby cities is the best idea."

"It is if they want quick access to medical care. We don't have the resources to do a wide distribution of things that are needed, at least in the short term."

"I know. Believe me, I know. A tech base needs to be built so they can start producing the foundation that'll make raising the standard of living here achievable."

Isaac regarded her for a moment. "I'm glad we got that sorted out. Now, can you stop being so uptight? You're starting to make me tense."

Lauren smiled dangerously as she stepped closer to him. He backed up. "What's the matter, Isaac. Cat got your tongue?"

A deep voice cleared its throat, and she saw Braun standing nearby, just beyond the curtain, his muscular arms crossed in front of his barrel chest.

She backed away from Isaac.

"We can't go back yet," Braun said.

She frowned. "How come?"

"I keep hearing about things happening in this place called the New Hope. It's some kind of city nearby."

"We've heard about that place, too," Isaac said.

"What did you learn?" Lauren asked.

"Public forums are discussing subjects such as 'the threat among us,' with the threat being hybrids. There are rumors of hybrids becoming Vemus, succumbing to some kind of latent instinct triggered by actual Vemus," Braun said.

Lauren frowned. "That's absurd."

"That's what I told them," Braun replied.

"Who's spreading these rumors?" Isaac asked.

Braun eyed him knowingly. "I know it's wrong to point a finger, but I think you know."

Lauren regarded him for a few seconds. "Spacers from Magnus Station? You're right, we shouldn't point fingers unless we have conclusive evidence."

Braun closed his eyes for a moment and exhaled through his nostrils. "Lauren, I've heard these kinds of things before. It's straight from the propaganda machine used on Magnus. They're coming here now, using the same old tricks as before. We need to do something about it. This needs to stop."

"You're right, Braun. These kinds of divisive efforts should be stopped, but not in the way you're thinking."

Braun frowned. "What do you mean?"

"I mean that if we start silencing people, it sends the wrong message, and those ideas will spread faster than they otherwise would have," Lauren replied.

"She's right," Isaac said. "Sometimes to defeat bad ideas, you need to bring them out into the light, exposing them for what they are. Then, you spread better ideas among people."

Braun shook his head, unconvinced. "You don't understand. This kind of divisiveness becomes violent. I've seen it happen before."

"Okay," Lauren said. "Let's finish up here and then head over to New Hope so we can investigate this for ourselves."

Braun nodded, looking relieved.

Lauren brought up her personal holoscreen and saw a message waiting for her. She opened the message and sighed.

"What's the matter?" Isaac asked.

She quickly finished reading and closed the holoscreen. "It's Ethan. He's on his way back to Earth."

Isaac frowned. "Wow, that was quick. Mission over already?"

Lauren shook her head. "I don't think so. He's been relieved of duty, pending an investigation."

Isaac's eyes widened. "An investigation! What the heck did he do?"

"I don't know. It was a short message he sent while in transit."

Isaac nodded a little and waited for her to look at him. "When it rains, it pours, right? We'll catch up to Ethan when he gets back."

Lauren nodded, still worried about her brother. She knew that formal investigations in the CDF were serious business. Ethan was in real trouble.

11

As much as Connor tried to recall what Earth had been like during his youth, he found that sometimes he had trouble doing so. He remembered snippets of a life before joining the NA Alliance Military where his family had moved around a lot. He'd spent a lifetime on the move, not really settling down until after surviving two wars. He'd had spans of quiet times between the Vemus War and the Krake War, but it wasn't until after the Krake War that he'd really found peace in his life. New Earth was his home, and until recently, Old Earth had been a distant memory.

The planet had changed, but some of the ruined cities teased memories out of his brain that he hadn't realized were there. He supposed this was a homecoming of sorts, but there were moments when he couldn't wait to go back home to New Earth. This was a long mission, and he'd known that when he agreed to it, and like all missions, it was right in the middle of it when the pull to go back home was the strongest.

Lenora sat next to him on the shuttle and they both gazed quietly out the window.

"It's still surprising to me just how much has changed," Lenora said and grimaced a little. "I feel like I keep saying that."

Connor chuckled. "I know what you mean."

"When you leave a place, you have this idea that it'll remain the same until you return. Not that I ever had any illusions of that happening on Earth, but still, it's what's been on my mind," she said and leaned back in her seat, crossing her arms. She glanced around and leaned toward Connor. "Sometimes it reminds me of New Earth—you know, finding the Ovarrow ruins and trying to piece together what had really happened."

Connor nodded. "It's almost like we're the aliens here."

Lenora's bright blue eyes widened, and she nodded. "That's exactly it. And it feels wrong to think like that."

Even though the human population was recovering from a huge decline, they were now a species who lived on multiple worlds—New Earth, Old Earth, and the second colony. Connor was sure there was a name for the colony. Noah must have mentioned it, but he couldn't remember what it was.

"What's that thought, love?" Lenora asked.

He shrugged. "Just thinking about Noah."

She smiled. "Oh yeah? I miss him."

When they'd first arrived at the colony on New Earth, Lenora had more or less adopted Noah as the little brother she'd never had.

"I can't remember what name they'd decided on for the second colony."

She frowned in thought for a few seconds and then shrugged. "Neither can I. He should be returning home from there by now. I can't wait to finally meet his son."

Connor smiled. He still remembered Noah as the unwilling recruit into the first Search and Rescue platoon for Field Ops, but Noah's contributions to the colony and humanity had changed the course of their entire species. For one, they wouldn't be flying through Earth's atmosphere if it weren't for Noah inventing FTL.

The shuttle flew over the city of Prism, which was one of the larger settlements on the North American continent. The city had been rebuilt using materials left over from the town that had been there. Those few people who'd taken refuge in a bunker had managed to build a new city next to an older one. Over the years, as the population grew, Prism had overtaken the old city. There was the lack of a central government that had been there before the Vemus Wars, making it similar to the colony where they'd had regional mayors that led a cooperative existence with their neighbors. But the people here had been trapped on Earth because the orbital platforms prevented anyone from leaving or coming to the planet.

"Looks like they were able to update the power grid," Lenora said, gesturing out the window.

"That's good. We still need an agreement for the central settlement site for the refugees. It's not right to just dump them in the various cities and expect them to be accommodated."

It was enlightening, dealing with people. The survivors of Earth were quite welcoming to refugees from the solar system, but they had very real concerns about their ability to accommodate them all. The spacers seemed determined to settle wherever they could, and most were happy to do that. It had been generations since they'd been on a planet. But there were a growing number of elites among the spacers that expected a certain level of deference to be given to them and the problems they'd faced for the past two centuries.

The shuttle flew Connor and Lenora right to the city square

where the seat of the local government was located. The city had been designed with a central park and campus for the local government to assemble and govern the regional residents. The briefing Connor had reviewed indicated that though the cities had separate regional authorities, they used the framework for laws that had been the foundation of the NA Alliance. Connor thought this was a good start and would make dealings between the colony and Earth that much easier. But there were other settlements across the planet that needed to be brought into the fold.

The shuttle landed at a designated landing pad where a CDF escort had been provided for their security. Connor saw that two other shuttles had already arrived.

"Looks like we're last to get here," Lenora said.

"You know what they say—save the best for last."

She rolled her eyes, amused. "Says the man who hates tardiness."

Connor shrugged. "I call that a healthy sense of punctuality. Showing up on time is common courtesy and shows respect for those you're meeting with." She eyed him and he sighed a little. "Okay, fine, there are exceptions for unforeseen circumstances."

"You've really evolved over the years."

"Or you just got used to how I do things."

Lenora smiled. "I love how you do things now. It took some work, but I got the job done."

She smiled at him mischievously.

"And I can say that I honestly sleep better knowing that no matter what happens, our shuttles have a remote override feature for pilots whose skills aren't up to snuff."

She pursed her lips. "Touché, and that's ancient history."

There were groups of people gathered outside various government buildings. Large holoscreens showed a live video of the Town Hall where their meeting would begin shortly. They were escorted through a side entrance where tall windows allowed the sunlight to bathe the entire area. The smart glass diverted the worst of the gleam, so the brightness was kept at an acceptable level.

They were escorted through a series of hallways until they arrived at the central meeting area. A large table was set on a stage in the center of an amphitheater of old. There were representatives from the neighboring cities, as well as placeholder holograms of participants who'd been invited from across the planet. Connor and Lenora headed toward the section of the table where the colonial diplomatic envoy was sitting. Fabian Dumont lifted his chin in greeting before standing to greet them formally.

"Need to put on a good show," Fabian said with a wry grin.

He kissed Lenora on the cheek and traded grips with Connor.

Qenirian stood nearby. The Ovarrow was as tall as Connor and had brownish skin with pointy protrusions that stemmed from his shoulders and elbows. He regarded Connor with almost feline-looking eyes.

"I think you're enjoying the attention now," Connor said.

"Only until the novelty of seeing a different species diminishes."

"That's when you really need to pay attention."

Qenirian stared at him for a few seconds with a thoughtful frown. "I am always attentive, especially for events such as these."

Connor sat down with Qenirian to his right. Lenora sat on his left and was speaking with Fabian.

"What do you think so far?" Connor asked.

Qenirian glanced around the large room. Rows of attendees filled up the space. "I remember the public forums I attended during our campaign to officially join the colony. Progress appears to move quite slowly, but that is an illusion. Much of the groundwork established here will influence the future for generations to come. I'm glad I can be a witness to some of it."

"It might be longer than you think it will be."

"Unless we experience some significant breakthroughs with what you humans refer to as prolonging."

Connor knew he was right. The average human lifespan had been extended to over two hundred years, and he was only now approaching what would be considered middle-aged. Ovarrow lifespans were much shorter in comparison, only approaching eighty years. Recent generations were expected to live longer, but Qenirian was correct. It would take a significant breakthrough to increase Ovarrow lifespans anywhere near what the current human lifespan was.

Connor frowned in thought. "Human lifespan" was the wrong term; it was "colonial" lifespan. People on Earth and throughout the solar system had lost the prolonging technology, whereas colonial scientists had improved upon it, so it was even better than what pre-Vemus-War Earth had been.

An older man approached the central podium, and Connor recognized him as Thomas Kessler, Mayor of Prism.

"Welcome," Mayor Kessler said. He had a voice like the aged wisdom of a man who had seen and done a lot of things. He reminded Connor of Tobias Quinn. Sometimes when the man spoke, it triggered Connor's memory of New Earth's first governor.

A hush swept over the large room.

Mayor Kessler turned to address those sitting at the long table. "Esteemed guests, both here and abroad, I welcome the opportunity to facilitate these early steps that will shape the future of us all. I formally acknowledge the presence of the colonial diplomatic envoy from New Earth. In the short time you've been here, I've personally seen the impact you've had in making Earth accessible again and in increasing the rebuilding efforts that will one day help us surpass anything achieved before."

Applause broke out among the attendees, and Connor watched as they stood, honoring them. He had to admit that it felt good to have their efforts recognized.

For the next half hour, introductions were made by all the participants in this Global Town Hall. Then presentations began. Connor watched as Fabian Dumont informed the people of Earth as to the current status of their ongoing efforts. He was at home at the podium and thrived when presenting to a crowd.

"I cannot emphasize enough the need for a central settlement site for refugees, but I think there should be consideration of going even further than that," Dumont said. "We're still compiling data from our analysis of this planet, about which we're learning more and more each day. This data has been and will continue to be shared. There are some continents that are better suited for rebuilding the human civilization here. I must stress that for some of the remote enclaves, where they've worked so hard all this time, it will be difficult to accept, but in the long term, the benefits far outweigh the costs.

"Our goal is to help improve the lives of all the people here —all lives—by providing the means and access to medical technology that has been lost and education that includes the latest discoveries. The future is bright for all of us, and on behalf of the entire diplomatic envoy, we are eager to lay a firm foundation on which we can build."

Fabian paused for a few moments and sipped from his cup before continuing.

"We simply don't have the resources to provide these things

to every city and enclave across the planet. Therefore, consolidation of habitats is required. One day, with enough of a tech base established, these things could be brought to remote enclaves where people have survived, but our estimate is that this is decades away. When I first learned of this, I felt that it would provide an unfair advantage to those places who receive access to these things first. I was not alone in this assessment, so we had to consider what was the best option to present for you moving forward that enabled us to achieve our objective while being fair, ensuring that no one was left behind. The best plan we could come up with is to help relocate the people living in remote enclaves to central cities on the North American continent."

A wave of quiet conversations swept over the attendees, and Connor was sure it was the same wherever the broadcast of these proceedings was being delivered. This was going to be difficult for people to accept. No one enjoyed being uprooted from their homes and moved to a place they knew nothing about, but he was somewhat biased because he'd witnessed the rebuilding of the colony twice during its short history. People could be resilient when they needed to be.

Fabian glanced at Connor. He'd asked him his opinion on the best way to deliver news that people would have trouble accepting. He gave a mental shrug. Connor had been the bearer of that kind of news more times than he could count. Over the years, the feedback he'd gotten ranged from him being entirely too blunt—or was it bleak?—to his presentation of troublesome news being more balanced in consideration of the recipients. Connor liked to think that he'd become better at communicating the older he'd gotten, but he knew that for the survivors on Earth the news they were hearing today might be a bitter revelation they would struggle to accept. By the sound of it, many were in the outright rejection or denial phase, but their future success depended on how quickly the people of Earth could adapt and accept that even more change would be required of them. The old alliances were dead, and the longer people clung to them, the more it would hinder the future that was being built.

Mayor Kessler joined Fabian at the podium. "Please quiet down. We were told this news would be difficult for us to hear, and the envoy has graciously agreed to answer your questions. This cannot happen until we have order."

Fabian returned to his seat, putting forth the image of someone who was thoughtful and earnest. It had endeared him to a lot of people. Fabian was a good man, and a seasoned diplomat. Connor had worked with all kinds of ambassadors over the years, and they were lucky to have a diplomat of Fabian's caliber.

Mayor Kessler waited for the room to become quiet, which it eventually did. There was a timer for the question-and-answer portion of this meeting, which would hopefully contribute to the spirit of cooperation.

"Jalen Ibanez, Mayor of Amtown. Why don't you start us off?"

"Thank you, Mayor Kessler," Ibanez said and looked at the colonial envoy. "We've been in the game of survival for a very long time, so I can appreciate what you went through to bring us these options. Will you make the data you used in your review process available to us so we can conduct our own analysis? Perhaps there is something we might bring forth that hasn't been considered."

"Absolutely," Fabian said. "By the end of today, we will transmit all the data used in our analysis for anyone to review, and we welcome all serious feedback."

Ibanez smiled and nodded. "Thank you." He paused, considering for a moment, then asked. "One of the questions I've been receiving is whether we will be welcome to travel to New Earth. Since your arrival, the wonders of humanity's second home have sent imaginations soaring, and many long to see it as well."

Kessler nodded enthusiastically. "This is a question I've received, too."

Fabian gave a sympathetic smile, the kind used to soften a blow. "That is an eventuality we hope will come to pass."

Ibanez nodded slowly, and looked as if he were going to ask a follow-up question, but Kessler interpreted his pause and opened the way for others to raise their own questions.

"Okay, our next question comes from Spacer Representative Pandu Mukhtar," Kessler said.

The spacer's delegation sat on the other side of the long table. Pandu Mukhtar had dark skin and was of average height. His dark eyes conveyed a keen intelligence as he stood and turned toward the Colonial Envoy.

"I think a follow-up on Mayor Ibanez's question is warranted here. General Gates, why is travel to your colony forbidden?"

Connor blinked. He hadn't expected to be asked anything. Fabian was designated to field questions. However, not being one to shrink from a challenge, Connor stood.

"Travel to the New Earth colony is not forbidden, Representative Mukhtar. It is an eventuality that there will be travel between our two planets."

Pandu Mukhtar considered this for a few seconds, looking puzzled. "Why do we have to wait? What if we wanted to go right now? Would we be welcome at your colony?"

Connor regarded his opponent for a moment. He knew a performance when he saw one, and right off the cuff, he knew that Pandu Mukhtar had an agenda.

"This is beyond the purview of the envoy."

The edges of Mukhtar's dark, thin lips lifted a little. He gestured toward the audience but kept his gaze on Connor. "So, we wouldn't be welcome. Thank you for being so forthcoming with your response."

Connor allowed a pregnant pause to let the tension build. It was a technique he'd learned over the years that yielded two results—it made people listen more intently when he *did* speak, and it sometimes eroded the will of his opponent, allowing their comments to crumble.

He tipped his head to the side a little and locked his gaze on the spacer representative. "I was not finished, and that is not what I said." He turned to address the audience. "We're all people, so no one is expressly forbidden from visiting the colony, but there is limited access to our ships and their capabilities to transport people back to the colony. The last thing we wish to convey is information that is misleading. We will deliver on all our promises."

"I see. Very well spoken," said Mukhtar and gestured toward Connor. "But you do function as the gatekeeper to interstellar travel. So, if you are unwilling or have limited capacity to take us to New Earth, will you share this technology with us?"

"Eventually," Connor replied. There were more than a few people voicing their disapproval of his answer, and it didn't perturb him in the slightest. These people were being manipulated by Pandu Mukhtar. "For the foreseeable future, our efforts will be focused as Fabian Dumont has already stated. Eventually, we will also rotate out of here so our citizens can return home to their families and allow others to come here."

Mayor Kessler looked troubled. "Thank you, General Gates. You are correct in reminding us that we have larger concerns than whether we will have access to FTL technology. All things in time."

Connor gave him an acknowledging nod.

"One more question for General Gates, if I may?" Pandu Mukhtar asked.

Mayor Kessler looked at Connor. If he put Pandu Mukhtar off, it would appear that he had something to hide. It was better to face his opponent directly.

Connor leveled his gaze at the spacer representative. "Go ahead."

His smile appeared just a tad smug, as if he'd achieved some kind of victory. "Thank you for indulging me, General Gates. There is a serious question that hasn't been raised as of yet, and I'm not sure whether it has even been considered. I would like to bring it up now. Is there a limit to the amount of assistance you intend to provide?"

Connor frowned. "I'm not sure what you're asking. Could you be more specific?"

He nodded. "Of course. Your colony benefited greatly from the sacrifice of our ancestors. Your survival was made possible because of us, and as such, I think we, the descendants of those who assisted your colony, are owed compensation for this. The terms of this compensation can be agreed upon, but it might be beyond what you deem appropriate."

Connor considered this for a few moments, more to strangle his growing irritation with the spacer representative than figuring out what he wanted to say. He knew *exactly* what he wanted to say. "Let me see if I'm understanding you correctly. You're asking me if I think we have a moral obligation to assist the people here as some kind of reparation, the terms of which you intend to set?"

Pandu Mukhtar made a show of considering his reply, and then nodded. "Reparations is precisely what I wish to discuss, and quite honestly, are long overdue."

Connor narrowed his gaze. "Long overdue!" he snapped, instantly calling to mind colonial lives lost since they'd come here, both from fighting Vemus remnants and outright betrayal. He clenched his teeth for a few moments and turned toward the audience. "The colony chose to send us back here to Earth because our probes had detected the presence of the Vemus here. We came to assess and remove the threat of the Vemus because we also learned there were survivors here. After such a long time, we finally had irrefutable proof that people had survived their war with the Vemus. Since we've arrived, we've done our best to understand the current state of things here now, as well as some of the history." Connor turned toward Mukhtar. "We are here to help, but any presumption or demands put on us through some misguided sense of entitlement will be met with staunch resistance. The way I see it is that you are owed nothing. And regarding the argument of the sacrifice of the people who redirected the Ark, they did so for the preservation of the species. It was with the best intentions that those people took those actions, some of whom were not strangers to us, meaning that we knew them. *I* knew them."

Pandu Mukhtar pursed his lips for a few seconds. "I believe your position on reparations is abundantly clear. Regardless of whether you think it is necessary, there is a growing majority of us who happen to believe it's appropriate and that we are within our rights to demand this from you."

"Demands," Connor repeated. He glanced at Lenora and noted her worried expression. "I could just as easily propose demands be placed on you. After all, who can say whether the Vemus would've found the colony if it weren't for the actions taken by the people here? I could go another step beyond that and say with authority that if we're going to continue this blame game you seem determined to play, then based on our analysis of the Vemus, we know it was scientists from here who modified the pathogen that made the Vemus hunt humans to the exclusion of all other mammals. Do you really want to pursue this line of thought here and now in front of the world?"

Pandu Mukhtar blinked, frowning with uncertainty. He'd thought to provoke Connor and, like many others before him, had gotten a lot more than he bargained for. The audience seemed to have been stunned into silence.

Mayor Kessler cleared his throat. "Thank you, General Gates and Representative Mukhtar. I think we should move on, as we have more questions."

Connor watched as Pandu Mukhtar sat down, and then he did the same. Lenora leaned over to him and whispered something about messing with bulls and getting skewered by the horns. He honestly didn't know whether she made these things up or had read them in some kind of historical reference of sayings and mottos.

"Something we should all remember," Mayor Kessler continued, "is that none of these questions have been planned. This Global Town Hall was put together rather abruptly, and it is our goal to create unity."

Fabian Dumont indicated he'd like to speak, and Mayor Kessler gestured for him to do so.

"I think it's important for us to look ahead to building our future rather than basing anyone's involvement or commitment purely on a historical reparations stance," Fabian said.

There was a round of applause, but Connor saw that not everyone participated.

The time devoted to questions and answers was soon used up. Promises were made and assurances were given before they exited the stage. Connor and the rest of envoy decided to meet in one of the conference rooms provided for them. It was a smaller room, as it was just the four of them.

Fabian was about to speak when Connor gestured for him not to. Fabian nodded, and Connor reached inside his pocket, bringing out a comlink scrambler.

"Should be good now," Connor said.

Fabian frowned. "What is that?"

"Just a precaution that gives us some additional privacy," Connor replied.

Lenora sighed. "We should've anticipated a stunt like this from the spacers."

Connor shrugged. "Only the ones from Magnus Station, or I should say the spacers who were part of the administration. We'll need to investigate who Pandu Mukhtar is."

"What concerns me," Fabian said, "is that he went right after you. I thought we were beyond this reparations nonsense after we deposed President Shao Fen of Magnus Station."

"He had supporters, even if they kept their heads down after we arrested most of their leadership," Lenora said.

Qenirian cleared his throat. "We haven't heard the last of this."

Fabian frowned toward the Ovarrow. "Why not?"

"Because this went almost exactly as Pandu Mukhtar expected. He knew we wouldn't commit to their reparations request. He just wanted to raise the issue in a public forum in order to get more support."

Connor considered it for a few moments and nodded. "And I played right into his hands?"

Qenirian frowned and shook his head. "Possibly, but that doesn't make the answers you provided any less valid. It's important that all parties involved know exactly where we stand on these issues."

Fabian banged his fist on the table a few times—not hard but enough to show that even he was frustrated by the turn of events. "Just because we're not committing to any silly notions of reparations doesn't mean we're not committing to helping the rebuilding efforts. We'd never leave these people in a lurch."

"That's not how it's going to be perceived," Connor said. Fabian frowned. "The perception is that something was taken away from the people of Earth—something they never really had or were owed—and they're now considering that perhaps they've missed out somehow on something they're entitled to. Ideas like this spread like wildfire." He looked at Qenirian. "I think you're right and hit the target right in the middle."

"It's behavior I recognize among my own species."

Lenora cleared her throat and raked her fingers through her long auburn hair. "Well then, we focus our messaging on what we *can* do. Fabian had the right of it in saying that we need to look ahead to build our future."

Fabian smiled and almost looked a little embarrassed.

Connor smiled. "Yeah, it's like you carry a storage container full of slogans."

Fabian laughed. "Have you listened to yourself? You inspire the best in all of us, Connor."

The others stared at him, acknowledgement in their eyes.

"If we keep going like this, Lenora is going to tell me that my ego is too big to fit on a battleship carrier."

Lenora grinned. "Oh, why stop there?"

Connor felt some of the tension evaporate following the jovial exchange. He shared a look with his wife and then looked at the others. "Well, now that the spacers have gotten their fifteen minutes of fame, we'll be better prepared to address their message, and we'll need to address it when it comes up again."

Lenora nodded. "Not only us, we need an official stance."

"I'll take this up with my team and see what we can come up with," Fabian said and frowned. "We might get pushback that requires us to take this up with the colonial government."

"Let's not get ahead of ourselves," Connor said. "They don't even have a global government here, and by the time they do, we would've laid the groundwork that will ensure cooperation between us."

Fabian stared at him, eyes intense, and Connor shrugged. "Not my first time dealing with this sort of thing. We have our own mandates to work within for the time we're here, and we should stick to working within those parameters. No need to borrow trouble from the future. It'll be here soon enough."

They were all quiet for a few moments.

"A question for all of you," Qenirian said. "Do any of you believe reparations are due to survivors here?"

Connor had already made his opinion known about this, so he was sure the question didn't really apply to him and waited for the others to respond.

"The heart of our mission to come here," Lenora said, "was a moral obligation we felt for everyone left behind. We were able to return, so we did. Once you add this framework of reparations due, the compulsory context around it will inhibit the entire process. This wasn't put forward through someone's misguided attempt at gaining justice. This is about consolidating power."

Connor smiled at his wife. She was among the most brilliant people he'd ever known.

"Is it really that insidious?" Fabian asked, looking at Connor.

"I think so. We'll need to keep an eye out, but it doesn't mean that anyone who brings the argument forward is pushing their own agenda."

Lenora nodded. "Yes, they could be pawns. So, we'll need to identify who the ringleaders are. Who stands to gain the most?"

"What about those who choose to follow this?" Qenirian asked.

"There's only so much we can do," Connor replied. "I think Thomas Kessler understands, and perhaps even Jalen Ibanez, but there were a lot of others at the town hall and attending virtually."

Fabian nodded. "And we just told them that their best shot at a prosperous future requires that many relocate their homes to the North American continent."

"All that was based on facts," Connor said. "There was a reason it was such a powerful alliance, even before the Ark left Earth. The whole planet was affected by their war with the Vemus. There are large portions that will take decades to recover, even with our help. The facts will speak for themselves. The only thing that's going to keep people from coming together is either fear or pride. We can help people with their fear through assurances and dealing with their concerns."

"Let's be clear," Lenora added. "The entire burden isn't on us. Everyone has a stake in this and will need to contribute."

Fabian nodded and then stared out the window. "The human population used to number in the tens of billions across the solar system. Now, between the colony and the survivors here, our population edges just over ten million. Why does it feel like we're still dealing with the same problems we were faced with before the Vemus Wars?"

Connor chuckled. "Because we are, at least to some degree. We're still the same, but hopefully we're a little smarter than before."

"And have a greater appreciation for the important things," Lenora said.

12

THE CDF HAD ESTABLISHED a temporary base of operations outside the city of Prism, which was where Ethan had spent most of his time since becoming a hybrid. He'd been put on temporary medical leave...again. Captain Waller couldn't relieve him of duty, so he did the next best thing—he'd raised concerns about Ethan's ability to function in the CDF. His actions were borderline insubordinate, which could be attributed to the unique situation surrounding Ethan in particular, and further medical evaluation was required. This was all a way of saying that Ethan was not to be trusted. Saving an entire platoon didn't count in the eyes of Captain Waller and his superior, Major James Racine.

Ethan should've realized this assignment was doomed to fail from the start. He'd been assigned to a platoon that had just come off a tough mission where it was suspected that hybrids were somehow colluding with the Vemus and were responsible for the deaths of CDF soldiers. It had made them less sympathetic and borderline hostile toward hybrids. When they'd learned that Ethan was a hybrid, it had gone downhill from there. Ethan could handle the adversity, at least he thought he could, but it was the sympathy that really hit him in the gut. The soldiers he'd come to know during the mission didn't hate him; they just didn't trust him, despite all he'd done. They pitied him. They viewed him as some kind of victim of circumstance and that he wasn't responsible for his own actions. It was enough to make him clench his teeth. Coupled with the colossally stupid decision to nuke the entire region where the mine and secret research facility had been was enough to make him scream. They didn't understand the importance of what the site had to offer, and now they would never know what secrets the research base would have revealed.

No one cares about the origin of the Vemus…

Part of the reason they'd returned to Earth was to understand where the Vemus had come from. It was secondary to helping the survivors, but there was no reason to destroy the entire site. They weren't in danger. The Vemus there were starving. They could've returned and been prepared to eliminate the threat while preserving the entire site.

What really set Ethan's teeth on edge was that there was nothing he could do about it now. The site was gone. He'd alerted his superiors as to the potential of the site, and they'd disagreed. Taking this further up the chain of command wasn't really an option. Sure, he had the contacts, but it would also confirm what some people always suspected of him—that he would use his family connections to further his military career. He had to function within the same confines of military protocol as everyone else, but he'd be lying to himself if he said he hadn't been tempted. He knew his father would've wanted that site investigated. But no, he'd filed his own report and sent it up the chain. Whether it made it to his father or General

Quinn was out of his hands. This wasn't the hill he was going to die on.

Ethan was assigned officer's quarters on the base, the same he'd been given before. It was almost like he'd never left. He glanced at the metallic gray walls of the temporary HAB unit and tossed his duffle bag onto the bed. He then transmitted his check-in to COMCENT, and they'd let him know when he'd be scheduled for evaluation. Shaking his head, he turned and left his quarters. Never being one to sit still for any length of time, he decided to take a walk.

A covered walkway connected the different HAB units, and he took the one that led away from the medical center. As he walked down the ramp, he glanced up at bright gray skies. It looked like they'd be getting some rain before long.

"Lieutenant Gates," someone said, and Ethan turned toward them.

"Ambassador Qenirian, hello."

The Ovarrow, at fifty years old, was considered middle aged. "I'm glad I found you before you left."

"Well, you're in luck. I was just about to take a walk."

Qenirian eyed him for a moment. "Not on duty today?"

Ethan shook his head. "No, I'm off duty for now."

Qenirian's gaze shifted to where Ethan had come from and noted the medical center. "I could use a walk."

Ethan saw that there were two CDF soldiers assigned to escort the ambassador.

Qenirian followed his gaze. "Part of the security protocols, I'm afraid."

Ethan lifted his chin toward the soldiers and then began walking. Qenirian walked next to him, easily keeping pace.

Ethan eyed him for a second. "Why do I get the feeling you didn't just happen to be in the neighborhood?"

He chuckled. "That's because I wasn't. You're as observant as your esteemed parents."

Ethan frowned a little as they walked. "Did you know I was here?"

He didn't reply right away, and Ethan waited him out. "You could say that I'm well informed."

"You must be if you have access to mission reports. What is it you want to talk to me about?"

"Actually, I was wondering if you wanted to speak to me."

They left the base, and several of the city's residents did a double take when they saw Qenirian, but they quickly recovered and continued on their way.

Ethan gave the Ovarrow a once-over and couldn't think of anything he wanted to speak to him about. He shrugged. "Meaning no disrespect, but I can't think of anything off the top of my head."

Qenirian tilted his head to the side and rubbed one of the pronounced brow ridges that extended to the side of his head. "You and I have a lot in common now."

Ethan's eyebrows pinched together. "We do?"

"Yes, we both have a foothold in two societies. Don't you see it?"

Ethan considered it for a few moments, and Qenirian gave him the time, waiting patiently. "You mean because I'm a hybrid now?"

"Precisely. You have a foothold in your old life as a soldier and colonist, and another foot in the world of being a Vemus human hybrid. It's not easy to maintain a balance or find peace like that."

Ethan pressed his lips together a little while he thought about it. "But you've been part of the colony for a while now."

Qenirian nodded. It was always a slow and deliberate gesture when the Ovarrow did it. "It's also something we still struggle with in some ways. We've embraced the ways of the colony while at the same time maintaining some of our traditions." He eyed Ethan for a moment, considering. "The traditions we were able to learn before the Krake."

The Krake was a race of beings who'd waged an interdimensional war on the Ovarrow in multiple universes. They conducted brutal experiments that ranged from biological impacts to psychological warfare. What followed was the elimination of entire worlds. The fact that even some of the Ovarrow traditions had survived all that was a miracle in itself.

"I guess I hadn't considered it, but now that you mention it, I can see what you're saying."

"Good, you should keep it in mind."

"What good will that do?" he asked, his tone a bit sharp.

Qenirian ignored it. "You cannot pretend to be what you were before."

"I'm not pretending anything like that."

Qenirian leveled his gaze at him. Ethan could feel his assertion begin to crumble, and he sighed.

"They'll kick me out of the CDF if I don't pretend. All the problems started when I revealed it."

"Problems for who? You, or the soldiers you served with?"

Ethan regarded him for a few seconds. "Did my father put you up to this?"

Qenirian raised one of his hands in a placating gesture. "I assure you that he has absolutely no idea I'm here. I'm not even sure if he's aware that you've returned to the planet. I've come to speak to you of my own volition."

Ethan looked away for a moment, considering. "What should I do? What did you and the other Ovarrow do when they chose to become colonial citizens?"

"We had to decide who we were going to be moving forward. We had to decide whether we're going to emulate you humans or try to maintain our own unique identities. It's something we continue to consider even now. We try to emulate the things we've observed that worked best and determine whether those behaviors are something that would improve us."

"I appreciate what you're trying to do, but being a hybrid is different. It's dangerous. We must constantly be attentive to changes that occur in us because they can be unpredictable.

"What kind of changes?"

"Sometimes it causes certain genes to express themselves, and that expression puts us in danger. There are people who've died because of it."

"Has this happened to you?"

Ethan shook his head. "Not exactly. I can hold my breath for a really long time now."

Qenirian frowned. "How long?"

"Ninety minutes."

Qenirian blinked, looking surprised.

"It's true. I can increase the amount of hemoglobin in my blood, which helps me maintain oxygen. It's something other mammals can do, but it does have some issues."

"Like what?"

"When I do it, I have to remember to breathe."

He frowned. "Remember to breathe?"

Ethan nodded. "Yeah, I'm not sure how familiar you are with the creatures of Earth. There are some mammals that live in the oceans who have to remember to breathe. It's not involuntary like it is for you and…well me, but only sometimes."

He stared at him for a few moments. "And this has put you in danger? This has hurt you?"

"Yeah, it scared my sister, Lauren. I hadn't realized I wasn't breathing, and well, as you can imagine, if you don't breathe, things tend to break down."

Qenirian looked both shocked and a little worried, as if Ethan was an anomaly they didn't quite understand. That was usually when the walls went up.

"Ready to run away?" Ethan asked.

Qenirian shook his head. "Never, but you must allow people to become acquainted with this information."

"That's just it," Ethan said and gestured around them. "These people have had what? Two centuries, maybe less, to learn to live with it, and look at how they are. Some portions of them embrace it. They had little choice because there weren't many people left in general, but the spacers were different. It caused huge divisions among them. People died for this. How am I supposed to have a foothold in any world while I'm like this?"

Qenirian regarded him for a few moments. "Patience."

Ethan blinked and nearly rolled his eyes. He hadn't realized how frustrated he was until now. "Patience! Are you serious?"

"You are so young. It goes against your gut instinct, which drives you forward. However, in this instance, a little bit of patience could go a long way toward long-term gains."

Ethan knew the ambassador was trying to help him, but he'd been patient. He'd exercised huge amounts of patience while the doctors measured and tested him for months. Then, he finally got his first mission and this happened. It felt like someone was working against him, but he also knew that wasn't true.

Ethan blew out a long breath. "I appreciate what you're trying to do for me. I'll think about what you've said, but I'm not sure if it'll help any. I'm noticing that the same divisions that have plagued the spacers have infected the CDF. If I go back to the colony, it might be worse."

Qenirian's eyes drew up in alarm. "*If* you go back to the

colony? Surely you can't mean to never return."

His first instinct was to deny it, but as the seconds went by, he found that he couldn't. "I don't know. I guess I have a lot to think about. If you don't mind, I'd like to be alone for a little while."

"Of course," Qenirian replied. "You know where to find me if you want to talk."

"Thanks," Ethan replied.

Qenirian turned back and began walking toward the CDF base. Ethan went in the opposite direction that took him farther into the city.

He still didn't completely understand why Qenirian had sought him out. It was clear that he'd wanted to help him, and Ethan supposed that the Ovarrow did have that impartial third-party perspective. He just wasn't sure it helped. So what if he had a foothold in two worlds? Many people did. His father was a soldier with a foothold both in the military and in the civilian world. His mother was an academic, renowned in her field, who had grown beyond that. But he was different. What had happened to Ethan was different. He'd been changed so much that he could never go back, so why did he find himself wanting to so badly? He wanted to get back to being a pilot, flying a Talon V space fighter. That seemed so far away now, and he was afraid he'd never get back to it.

Physically, he'd never been as strong as he was now, and his mind had never been as sharp, so what was holding him back? Thinking back to his last mission, he'd done things in that mine that elite soldiers in combat suits would be hard pressed to match.

Ethan walked through the city. It was a bit of a stretch thinking of this place as a city. It was so spread out that it sprawled across the countryside. He'd been going for hours, walking without a destination. He wasn't even tired or hungry. He could go on like this for days if he had to. At some point, he decided to begin heading back to the CDF base. He must've been moving quicker than he thought, because it hadn't taken him long before he stood outside his room.

He paused in front of the door for a few seconds before transmitting his authentication. The door opened, and he walked inside. There was a workstation next to the window, and the holoscreen powered up. A video comlink chimed from his sister.

Ethan walked to the workstation and sat, accepting the link.

Lauren peered at him. "Where have you been? I've been sending messages to you all day."

He frowned and glanced at his wrist computer. "Sorry, I took a walk and enabled the privacy mode on my wrist computer."

She stared at him for a few moments, doing some kind of quick assessment. "Are you okay?"

A flicker of annoyance must've shown on his face.

"Come on, Ethan, you know what I mean."

"Honestly, I'm a little annoyed to be back here. There's nothing wrong with me, Lauren. I don't understand why they have to do yet another evaluation."

"Yes you do. They'll make you do as many as it takes for them to be convinced you're not a danger to yourself and others."

Ethan rolled his eyes. "I'm a soldier. By definition, I've been trained to be dangerous."

She gave him an exasperated look and then laughed. After a few moments, he began to chuckle himself.

"Thank God for that," Lauren said. "If you hadn't loosened up, I'd have had to start reminding you of all the embarrassing things you've done."

He regarded her for a second. "Well, there's plenty of that to go around."

They shared a moment and then Lauren said. "What if there was a way to reverse it?"

He frowned. "Reverse what?"

"You being a hybrid."

He stared at her. She was serious. More than serious—she was excited.

"I didn't think it was possible."

"I said *we* haven't figured it out."

"And have *you?*"

"I'm getting there. I've come across some things that might make it a real possibility."

Ethan leaned back in his chair with a thoughtful frown.

"What's the matter? I thought you'd leap at the opportunity."

He pursed his lips for a second, feeling conflicted. "I don't know. I guess I'm just surprised."

Lauren nodded. "Understandable, but what do you think? Would you do it if you could?"

Ethan swallowed hard and considered it. What had been so clear before seemed to have blurred in the last few minutes. "Hypothetically, I'm not sure. I'm still trying to learn to live with it."

"Why the hesitation? Is this because of Cynergy?"

His gaze flicked toward the door. He'd long since become accustomed to the connection he shared with Cynergy.

Lauren cleared her throat and he looked at her. "She's part of this. She's part of me."

Lauren blinked a few times. "She can be cured, too."

Ethan scowled and shook his head. "Don't put it like that."

Lauren looked away for a second, abashed. "I'm sorry. I know it sounds derogatory, and that's not how I mean it, but the Vemus were a pathogen. It's a disease. Just because an adaptation inside of us allowed for some kind of hybridization to occur doesn't change the fact that this stems from a disease, and we need to think of it as such."

Ethan could make a pretty good guess as to how Cynergy, Clip, and other hybrids he knew would react to that. So much of their identity was wrapped up in what they were.

"This could be a way to reverse what was done to you and finally put things back to normal. Isn't that what you want? To be back with the 7th flying missions and doing what you do best, little brother?"

Ethan was quiet for a few moments. "Yes," he said and shook his head. "No. Heck, I don't know. I want that, but at the same time—I just didn't think this was an option."

"It's going to be an option. It's your best option."

"But you haven't done it yet. This is all theory, right?"

"I'm getting close. I've learned some things recently that are promising," she said, eyes gleaming, and she smiled.

She was really fighting for this, doing what she thought was best for him.

"Just for the record, so I'm clear. If a cure was really an option, would you take it?"

Ethan sighed. His answer was on the tip of his tongue, but his mouth wouldn't form the words.

A loud slam came from his door, and he spun his chair around.

"What was that noise?" Lauren asked.

Ethan stood and peered out the window. He saw Cynergy storming away, lengthening her stride.

He looked back at the comlink. "I've gotta go. I'll speak to you soon," he said.

He hastened to the door and was through it before Lauren could respond.

Ethan ran down the corridor, shouting for Cynergy to wait.

13

ETHAN KNEW Cynergy had heard him, even though she was more than fifty meters away from him and the area was a buzz of activity. Highly acute hearing was one of her specialties, and with their connection, it was all but a given that she'd heard him.

As he ran after her, he wondered how much of his conversation she'd overheard. He watched as she scowled at a soldier who approached her. Her skin had darkened, but her long blonde hair trailed behind her.

Ethan closed the distance. "I've got this, Private," he said.

She was still a short distance ahead, and he knew that if she really wanted to run, she could go much faster than this.

Cynergy stopped and spun toward him, regarding him coldly. She'd told him she couldn't read his thoughts, but she must've sensed something. All he was getting from her was cold fury and a sense of betrayal.

More than a few people stopped to look at them, sensing that something was about to happen.

"Let's just talk," Ethan said quietly.

Cynergy narrowed her gaze. "What's that? I can't hear you. I think you're mumbling."

Her skin color went back to pale and she glared at him. "Is this what you prefer?" she asked, striding toward him.

Ethan's mouth hung open a little and he was momentarily at a loss for words.

Cynergy paused and her skin changed again. As she embraced her hybrid nature, she became dark with a purplish sheen, and her voice deepened. She turned toward the people staring at her and hissed. "Isn't this what you're waiting for? This is what I am. I shouldn't have to hide it from anyone," she said and looked at Ethan. A pair of blazing, emerald-colored eyes stabbed him right in the chest. "This isn't something to be ashamed of or that needs to be cured."

Ethan held her gaze and stepped toward her. He didn't need to rely on the connection they shared to know she was hurt. She was hurt because she'd overheard his conversation with Lauren and now believed that he wanted to be changed back.

He inhaled a deep breath. "You only heard half a conversation."

"I heard enough," she snarled.

Cynergy had had a tough time among the spacers where the very real possibility of dying was part of her everyday life.

He held up his hands in a placating gesture. "Please," he said gently.

Her bottom lip trembled, and her cold facade began to crumble. Then she clamped her jaw shut.

He came closer to her. "Let's go somewhere so we can talk. Privately," Ethan said with a slight tilt of his head.

Cynergy blinked and glanced over at the people.

Ethan had had just about enough of the audience they'd gathered. He turned toward them. "Show's over. Go on."

The small crowd began to move, slowly at first, but then at a normal pace.

He came to stand in front of Cynergy. "Come on. Let's get out of the street here."

They walked to where a group of rovers were parked, then moved past them and were soon away from the base.

Prism had been built over an older city that Ethan didn't know the name of, but there were still some partially intact buildings among the shrubs and trees.

Sighing, he decided to speak first. "There are a lot of places like this on New Earth."

Cynergy frowned toward him with honey-brown eyes.

He gestured ahead of them to a partial wall that was covered with thick green vines. The wall was angled, as if it had been falling and the only thing keeping it up was the vines. They grew past the wall and clung to the nearby trees.

"Ovarrow ruins. I spent a lot of time exploring them when I was younger."

Cynergy crossed her arms over her stomach. "It looks depressing." He blinked and stared at her, waiting for her to continue. "I've lived on old ships and stations my whole life. Earth was always a mystery to us, something we learned about. We finally get back here and it's like the entire planet is one giant cemetery."

"That's pretty bleak, Cyn, even for you."

She looked at him and there was something in her gaze that just made him feel exposed, as if she really could read his mind. "Do you want to go back to your home?"

He shrugged. "Maybe one day. I'd love to show it to you."

Her gaze hardened a little. "Would I be allowed to go?"

"Of course you would be. Why would even say something like that?"

"You still don't understand."

"Understand what?"

"They're never going to trust you again. You're exiled, Ethan."

"That's absurd." But his words sounded hollow even to him.

She gave him a sympathetic look, and he had flashbacks to how Hayman and the rest of the platoon had regarded him post mission.

"The CDF is being understandably cautious," he said.

"Ethan," she said evenly, "I've lived with this my whole life. Sometimes people do accept it, but they also want to keep you at arm's length, so we're never truly accepted."

"I understand that, but that doesn't match how Elias regarded you when we first got here. Colonel Cooper and the rest of his soldiers welcomed you. The people here are more tolerant than the spacers were."

She nodded slowly. "And how long before those prejudices spread to the people here? Can you tell me it won't happen? You can't because it's already happening."

"Let's just say you're right. Ideas spread. I understand that, but there has got to be a middle ground for coexistence. We found it with the Ovarrow. Why can't we find it with hybrids?"

She tilted her head to the side, her long, dark-blonde hair shifting a little. "I want you to be right about this, but I've got a lifetime of experiences that say otherwise."

"Time will tell then," Ethan said and paused for a moment, considering. "About what you heard...What *did* you hear?"

"That Lauren is working on a cure to rid the world of hybrids. That you would take it if it was available to you."

Cynergy had risked her life to save him. They'd been crashing to the Earth and he was already dying. By changing him to a hybrid, she'd nearly killed herself.

"Cyn," he said, reaching out to grasp one of her hands. She

let him take it. "Lauren is trying to help. There are hybrids who have been a lot less fortunate than us, who have a really hard time surviving, let alone actually living. It's those people she wants to help."

Cynergy gazed into his eyes for a long moment. "And she wants you back to the way you were."

"She's trying to protect me. That's all she's doing. It's not because she hates you or any other hybrid out there."

"She might not, but there are other people who will use this to push a cure on us. We'll all be exiled. It'll be like Magnus Station all over again."

Ethan shook his head. "It won't."

She narrowed her gaze and pulled her hand away from his. "How do you know?"

He inhaled a breath and sighed. "Well, number one, Earth is open to you. There's plenty of room here for people to live. Two, the envoy won't condone those actions."

"But would they give us their support if it came down to it?"

Ethan frowned and considered it for a few moments. "You know I can't answer that. They'd work to prevent it from coming down to an us-or-them decision matrix."

She looked slightly amused. "Decision matrix?"

He smiled. "Would you prefer a common framework from which to base a decision?"

"Now you're just showing off."

"One likes to rise to a challenge."

She rolled her eyes, but then her expression became serious. "You never answered me."

He looked away from her for a moment. "I'm not sure. Don't get insulted. This isn't even a real decision. Wouldn't you consider it? I mean, really consider it?"

"It's part of who I am. It's part of who you are, too, whether you want to accept it or not," Cynergy said and paused for a moment. "My initial reaction might have been too abrupt. I do believe that your sister's intentions are good. I just worry about how others will take advantage of it."

A question came to his mind that he was afraid to ask, but now that it was there, he knew that if he didn't, it would gnaw away at him.

"Things would change between us if you were cured," Cynergy said.

He swallowed hard and clenched his jaw for a moment. "Why? Why does it have to change anything?"

She shrugged. "It's just a feeling," she said and patted her heart.

She was saying that if a cure became available, and he used it, they might lose each other.

He leaned toward her. "We're more than that, Cyn. We have to be."

She blinked and looked away from him. He couldn't tell whether she believed him or not.

"What happened to you on Mars?" she asked.

He told her and she listened.

"So this research base and communications were from someone on Earth before the planet was quarantined?"

Ethan nodded. "And they were coming to Mars. It was the best clue with a real link to the Vemus origins."

"What are you going to do? They destroyed the site. The data is lost."

"I'm going to look for it here," Ethan replied.

She frowned. "How?"

"There has to be a way."

She arched an eyebrow. "You don't know?"

He grimaced, then widened his eyes and smiled. "Find a way

to trace it. And before you ask how I'm going to do it, I'll just tell you." Her full lips lifted at the edges. "Remember all the satellites we saw when we went to the orbital platforms? Many of them were for communications, so it stands to reason that whoever sent that transmission to Mars was on Earth and had to use one of those. I need to figure out how to narrow it down, though."

"We could ask Clip. He wants to see you, anyway."

"About what?"

"He doesn't think you should just be waiting around, doing nothing."

"I'm not."

She stared at him.

"Not anymore. Let's go find Clip."

14

_____

CYNERGY TOOK Ethan to a camp about fifty kilometers outside the city.

Ethan watched the landscape from the rover's windows. "What's he doing way out here?"

"He likes the space out here."

He frowned. "Really?"

She nodded. "And it's private."

Clip was a hybrid leader who rescued people who'd been exiled from Magnus Station.

"Doesn't like the city, I guess."

She considered it for a few moments and then said, "You spend your life aboard old ships and small outposts where space is extremely limited, and you finally get here." She gestured out the window. The rover's windows were down, and they were traveling along an ancient road through the foothills of nearby mountains east of them. She glanced at him and then arched an eyebrow. "What?"

Ethan shrugged. "It's just interesting seeing how spacers react once they get here. You finally get to visit a place you've only read about or seen from far away. Some of you take to the cities where it's convenient and there are lots of people, while others prefer to be away. I don't know if it's solitude, or they just don't trust each other."

"It's both," she replied, and patted her palm on the steering wheel. "We can't just erase decades of skirmishes and conflict."

He nodded. "I get it."

"But you want us to move past it."

"Yes."

"Easier said than done."

He agreed. "Doesn't explain why he's this far out."

"You can ask him yourself. We'll reach camp in a few minutes."

The camp was home to about fifty people. They looked to be mostly ex-spacers, but Ethan recognized the tan uniforms of Prisms Field Ops people. Clip must be coordinating with Colonel Elias Cooper. Ethan wondered if Cooper was at the camp. It had been a couple of months since he'd last seen him.

Cynergy parked the rover and checked in with Clip through comms. "Yes, I have him with me. I'll bring him." Something Clip said made her laugh and she glanced at him. "I'll tell him."

They climbed out of the rover and Cynergy led him through the camp.

Ethan cleared his throat. "Aren't you supposed to tell me something?"

She frowned for a second. "Oh, that's nothing. He wanted me to make sure you weren't moody."

He rolled his eyes. "That was one time."

His adjustment to becoming a hybrid had its challenges, which had initially presented by making his emotions seem like a ship with its maneuvering thrusters all misfiring. That part had been temporary, but Clip had been around for some of it.

"He still has the scars to prove it," she said.

"That's because he refuses to get rid of them."

What had begun as a friendly wrestling match between hybrids had escalated, and there were a few broken windows in an old warehouse. Clip had been showing him a few new tricks that were unique to hybrids. Not only did he finally learn some of his physical capabilities that day, but he'd learned to manage his emotions. Lauren had informed him that his biochip reported his hormones were chaotic for a time and then returned to the familiar pattern that had been recorded in his records. It was as if he'd been reborn, and it affected his entire body.

They found Clip standing at a workbench, reassembling a rifle. He was tall and broad shouldered, with dark hair and a grizzled brown beard. He looked up from his work and smiled, dark-brown eyes gleaming.

Ethan returned the smile and tipped his head to the side where Cynergy stood. "I see you sent out the big guns to get me here."

Clip grinned. "I knew she'd get the job done."

"How'd you know that I'd be back so soon?"

Clip scratched his chin and glanced at Cynergy for a second. "Call it a hunch. Regardless, you're here. What I want to know is whether you're able."

Ethan frowned. "Able to do what?"

"We'll get to that in a second. Cynergy tells me there's something you want my input on."

A message alert appeared on his internal HUD. The message header contained the CDF emblem. "Excuse me for a second," Ethan said and stepped away from them.

He opened the message and quickly read it. Then, with a slight shake of his head, he turned back to the others.

Clip regarded him for a few moments. "More good news?"

Cynergy frowned. "What is it?"

"My request for resources to investigate what I found on Mars has been denied."

Clip tilted his head to the side with pursed lips. "What's this about Mars?"

Ethan told him about the mission and finding the hidden research base.

"Better Research, Better Tomorrow..." Clip said and considered it. "I've never heard of them." He shrugged. "No one really keeps track of corporations from that long ago."

Spacers had spent the better part of two centuries salvaging what they could from what the Vemus left behind. Why would they pay attention to the corporation names? He could see how those names would lose meaning as the decades went by.

"They destroyed the mine then?" Clip asked.

Ethan nodded and Clip looked as if he'd expected it.

"You can't be that surprised, Ethan."

"They could've waited. There was so much we could've learned from that site."

A shuttle flew high above them, and Clip glanced up at it. Then he looked at Ethan and shrugged. "The priority is to rid the entire solar system of the Vemus. The site is marked for future reference as a potential place where resources can be found."

"The Vemus were half dead already."

"You say that like it's a bad thing. They're still dangerous, even if they were starving," Clip said and gave a slight shake of his head. "It's remarkable that they survived all this time."

"I didn't have time to consider it."

Clip chuckled. "Point taken, Ethan."

"So, what do you intend to do now?"

"The last communication to the research base indicated that they were moving Vemus research operations away from Earth. Other facilities had gone offline."

Clip nodded. "Presuming they'd lost control of whatever experiment they were conducting, I'm afraid you've set no easy task for yourself. What I can't figure out is why you would bother when there are so many other things that need to be done."

Ethan inhaled a breath and thought about it. "It's important for us to understand the origins of the Vemus."

"That's easy. Early records indicate it came from the Pacific Ocean," Clip said.

"Suspected origins," Ethan corrected.

Cynergy frowned. "What do you mean by that?"

"I mean that there are no actual records indicating that we know where the origins were. The little we gleaned from their invasion fleet was that they first appeared in the Pacific Ocean and began attacking Asian Alliance territories."

She nodded. "Leaving a search area of roughly half the planet. The thought of spending years aboard a submarine doesn't appeal to me."

He smiled. "Me either, but my point is that all we have are rumors. The records were lost when Earth was quarantined."

"Not entirely," Clip said. Ethan's eyebrows raised. "There were many origin stories concerning the Vemus that occurred during the fall—so many that it became obvious that no one had any idea of where the origin actually was."

Ethan held up his finger. "Or they were hiding it in plain sight. If they couldn't contain the location of the Vemus origins, they could bury it amid a barrage of false leads, essentially squandering all attempts at finding it."

Clip regarded him for a few moments. "I thought you were supposed to be a pilot."

"I'm also a pilot."

Clip arched an eyebrow.

"I spent most of my childhood chasing mysteries with my parents—Ovarrow, Krake, ryklars, and more."

"I'm familiar with the Ovarrow, but those others I've never heard of. New Earth must really be something," Clip said.

Ethan nodded, thinking about home. "I'll tell you about it sometime, but do you understand why finding the Vemus origin is important?"

Clip's expression became serious. "It depends on what you find."

He glanced at Cynergy, and she looked serious as well. "Why?"

"Because, Ethan, whatever you eventually find could be used as justification for certain kinds of decisions that have no standing now."

Ethan blinked. "I don't understand."

Clip glanced around, making sure they weren't overheard. "The CDF still has no idea as to the identity of the aliens who moved your probes here. Correct?"

"No, they don't. We just know that there is no natural occurrence that could explain it. There had to have been a third party involved with it, but we haven't found any evidence to support it. They left no trace, and the probes were gone."

Clip nodded. "We must then seriously consider that the Vemus are of extraterrestrial origin."

"Wait. What?" Cynergy asked.

"It's a theory," Ethan said.

"More than a theory, I should think," Clip said.

"Unless there is proof, it can only be a theory."

Cynergy shook her head. "Wait a second. How could the Vemus be from aliens?"

Clip lifted his chin toward him, and Ethan nodded.

"First off, it's a theory. The Vemus pathogen represents a symbiotic relationship between a virus and a bacteria, and it's the viral portion that enables the bacteria to alter the DNA of the host. It spread itself among mammals, first in the ocean and then on land. Diseases that cross species aren't common and are difficult to manufacture. That's as much as I know about it. My sister is more of an expert on it and could explain it better."

"I still don't see how the extraterrestrial origin fits into all this," Cynergy said.

"I don't know that it does," Ethan said.

"Indeed," Clip said. "But it *is* a real possibility, and if we chase that possibility to its conclusion, it could cause even more of a division among us."

Ethan shook his head. "You're making a whole lot of assumptions."

Clip shrugged.

"I'd rather know the truth."

Cynergy stared at him. "Why? Why do you need to investigate this at all? It's in the past."

Ethan considered his reply for a few moments. "Because it could give us a clue about the aliens that transported the probes."

She frowned and looked at the ground for a few seconds. "Are you worried about them? Is the CDF concerned about them?"

"They're an unknown, and they've demonstrated that their technology—at least as far as traversing space is concerned—is superior to ours. If there's a link between the Vemus and whoever these aliens are, it's something we need to investigate."

Cynergy looked as if she wasn't sure whether to believe him. She glanced at Clip.

"Those are obviously valid concerns, but my concern is a bit closer to home. Finding this will cause divisions among us even more than there already are," Clip said.

"Not investigating this could hurt us even more in the long run."

"You both have made your points," Cynergy said.

Ethan wanted to push further. "I don't want to cause even more trouble for hybrids."

"I know that," Clip replied.

"Will you help me investigate it?"

Clip pressed his lips together. "I need some time to consider it. It's not that I don't want to help, but I only have so many resources available. Actually, that's one of the reasons I had Cynergy bring you out here."

Ethan shared a look with Cynergy. "Something about not having enough to do."

Clip smiled. "More to the point, Ethan, I can use your help. If the CDF doesn't want to use you, then I could."

"What do you need my help with?"

"There have been reports of encounters with strange animals west of here. Cooper has gotten reports from hybrids of encounters with Vemus west of here also, but they don't measure up to what we know about them."

Ethan rubbed his chin and considered this for a few moments. "Why doesn't Cooper bring this issue to the new alliance being proposed?"

Clip stared at him for a moment. "The new Earth Alliance hasn't been formed yet. He's concerned about the reactions to it, so he's asked me to take a group to investigate."

Ethan glanced around the camp. "Just hybrids?"

"It'll be a mixed group, much like what I had up there," Clip replied, gesturing toward the sky.

"I could try to get the CDF to put some people on it."

Clip shook his head. "Not yet. They're spread rather thin these days."

He looked at both of them. They seemed to have expected this from him. "I need to think about it."

Clip nodded. "I expected no less from you."

Ethan smiled. "That's good. I almost thought you were going to insist that I make a decision right now because you were about to leave."

Clip chuckled. "No. No, that wouldn't be fair. I can delay for a day, but not much more than that. I have some scouts yet to come in."

Ethan looked around the camp and nodded.

Clip stepped toward him. "Look, if you help me with this, I promise to help you investigate the Vemus origin. Call it a trade. How does that sound?"

Ethan regarded him for a few moments. "It sounds good, but I still need to think about it. Make sure I'm not in violation of some kind of restriction."

"They sidelined you, Ethan. They don't know what to do with you."

He didn't like to be reminded that the CDF didn't seem to know what to do with him, but that didn't make what Clip was saying incorrect.

"I don't get it, Clip. You've got lots of people available who would help with this sort of thing. Why are you so keen on getting me on board?"

Clip scratched his beard and then stretched his arms out in front of him for a second. "You're right. I do have other people I can bring with me, but you're good. Really good—one of the best I've ever worked with. You've got a good sense of things, and you don't lose your head when things get tense. If all I needed was a couple of scouts with rifles to do the job, I wouldn't be asking you for help. You know things. Both your training and your upbringing make you unique. If the people running the CDF are too stupid to put such an important resource to work, all the better for me." He paused for a moment. "Plus, you're one of us. We both know it. That doesn't mean you're not in the CDF or even a colonist, but still, you've got a stake in this."

Ethan sighed. "A foothold in two worlds..." Clip frowned, and Cynergy stared at him, looking concerned. "It's something Qenirian said to me. He's the Ovarrow ambassador."

"What did he say?" Cynergy asked.

"He said pretty much what Clip just said. I'm part of two worlds now," Ethan said and paused for a moment. "I appreciate it, Clip. I just need a little bit of time."

Clip smiled. "Good, because a little bit of time is all I can give you."

Ethan and Cynergy walked back to the rover. It was a quiet ride back to the city.

"What are you going to do?" Ethan asked.

"Clip has me gathering some supplies. What are *you* going to do?" she asked.

Ethan couldn't help but think that he'd somehow disappointed her. He reached out and covered her hand with his, giving it a gentle squeeze.

"I'm going to weigh some options."

She sucked in her bottom lip for a second. "Ethan, I know that being part of the CDF means the world to you. Okay, I know it. I respect it."

He stared at her for a moment. "But?"

She covered his hand with hers. "That's it. I just wanted you to know that I understand how caught in the middle you are. I'm with you no matter what you decide."

Ethan leaned in and kissed her. "Thanks. I really appreciate it."

He watched her for a few seconds as she drove away.

15

ETHAN DIDN'T RETURN to his quarters after Cynergy dropped him off. He went to a mobile workspace and began using one of the open workstations. It was a small office that was available to him, and he'd shut himself inside. He opened a holoscreen and stared at it for a few minutes, unable to decide what he should do first.

He thought about his conversation with Lauren. She seemed determined to find a way to reverse hybridization. He didn't want to think of it as a cure. He didn't know what it *should* be called, but referring to it as a cure put a lot of negative connotations on hybrids.

He opened a data session and scanned for nearby communications arrays. A network had been established between the major cities in the area, but Ethan knew of a small array that was dedicated to scanning for open communication sessions and cataloging the hits it received. There were satellites orbiting the planet that were in low-power mode. Power cores became depleted over time, but what they'd discovered was that during the quarantine of Earth, a general configuration update to communication systems put them into low-power mode to conserve the energy required to keep those systems running. Ethan didn't think the people who'd executed those orders thought it would require those protocols to preserve functionality of those systems for over two centuries. Over the short time that the CDF had been here, it had built up a catalog of satellites and other communication systems that were still online, even if they were on standby.

Ethan configured his query to trace communication signals during a specific period within an acceptable window around the time the research station on Mars received the update. He assigned the query a medium priority so it wouldn't impact the higher priority work that was already being done. He was hoping his query would avoid notice. If there was a discovery made, he'd have a decision to make.

He set up a separate data storage allocation and a check-in from his personal wrist computer. It was an added step, but it would also help him avoid attracting attention. His was just another query running among thousands of others at the same time. The system was available for him to use, so he wasn't breaking any rules, but if he was discovered he could be ordered to stop.

He closed the data window and leaned back in his chair, staring at the holoscreen for a few moments and thinking. Then he opened the communications interface and paused. If he contacted his father, it would likely result in him being reassigned. His father could override a lot of bureaucracy because of his rank. But that assumed there was absolutely nothing wrong with Ethan. He didn't think there was anything wrong with him that would make his performance unpredictable while on duty, but he didn't want to make that call to his father.

Technically, he was under General Sean Quinn's battle group. Anyone who knew anything about General Quinn knew that he'd been a close family friend, and he'd been referred to as Uncle Sean growing up, despite having no actual familial relationship with him. At some point, Sean would be made aware of his current status and would make a decision. He just hated being sidelined when he was fully capable of carrying out his duties. He'd gone from leading a Talon V strike group to a glorified lab rat in the span of a few months, and he was getting tired of it. Also, he didn't want to put his father in a position where he'd be inclined to give him special treatment. It was an unspoken rule between them. His father would never compromise himself like that, and Ethan would never position himself where it became an issue for either of them. Stubbornness was a family trait.

Ethan sighed, feeling a little isolated. There was one person he could contact who had no direct ties to the CDF, but he knew she was busy. He also knew she'd always take his call. He keyed in his mother's comlink and she answered.

"Ethan! How wonderful to hear from you," she said and frowned, glancing at the upper left corner of her screen. "What are you doing back planet side? I thought you'd been reassigned."

News hadn't traveled fast.

"Uh, I was, and now I'm back for further evaluation."

He watched as his mother walked into a quiet room and sat down. "Oh, I wasn't aware of that."

He smiled. "It's only been a day or so. Are you busy?"

She smiled. "Not for you, I'm not. If you've got some downtime, why don't you come join us for dinner?"

Ethan frowned. He could arrange transport to them, but they were in another city and he didn't want to leave Cynergy. "Mom, I can't tonight. I need to work on something, but I could also use some advice."

His mother's eyebrows raised a little and she smiled. "Well, you've come to the right place."

He blew out a long breath and smiled a little. "It seems like they don't know what to do with me," he began. "I can't go into all the details, but I don't know what to do. How long should I cooperate before I draw the line and start pushing back?"

She frowned. "Who doesn't know what to do with you?"

"Sorry, I guess I came at you in mid thought. There's a reason I'm calling you. I needed to speak to someone outside of the CDF, and…" He didn't want to say someone who wasn't a hybrid either, but he was sure his mother could guess.

She bobbed her head once. "I think I understand," she said and paused for a moment, considering. Then she smiled at him. "You're so much like him, you know."

When Ethan reached a certain age, that was the one consistent thing that was said of him by close friends and family. The people who knew his father well often remarked on how Ethan reminded them of his father. It was something he'd learned to embrace and draw strength from.

"As a general rule," his mother continued, "I would tell you to follow your heart, but that doesn't mean blindly push forward. It means that after careful consideration and perhaps some consultation, if whatever you have in mind holds up then maybe you should listen to it."

Ethan looked away from the screen for a moment. "Dad didn't wait around to ask for permission and neither did you, so why should I?"

His mother regarded him for a long moment. "Sometimes it's necessary, but what's the worst that can happen if you wait? Have you asked yourself that?"

Ethan didn't have an answer for that. The fact that he'd been unable to retrieve all the data from the research station on Mars had instilled a sense of urgency in him that tracing the Vemus origins was massively important, and it was being overlooked by everyone.

His mother cleared her throat and he looked at her. "Why don't you tell me what has you so conflicted, Ethan?"

He pressed his lips together while he considered it. "It's probably better if I don't."

She arched an eyebrow and speared a look at him. "Better for whom?"

"Everyone. Do you know Lauren thinks she's…not close per se, but there's been some developments in finding a way to reverse being a hybrid."

His mother blinked in surprise, and a range of thoughts flashed. "What do you think about that?"

"I know you want me back to how I used to be." He paused and she waited for him to continue. "I don't know what to think about it. Being a hybrid isn't all that bad. I'm able to see and do things that I never thought were possible."

His mother pursed her lips for a few seconds. "I worry about its unpredictability. That's what concerns both your father and me. We don't mean to take anything away from what Cynergy did for you. You do understand that?"

He nodded. "I know you're looking out for me."

"How does Cynergy feel about this?"

"She's worried that it'll be forced on hybrids. That it'll be used as a means to control them. Cause even more divisions."

His mother gave him a knowing look. "She's not wrong."

Ethan blinked, and his mother snorted, then shrugged. "She isn't. Never underestimate someone's willingness to push their own agenda."

"I understand that, but that's not what Lauren has in mind."

"I know that as well. But still, divisions aside, if reversing it is an option, is it so bad that it's available? I think this issue is an eventuality we'll need to deal with. And I don't mean just the envoy but everyone."

"Given what Cyn has told me about what happened before, I understand their reluctance at having anything to do with it. They've been down this road before."

His mother regarded him for a few moments. "Don't think I don't see what you did. I'm not going to press. All I'll say is that I trust you. I trust your judgement. However, be careful."

Ethan met his mother's gaze and held it. "I will."

She gave him a small nod. "Is there anything you want me to pass along to your father?"

Ethan considered it for a moment. "Just say hello from me." She exhaled a long breath. "What?"

"This tiptoeing around. It does more harm than good. Surely you can speak with your father and not talk about the CDF."

"We do, but look where I'm at. It's kinda obvious that I'm dealing with a few obstacles, and he doesn't need to deal with it. Please don't tell him."

She narrowed her gaze, and she might've clenched her teeth a little. "You're trying to protect your father. I understand that. However, he's more than capable of dealing with those gray issues that come with you being in the CDF."

"I don't want to make his job harder."

She chuckled. "Really? Then you might've picked a different career." She winced and held up her hand. "I'm sorry. Look, at some point you need to stop allowing the CDF to impact your relationship with your father. He deserves better than that from you."

It was a rebuke and one he deserved. He lowered his chin. "All right, I'll talk to Dad about this. Okay, I promise."

"Sooner rather than later."

"I will."

They ended the comlink, and Ethan sat at the workstation with a barrage of thoughts banging around in his brain. After a few minutes, he stood up and closed the holoscreen. As he left the mobile work area, he noticed that the sun was setting and evening would soon be upon them. Having no desire to return to his quarters, he decided to take a walk, which led him to the southern outskirts of the city in the opposite direction of Clip's camp. His vision adjusted to the darkening skies, and the cool evening air felt good to breathe in.

He began jogging down an old road. There were few rovers using it as the settlements south of Prism were so far away that they required the use of a shuttle or aircar. Ethan settled into a rhythm, enjoying the solitude. His thoughts flatlined and he focused all his attention on what was in front of him. At some point he'd slowed his breathing so much that his biochip flashed a warning on his internal HUD. He hadn't even realized he'd switched to his voluntary nervous system that required him to remember to breathe. He couldn't just switch back to normal or he'd pass out and run the risk of cardiac arrest.

He inhaled a long, deep breath and held it for a few moments before exhaling it. After repeating that for a few minutes, the alert changed from red to green, and a prompt appeared, asking if he wanted to report the activity. A flash of irritation made him clench his teeth. He didn't report the activity.

He stopped running and stared up at the night sky. The moon was bright and full above him. He could see the massive chunk that had been removed sometime during the Vemus Wars. The inhabitants of Earth were lucky that the lunar chunk hadn't crashed into the planet. If it had, it would've been an extinction-level event.

A message chimed on his wrist computer, and he looked at it. Results from his query were in and data extraction was available. He wiped the sweat from his brow and opened his personal holoscreen. There were partial data dumps that had been reassembled from multiple data sources. He ran an analysis engine on them that highlighted key phrases and concepts. As he read the results, his pulse began to quicken.

He peered at the data and blew out a breath. The researchers had been attempting to communicate with the Vemus. This must've been during the time when Syndicate scientists had altered the Vemus pathogen to target humans.

"This can't be right," he said.

He needed to get back as quickly as he could and review everything that had been gathered. His mind raced nearly as fast as he was moving. Judging by the data he'd found, centuries-old scientists had made quite a few startling discoveries about the Vemus. He wanted to stop and review it all on his wrist computer, but it would be twice as hard with such a small screen. He needed to get cleaned up and eat some food to come at this fresh. He wouldn't be getting any sleep tonight, that much was certain.

16

ETHAN HAD RETURNED to his quarters sometime in the middle of the night. It was the only place he could work in private. At some point, he'd fallen asleep with his head on his desk.

His cheek was pressed against the desk and there was a little wetness under it. He groaned and wiped away the drool. After splashing some water on his face, he took a quick shower and dressed. Feeling a little less tired, he stared at the active holoscreens. He'd been working for hours, perhaps even until sunrise, but he couldn't be sure about that. He'd snatched about four hours of sleep.

He waved his hand in a swiping gesture, and the holoscreens went on standby. He shut down the data sessions he had going and retrieved his all-weather gear. He wouldn't be coming back to this room for a while.

He'd left the room and was securing the door when he saw Cynergy walking toward him.

She smiled at him tiredly, looking as if she hadn't slept much either. "Something keep you up all night?"

He nodded. "I was just coming to find you."

"So was I," she said.

They'd left the temporary HAB units, and she pulled him aside. "Ethan, I need to apologize to you."

He frowned. "No, you don't."

She shook her head. "Yes, I do. I've put you in the middle of all this, insisting that you choose between being a hybrid or not. It's not fair. It's not fair to you."

"There's a lot that isn't fair, Cyn. You're not making me do anything I don't want to do. You're making me face what I don't want to see." They shared a look that was both unrelenting and acknowledging. "Actually, that was one of the reasons—" He stopped speaking as a prompt from his biochip appeared on his internal HUD. He was overdue for a check-in. He stared at it for a few seconds. The prompt seemed to demand his compliance, and his gaze narrowed.

"What's wrong?" Cynergy asked.

He brought up his wrist computer and opened his biochip interface, then selected the option for privacy mode and marked it as permanent.

She shook her head. "Ethan, you're supposed to check in."

He closed the interface and looked at her. "I'm done checking in. This has gone on long enough. The CDF has all the data it needs to decide whether I can serve or not."

Her dark-blonde eyebrows pulled together in concern. "Are you sure about this? I mean, really sure? They could use this as a means to have you discharged from serving."

He felt like a weight had been lifted from his shoulders, but he didn't know the consequences. "You're right, that could happen."

"What will you do if it does?"

"I don't know, but I'm done being a lab rat. I've been stable for months now, and I'm tired of being sidelined, so I thought I'd make myself useful and lend Clip a hand."

She stared at him searchingly for a long moment. "He'll be happy to hear that."

Ethan smiled. "I thought he might."

She shook her head. "You don't understand how highly he thinks of you."

"That's because of you."

She rolled her eyes. "Please. I've known Clip a lot longer than you. He's rarely forced into doing anything. He's got an eye for talent and so do I."

He stared at her, pretending to be shocked. "I'm glad to hear you finally admit it…again."

She sighed. "And just like that, you killed the moment." She gestured toward the rovers. "We should go."

"Or…" he said, drawing out the word, and she raised her eyebrows. "I've got a quicker way," he said with a smile.

She quickly grabbed a few things out of the rover, and they headed toward the transport station.

Ethan walked up to the requisitions officer. "Lieutenant Gates here to pick up a requisition." The soldier peered at his holoscreen and then gave Ethan a once-over. "Is the kit ready?" he asked, and the soldier's name appeared on his HUD, "Corporal Stephano."

"Everything is in order, Lieutenant Gates. But it says here you're not cleared to return to the lunar base."

Ethan smiled. "That's a relief because I'm not going to the lunar base. I'm taking some equipment to a camp away from the city. It's a cooperative scouting mission between Alliance Field Ops and the CDF."

Corporal Stephano blinked. "I didn't think the Earth Alliance was ratified yet."

"It's not, but you know how it is. Militaries align faster than civilians." He tilted his head to the side. "Don't you know your CDF history? We had Ovarrow soldiers serving with us in joint task forces long before they officially became part of the colony."

Corporal Stephano's eyes widened. "I didn't know that."

Ethan smiled. "Well, it looks like you've got some reading to do. Anyway, this won't take long. I'll have the aircar back before the end of your shift."

The corporal considered it for a few seconds and then nodded. "Okay, I'm sure it's fine. You're at landing pad six."

Ethan did a double tap on the desk. "Thanks. I'll be seeing you."

"Safe travels, Lieutenant."

Ethan left the office and Cynergy eyed him.

"How did you get authorization?"

He chuckled. "I didn't, not really, but he doesn't realize it yet."

Cynergy's eyebrows raised in alarm. "Then how did you get clearance?"

"I'm not officially banned from using equipment on the planet, and I'm only going a short distance away."

"He mentioned a field kit. What did you request?"

"Oh that. It's just some stuff for us. You know, a couple of things I thought we could use."

She narrowed her gaze at him. "You're being deliberately vague and I'm really not in the mood."

"I hear and acknowledge your complaint." He laughed as she jabbed his side. "Okay, look, I was able to get a couple of MPS suits, AR-74s, and a couple of other things we'll need."

They walked past a few landing pads and Cynergy looked as if she was considering something.

"They just let you take a couple of rifles and that other equipment?"

He frowned. "Yeah, I'm still in the CDF. It's not like I asked for combat suit, heavies, powerful ordnances, or anything like that. Like I said earlier, I'm definitely sidelined but not quite off duty. It's a loophole to be sure, but why not take advantage of it while it's available?"

If he was in for a penny, he might as well be in for a pound.

Ethan opened the aircar's storage compartment and found the field kit had been stowed. He helped Cynergy load her belongings and they climbed inside.

Ethan transmitted his clearance to the local operations center and was cleared to leave. The aircar rose into the sky and they flew toward Clip's camp.

Cynergy eyed him thoughtfully. "You love this, don't you?"

He frowned. "Love what?"

"Flying."

He smiled. "Yeah. It's not a space fighter, but it'll have to do."

"What aren't you telling me?"

He feigned innocence. "I don't know what you mean."

"I can tell you're holding something back. You've learned something since yesterday. What is it?"

"Maybe I'm just enjoying the pleasure of your company and to finally be doing something."

There was something in the stubborn set of her jaw that indicated her patience was wearing thin.

"Let's just say that what Clip is investigating and what I'm looking for aren't entirely off the mark."

Cynergy frowned in thought. "They're related? How?"

"I was able to retrieve data from some of the older satellites. There were some old security protocols in use, but that's easy to bypass. They were doing all kinds of research into the Vemus before the quarantine went into effect."

"What kind of research?"

"Communication, for one."

A message appeared on the holoscreen. It was a status indicator that told him he was almost at Clip's camp.

"Communication… you mean with the Vemus?"

Ethan nodded. "And there's something else, but I'm not sure if I should tell you."

She arched an eyebrow. "You'll regret it if you don't."

"What if I told you there's a possibility that hybrids aren't some crazy adaptation we've evolved into?"

Cynergy blinked as she considered that for a few moments. Her eyes widened. "Are you saying hybrids were created?"

"Maybe. I don't have actual research data, but there were snippets from different communications channels that my analysis AI was able to piece together. At the very least, it was implied—a strong maybe."

Cynergy looked away from him. She crossed her arms, and Ethan thought she looked upset. He hadn't expected that. He thought she'd be surprised, but this was something else.

"Are you okay?" he asked.

She kept staring out the window.

"Look at me. What's the matter?"

She finally turned toward him. "What's the matter? You just told me that hybrids are the result of some kind of lab experiment that somehow survived the Vemus Wars."

He frowned. "What's wrong with that?"

She gestured toward the main holoscreen. "You have to set us down."

He altered course and flew them away from the camp. "We have as much time as we need."

A comlink request from the camp pinged their aircar, and Ethan gave a quick reply before putting them in standby.

"I'm not setting us down until you tell me."

She turned toward him, honey-brown eyes blazing. "Don't you understand yet? Don't you get it? Do you have any idea how many people died because of this? And you just casually drop that hybrids might've been engineered, like it's not a big deal."

He blew out a long breath. "For the record, I did say I wasn't sure if I should tell you."

"Don't give me that. Anytime someone says that, it just makes the other person want to know more."

He enabled the autopilot and the aircar slowly made a sweep of the area. Then he held his hands up in a placating gesture. "Fine, I did bait you a little bit. So what if it was engineered? We can't change history, but we can try learning from it."

Her gaze sank to her lap, and she shook her head. "You've only been a hybrid for a few months. Everything is still new to you, and you're lucky the transition has been going well."

Sometimes the transition was deadly, or it changed a person so much that their entire personality was altered.

He gave her a solemn look. "I know, Cyn. I know I don't have years of experience with this and that I haven't seen the hardship you have. But this knowledge will help us."

"It'll also hurt us."

"So can anything. We shouldn't hide from it. Just like you don't want to hide being a hybrid."

He waited a few moments for her to consider it.

"Most of the time, knowledge isn't inherently bad or good. It's people that make it one or the other. Regardless of what you and I do, someone somewhere is going to study hybrids—how we are able to do the things we can do and survive wounds that would kill other people but also deal with our vulnerabilities.

Those same strengths also express themselves as weaknesses. That's what Lauren is trying to do."

She lifted her gaze toward his. "I hope you're right."

"Which part?"

"All of it. They tried to wipe us out before and came close to doing it."

Ethan considered her words for a few moments. "Those are decisions made through ignorance. Knowledge and research are how we learn. It's how we improve."

She regarded him and exhaled a long breath. "You're such an optimist."

He smiled. "We balance each other."

She frowned. "How?"

"Because you're a realist."

She shook her head. "No, I'm not. You can't just put a label on me and that's all I can be."

"Well, when you put it like that," he said and paused for a moment. "Are we okay?"

Their gazes locked, and he felt something warm spread across his chest and arms.

"What do you think?" she asked.

He remembered when he'd first felt the hybrid connection to her. It had made them sensitive to each other in ways that normally took years to achieve. It was a level of intimacy that he'd only witnessed with people like his parents. Their love for each other was obvious to him.

As he looked at Cynergy, he remembered there being some attraction between them before she'd saved his life. The mere four months or so since then had only strengthened their connection. At first he'd been suspicious of it, believing it to be a byproduct of her changing him into a hybrid, but he was wrong. He hoped he wasn't wrong about pursuing the origins of the

Vemus. Cynergy's caution was understandable. Sometimes the past should remain hidden, but all his instincts pushed him toward pursuing it.

He set the aircar down just outside the camp. As they offloaded it, Clip came over to them.

"I guess it's safe to assume you've accepted my offer?" Clip asked.

"How could I pass up an opportunity to tour the countryside?" Ethan replied.

Clip grinned. "I see you've brought your own equipment. Good." He lifted his chin toward the vehicle. "Does that include the aircar?"

Ethan shook his head. "Nope, I've got to send it back."

He checked the storage compartment to see if anything was left inside and then closed it. He used his wrist computer to set the coordinates for the autopilot, and the aircar lifted into the air and flew away from them.

Clip watched it, looking thoughtful.

"What's wrong?" Ethan asked.

"One of our vehicles is down and the replacement parts won't be available in time."

They walked toward the camp, and Clip grabbed a storage container from Cyn.

"I was able to get just about everything you asked for," Cynergy said.

Clip nodded. "Good. We're still waiting on a scout team to return, and then we'll leave."

Ethan glanced ahead and saw what looked like an old personnel transport carrier. Though it was over a hundred meters away, he could see it clearly, as if he were standing just outside. The loading ramp was down and there were smaller vehicles inside.

"That small shuttle next to the carrier, is that the one that's down?" he asked.

Clip nodded. "Unfortunately. The power relays are shot, and the landing gear is jammed. Hash thinks it's because someone bent the components during a botched landing."

The shuttle looked old and probably shouldn't be used. He was glad they weren't flying in it. He glanced at the carrier.

"It's safer than it looks," Clip said.

"As long as we stay close to the ground."

He nodded. "It'll never escape the atmosphere."

Clip guided them into the camp.

Cynergy peered over at the carrier and then at Clip. "Smaller team than you'd hoped."

He nodded. "Yeah, but time is against us."

"Why?" Ethan asked.

"We've had a few hits from our scouting parties, but one team hasn't reported in yet."

"Should we go after them?"

Clip shook his head. "Not yet. They asked for extra time to investigate a lead."

"Which team?" Cynergy asked.

"Cowen and Taylor," Clip replied.

Cynergy nodded and looked at Ethan. "They're excellent scouts. Had lots of practice on salvage runs."

Ethan frowned a little. "Yeah, but they're spacers. They've only been back a few months, like us."

Clip smiled. "They've been practicing with the locals ever since we arrived."

"With that kind of help, how can we lose?" Ethan said, and then quickly added, "Seriously, couldn't Cooper send some of his people over?"

"Unavailable, and he wants to keep this quiet."

"He wants to keep the news about the strange animals quiet?"

Clip regarded him, looking slightly amused. "Already regret coming along?"

Ethan shook his head and was about to reply when he heard a squeal of delight coming from a young woman as she ran to Cynergy.

The two hugged. "Emma, what are you doing here?"

Emma glanced at Ethan.

"Emma Lane, this is Ethan Gates."

"Hello," Emma said.

Ethan returned the greeting.

"What are you doing here? I thought you were staying in Arcadia to work in one of the clinics," Cynergy said.

Emma looked at Clip, positively preening. "I'm coming with you. Clip is letting me come."

Cynergy's gaze swooped toward Clip. "What!"

"I'm fully qualified," Emma said quickly.

Cynergy looked at her. "To work in the clinic."

"It's more than that," Clip said.

Ethan glanced at Emma. She had long brown hair that was tied back in a loose ponytail. She also had the pale skin that was common among spacers, and her large brown eyes seemed full of life.

Emma reached out and grabbed Ethan's wrist. Her touch was warm, as if she'd been clutching something hot.

Emma's eyes widened and she looked at Cynergy. "Twenty-two years of age. Healthy...really healthy. My God, you're strong. Hybrid—no surprise there. Peak physical condition, and wow does he love you. It's amazing!" She glanced at Cynergy and then looked at Ethan. "You're amazing. I have to admit I'm a little envious, Cyn."

Ethan thought she had to be joking, but she seemed so earnest. "Uh, thanks?" He looked at the others. Clip nodded approvingly, but Cynergy looked irritated.

"That's enough," Cynergy said and looked at Clip. "You can't be serious about this."

"I certainly can. Her empathic abilities make her the best medic around," Clip said.

Ethan glanced at Emma's hand, which she still had on his arm. He arched an eyebrow, and she pulled it away, looking embarrassed.

"Yes, and she was to be trained as a doctor, Clip. She shouldn't be traipsing all over the continent."

Clip gave Cynergy a once-over. "Tell me, how old were you when you first joined my crew? I seem to recall you being rather insistent about it, too."

A small grin escaped Ethan's lips, and he gave Cyn a one-shouldered shrug.

"That's beside the point and you know it," she said and turned toward Emma. "You need to go back to the city. Work in the clinics being set up by the colonials. Learn all they have to teach."

Because of Emma's young age—and he assumed she couldn't be more than seventeen or eighteen years old—he thought she'd assert herself with all the gusto of someone inexperienced in life, but she didn't. Emma calmly met Cynergy's gaze.

"I love you, Cyn. You've looked out for me ever since I was a scrawny spacer rat at Clip's outpost, but it's time for me to pitch in. This is a short trip, and after we're done, I'll be back at the clinic learning all I can. I promise."

Cynergy stared at her, and Ethan finally noticed the sisterly affection between them. "Out here it's the same as up there," Cynergy said, gesturing toward the sky. "You do as you're told when you're told, or I'll personally tie you up and bring you back myself. Do you understand?"

Emma nodded, the edges of her lips lifting. "I promise, Cyn."

Clip nodded. "There, now that this is settled, Emma, why don't you go check on our medical supplies. Make sure we're adequately stocked for the trip."

Emma smiled and tossed Ethan a quick wave before leaving them.

Clip was about to speak, and Cynergy jabbed a finger toward him. "No! Not another word," she said and ran to catch up with Emma.

Ethan noticed how their hair seemed to bob as they walked in unison.

He glanced at Clip.

"Family makes things complicated."

Ethan frowned. "Family? Cyn never mentioned a sister."

They started walking and Clip shook his head.

"Strictly speaking, they're not actually sisters, but they're close. Cynergy is very protective of Emma. Always has been."

Clip led him toward some HAB units. "We've got some downtime, and it looks like you could use some sleep."

Ethan had gotten just enough sleep to know that he wasn't going to be able to sleep again for a while. "I'm fine. I'd rather you told me more about what we're doing."

Clip eyed him for a few moments. "Are you sure?"

Ethan nodded.

Clip gestured for him to follow. "There's a reason for all the secrecy, so I'm going out on a limb here. I need you to be discreet with what I'm about to share with you. Not everyone here at the camp knows all of it."

Ethan nodded once.

"All right, these strange creatures that are believed to be some kind of Vemus are an inaccurate description of them. They're some kind of hybrid but not like us. They're almost feral. The few encounters with them are confusing. Accounts range from just a sighting to some explorers being attacked."

Ethan blinked a few times. "Feral hybrids but not fully Vemus?"

Clip nodded. "Definitely not Vemus but different from us."

Ethan frowned. "Who was attacked?"

"That's just it. There've been several encounters reported, and the accounts are spotty. They could've just come upon a bear. The encounters happen at night, so conditions aren't ideal."

"But who was attacked? Were they humans, or were they other hybrids?"

Clips pursed his lips approvingly and gave him a small nod. "Both."

"Has anyone been killed?"

Clip shook his head. "No. But there have been wounds, and again, the behavior described is strange."

"What kind of behavior?"

"They're like someone afflicted with a disease that makes them unpredictable. Irrational."

"How do you know they're feral hybrids?" Ethan asked and then shook his head. "Now, that sounds strange."

"Agreed. That's why we need to investigate this. We need to know if these things are, in fact, hybrids, and whether they're suffering from something that made them this way. Or maybe they're some kind of offshoot."

Ethan glanced at the other hybrids in the camp. "Were the people who were attacked…changed?"

Clip regarded him for a few moments. "Nothing that has been reported."

He stopped short and stared at Clip. "What does that mean? Why wouldn't they report it?"

"Tell me, Ethan. Is your biochip transmitting data back to COMCENT?"

Ethan shook his head. "No, I disabled it."

Clip tipped his head to the side. "You wanted your privacy. Regardless, we tried to observe the people who reported the attack. So far, they appear to be normal."

"But you're concerned about it. Colonel Cooper is concerned about it."

"He is. This could cause panic if we don't understand what's happening. We need to confirm what they are and whether they're a danger to anyone. Come on, I'll show you the planned route I intend to take."

17

FOR THE NEXT SEVERAL HOURS, Clip went over the plan he'd
come up with. Scouting parties had been sent out in the regions
where the creatures had been spotted. All were hundreds of
kilometers away from the city. Mainly salvage teams had
experienced the encounters.

During Clip's review, Cynergy joined them. She looked
calmer than she'd been before, but Ethan could tell she was still
irritated with Clip for allowing Emma to come along. He had his
own suspicions about it but decided to keep them to himself. It
was always advisable for deep scouting missions to have at least
one person trained in field medicine. Emma's unique hybrid
senses gave her empathic abilities, which made Ethan wonder
whether her medical training was the only reason she was joining
them.

Clip had stepped away because he'd received a comlink,
which left Ethan and Cynergy alone. The field holotank showed
the rugged terrain of mountains almost in the middle of the
North American continent.

He looked at Cynergy. "I think this used to be referred to as the heartland."

"How poetic. All I see are kilometers of wilderness that are broken up by mountains."

He eyed her for a moment. "Are you worried about the mountains?"

Cynergy shook her head. "Not really. I've been on salvage runs on outposts located on the icy mountains of Titan." She was quiet for a few moments, staring at the holotank. Then she looked at him, giving in to curiosity. "Why did they call it the heartland?"

He smiled a little. "Because it was in the middle of one of the founding nations of the NA Alliance, some kind of traditional reference or something. That's about the extent of what I know about it."

He'd added the last because he knew she'd begin asking him questions that he didn't know the answer to, so he thought he'd save himself by disclosing his lack of knowledge right off the bat. Cynergy could fire questions at him almost as fast as an AR-74 could shoot on full auto. He didn't mind the questions, but sometimes they came so fast that he couldn't think of an answer before the next volley.

The holotank showed an HD image of the terrain. The trees were awash in rusty browns and pale greens due to the change in the weather.

"It'll be beautiful here. There's nothing like crisp, clean, fresh mountain air," Ethan said. She smiled a little, but it looked as if something was weighing it down. "Clip told me you're close to Emma. I'll help you keep an eye on her."

When she smiled this time, she was much more at ease. "Thank you, Ethan. I really appreciate it. What did Clip tell you about—"

She stopped speaking.

Clip returned to them, bringing a man and a woman with him.

"Introductions are in order," Clip said. "This is Will and Coreen Cowen, and according to Cooper, they're some of the best scouts he has."

Will Cowen was of average height with an athletic build and the tan skin Ethan had come to expect from an outdoorsman. His dark hair was just long enough for him to be able to tie it back. He looked to be in his late thirties or perhaps early forties. Ethan couldn't be sure. Prolonging had disappeared for the people of Earth. If he'd met Will back on New Earth, his assumption for age would've been that he was just over a century.

Coreen Cowen had smooth, dark skin and high cheekbones, with expressive almond-colored eyes. She had an easy smile and looked as fit as Will. Ethan was surprised to learn that she was about the same age as Will and the two had been married for over twenty years.

Coreen regarded him for a moment, noting his surprise. "Didn't expect that, did you, Ethan?"

He laughed a little and bobbed his head once. "No, I did not."

Will chuckled. "That's because you still look as young as the day we met."

Coreen smiled as she shared a look with her husband. "Sweet talker."

Will looked at Ethan and grinned. "Tell me I'm wrong."

"Will, stop! You're embarrassing me," Coreen said.

"I have an uncle," Ethan said. "His name is Juan Diaz, and he would always say that some people just age better than others."

Coreen grinned and shook her head. "Don't encourage him, Ethan." Then, she playfully narrowed her gaze at her husband. "Love blinds you."

Will let out a hearty laugh. "If love is what's making me blind, then I don't ever want to see again."

"Yes," Clip said, sounding amused. "Why do I suddenly feel as if I'm the odd man out amid all the couples here?"

Ethan shared a quick glance with Cynergy.

Coreen saw it and leaned toward Will, whispering something to him. He nodded.

"If you want, Clip," Cynergy began innocently, "I could just put the word out—"

"No thank you, Cyn. I can take care of that myself," he said quickly while waving away the comment.

Ethan sensed that this wasn't the first time this subject had come up.

Will snickered. "The next time we have some downtime, I know the perfect woman for you. She lives in Arcadia."

"Don't *you* start now," Clip said with mock severity.

Despite Clip's calm facade, Ethan saw that he was getting a little uncomfortable.

Ethan arched an eyebrow. "I don't know, Clip. Didn't you say that sometimes you just need a little push?" he asked with a glance toward Cynergy.

Clip shook his head and laughed. Then he sighed. Building up camaraderie in a team was important. It forged bonds and delivered greater performance from everyone.

Cynergy smiled sweetly at Clip, her eyes gleaming. "I know *I* feel better now."

Clip regarded her dryly. "Truly, now my day is complete."

Emma walked inside the command tent.

She smiled, sensing the jovial mood. "Oh, I missed it," she said, looking disappointed.

Cynergy smiled. "Not to worry, I'll fill you in."

Clip made quick introductions and then continued. "Okay, the only person who's missing is Hash. Most of you have met him before. He's a tech expert and has gotten us around more than a few obstacles."

Will frowned. "We're going into the field. Do we really need a tech expert?"

"Yes," Clip replied. "We don't know what we'll encounter out there, so I've built a team that covers a wide range of talents and expertise, some of which overlap, but that's to be expected. Ethan here, in addition to being a CDF officer, has extensive experience exploring ancient ruins."

Coreen glanced at Ethan curiously, then looked at Clip. "This is more than a deep scouting mission."

Clip nodded. "It is," he said and proceeded to tell the others about the suspected feral hybrids. "We don't know for sure, and that's what we intend to find out."

"So, we find some of these..." Cynergy hesitated. She was just as reluctant to call them hybrids as Ethan had been. "Let's call them creatures for now, until we know for sure. And what are we supposed to do?"

"Observe and collect samples," Clip said and gestured toward Emma. "If we cannot readily identify what species of animal this is, we'll need to collect a sample of its blood."

Will had sobered over the past twenty minutes that Clip had been telling them the purpose of the mission. "Coreen and I have hunted all kinds of creatures, but we've always stayed within the region of the cities, maybe going a couple of hundred kilometers away. We can track them if and when we find them. But if these are feral hybrids, do we need to be worried?"

"I am," Clip replied. "We don't know what we're dealing with. We don't know if they've always been here, or are these hybrids afflicted with some kind of disease?"

Ethan cleared his throat. "Has there been any missing persons reports recently? Maybe there's been a spike in events."

Clip shook his head. "Not that anyone has reported. Also, it's hard to get access to that kind of data. It's local, and it's not as if the cities are networked all that well, so we're in the dark. All we've got to go on are various sightings."

"Deploying communication systems is one of the priorities the expeditionary force is implementing," Ethan said.

"Understood, and more and more places are coming online every day," Clip replied.

Will sighed. "About the sightings. Not all of them have panned out, but I've just sent you an update. We've got a region to start with."

"Very well," Clip said. "There's one more thing I'd like to cover. This is a volunteer mission, but for the sake of keeping things in order, Ethan is going to be my second."

Ethan blinked, not sure he'd heard Clip correctly. "Me?"

Clip nodded, and the others looked at him. "Yes, you. You've led teams before and have the training, plus I think it's time, don't you?"

Ethan glanced at Cynergy. "This isn't the CDF. I thought Cynergy was your second."

Clip shared a look with her. "She gets kinda bossy."

Ethan frowned and looked at her.

Cynergy rolled her eyes a little. "Clip already spoke to me about it. He's right, you've got more field experience than I do."

Ethan nodded slowly and smiled with half his mouth.

"Now don't say something you'll regret," she warned.

Ethan chuckled, resisting the strong urge to make some kind

of quip. Instead, he looked at Clip. "All right. And thank you, I'll do the best I can."

"That was the last thing I had. I want you all to get a good night's sleep. We'll be leaving quite early," Clip said.

They left the command tent, but Clip stayed behind.

"I'm going to check on Hash," Emma said.

Will and Coreen went to get cleaned up, leaving Ethan and Cynergy alone.

He glanced back at the command tent. "I wonder if I should go back in there."

She shook her head. "He wants to be alone."

"How do you know?"

"I spent years with him, remember? I know. Besides, I'm hungry and I know you're hungry, too. Let's go get some food and then find a place to settle down for the night."

"That's already taken care of," Ethan said as they walked toward the cooking tents. He wasn't sure what they were cooking, but it sure smelled delicious.

They ate dinner and were soon in a temporary HAB unit that Clip had shown him earlier.

"Clip's worried," Ethan said.

"I know."

"Are you?"

"Of course. Look at the potential outcomes of this. We could find that there are feral hybrids out there or something is causing hybrids to become feral, or maybe someone has found a way to make them this way, or a bunch could've been locked up and someone released them. See what I'm saying here? This could end very badly."

He eyed her in the dim light, then arched an eyebrow. "Hey, Captain Dismal, stop looking on the downside of everything. At least we'll be out there doing something about it."

Cynergy was quiet.

"Hey, even if any of those things are true, we can deal with each and every one of them. Personally, I'd rather know about a problem than not. That way we can solve it."

Cynergy's sigh turned into a slight chuckle. "You're like my own little crusader."

He frowned. "What?"

She turned onto her side to face him. "Crusader. You know, champion of causes, standing up for righteousness. Also known as a hero."

Ethan shook his head. "Yeah, that's me."

"It *is* you."

He regarded her for a moment. "Well then, so are you. I wouldn't be here if it weren't for you."

She lay on her back and stared up at the ceiling. "So you're fond of pointing out to me."

Ethan nodded. "Well, yeah. I really didn't want to die."

"And yet, you throw yourself at the biggest kinds of trouble. It's a wonder you're still alive."

There was a bit of an edge to her tone, so he leaned toward her. "Cyn, you don't need to worry about me. I mean, yeah it's in me to risk my life, but I'm not going to throw it away."

She looked at him, almost glaring. "You better not."

"I'm stubborn that way."

She rolled her eyes. "Or you just like to tempt fate. Sooner or later, it'll catch up to all of us."

Ethan considered that for a few moments and recalled a few conversations he'd overheard his parents having over the years.

"I'll make a deal with you," he said.

"Stop."

"No, I'm serious."

"I know. I just don't want you to do it."

He peered at her. "Don't you even want to know what the deal is?"

She shook her head once. "No. Not interested."

He sniffed. "That's a shame, because you would've really wanted it." She ignored him. "Yup, now I'm going to have to take point on anything that's remotely dangerous. The lower the odds of surviving, the better. I can't wait to just leap—Ouch!"

She'd elbowed him in the stomach, and it surprised him more than it actually hurt. Then she crawled on top of him with a sneer. "Don't. You need to stop."

Ethan's eyes widened. If it weren't for the shackled fury in her eyes, he'd have thought how beautiful she looked atop him. "Take it easy. I was only joking."

"Well, it's not funny."

He eyed her for a moment. Her long blonde hair cascaded to the side like a curtain.

"What are you so afraid of?"

She glared at him. "Are you really this stupid?" She didn't wait for an answer, instead she pushed herself off him and hastened toward the door.

Ethan sprang up and intercepted her. "Hey, come on," he said gently.

Cynergy did the last thing he expected her to do. She hugged him, holding him tight. He wrapped his arms around her, feeling extremely foolish for having upset her.

AFTER A SHORT WHILE, she backed away from him. "You," she said, drawing out the word. "You make me so mad sometimes." He looked away for a moment and then turned back to her. "Don't you dare give me those eyes. I'm not done being angry."

"I'll try not to anymore—the making you angry part. I can't

help how I look, but I feel like all this is coming out of nowhere."

She stared at him. "Believe it or not, I had a life before you arrived."

Why was she assuming he wasn't aware of her life before? The question popped into his mind, but he refrained from bringing it up. "Seriously?"

Irritation gave way to exasperation until her expression became somewhat neutral, which was probably more dangerous than the others.

"Look, I'm sorry about that. It's how we break up the tension. I don't want to lose you either. All kidding aside, of all the things that have come my way, you are by far the best of them. And that is in spite of you saving my life. I mean it," he said and leaned toward her. "You're never going to be rid of me."

She gave him a small nod and placed her hand on his chest. "I've lost people, Ethan. Over the years. People I've really cared about. Sometimes I get reminded of it. They've all had this bravado, as if they could never be hurt right up until it was too late."

He frowned a little. "Is this because of Emma?"

She thought for a few moments. "Maybe. Regardless, it's hard for me to watch you struggle with being a hybrid, knowing that I was the one who changed you. I don't regret it or anything like that, but I'm worried about the price you'll pay because of it."

"Somehow I feel that telling you not to worry is exactly the wrong thing to say, so I'll go with this: Whatever price I have to pay for being who or what I am is mine, not yours. You did what you had to do, so you don't need to borrow any of my burdens."

She shook her head. "You're wrong, Ethan. They're *our* burdens. What affects you will affect me. The same goes for the other way around. I know we haven't really discussed the future, other than some vague comments, and I'm not saying we need to do this now, but eventually we'll need to."

Ethan blinked and felt like his stomach had plunged toward his feet. He didn't want to say the wrong thing. She was being serious, and this was important to her, so it was important to him. "Okay. When this is done, we'll sit down and figure some things out."

They returned to bed and both quickly fell asleep. Just before he passed into oblivion, he felt a calmness he hadn't felt in a while. Maybe Cyn was right and they needed to sort out their future together. They were of two different worlds. What would they need to change to accommodate being together?

18

THE NEXT DAY, before sunrise, Ethan and the others gathered by the old troop carrier. It had a pair of engines on wings that could pivot and rotate as needed, and Ethan spotted the smaller maneuvering thrusters. Several of them had red slashes painted over them. The hull was brownish with the kind of dirt and decay that came from being hundreds of years old, making him wonder where the old troop carrier had been found.

Hash jogged down the loading ramp to the carrier and waved at Ethan as he came over.

Hash gestured toward the carrier, smiling excitedly. "Can you believe this baby?"

Ethan frowned. "It looks like an old troop carrier, but it doesn't have any weapons. Not even the mounting for them. Where did it come from?"

"Oh, it's not a troop carrier, at least not a military carrier. This was used for support personnel traveling to remote regions. It served any number of tasks. It could haul equipment and people and has an impressive range. We could easily reach the ocean without giving the power core a chance to recycle."

Ethan glanced toward the middle of the carrier where the power core was. "Did you say recycle? How old is this thing?"

"We found them in that warehouse you took those old space fighters from. The power core was built with early fusion tech. It'll diminish over time because the core containment unit doesn't have a large capacity. They knew that going in, so there's a recycle function that allows the power core to replenish the battery reserves."

Ethan nodded, finally understanding. The carrier didn't draw power directly from the core. They were traveling with a portable power core that kept the batteries charged. "What did the diagnostic on the batteries show?"

Hash smiled. "They're fully operational. They were held in cold storage and are fully functional. Their output isn't anything near what I've seen on CDF shuttles or other small vehicles, but it works well enough for what we need it for."

"Yeah, we've had a few advances on that front. Have you taken this thing on a test flight?" he asked while hoping Hash wouldn't be insulted. The young spacer was quite excited and proud of the carrier. Ethan wouldn't be surprised if he'd slept on the ship last night.

"Of course we did. The question that remains is whether *you* can fly it?" Hash asked, waggling his eyebrows with a grin.

"I can fly anything, but this thing looks like it'll be sluggish."

"Name me any kind of hauler that isn't sluggish," Hash said and then frowned. "Unless you've got them as well in that fleet of yours."

Ethan calmly returned his gaze. "I'm not at liberty to discuss CDF fleet capabilities."

Hash blinked and then glanced at Cynergy, who gave him a nod.

"He's serious," she said.

Ethan shrugged. "Focus, Hash. Take me through what you've been doing to get the ship flight ready."

Ethan and Hash circled around the outside of the ship, doing a visual inspection. Then they walked up the loading ramp to the inside, and he saw a group of motorcycles secured in place right on the floor. They were white, with adaptive tires meant for rough terrain. Hash explained the smart matrix fibers that helped the tires adapt to different conditions, making them versatile in the field. In the standby mode, they looked like a round piece of battle steel, black with a hint of bronze in them.

"These are a lot of fun to ride. Have you ever used one?" Hash asked.

Cynergy looked over at him. "Oh, I bet he has."

Ethan tipped his head to the side. "They were the alternatives to smaller rovers. The ones we have back home have a lot of range. Good in tight places."

Cynergy stared at him.

"Let me guess—you've used them on salvage runs?"

She nodded. "Yeah, it wasn't practical to walk or fly everywhere. But ours were a bit different."

Ethan nodded. "Makes sense. These look to be designed for use here only, while the ones you've used are likely meant for harsher climates."

They would take the carrier to a particular area, then take the motorcycles out for scouting runs. That would make things easier since they didn't have access to Nexstar Combat suits.

They were joined by the others, and the carrier was large enough with plenty of room to spare. They could have fit another ten people easily and been fine.

Clip palmed the ramp controls to retract it.

Will yawned several times, looking as if he'd fall back asleep at a moment's notice.

He lifted his chin toward Ethan. "I'm going to get some more sleep. Wake me when we reach the first stop." He shuffled over toward a row of seats and laid down, using his field coat as a pillow.

"He'll sleep anywhere," Coreen said.

"Didn't he get any sleep last night?" Cynergy asked.

Coreen smiled a little and twitched her eyebrows. "A little."

Emma's eyes widened and Cynergy frowned a little. Hash laughed.

Ethan wasn't sure how to react to that exchange. "Will's a lucky man," he said as he headed toward the cockpit.

Coreen laughed. "He knows."

Another round of laughter erupted from them.

Clip was already at the controls when Ethan reached the cockpit. He sat in the copilot's seat and brought up his own HUD.

"I'll take first shift," Clip said.

Ethan nodded. "Sounds good to me. We've got three pilots, so we'll each take a turn."

Clip eyed him briefly. "Not going to let Cyn off, then?"

Ethan snorted. "Do you think she'd let me?"

Clip tipped his head to the side, then began preflight checks.

Ethan opened a broadcast channel to the rest of the ship. "Ladies and Hash, we'll be leaving momentarily."

Will shouted something unintelligible and Hash laughed.

"Just seeing if you were listening, Will. All right, we're leaving, and..." he paused. Clip engaged the engines and the carrier lifted into the air.

"I like to keep them on their toes," Clip said.

Ethan glanced at the camera feed and saw that they'd all grabbed a seat, and none of them had fallen.

"They're ready."

Clip nodded. "Good."

He set a course and switched the pilot controls to auto.

Ethan felt a rumble in the pit of his stomach. He reached into his backpack and pulled out a protein bar, offering one to Clip, but he shook his head.

He put up a regional map on the main holoscreen. There were several waypoints spread throughout.

"These are where the scouts have been, but Will and Coreen reported that there were several sightings in this region along the western ridge of these mountains."

Ethan frowned at the holoscreen. "So, we're hoping to spot a few of these things just wandering around?"

"If we're lucky. Hash is going to set up a monitoring station in the back so the others can help with that. It'll take us about ninety minutes to reach the area. Then we'll put down and begin our own scouting run on the bikes."

Ethan nodded. It really was the only way. This was going to be an extended run in hopes of crossing paths with the creatures.

They were a couple of hours before sunrise, but since they were traveling west, they were effectively moving away from the sunrise.

The carrier had a rudimentary sensor array that was able to show them the landscape but very little else. Not that Ethan expected anything like the precision scanners they had with the CDF, but neither had he expected something so dated.

They flew over older towns that had been abandoned and destroyed during the Vemus War. There were still roads in use as they were within range of the nearby cities.

While growing up, Ethan had traveled all over the super

continent on New Earth. There were ruins there showing different eras of Ovarrow architecture, but here it was different. There were building shapes that reminded Ethan of the colonial cities and of the cities he'd been to here. As he watched the darkened landscape artificially enhanced by the sensors, he thought about the people who must've lived here. Before the Vemus War, Old Earth's population had been well over twelve billion, just on the planet. New manufacturing methods and food-producing breakthroughs had enabled the human population to soar well beyond what had once been unthinkable. Ethan couldn't imagine so many people in one place. The colony had close to three million people, and hundreds of thousands of people lived in colonial cities. It was similar on Old Earth, even with the spacers returning. Even still, it was nothing compared to what had been before—so many people going about their daily lives—but over the span of two decades the human population had been decimated. Almost all mammalian life had suffered a similar fate, and what had survived appeared to be different from their predecessors.

"It's really unbelievable," Clip said.

Ethan frowned. "What?"

"All the buildings. The towns. It reminds me of salvage runs on old outposts and space stations."

He nodded. "It's almost like the entire planet is one huge cemetery."

Clip turned toward him, pensive. Then he shrugged a little. "You're not wrong."

Ethan sighed. "When the Ovarrow came out of stasis and we brought them to old abandon cities that had fallen during their war with the Krake, they had to take time to adjust. Some of them recognized the places we took them to. My mother was always sympathetic toward them, but I never really understood until now. We're flying over...We're flying over..." his voice trailed off as he couldn't find the words he wanted to say.

"Hard to come up with the right word to represent the ruination of mankind," Clip said.

Ethan nodded. "My father warned me about this. He said at some point we'll be faced with the realization that we're on the opposite end of an apocalypse. We're the survivors and the only ones left to be a voice for those who had died."

Clip blew out a long breath. "Your father is quite a man, and I don't say that lightly. He has the look of someone who's seen more than his share of dark things that no one ever wants to think about. He's the kind of man who will get you through whatever hell comes at you. I saw it in how people from your envoy deferred to him, but I also see that he carries the weight of it."

Ethan stared at him, and Clip returned the look with a solemn one of his own.

"Those kinds of burdens have a way of wearing on you," Clip said.

Ethan was quiet for a few moments, thinking about his father. He remembered some of the conversations he'd overheard his parents having when he was a lot younger, but they didn't make as much sense anymore. His father had seen terrible things, but to him he'd always had peace. The older Ethan became, the more he recognized that for as much as he knew about his parents, there were things regarding the decisions they made with their lives that he was only beginning to understand.

"You have some of his mannerisms, you know," Clip continued. "That ability to perceive a situation and then take action. It's not something you can teach; it's something you're born with. The older you get, the more you'll learn to recognize it in others."

Ethan considered that for a few moments. "So that's why you wanted me to come along."

Clip chuckled. "You've got a lot of talent, Ethan. I'm just glad I get to make use of some of it while you're still among us."

He frowned, and Clip held up his hand. "Now, don't go reading too much into that statement. You're here, but that might not always be the case. Eventually, you'll move on. We all will. That's the way life goes for all of us."

"For a second there, I thought you might've overheard a conversation Cyn and I had last night."

Clip shook his head. "No, but it's not a surprise. I imagine that as time goes on, both of you will have some important decisions to make about the future."

"Any advice you'd like to share about that?"

Clip chuckled. "Don't take advice from me. I'm not exactly the beacon of stability when it comes to that sort of thing."

Ethan was well aware that Clip kept his private life very private and decided not to press him on the matter.

They were almost at the waypoint, making it there a little ahead of schedule. Clip set the carrier down just outside of the remains of a town nestled near a lake surrounded by mountains. They weren't especially tall, but Ethan had no doubt that they made for quite a sight during the day.

As the loading ramp descended to the ground, a crisp breeze blew in. It tickled at Ethan's nose and Emma sneezed.

It took them a few minutes to unlock the motorcycles and roll them down the ramp. Each of the bikes had a storage compartment in the rear where they stored their field kits. Ethan strapped his AR-74 to his back. The others had various types of rifles and smaller firearms with them.

Ethan wore an MPS suit over his clothes and set the

configuration toward general protection mode. The smart fibers would be flexible unless met with a certain level of blunt force. Plus, the suit computer could detect and adapt itself toward whatever movement Ethan made. Cynergy had put hers on as well.

The others wore field helmets that offered some protection but also contained cameras to record their encounters. Ethan's implants could record what he saw to his wrist computer, and the MPS provided plenty of protection. A helmet could form over his head in a fraction of a second, so neither he nor Cynergy needed the field helmets.

"Okay, we'll divide the area up into three quadrants," Clip said. "Hash and Emma, you're with me. Will and Coreen will take the town's southwest area and the outskirts. Stay within forty kilometers of the town. Ethan and Cynergy, you'll be on the opposite side along the north, extending into the mountain areas. Remember, if you come across anything, we need evidence of their behavior. Observation is the goal here. If you can get close enough to place a tracker on them, go for it. However, I must stress the need for caution. All the encounters indicate a level of unpredictability, so be on your guard."

"And if they attack?" Coreen asked.

"Defend yourself," Ethan replied, and Clip gave him an approving nod.

"Ethan's right," Clip said. "Avoid a confrontation if you can, but if it comes down to it, shoot to kill."

Vemus fighters were extremely hard to kill because they were able to regenerate from injuries quickly. Hybrids could as well but at a much lesser rate. Regardless, if these were some kind of feral Vemus hybrids, there was a danger they needed to be prepared to face.

They split into pairs, and Ethan went over to his motorbike.

It was remarkably well preserved. Clip must've found a stash somewhere that he hadn't reported in.

He powered on the vehicle and a high-pitched whine stretched out for a few seconds until it became barely audible. The vehicle went through a quick safety check and reported all systems operational. He glanced down at the tires. They'd gone from a seemingly solid disc to a wheel configuration meant for off-road.

Ethan pressed down on the handlebars and the shocks only gave a little bit. He looked over at Cynergy. "Want to take a ride?"

She grinned as she straddled the seat of her bike. Then she leaned forward. "See if you can keep up."

She sped off ahead of him, and Ethan raced after her.

The motorcycles were extremely quiet, and only a slight trill came from the gearing inside.

They crossed a small field and reached a road. The bikes had a small holoscreen over the handlebars that projected a HUD. The waypoint flashed in the distance, and they rode toward it.

Both he and Cynergy could see well in the dark. Ethan had to find a balance between what his hybrid abilities enabled him to do and what his military implants were capable of. His implants were specialized for flying ships, but his hybrid capabilities enabled him to keep up with field units. It came down to personal preference but also the right tool for the job. His implants could link up with a recon drone, which provided another layer of insight into an area.

The roads weren't smooth, but the bikes did a good job of absorbing the uneven terrain. They took an old road that allowed them to see the town at a higher elevation. The skies overhead were beginning to brighten as dawn finally caught up to them.

They stopped and Ethan peered down. It looked as if a

couple of towns had formed around the huge lake, which had become a large community centered around recreation.

"I don't see anything down there," Cynergy said.

He nodded. "We still need to explore it a little bit. There are lots of things we can't see from up here."

"I wish we knew more about them."

He frowned. "The people that used to live there?"

She shook her head. "No, the creatures. All we have to go on are some random encounters in uninhabited places." She paused for a few moments and sighed. "I'm trying not to think about the people who lived here. It's…"

"A lot to take in."

She nodded, and he thought he saw her wipe one of her eyes. She didn't say anything else; instead, she started heading toward the town.

Ethan followed her.

They rode down a main thoroughfare of the town. Many of the buildings had suffered some kind of damage and looked as if they could crumble at any moment. In the silent morning, the birds' chirping was only broken up by the soft groans of ancient buildings teetering on the brink of destruction. He thought all it would take was a powerful storm to blow through.

There were neighborhoods where the houses had collapsed, but among the shrubbery he spotted metallic fences atop the stone walls. Stone steps led up to an overgrowth that looked almost impregnable.

They paused at a major intersection and Cynergy shivered.

He knew she wasn't cold; it was this place. Spend enough time in abandoned places, and it was enough to rattle anyone's nerves for those who weren't used to it. He was used to it, but he supposed it was affecting him too.

They moved on, making their way toward the lake. Several

species of furry animals had taken up residence in the area. They turned a corner, taking a long, curving road that followed the lake. He spotted a pack of wild dogs running right near the lake shore. They were mainly brown and stocky and let out a few yips.

Ethan slowed his bike to barely a crawl as he watched the dogs. They didn't look like wolves. Their fur was different, but they were just as big. He was sure that the length of their bodies would make them taller than he was. Several of them circled around a patch of ground, but Ethan couldn't see anything. Their snouts lowered to the ground for a few moments, and then they darted away, several of them picking up a trail.

"Come on. Let's follow them," Ethan said.

They rode on, keeping their distance from the pack.

"What do you think they're tracking?"

"I have no idea, but it beats riding aimlessly, hoping to encounter something."

She nodded. "I'll send Clip an update."

The pack moved quickly as they tracked something that led them away from the lake. They went deeper into the forest, away from any roads. There were no paths but the ones they made. More than a few times, Ethan would've liked to have a recon drone to fly ahead of them so they had an idea what they would encounter.

They followed the pack of dogs for over an hour, and they showed no signs of slowing down.

"How long can this go on for?" Cynergy asked.

"I really don't know."

She stared at him for a moment. "Didn't you encounter animals like this on New Earth?"

He nodded. "Yeah, but the predators there are different. More intelligent. It's a different world. There are creatures there called berwolves. They'll track something for days if they've gone without food for a while."

"Well, that's not going to work here. We don't have that kind of time."

"Let's keep—"

Several of the dogs began a barking howl combination, and it spurred the rest of the pack to move more quickly. Ethan marveled at their endurance. They'd been moving at a high-energy pace to begin with.

They came to a clearing, and Ethan peered ahead. Something larger had just moved into the forest across the way. The pack of dogs sped toward it and left very little doubt that they were finally closing in on their prey.

Ethen put on a burst of speed and the motorcycle rocketed forward. The rough terrain caused it to buck, and he knew he was probably going too fast, but he needed to see what the pack was hunting.

"Did you see it?" Cynergy asked, her voice coming over their comlink.

"Not clearly. It's big, whatever it is."

They flanked the pack of dogs as they sped into the forest, but the dogs didn't seem to care. Some kind of dark shadow lumbered ahead of them, and he thought it might've been a bear. It moved at a trot on all fours, but then it rose on two legs and grabbed the base of a thick tree to heave itself forward. The creature leaped through the air, grabbing another tree. It spread its arms wide, and Ethan saw large human hands. The skin was almost black.

They stopped just under fifty meters from where it was.

The creature climbed up a tree and swung a shaggy head toward the pack of dogs tracking it from the ground. The dogs leaped up, their claws digging into the tree as they attempted to reach the creature. Ethan's heart raced as the creature climbed higher and then swung its gaze right toward them. He saw large brown eyes peering at him through matted hair.

He felt a rush through his body as his own hybrid nature responded to the presence of another. There was no doubt in his mind that the creature was a hybrid, but in its gaze was a wild fury.

It lowered its head, growling at the wild dogs. The hybrid howled and the sound of it overtook the sound of the dogs until echoes of their combined songs permeated the area. Then the hybrid lunged toward the nearest dog, tackling it to the ground. The dog bellowed in sharp pain. Ethan heard a sickening snap, and the hybrid flung the dog to the ground.

The hybrid was much bigger than he'd thought. Even squatting, it was as tall as he was, which meant that when he stood up straight he was about eight feet tall. The hybrid grabbed two dogs right by their muzzles and flung them into the tree, but the others seized the opportunity and attacked.

The dogs surged to the hybrid, biting its back and legs. The hybrid howled in pain. His arms whirled around, flinging the two dogs. They collided with some of the other dogs, scattering them.

Ethan hopped off his bike and grabbed his rifle.

"What are you doing?"

"I'm going to help it. Cover me from here," he said.

Then, without waiting for Cynergy's reply, he ran toward the attack. He crossed half the distance and came to a stop, aiming his rifle. Two of the dogs lunged toward the hybrid, but before they reached it, Ethan fired his weapon. A three-round burst of high-density darts ripped into the dogs, and the explosive rounds released a payload, killing the dogs.

The hybrid backed away, surprised that the anticipated attack never happened. More of the pack lunged toward him and he swung a ham-sized fist. Ethan spotted dark blood leaking from dozens of wounds. They weren't healing. The wild dogs would kill the hybrid if Ethan didn't intervene.

He closed in further, working his way around the trees to get a clear shot. He killed a few more dogs, and they finally realized they were being attacked. Several of them looked over in Ethan's direction, canine faces alert as they assessed the threat. Then they glanced at the hybrid. More than half the pack was dead or dying on the ground nearby. The hybrid clutched its side, but it kept a wary eye on the dogs.

One of the dogs let out a series of singsong barks, and just as suddenly as the attack had begun, it ended. The dogs quickly beat a hasty retreat, moving out of the area.

The hybrid watched them go, its breaths coming in ragged, heaving gasps. It watched Ethan for a few moments, clutching its side. Between the dark skin and all the hair, the hybrid looked more like a beast than a man.

"I'm not going to hurt you," Ethan said, lowering his weapon so it pointed at the ground.

The hybrid shook its head, and long dark hair swung away from its face. It had pronounced facial features—huge cheekbones and a thick brow. Its mouth hung open a little, revealing thick teeth that looked more or less human except for the size of them. The hybrid looked as if it could chew rocks, and with all that muscle, it could break boulders if it wanted to.

The hybrid let out a harsh moan that ended in a shout. Ethan thought he was posturing but didn't want to agitate it further by moving closer, so he stayed where he was.

"Just take it easy. Can you understand me?" Ethan asked.

The hybrid swung his head toward where the dogs had gone and then back to Ethan.

Ethan embraced his hybrid nature and felt the change take over almost immediately. He repeated his question.

The hybrid's eyes widened, and he spoke in a language Ethan couldn't understand. It sounded like mumbled gibberish. The hybrid bellowed to the sky, then grabbed the body of one of the dogs and ran off. He lengthened his stride and was soon far away from them.

"Ethan," Cynergy called out to him, "come on. We need to follow him."

Ethan spun around and ran back to his motorcycle.

"I don't think he understood me," he said as he climbed on. He secured his weapon in the front storage compartment so it was within easy reach.

"It's hard to tell," Cynergy replied as they started moving.

They didn't rush, as they didn't want to chase it.

"I definitely got a response when I showed it that I was a hybrid."

"I saw, but I don't know why it ran away. It's the biggest person I've ever seen."

Ethan nodded. "It wasn't wearing any clothes. Did you see all that hair? It's been running around out here for who knows how long."

"I don't understand why the dogs attacked it. I know they hunt for food, but they were determined. They lost half their pack, and it was only after you intervened that they decided to back off."

"They looked at me as if wondering why I was attacking them. It was strange. We need to report this to Clip and the others."

Cynergy peered ahead, trying to spot the hybrid. It must have been moving at a quicker pace than they thought.

Ethan opened a comlink and told Clip what had happened.

"Amazing. Were you able to get a tracking dot on it?"

"Negative, I didn't get close enough. We're tracking it now."

"Understood. Stay on it. We'll finish our sweep and then catch up to you in the carrier. I'll let you know if anything changes."

The comlink closed, and now that Ethan could focus on driving, he increased the motorcycle's speed.

They were definitely chasing a hybrid, and it looked feral. He kept going over the encounter in his mind, trying to squeeze every ounce of insight from it, but eventually had to let it go. He'd review the recording of it after they stopped.

They tracked the hybrid from the blood on the trail. It wasn't dark like what he'd seen coming from the hybrid's wounds. The blood on the trail was red, and it came from the dog's body.

They found the dog's body an hour later. It looked as if it had been gutted and tossed up on the branch of a tree.

Cynergy looked disgusted by the sight and quickly averted her eyes. "How are we going to track it now?"

"I've got an idea," he said.

He brought up his wrist computer and accessed his implants. They came preloaded with configurations meant to address different kinds of circumstances. He found one related to tracking and focused his gaze on the hybrid's footprints found near the dead dog. Soon, the analysis engine on his wrist computer began projecting a probable path the hybrid had taken onto his personal HUD.

"I can track it," Ethan said, tapping the side of his head.

They climbed back on their motorcycles. The power cores were highly efficient, and they still had over ninety-five percent power available. They had a range of over twelve-hundred kilometers before they'd need to go through a power recycle mode.

Ethan took point, and Cynergy followed.

The hybrid seemed to be following an older road. It was barely large enough to accommodate a rover, so Ethan knew it wasn't one of the superhighways used before the Vemus Wars. This must've been a back country road that could've been abandoned long before the wars had even begun. The ancient concrete was uneven and broken throughout, but it was much better terrain than going through the forest.

They reached a long stretch of road that went for kilometers ahead of them, but what they didn't see was the hybrid.

"We're falling behind. Are you sure you're able to track it?" Cynergy asked.

Ethan glanced ahead of them. The tracking application highlighted the recent passing of the hybrid.

"It's got a high probability of being accurate. I know the application works. It's widely used back home."

"Then we need to move faster. A lot faster."

He couldn't argue with that, but they were already nearly a hundred and fifty kilometers away from the town. Their location was traceable through their personal comlinks and a beacon on their motorcycles. Whenever Clip did return to the carrier, he'd be able to catch up to them.

Ethan snorted and shook his head as they rode. Cynergy, riding next to him, heard it.

"What is it?" she asked.

"We're supposed to divide piloting duties among me, you, and Clip. We're way out here, so it's all on Clip."

"Hash could probably fill in, and maybe Emma."

Most spacers had at least a rudimentary knowledge of flying shuttles, but atmospheric flying was different, and Ethan said so.

"I just meant that Clip had options he could use if it came down to it."

Ethan nodded.

They didn't talk much after that because they went as fast as they could go. The last time Ethan had used this configuration of his implants was during his CDF training. However, since he'd spent the last few years training to be a pilot, he found that he was impressed with what his implants could do. The faster they traveled, the less time his wrist computer had to make a determination about the tracks they were following. He noticed that the probability indicators for the tracks lowered, but not by any great amount.

A couple of hours passed, and they still hadn't seen any sign of the hybrid. Clip checked in with them and told them to keep going. The other teams hadn't found anything, so theirs was the best lead so far.

The mountains gave way to foothills, and the tracking application was struggling to find the hybrid's tracks. The probability indicators lowered substantially.

The motorcycles were fast, but could the hybrid really have traveled this far this quickly?

"There's another town that way. Maybe it went there," Cynergy said.

"Let's check it out."

By the time they reached the town, the land had become flat, and all indications that they were still tracking the hybrid were virtually nonexistent.

The town was much smaller than the others they'd been to earlier that day. Ethan was getting anxious to be off the motorcycle, and he knew Cynergy felt the same. They'd been periodically standing up while riding, allowing their legs and backs to stretch before settling back down.

Trees had overtaken the small town and limited their visibility of the surrounding area.

A loud shockwave sounded from nearby, and Ethan squeezed the brakes, causing the motorcycle to skid to a halt.

Cynergy stopped next to him, and they both cocked their heads to the side, listening.

Several loud bellows sounded from nearby on one of the other streets, which was followed by the unmistakable sound of CDF weapons fire—explosive rounds by the sound of them.

"High-yield rounds," Ethan said.

Cynergy frowned for a second, and then her eyes widened a little. "The CDF is operating out here?"

"Let's go find out. Slow and steady. Let me take the lead."

They drove toward one of the side streets and Ethan heard the high-pitched whine of a Hellcat's engines. It sounded like it was exerting a lot of force. Then a loud rumble sounded and the ground shook. Ethan rounded the corner and saw the flaming wreck of a Hellcat.

19

SMOKE BILLOWED into the sky and Ethan felt waves of heat. He peered at the flaming wreck, looking for survivors. Something large struggled on the ground nearby, and it looked like the large hybrid they'd been tracking, or what was left of it. It was desperately crawling along, dragging the remains of its legs. Suddenly, the hybrid jerked to the side as it came under fire. It didn't cry out and must've died instantly. A bright orange blaze engulfed the body, quickly devouring it.

Several CDF soldiers in combat armor circled the remains of the Hellcat, and one of them saw Ethan and Cynergy. They raised their weapons.

"Wait," Ethan shouted, holding up his hands.

"Identify yourselves," a man said in a burly voice.

"I'm Lieutenant Ethan Gates of the CDF. Transferring my identification to you now. Don't shoot me."

Several of the soldiers lowered their weapons, except for the man who'd spoken.

Ethan used his implants to transfer his ID to them and then

gave them a few seconds. "Am I free to approach?" He peered at them, and their names suddenly appeared on his internal HUD. Some of them were familiar.

The man who spoke lowered his weapon. "I apologize for the confusion. Cleared to approach."

Ethan and Cynergy rode toward them and then climbed off their motorcycles.

The man who'd spoken to him was Sergeant Wade Handler, and as he retracted his helmet Ethan noticed a seemingly permanent scowl, along with an attitude that barely tolerated others. Ethan knew the type. They led their squads efficiently, but their attitudes were off-putting.

"What's going on here? What happened to the Hellcat, Sergeant?" Ethan asked.

"We were attacked by some kind of..." Sergeant Handler paused for a moment, looking at Cynergy. Ethan waited him out. "We were attacked by hybrids."

"You'll need to be more specific," Cynergy said. "That's like saying I was attacked by a soldier and that all soldiers are out of control."

Handler glared at her.

"Why don't you stick to the facts, Sergeant?" Ethan said.

Handler stared at Ethan for a moment.

"Excuse me, Lieutenant Gates?"

Ethan turned toward the soldier who'd interrupted. She retracted her helmet, but he'd already recognized the name and smiled. "Corporal Nance," he said and looked at the rest of the squad. He saw Armstrong and Logan. "Sir," they said.

He then saw Specialist Gutierrez walking with Jared Andrews. As they came around the wreckage, Andrews looked at Ethan in shock.

"Sir," Corporal Nance said, "we were attacked by some kind

of hybrid. It wasn't a full Vemus, but they weren't like you either. We're not sure what they were." She glanced at Cynergy for a moment.

Jared Andrews was a science officer and had the rank of lieutenant, but the way Sergeant Handler moved toward him seemed to indicate that Andrews was commanding the squad.

"Gates, I'm...you're the last person I expected to find out here," Andrews said and looked at the motorcycles behind them. "You're a long way from the nearest city."

Ethan considered his response for a few moments, not sure how much he should share with them. "Just happened to be in the neighborhood."

Andrews arched an eyebrow. "Indeed." He looked at Cynergy. "Hello, I'm Jared Andrews."

"Cynergy," she replied.

Andrews bobbed his head slowly. "Okay, looks like explanations are in order. As you can see," he said, gesturing toward the Hellcat, "our transport has been destroyed. We were attacked by some kind of Vemus hybrid. We'd been tracking a group of them south of here. Several more appeared in this town, so we landed a short distance away and were scouting the area."

"You're leading this team?" Ethan asked and looked at Sergeant Handler.

"Yes, Lieutenant Gates. This squad has been assigned to Lieutenant Andrews for the purposes of this mission."

Ethan looked at Andrews. "What happened to Burk?"

Corporal Nance stiffened for barely a second.

"He's been reassigned," Andrews said and stared at Ethan a few moments. "Just the two of you way out here?"

The question implied that Andrews already suspected they weren't alone.

"No, we're not here alone," Ethan said and sighed a little.

"We were tracking a hybrid ourselves. It was different, feral. It led us here."

Andrews frowned in thought. "Fascinating. Any idea why it led you here?"

Ethan shook his head. "No. Not at all. We first encountered it about two hundred kilometers east of here."

Andrews's eyes widened. "And you tracked it on those?"

"Yeah, on those. We lost sight of it, and I thought we'd lost the trail until I heard the Hellcat."

Cynergy cleared her throat. "You said it attacked you. Any idea why? When we encountered him, he didn't attack us."

Andrews arched an eyebrow. "Him?"

She narrowed her gaze. "Yes, him. He was in trouble." She lifted her chin toward the wreck. "Did you just shoot him, or did you at least pause first?"

Andrews scowled. "I don't answer to you. I said we were attacked. Who knows what triggers a hybrid to finally give in to the Vemus inside them?"

Cynergy reached for her sidearm, and Ethan quickly stepped in front of her, urging her to calm down.

Ethan turned toward Andrews. "That was uncalled for."

He sighed. "I forgot who I was speaking to. You're one of them."

Ethan leveled his gaze at the man. "Careful now. Don't say something you'll regret later."

Andrews looked away and winced. "You're right. That wasn't fair. I apologize."

He sounded sincere.

"No harm done," Ethan said.

Both he and Cynergy heard the carrier's engines before anyone from the CDF squad.

"Our companions," Ethan said.

The carrier swooped overhead and landed nearby.

Ethan glanced at Nance, and she gave him a fraction of a nod. He wondered what had happened to Burk, as he was more level-headed. Handler reminded him of a blunt instrument—dangerous but somewhat predictable.

Cynergy looked at Ethan. "I'll go check on Clip and the others."

He nodded, and Andrews came over to his side. "What are you doing way out here?"

Ethan eyed him for a moment, considering. "Did you expect me to be somewhere else?"

"Honestly, yes. Last I heard from Waller was that you were sent back to the planet for medical reevaluation," Andrews replied.

Ethan snorted and shook his head. He supposed he should've expected something like that from Captain Waller. "It's ongoing," he said, and pursed his lips for a second. "You're almost a doctor. Do you really think I need another evaluation?"

Andrews chewed his bottom lip for a second and shook his head. "I wasn't on the mission. I just monitored it from the shuttle, which is where you should've been."

"If I'd remained on the shuttle, Hayman's platoon would've been dead."

Andrews looked away for a moment and then shook his head. "I'm outside my depth here and I really don't know what the right answer is."

"The right answer would've been for them not to have nuked the entire site."

Andrews frowned, looking a little suspicious, and Ethan stared at him. "You found something."

Andrews's gaze went skyward, and he made a noncommittal shrug. "Maybe. I don't know. We're still searching."

Ethan blinked. "Well, don't keep me in the dark. Tell me what happened. You were with me at the research base, and you know what *I* found."

Andrews nodded a little. "Yeah, well, the site is gone, but I was able to pull some communication logs from the satellites orbiting Mars. I had Gutierrez run a trace on them, which led us back here."

Ethan frowned. "They gave you a team to come investigate?"

Andrews regarded him for a few seconds and then nodded.

Ethan was both elated and angry at the same time—elated that someone was at least looking into this. The origins of the Vemus were more important than most people realized. But why hadn't they assigned him to this mission? Andrews never left the damn shuttle.

"It's not personal," Andrews said.

Ethan blew out a breath and scowled.

"So why were you following that hybrid?" Andrews asked.

"Because of some reported sightings. We weren't sure exactly what he was until I came face-to-face with him."

"What happened?"

Ethan told him about the encounter. The other CDF soldiers listened to his account.

"He didn't attack us, and he could've."

"That's because you're like them," Handler said. There was an unmistakable accusation in his tone.

"Maybe," Ethan replied. Regardless of what he thought of Handler's tone of voice, he had to concede the point. "He also didn't attack before I showed him what I could do."

Armstrong smiled and gave an approving nod, but Handler nearly sneered at him. "You've should've seen Lieutenant Gates in action, Sergeant. I'll never forget it," Armstrong said and looked at Ethan. "I don't care what happens with your skin. You're all right in my book, sir."

Handler shook his head. "Logan, take Armstrong and make a circuit around the area. We don't want to be blindsided by anything."

The two soldiers left.

"It's interesting," Andrews said, "that it recognized some kind of kinship."

"That's the thing. I don't know if he did recognize a kinship of any kind. He'd just been attacked and was wounded," Ethan said.

"And yet it was able to cover so much distance. How wounded could it have been?" Andrews asked.

"Vemus can regenerate," Handler replied.

"True," Andrews replied.

"What drew them to the Hellcat?" Ethan asked, looking at Handler.

"We were trying to outrun them. I initiated a remote pickup and didn't know that the hybrids were anywhere near it."

"We're going to have to come up with a different name," Ethan said.

Handler regarded Ethan for a second. "Whatever you want to call them."

Andrews cleared his throat. "Feral hybrids seems to fit, but we don't know why they became feral."

Something felt off about the entire exchange, as if Ethan was only getting half the information. "It's a concern. We were tracking them and were going to collect samples of their blood for analysis."

"There isn't anything left of it to collect a sample from," Andrews said.

Clip and the others had exited the carrier and came over to

them. They were all armed. Cynergy had probably made sure of that.

Clip smiled as he approached. "I see you've had a problem with your ship. Perhaps we can be of assistance."

Ethan made quick introductions but kept back the fact that Clip and others were hybrids.

"Our communications equipment was on the Hellcat," Specialist Gutierrez said.

"I'm not sure we can be of much use then," Clip said. "Our comms capabilities are somewhat limited."

"Surely you can reach the nearest city," Andrews said.

Ethan thought he saw Sergeant Handler twitch a little and frowned.

Clip glanced at Hash, who gave him a small nod. "Shouldn't be a problem."

"Thank you," Andrews said and turned toward Handler. "Can you see if there's anything that can be salvaged from the Hellcat? I'll see about getting us another transport."

"Understood, sir," Sergeant Handler said, and he and the rest of the soldiers went with him to the Hellcat.

"Hash, set up our friend here with some comms so he can reach the CDF," Clip said.

Hash and Andrews began walking toward the carrier, but Ethan ran over to them.

Hash frowned at him.

"This will just take a second," Ethan said.

"I'll get the portable and come right back," Hash said and disappeared up the loading ramp.

"Look, Andrews," Ethan said and sighed, "I'd rather you not report this, about me, I mean."

Andrews blinked and seemed to consider it for a few

moments. "You're asking me to withhold information from an official report?"

He shook his head. "No, I'm asking you to delay sending an official report. You're just going to check in and request another transport."

Andrews frowned, and Hash returned with a portable communicator. It was the size of a helmet and looked as old as the carrier.

Hash showed him how to enter the communication protocols and then left them.

Ethan lingered behind and watched Andrews with raised eyebrows.

Andrews sighed. "Very well. I'll keep you out of my initial report. Now, if you don't mind, I'd prefer a little privacy."

Ethan nodded a little and went over to join Hash.

The young man leaned toward Ethan. "Well, this just got interesting."

"What did Cyn tell you?"

"Not much, just a recommendation for us to bring our weapons with us. What's up with this squad? They look kinda tense."

"They said they were attacked by the feral hybrids."

Hash regarded him for a few moments, and Ethan knew he was trying to get a read on Ethan's emotions.

Ethan sighed. "Do you have to be so obvious about it?"

Hash blanched and shook his head. "Sorry, Ethan. It's kind of a habit. Did you see the attack?"

He frowned for a moment and shook his head. "No, we heard the Hellcat explode and went to investigate."

Hash pressed his lips together thoughtfully. "That's strange. I didn't think Hellcats were easy to destroy."

He shrugged. "It sounded like it was under a significant load. It wouldn't take much to damage the engines."

Hash nodded a little and tipped his head to the side, as if he were having a private conversation with himself.

"What?" Ethan asked.

Hash winced. "It just doesn't add up in my brain. The hybrid you described was big, to be sure, but for all our abilities, we can't tear through battle steel."

"Well, yeah, you're right. I don't know all the details about the attack."

Hash nodded. "I'm sure there's more to it than that." He smiled and grinned a little. "You know me."

He did. Hash had a naturally inquisitive nature, and his questioning of the details of the attack was right on the mark. Ethan should've thought of them and chided himself for not doing so.

Andrews closed the portable communicator and handed it to Hash. He looked troubled.

"What did they say?" Ethan asked as they walked toward the others.

"Transports are going to be delayed," Andrews said, frowning. "I didn't say anything about you, but I did tell them that outside help arrived."

Ethan thought about that for a few moments, and Sergeant Handler came over to them.

"Transport has been delayed," Andrews said.

"How long until we can expect a pickup?" Handler asked.

Andrews looked at Ethan for a moment and then at Clip and the others.

Emma leaned up toward Clip and said something Ethan couldn't hear, but judging by her expression, it was some kind of warning.

Andrews gave Ethan a guilty look. "I'm sorry, Ethan. We're to commandeer the carrier and return to the city."

Ethan frowned, and Sergeant Handler looked as if he'd received an early birthday gift. Maybe it was a new combat knife set.

"That's not going to work," Ethan said.

Clip joined them. "Did I hear that right? You intend to take my ship?"

Handler gripped his weapon, and as he started to raise it, Cynergy pointed her rifle at him.

"I wouldn't do that if I were you," Cynergy said.

The other CDF soldiers aimed their weapons, each picking a target. Will had his weapon up, but Coreen and Emma had been caught by surprise.

"Let's not do anything hasty," Clip said calmly.

Ethan speared a look at Handler. "Lower your weapon, Sergeant!"

Handler sneered toward Cynergy. "Go ahead, shoot me. It'll be the last thing you do, sweetheart."

Muttering a curse, Ethan put himself in the line of fire between them, arms upraised. "That's enough. This ends now. Lower your weapon. That's an order."

Handler glared at him for a long moment, and then slowly lowered his weapon.

"The same for the rest of you," Ethan said to the others. "Commandeering doesn't mean you shoot the owners of the vehicle."

"What do you expect us to do? Those are our orders...sir," Handler said.

"Those aren't your orders, are they, Andrews?" Ethan said.

Andrews sighed. "It was more of a suggestion. If it's not an option, we'll need to camp here until transport can be arranged."

Ethan went to stand by Cynergy's side. He didn't think Clip would leave them stranded.

Clip looked at him as if he'd guessed what Ethan had been thinking. He raised his eyebrows.

"We're looking for the same thing," Ethan said.

Clip turned toward Andrews. "What exactly are you searching for?"

"It's just like Ethan said. We're searching for the feral hybrids. They seem to be moving west for some reason, and they're exhibiting erratic behavior. I'm not sure what he did to trigger them to attack."

"How many of them were here?"

"There were eight that attacked our ship."

Clip considered that for a few moments and Andrews continued. "We're also tracking the communication that was sent to a research base on Mars. The evidence we found indicates that it came from a region west of here."

Clip's gaze darted toward Ethan.

"The two might be related. Only one way to be sure, though," Ethan said.

"Indeed," Clip said and looked at Andrews, then at Handler. "Which one of you is in command?"

"I am," Andrews said.

Sergeant Handler nodded once.

"All right, then," Clip said. "Commandeering my ship is out of the question. However, I'd rather not leave you stranded here, either. It seems that our objectives are similar. We are also tracking the seemingly feral hybrids. We need to understand what's wrong with them. I won't condone wholesale slaughter, but I won't find fault with anyone defending themselves. If you can agree to that, you're welcome to come with us. But I must emphasize that any more displays like what just happened, and I'll put you off my ship. Am I clear?"

Andrews shared a look with Handler. "That will be fine," Andrews said and frowned. "Are you a captain, or is there another title you use?"

Clip snorted. "Heavens no. I'm not in a military. I'm a former spacer and I'm in charge. Ethan—Lieutenant Gates—is my second and has agreed to assist us in an unofficial capacity."

Andrews looked at Ethan.

"Technically, I'm off duty."

Andrews nodded. "Are we ever really off duty?"

Ethan smiled with half his mouth. "No. Okay, let's pool our intelligence and see if we can agree on a way forward."

"Agreed," Clip said. "We'll camp here tonight."

Cynergy gave Ethan a look that seemed to convey she'd rather camp anywhere else but where they were. She was slow to trust, but something nagged at the back of Ethan's mind. There was something off about this squad, and he made a mental note to try to speak with Corporal Nance alone. She might have a few insights to share with him about the others.

20

THIS WASN'T the first time Lauren had lived at a medical clinic over the past few months. Sometimes they were little more than tents, but in the city of New Hope, their accommodations were part of an existing hospital. They even had a small lab where she spent most of her early morning hours before the sun came up to start the day.

The lab was home to a couple of sterile rooms used for research, mainly devoted to agriculture. With a growing population, the resident's priorities were increasing crop yields while ensuring the replenishment of nutrients to the soil.

Lauren managed to secure lab time by agreeing to use it from the wee hours of the morning until about seven. She knew Isaac would wander in before that but was adamantly against doing any kind of focused work before half-past five in the morning. They shared a small bed, and she bet he didn't mind the extra space when she left. He complained that she liked to spread out when she slept.

She sat at a black workbench. Bright lighting overhead was

enough to fool her brain that it was already daytime, which meant she'd be yawning and craving sleep shortly after dinner. She'd maintained this schedule for the past week or so since they'd arrived at New Hope. They hadn't intended to stay this long, but it couldn't be avoided. The city had a much larger population than the surrounding towns, and people began journeying from outside the city to see them.

Both she and Isaac had developed a good reputation among the residents, and it gave them time to investigate the different factions in the city. Isaac took the lead on that. He made time to go into the city alone, performing traveling doctor duties and more incognito work. When they were out together, they met and worked with the local medical staff, who were quite resourceful and eager to learn from them.

The windows on the holoscreens along the workbench refreshed with new data, and Lauren checked on the scheduled reports she'd been waiting for. As she read through the list, she began to frown. One very prominent one had been missing for days, and she pursed her lips in thought.

She opened a message window, intending to send Ethan the question that had been bothering her for the past few days. His biochip had stopped checking in, and at first she thought it was some kind of glitch, but after days of no check-ins she realized she'd been wrong. Ethan must have stopped allowing his biochip to send in his health data by enabling his privacy settings, but he hadn't told her why he'd made that change.

The door to the lab opened, and she spun around in her chair to see Isaac making his way toward her. He threw her a tired grin and gave a slight shake of his head as he yawned.

"I don't know how you get up this early," he said, checking his wrist computer and then looking as if it had betrayed him.

Lauren smiled. "Good morning, sunshine."

He smiled and wrapped his arms around her. She leaned into him, enjoying his embrace. She could smell the soap he'd used, and she inhaled contentedly, taking in the masculine scent that ticked all the right boxes to start her day.

"You smell so good," she said, nuzzling into his neck.

He shivered a little because it was one of his ticklish spots and then peered at the holoscreen, eyes quickly scanning.

"Ethan's still waging his rebellion, I see."

Lauren nodded. "I don't know why."

He chuckled. "I think it's obvious. He's tired of being treated like some kind of lab animal. I'm surprised it didn't happen sooner."

Lauren's shoulders slumped a little. "But he knows how important it is. We have to monitor his health and the adaptations that present from being a hybrid."

Isaac held up his hands in a placating gesture. "You're preaching to the choir here. You don't have to convince me."

She nodded and turned toward the message. Isaac cleared his throat and she turned toward him.

"Maybe hold off on sending him a message about that for now."

She frowned. "Why?"

Isaac pursed his lips for a moment. "Because he's taking a breather. That's all this is."

She blinked, and a half-formed scowl appeared on her face. "This isn't the time for that. He could jeopardize his position in the CDF."

"He's more aware of that than we are. I know the CDF is in your blood. I get it. Between both our fathers, it's got a powerful draw. But Ethan didn't do this on a whim, even if it appears that way."

"Be that as it may, he's putting himself at serious risk. You know there are times when he has to remember to breathe? He was so excited about it. It's as if he'd never considered what could happen to him if this presented itself while he was sleeping."

Isaac regarded her calmly, and it threatened to spike her irritation. "I read the report too, and it's really quite something. But his biochip has the protocols to inform him when that happens, so he's covered."

She rolled her eyes. "But what if something else happens? It's so unpredictable that it's impossible to foresee what will happen to Ethan or any of the hybrids. I don't know how they can live like that."

Isaac regarded her for a few moments, drawing his fingers over his goatee.

Lauren sighed with a small shake of her head. "It feels like Ethan's just one adaptation away from dying." She stabbed a finger toward the ceiling. "One! You know what I've been finding with all the samples we've been collecting?"

"That it's too soon to come to any conclusions?"

She narrowed her gaze for a second. "All it takes is an adaptation to misfire and it can cause almost instant death. There have been reports of it in the past."

"But none recently," he said, and she frowned. "You won't like hearing this, but will you hear me out?"

Lauren inhaled a deep breath and sighed. "Of course."

He nodded. "Good. What if the best course for us to take regarding the hybrids is simply doing nothing? Tweaking and helping to deal with obvious ailments is fine. We've already come up with protocols that help guide the adaptations so they don't hurt or cause severe symptoms. Maybe it's enough."

She shook her head. "It's not."

"You haven't even considered it."

"Yes I have. What do you think I've been doing every

morning working here, and before that at all the other places we've been to?"

"You've been working very hard with minimal resources and not getting enough rest."

She leveled her gaze at him. "I'm fine."

He just looked at her for a few moments. "I'm just saying we're both getting a little tired, and this place isn't helping."

He wasn't wrong about that. The city of New Hope demonstrated divisions that grew in intensity each day. Where once hybrids had lived in peace, they were now viewed with scorn and mistrust.

"I'm close to reversing it," Lauren said. "Maybe not for everyone but definitely for some of them. They can be free of it."

Isaac's eyebrows drew up in alarm and he shook his head. "Maybe, Lauren, but this has nothing to do with you. Your research must go before a review committee, and then comes clinical trials. The research and data have to be documented, before a decision can be reached."

She licked her lips and nodded. "I know that. And it'll come under more scrutiny because we'll need buy-in from the people we're trying to help. But I'm telling you, I've made some real progress. Let me show you."

She walked to the end of the workbench and brought up a holoscreen. "There are several compounds I've been using to treat the cells that are associated with the Vemus. I've built on what colonial scientists have done with some of the New Earth compounds discovered there."

A data window appeared among other reports she'd been steadily updating.

Isaac peered at the holoscreen, then manipulated some of the views to delve further. "Wow! These look really promising."

Lauren smiled. "I know. This could impact a lot of people.

I've created a few formulations based on the results I've gotten thus far."

"Really?"

She nodded. "I'm going to test them with some of the samples we've collected. Do you want to help me?"

Isaac nodded and then glanced at his wrist computer. "We'll have to do it later. We're taking the mobile unit out today. Plus, there's a place I want to take you for breakfast."

Lauren looked at the time and did a double take. Where had the morning gone? Her lab time was just about up.

"I've got some protein bars…" she was saying and stopped.

Isaac arched an eyebrow and shook his head. "Not today. No prepackaged meals. We're going to have real food prepared for us. It's time we sampled more of the local delicacies."

Lauren was more a creature of habit, willing to eat whatever was convenient, but Isaac came from a family that loved to prepare big meals of fresh food. He abhorred anything prepackaged unless they were in the field, and even then, she could tell it was barely tolerated.

They quickly cleaned up the lab, making it ready for the next group that had it reserved.

"I miss having my own lab," she said as they left.

"It would mean returning to one of the ships."

She shook her head. "No, it's too far away from here. We need to build a facility out here."

He nodded. "In time, but come on, let's go," he said, pulling her along after him.

Lauren grinned as they started to jog. She'd needed to move around, and her stiff muscles loosened after a few minutes. Maybe Isaac was right and she'd been pushing herself too hard—another family trait.

After breakfast, they took one of the vehicles that they'd

designated as the mobile clinic and restocked it with basic medical supplies, essentially going on a tour of the city. There were new neighborhoods being built for all the refugees coming to the area. A significant portion of the influx came from spacers who'd been forced by the quarantine to survive in the solar system, but others were from smaller, remote settlements around the planet. Humanity was getting a chance to regroup, and the best way forward was for them to live in peace and harmony. These sentiments were what Lauren often heard from regional leaders, but it wasn't trickling down. There was serious unrest, and she'd witnessed several brawls break out near the mobile clinic. They'd patch them up, but some of the vitriol was alarming.

The day went on, and they moved toward another section of the city, not far from where they'd begun that morning. They set up shop, and people visited with their list of ailments. She'd even convinced a few hybrids to give a blood sample for them to analyze.

"What good is this going to do? I've given samples like this before," Greta said. She was an older woman, in her early seventies, and walked with a stooped posture.

Lauren packed the blood sample into a portable bio containment unit. "It'll help us understand the extent of hybridization."

Greta eyed her for a long moment. "Your heart is in the right place, but at this point, I doubt anyone will figure it out."

She smiled a little. "Well, I haven't given up yet," she said and paused for a moment. "You've lived with it for a long time. Do you have any insights you can share?"

Greta's gaze softened. "Sure, you take that young man over there and get married. Don't look back or be worried about what anyone thinks."

Lauren felt her cheeks redden and she grinned a little. "That's not what I meant."

Greta arched an eyebrow. "But is it what's important?" She regarded Lauren for a moment. "Many people...doctors have tried to figure out how hybrids came to be. Some even tried to fix it, and over all my years, I'm not sure anything good came of it. I wish I could be more helpful, but that's all I've got to offer."

"You've been a big help, Geta. Maybe we'll think of something that hasn't been considered before."

Greta rolled down her sleeve. "I hope so. With all the uproar out there, it reminds me of the Amtown uprising, except they were fighting about access to salvaged materials. Amtown proper —the old city—could process the materials for reuse, but the new Amtown was able to collect it with efficiency. This was about fifty years ago. I was just a young woman then, much like yourself."

Lauren smiled. "What happened?"

"They got tired of trying to outdo each other and began to work together. They combined operations, and Amtown prospered because of it." She eyed Lauren. "I served on the council that bridged the gap between the two. Things like this that're going on out there will eventually pass."

She sounded so sure that Lauren found herself agreeing with the older woman.

Greta stood up and gave Lauren a wink. "Remember what I said about that cutie you've got eating out of the palm of your hand."

Lauren laughed, and Isaac glanced over at them from outside the exam area. "I'll keep that in mind."

"You do that, and if I was forty years younger, I'd give you a run for your money." Greta chuckled as she left.

Isaac finished with the person he'd been treating and walked over to her. "What's that all about?"

Lauren raised her eyebrows and tilted her head to the side. "What do you mean?"

He frowned. "I felt like that older lady was sizing me up for a meal."

Lauren laughed. "She was!"

Isaac's eyes widened and he turned toward the street. "I can't exactly argue with her taste in men."

Lauren rolled her eyes. "You're so full of yourself."

Isaac looked on the verge of replying but didn't. His attention had been caught by a pair of black rovers driving toward them, the New Hope emblem showing proudly on the vehicle's front.

The sidewalks were full of people going to and fro, but many stopped to watch the rovers.

The vehicles stopped and several armed enforcers exited. They wore the brown uniforms of New Hope's law enforcement division, and they walked toward her and Isaac with a determined stride.

"Doctor Lauren Gates?" a man asked.

Isaac stepped a little ahead of her, shoulders back and his chin raised. "Who wants to know?"

Lauren saw that one of his hands moved toward the small of his back where he had his sidearm concealed.

The uniformed officer ignored him and stared at Lauren. "Doctor Lauren Gates?"

"I heard you," Isaac said. "But you didn't answer me."

Several of the officers drew their weapons, sidearms of their own, while others held some kind of stunner.

"Step back and don't interfere. I'm Captain Mitchel of New Hope Security. Doctor Gates, you need to come with us."

Isaac barked out a laugh. "Like hell she does. You don't have the authority to hold us."

Lauren came to stand beside Isaac. "What's this about?"

"It doesn't matter what this is about, you're not going with them. She's not going with you." Isaac pulled out his sidearm so quickly that Lauren wasn't sure if she'd seen it happen. "Back off, now!" he bellowed to one of the approaching officers.

The officers swung their weapons toward Isaac. He was going to get himself killed if she didn't do something.

"Captain Mitchel," she said, "we're part of the colonial diplomatic envoy. You need to tell us what's going on."

She glanced at Isaac. She'd seen him under pressure before with their lives in danger. While other people became angry and on edge, he became cold and calculating. It was a side of him she wasn't accustomed to but had witnessed a few times.

Captain Mitchel sighed. "Doctor Gates, you're wanted in connection with several murders that took place this morning."

Lauren blinked a few times and frowned. "What? I haven't killed anyone. We've been in the mobile clinic all day, going all over the city."

"I have my orders, Doctor Gates. And they're to bring you in for questioning."

"That's not going to happen," Isaac said. "She's not going anywhere with you."

The officers looked as if they were moments from taking action. Lauren moved in front of Isaac, cutting him off from the others.

"Think, Isaac. Think. You're not going to kill anyone," she said.

He somehow still had his sidearm pointed at the officers. "You're right. Just a few leg wounds and we'll get out of here."

"And go where?" she asked, and Isaac frowned. "We can't run from this. *I* can't run from this."

He glared at her. "I'm not letting them take you away."

"You're not. I'm going with them," Lauren said. She reached toward his wrist and pulled his arm down. He resisted for a second and then relented.

"This is a mistake," he whispered.

"I hope not," she said and turned toward the officers. She raised her hands over her head. "I'll come," she said, walking toward them.

Captain Mitchel gestured toward one of his officers. "Take her in."

An officer strode over to her and put metallic bindings around her wrists. As she was being led away, she glanced toward Isaac. He looked furious.

"Captain Mitchel," Isaac said, "if anything happens to her, I'm coming for you first."

Mitchel regarded him for a second. "Are you threatening me?"

Isaac shook his head. "Not a threat—a promise."

Lauren used her wrist computer to send a message to the envoy. She hadn't killed anyone and had no idea why anyone would suspect her of anything. This had to be a huge misunderstanding.

The officer opened the back of the rover and helped her climb inside, then sat next to her in the back while another came to the other side. A third sat across from her. She frowned. Who did they think she was?

21

CONNOR FURROWED his brow as he tried to quickly review the messages waiting in his inbox on his wrist computer. The closed-door session with regional representatives of what would hopefully become the Earth Alliance Council had begun their afternoon meeting a short while ago.

Lenora walked over to the table of refreshments and poured herself a cup of water, and he watched her eye the platter filled with pastries. As if sensing his gaze, she turned toward him, arching her eyebrow, and tilted her head a little toward the platter. Though he was on the other side of the large room, she knew he could see her clearly, as if she'd been standing right in front of him. He'd never given up the military implants that enhanced his senses.

Connor nodded, and Lenora made a couple of sweet selections.

The people in the meeting were returning to their seats as their break was ending and it was time to resume.

Lenora smiled at him as she sat down.

He went to reach for one of the pastries, and she pulled it away. "Uh, these are mine. Yours are still on the platter over there," she said, gesturing back the way she'd come.

Connor regarded her for a moment. "That really hurt my feelings."

She laughed. "I'm sure. Here, have this one," she said and gestured toward the one with orange frosting.

At the last second, Connor stole the one with the white frosting and quickly took a bite out of it to seal the deal.

Lenora narrowed her gaze and then shrugged. "I dropped that one on the floor, anyway."

He'd been chewing and her comment made him laugh, so he began coughing. Clearing his throat, he took a sip of his water.

"You deserved that," she said, eyes gleaming playfully.

"I can take it," he replied and eyed her for a second, then leaned toward her. "You won't know when I'll exact my revenge, but know that I will."

She grinned.

The meeting began again, and their momentary reprieve was done.

Claire Worthington brought up the next item on their agenda. She was a tall, dark-skinned woman. "The issue that keeps coming up is the subject of reparations." She paused for a moment, her gaze lingering on the colonial delegation.

Thomas Kessler cleared his throat. "That subject was addressed in the public town hall we had last week. I don't think there's a need to revisit it."

"I understand that the subject was raised during the town hall, and since then my office has been getting regular inquiries about it. We need an official statement on this."

Kessler glanced at Connor for a second and the two shared a look. Kessler was the mayor of the city of Prism. The city had one of the larger populations in the region, but Claire Worthington was also a mayor of a city whose population was enough to rival it in terms of resources and demand.

"An official statement as the Earth Alliance would be premature since we're still in the process of forming it," Kessler said.

Connor looked at Fabian Dumont, who looked on the verge of speaking.

"Our position in regard to reparations has not changed," Dumont said.

Kessler lifted his hand, gesturing toward the colonial ambassador. "There, you see, Claire? I don't understand the logic in raising this again."

"The issue is that it's been coming up in New Hope. We've taken in the largest group of refugees, and since then, ideas have spread. The concept of reparations is gaining traction."

Connor leaned forward, clearing his throat. "So, the idea is gaining popularity. That doesn't make it any more tangible than it was last week."

"Excuse me," Jalen Ibanez said. "I don't mean to throw fuel on the fire, but I've been seeing the same thing in Amtown as well."

A general statement of assent went around the room. Connor frowned, surprised by the speed at which this pathetic idea had taken root.

"You're supposed to be leaders of your respective cities. That also means that sometimes it's required of you to set the record straight," Connor said.

Claire frowned in thought for a moment. "What if we were to change the messaging of the aid you're providing? That could go a long way toward calming the rising tensions among the citizens."

Connor blinked. "You're proposing to give in to the whim of a mob? Is that what you're really saying?"

Claire looked taken aback for a second. "No, of course not. I just want to avoid more civil unrest."

"Then I suggest you stick with the truth," Connor said, feeling a spike of irritation. He shook his head. "Someone is campaigning this nonsense through the cities." He paused for a few seconds, looking at the others. He wasn't seeing any shock or denial. Some of them looked uncomfortable, as if they were afraid. "What's next? A lottery to define who qualifies for colonial assistance based on whose sob story gains the most traction with your voters?"

The seconds went by as a gathering tension filled the room. All Connor could think of was how disgusted he was with the situation.

Thomas Kessler began to speak and stopped to clear his throat. "I think we should table this discussion."

"I don't agree," Lenora said. Connor turned toward his wife, shocked. "If we can't discuss this among ourselves, how are we supposed to address it with our staff and other people?"

Connor considered that for a few moments and then nodded. "Maybe we shouldn't be part of this discussion. Perhaps the envoy should recuse themselves from this meeting and let the representatives discuss it among themselves. Get a real consensus before we move forward at all."

Lenora nodded.

Claire Worthington gave him an appraising look.

"Connor makes an excellent point," Fabian Dumont said.

They all shared a look and stood.

"Wait," Kessler said, looking uncomfortable. "I don't think that's a good idea. This is like taking a step back when we should be moving forward."

"It's necessary," Dumont said. "If the Earth Alliance is to have any kind of future, you'll need to decide what issues are important. It's essential to keep people's concerns in mind, but I agree with Connor—you cannot give in to the whims of a mob. And it's not appropriate for us to participate in whatever way forward you choose. However, it is my profound hope that you reach a reasonable consensus, keeping in mind the long-term implications of whatever decision is made here in this room."

They left the conference room and received more than a few surprised looks from the people who were outside. Connor ignored them and led the others away.

They rounded a corner and Lenora spotted a small breakout room used for impromptu meetings. The three of them went inside and closed the door.

"I didn't see that coming," Lenora said.

"Neither did I," Connor agreed.

Fabian shrugged. "I didn't think we were free of it, but it looked as if some of the people in that room were seriously considering it."

"Not Tom Kessler. He just wants to move forward," Connor said.

"Nothing good will come of this," Lenora said.

"That's the whole point. Whoever is promoting these ideas wants us to be divided. This is a power grab."

Fabian regarded him thoughtfully. "You obviously have someone in mind."

Connor chuckled. "Isn't it obvious? It has Pandu Mukhtar's grubby little hands all over it."

Lenora pursed her lips for a moment. "We can't make accusations without supporting evidence."

"You heard Worthington. She said New Hope has taken in the most spacers of all the cities."

"This could get ugly really quickly," Fabian said. He crossed his arms and rubbed the stubble of his beard for a moment. "We will push back on this, especially if the Earth Alliance pushes for it. All of this will add pressure to a challenging situation."

"And," Connor said, "it'll distract from more important things."

"We should be consistent with our stance, but it couldn't hurt to remind people of what we're trying to accomplish. Convince people that it's in everyone's best interest to work together instead of making demands that have no basis," Lenora said.

Connor arched an eyebrow. "Use their own message against them. That could work—"

His and Lenora's comlink chimed at the same time with a high-priority message.

Connor looked at the message and his brows pushed forward.

"What is this?" Lenora asked. "This can't be right."

Connor read the message. It had come through the CDF soldiers assigned to Lauren's protective detail.

"What's wrong?" Fabian asked.

Lenora looked at Connor in complete shock. He clenched his jaw and looked at Fabian. "Our daughter has been taken into custody."

"What?" Fabian gasped. "What for?"

"They're saying she murdered someone," Connor said, and summoned his own security detail. "We're going there right now."

"Where?" Fabian asked.

Connor walked toward the door. "She's being held in New Hope."

Lenora followed him but turned back to Fabian. "You stay here."

Fabian followed them out into the hall. "I can't do that."

Connor sent a quick message to Major Daniels to assemble two platoons to meet them at the base. He'd have three more meet them in New Hope.

"What are you going to do?" Fabian asked.

Connor closed his personal holoscreen. "I'm going to get my daughter."

Fabian regarded them for a second. "Please wait."

"For what?"

Fabian glanced around, pressing his lips together. "Look, we need to be cautious about this. We can't just go in there and do a military extraction."

"That's exactly what I'm going to do."

Connor began walking down the corridor, and Fabian hastened in front of him.

"Connor, please, just listen to me. I'm trying to help you."

There was something in his voice that made him stop. He'd worked closely with Fabian since they left New Earth.

"Connor," Lenora said, "maybe we should."

Connor closed his eyes for a second and then looked at Fabian. He inhaled a deep breath, setting aside that Lauren had been taken into custody.

"Just hear me out," Fabian said.

Connor lowered his chin in agreement.

"We need more information. They didn't just arrest her on a whim. It's better if we secure her release through diplomatic channels."

Connor considered it, going against every instinct he had as a father, but there was a part of him that knew Fabian was right. He shared a look with Lenora.

"We're still going there," Connor said, his tone leaving no room for argument.

"I'm going to contact her," Lenora said.

She brought up her personal holoscreen and tried to reach Lauren. The comlink wouldn't connect. She looked at Connor.

"They're using a suppressor to block the signal," Connor said, gritting his teeth. "Fabian, go through diplomatic channels, but Lenora and I are going to New Hope."

Fabian nodded. "I'm going back to the conference. Claire Worthington will be able to get answers for us. I'll contact you with an update."

Connor and Lenora strode down the corridor with their CDF escorts nearly running to catch up.

"Where is Isaac? Where was her escort? Why would they let her be taken like that?" Connor asked.

"I'm trying to reach Isaac," Lenora said, and then blew out a breath. "She traveled so much that her escort might not have been with her."

Connor nearly growled and brought up his comms interface. He sent a priority comlink to Isaac, and there was no response. "He knows better than this."

He quickened his pace and Lenora ran to catch up.

"Slow down," Lenora said.

Connor did as she asked.

"Isaac *does* know better. He wouldn't have let anything happen to her."

"Then where is he?"

"He wouldn't leave her. That's probably why we can't reach him."

Connor's comlink chimed. It was Isaac. "What happened?"

"I'm sorry. I should've contacted you sooner. They just arrested Lauren, and I didn't realize they had a suppression field active until just now. They said it's standard procedure when they take people into custody."

Lenora came next to him, and they both stared at Isaac's face on the holoscreen.

"She's been brought in for questioning regarding a recent murder," Isaac said.

"Are you able to get to her? We'll be there in thirty minutes. I've got the CDF en route."

"Isaac," Lenora said, "is she all right?"

"I didn't want her to go, but..." Isaac paused for a second, looking frustrated. "Have you ever tried talking her out of something once she's made up her mind?"

Connor frowned. "What do you mean? Are you saying she surrendered?"

Isaac nodded. "She went with them. They shouldn't have the authority to arrest us, but they told me there are exceptions for people linked to violent crimes."

Lenora gave Connor a level look, and he knew he wasn't going to like what she was going to say.

"We can't go in there with the CDF," Lenora said.

Connor inhaled a breath to reply that not only *could* they go in there, but that there wasn't anything anyone could do to stop them.

"We can't. You can't do this."

Connor gritted his teeth. "Why? Why can't I do this?" he asked, shaking his head. "First, this reparations nonsense, and now this. This is just another thing atop of all the rest."

Lenora looked at Isaac. "We'll contact you."

"I'm going to get in to see her, but first I'll find a way around the suppression field."

Connor shook his head. "It'll only be in use for transit. You should be fine once they get her wherever they're going to question her."

"Understood," Isaac said and closed the comlink.

Lenora stared at Connor and leaned close. "Listen to me. I know you want to go in there and get her. I want you to as well, but we need to be smart about this."

"They can't hold her."

"I know, but you said it before."

Connor blinked. "I don't know what I said. All I can think about is Lauren."

"You said that this is just one more thing on top of everything else. Don't you think the timing of this is just a little too...timely?"

Connor blinked, and it was as if everything clicked together in his brain. He should've seen it before, but because it was his baby girl he'd been blinded.

Lenora saw his recognition of the situation as it dawned on his face, and she nodded. "This is exactly what they want you to do. What did you always tell me about that?"

"Never give the enemy what they want," Connor said and sighed. "You're right. We need to bring her help."

Lenora nodded. "We need to find out who's behind this."

"We do. We need to get Lauren some help. Someone with legal expertise."

Lenora frowned. "Who?"

"Fabian has someone on his staff. We'll pull them out of whatever they're doing and bring them with us." He paused for a few seconds, thinking. "She's smart."

"Who?"

"Lauren. She knew that surrendering to them and meeting this thing head-on is the best way forward, but prison camps aren't the nicest places," Connor said.

"I really wouldn't know."

Connor had seen enough, probably too much, both when he was an NA Alliance officer and during the war with the Krake.

"What are you thinking?" Lenora asked.

"I think we should still go to New Hope with a CDF escort. I want teams on standby. I just want to be ready to take action if the situation becomes untenable."

Lenora frowned. "Untenable…"

"She'll be vulnerable wherever she's being held. Lauren didn't kill anyone, so whoever is trying to frame her for this would have to be willing to take other steps to ensure they get the desired result." Connor shook his head. "I should've anticipated this."

Lenora shook her head. "Don't do that. We took the precautions we thought were enough. Let's get to New Hope."

He stared at her for a long moment. "Lenora, I might have to do some things, and they might appear to be irrational."

Lenora stared at him. She didn't blink. "I trust you, Connor. Now and always."

22

LAUREN SAT IN THE ROVER, wedged between the two men. They tried to make room for her, but it wasn't the most comfortable ride she'd ever had. There was also a smell that gave away the fact that the two men were very much in need of a shower and a change of clothes.

She went over the recent events in her mind. This had to be some kind of misunderstanding. Captain Mitchel sat in the front passenger side of the rover and looked to be entering a message on his tablet computer. She considered asking him for more information but then thought better of it. Why had New Hope Security sent out a captain to bring her in? If New Hope Security was in any way similar to Field Ops and Security on New Earth, then this task was several levels beneath his rank.

The rover turned off the street and drove through a security checkpoint and into a parking complex, coming to a stop at the entrance to the building. One of the officers helped her out of the vehicle.

Captain Mitchel stared at her for a moment, giving her a

once-over as if he were considering something, then led her up the stairs and into the building.

As she approached the front desk, she looked down at her wrist computer. An alert appeared, indicating that communications were offline. She frowned and looked at Captain Mitchel.

"I'd like to contact the colonial envoy," she said.

He approached a kiosk and gave a nod to the officer on the other side of the counter, then glanced at her. "We'll get you processed first and then bring you in for questioning before communications are permitted," he said and turned back to the holoscreen, bringing up some kind of check-in form.

"That's not going to work for me."

Captain Mitchel shared a look with the man behind the desk and slowly turned toward her, looking bored. Then he cocked his head to the side. "Are you saying you're not going to cooperate?"

Lauren shook her head. "Not at all. I will cooperate, but I won't answer any questions without legal representation." Mitchel blinked and snorted. Lauren smiled. "Come on now, Captain Mitchel, did you think I'd help you make your own case against me? Certainly not. I will not say another word until I have legal representation and after I've contacted the colonial diplomatic envoy."

Mitchel's gaze narrowed as she spoke. He pursed his lips, considering, then smirked. "Very well. Have it your way, Doctor Gates," he said and looked at the officer behind the desk. "Put her in General Holding."

Lauren frowned, not knowing what "general holding" meant.

Captain Mitchel gave her a smile that didn't reach his eyes. "Don't worry, Doctor Gates. We'll send a message to your envoy.

I think the average turnaround time for a response is about two weeks. Enjoy your stay."

Several officers came from behind the desk. One of them held her arm firmly while the other walked in front of her. She got the impression that they'd either drag her or she could walk, so she decided to walk.

They brought her through another security checkpoint that led out of the area, and a man stood in the doorway of one of the offices. He was of average height, with sandy-colored hair, and he regarded her with pale blue eyes that displayed a curious expression.

Lauren was guided past him, and she thought he was going to speak to her, but he didn't. She'd walked past several other offices when a man called out to them from behind.

"Hold on a second."

The officers stopped.

The man she'd seen in the doorway came to stand in front of her. He regarded her with a thoughtful frown. "Doctor Gates?"

"Yes," she replied.

He nodded as if he'd just checked something off a list and looked at the lead officer. "Bring her to questioning in room 301," he said.

The officer frowned. "We're supposed to bring her to General Holding, sir."

"Change of plans."

"She said she wouldn't answer any questions, sir."

The man regarded the officer for a moment and then glanced at her for a second, considering. "Understood. Please do as I ask," he said and went back the way he'd come.

Lauren glanced over her shoulder and read the name posted outside the office door. Investigator Hal Demming.

Shrugging, the officers brought her to a room that had a

single table and two chairs. They guided her to a chair and left the room. She still had wrist restraints on.

The room sported pale-colored walls with a few small cameras throughout. She also spotted a couple of other biometric sensors that were no doubt measuring her at this very moment.

The door opened and Demming walked in. He carried an old tablet computer, and the case looked worn and scratched.

He sat across from her. "I'm Investigator Hal Demming. For the record, could you tell me who you are?"

"Doctor Lauren Gates of the New Earth Colony."

The edges of his lips lifted a little and he bobbed his head once. "Do you know why you're here?"

"They told me I was connected to several murders," she replied.

She was just stating the facts as she understood them and didn't plan on cooperating any further than that.

Demming regarded her for a few long moments, waiting for her to continue. She knew the tactic well. Long pauses enticed people to start speaking. She stared back at him and waited him out.

He gave a small nod with a slight purse of his lips. "Is that all you have to say for yourself, Doctor Gates?"

"Not without legal representation and someone from the colonial envoy, Investigator Demming."

"And the fact that you're going to be charged with murder doesn't make any difference to you?"

Lauren blinked, and her pulse quickened. They were going to accuse her of murder? Why were they going to do that? Captain Mitchel had said they wanted to question her in connection with "several murders."

She began to deny it, but clamped her mouth shut at the last second. Demming had wanted to get a response out of her, and she'd almost given in. Instead, she inhaled a deep breath and stared at him. She wasn't going to be intimidated by him or fall for his catch-you-off-guard questions. He was fishing for her to condemn herself for a crime she would never commit.

Demming sighed and leaned forward a little. "You really don't want to go into General Holding. Trust me on that."

His voice was smooth and even gave the illusion of reassurance.

"So don't put me there," she said and chided herself for doing even that.

The edges of his lips twitched. "You're not leaving me much choice."

Lauren chuckled. "Does this tactic really work for you… Investigator Demming?"

He leaned back and smiled. It looked genuine. He exhaled a long sigh, then brought up a holoscreen. It showed six people lying on the floor, looking as if they'd been frozen in agony. The breath caught in Lauren's throat, and a shiver rushed down her back. Three of them were children. She stared at the images, unable to look away. All of them looked as if they'd experienced the most profound agony, faces frozen in torment. Her heart froze and her eyes tightened.

"Do you recognize these people? Any of them? They've been to your clinic. You treated them. Maybe you did a little more than treat them, Doctor Gates."

Clenching her teeth, she tore her eyes away from the ghastly images. Shaking her head, she exhaled forcefully through her teeth, anger and revulsion spiking through her. How dare he accuse her of this! She'd spent her life helping people, learning to heal the sick and injured.

Demming leaned across the table, eyes hard and unyielding.

"Do you recognize them? You do, don't you! You recognize them. You know who they are!"

Lauren sneered, wanting to tell him that he was wrong, that she'd never seen them before, but her gaze strayed toward the holoscreen as if there was some kind of unyielding force drawing her in. She stared at it, recognizing them, the family she'd treated, and her throat became thick with sorrow. She recognized them and cursed her perfect recall. She never forgot a face or a name.

Demming leaned back, looking satisfied. "You do know them. Thank you for that, Doctor Gates."

She hadn't said a thing, but she hadn't needed to. The answer to his question was written on her face. Her vision blurred, filling with tears for the fallen.

They'd been murdered.

Demming closed the holoscreen and stood. He walked over to the door and gestured to the officers waiting outside. "Take her to holding. I'm done with her." He glanced back at her, and she was barely aware of him. "For now," he added and left.

Lauren didn't remember standing or walking through the building. She might've walked for a good length of time. The horrifying images replayed in her mind, tumbling in succession, and her brain began putting the pieces together of what their last moments had been like—all that fear and pain and suffering.

Eventually, her emotions flattened, as if she'd come to a barrier in her mind that held them back, but they weren't gone. They were like a raging storm with gales of wind and rain banging down the door—a door she leaned against that held her up. She was used to treating injuries and had seen people who'd died before, but murders in the colony were few and far between.

A metallic door clanged behind her, and she stood in an

open area filled with other people. She rubbed her wrists, noting that the restraints were gone. She hadn't realized they'd been taken off. Inhaling a deep breath, she looked around, realizing she needed to pay attention.

People clustered together in groups like fortifications on a battlefield. Lauren glanced behind her at the heavy steel door. She had no idea where she was supposed to go or what she was supposed to do.

The area looked like an old cafeteria, but there was no food being served. There were tables with benches attached to them. There were easily a few hundred people being held here, waiting. If this was General Holding, where did people sleep? Were they expected to sleep on the ground?

Knowing she couldn't just stand there, Lauren decided to walk along the outskirts, away from clusters of people. There was nowhere for her to get lost here. The large, open area was just a rectangle. More than a few people looked in her direction, but she didn't hold their gazes for long. The tension in the air was palpable, and there seemed to be a general suspicion.

An obese man with thick eyebrows glowered at her as she walked by. Lauren angled away from him, which he took as some kind of insult.

"There's nowhere for you to run, and no one is coming to save you!" he shouted.

Lauren looked at him as he pushed off the wall and strode toward her. He was a lot taller than her, and he wore a mean scowl on his face. She could either hasten away to become someone else's target of humiliation or dominance, or she could meet this threat head on and set the tone for her stay here.

She turned toward him, lifting her chin. "Careful there, big guy, you might work up a sweat."

He grinned. "I'm bored and I've found my new plaything."

Lauren stared up at him. He frowned as he closed in on her.

"You're supposed to run away."

Two ham-size fists lunged toward her, and Lauren easily sidestepped out of the way.

The man let out a moan of pain and he stiffened, with one of his shoulders hitching up.

She saw the large welts on his back. They were caked with dried blood, but some of his wounds began bleeding again.

"Lee!" a woman shouted, running over to him. "I told you not to move away from the wall. Your wounds are going to open up."

Lee limped to the side and glanced at Lauren. He looked apologetic, as if this was all a game to him.

The older woman came over to Lee's side and he slung an arm over her narrow shoulders. Lauren paused for a moment and then came to Lee's other side.

They helped Lee to the wall, and he sank down to the ground, gasping.

"He needs treatment," Lauren said.

The older woman was of Asian descent, and she had long brown hair that was stringy with age. She gave Lauren a once-over. "They know about his condition."

Lauren frowned for a second. "Who did this to him?"

"No one. He did it to himself."

Lee sat back with his eyes closed. He wasn't sleeping. His face was scrunched in concentration. The skin around his wounds darkened and the bleeding stopped. He winced, suddenly moving froward. "It itches so much."

Lauren looked at his back. The wounds had closed, but the skin was bright red, as if he'd had an allergic reaction to something. She instinctively reached for a medical kit that wasn't there.

The older woman saw it and frowned. "What are you doing?"

"I'm a doctor. I know how to treat his wounds."

She frowned, eyes narrowing a little suspiciously. "You're a colonial?"

Lauren nodded and introduced herself.

"I'm Mary. This is Lee Hailey."

Lee had curled up on the ground, eyes tightly squeezed shut.

"What's he doing?" Lauren asked.

"He's trying to stop the itching."

Lauren blinked. "How?"

Mary regarded her for a few moments. "Don't see many hybrids, do you?"

Lauren glanced at Lee. "Yes, I've seen quite a lot of them, actually."

Mary sniffed and gave her an appraising look. "You can't let your guard down here. Not even for Lee."

"Why?"

A man cleared his throat. Lauren hadn't seen him approach them. He had a time-worn face with hooded gray eyes, and his clothes seemed to hang off him, but he looked strong.

"Because he's dangerous. Unpredictable. You should stay away," he said.

Mary looked up at him. "Couldn't wait to come over, Jankle?"

He shrugged. "We're all in the same mess, aren't we?" He looked at Lauren. "Always more of us getting taken."

Jankle stared at her for a long moment, and then his eyes widened. "She's not a hybrid."

Mary shook her head. "No, Jankle, she's not."

He stepped back. "Then you should go over to the other side."

Mary rolled her eyes. It looked like something she did a lot. "No, she doesn't need to. Don't start that nonsense."

"She belongs on the other side. If she isn't a hybrid, she shouldn't be here!" Jankle nearly shouted.

Lauren stood. "Why do I need to leave?"

Jankle sneered. "Stay here too long and they won't have you either."

He hastened away from them, shaking his head.

Mary sighed, and they walked away from Lee. Lauren looked at her with raised eyebrows, and Mary sighed. "Sometimes, Lee isn't in his right mind."

"What happens?"

"It's like he's stuck in a dream—sleepwalking—but he's awake. He lashes out sometimes."

Lauren thought about that for a few moments. "Where does he sleep?"

Mary titled her head to the side. "In a cell. A holding room. You'll be assigned to one, assuming you'll be here."

She considered asking why Mary was there, not able to imagine why New Hope Security would need to arrest an old woman. "How long have you been here?"

Mary gave her a long look. "Eight days."

Lauren blinked. Mitchel had hinted that it would take two weeks to get a response from the colonial envoy. She shook her head a little. Isaac would contact them, if he hadn't already. Someone was on their way here right now.

"A lot to take in, isn't it?" Mary said.

Lauren nodded. "If you don't mind me asking, why are they holding you here?"

Mary's gaze hardened a little, and she sighed. "I'd rather not say."

"I'm sorry."

Her gaze narrowed a little. "I doubt you'll be here long enough to find out anyway. You're a colonial, right? A doctor, no less."

The way she said it made it sound like an accusation.

"We're trying to help."

Mary looked away from her and gestured toward the holding area. "Does it look like you're helping?"

Lauren's eyes widened. "What does me being a colonial have to do with this?"

Mary shook her head. "You really don't get it. You show up here in your ships and open up the world to all sorts of nonsense. Now nothing is the same. Too many new faces, new ideas, everyone with an opinion on how things ought to be run."

"Things will improve, Mary. That's what we're working towards."

Mary waved away the comment and began to walk away.

Lauren kept pace with her.

Mary paused. "What do you want now?"

"You never answered my question."

She blinked. "I'm old and I'm tired. I can't keep up with all the questions. Leave me alone."

Lauren chuckled, and Mary wrinkled her nose. "That 'old' argument isn't going to work on me."

Mary's gaze went skyward for a second. "Fine, look around. See any similarities among the people here?"

Lauren looked around the holding area, unable to see anything. She shook her head. "What am I supposed to see?"

"People being held here are either hybrids or people close to them."

Lauren took another look around. Hybrids looked like humans if they wanted. There were a couple whose skin was almost entirely black, their features more pronounced, but there weren't many of them. She honestly couldn't tell the difference, but when she turned to tell Mary that, she was gone.

Lauren frowned, looking around for the older woman. She finally spotted the back of her head, and she was sitting with a group, none of whom looked particularly friendly.

She decided not to bother her anymore, instead going back toward Lee. She didn't get too close but was within a few feet of him. She sat with her back to the wall, thinking about what had happened to her.

Since she'd never been in trouble with any authority, she'd assumed they needed her expertise, but she was being accused of murder. She only had a cursory knowledge of standard law practices among the colony, but she knew enough not to answer questions and to request the presence of someone who knew the law to represent her interests. She thought about Investigator Demming. He'd gotten her to talk, despite her being determined to be quiet. Had she made a mistake?

That family was dead, and they thought she killed them somehow. She recalled the images Demming showed her and tried to remain as clinical as possible. She pushed from her mind what she was being accused of and peered at each of the victims in her mind. She began with the adults because it was much easier for her to concentrate on them than to recall the children.

The images looked to have come from the angle of a tactical helmet. She focused her attention away from their facial expressions and searched for an indication of the cause of death. None of the victims' bodies looked to have been struck or shot by a weapon.

She glanced over at Lee. He still lay on his side, staring off at nothing.

Lauren closed her eyes and recalled the images again. Judging by the way their bodies lay on the ground, they looked as if they'd been in pain. They might've been poisoned, but without a toxicology report, she couldn't guess what had been used. She kept thinking of different causes of death and grouped them in her mind according to plausibility.

She leaned her head back against the wall and sighed, opening her eyes. A group of people were walking toward her. Some of them gestured to her, looking accusatory. Did they know why she was there? Did they suspect what she was being accused of doing?

A chime sounded overhead, and everyone in the holding area looked up toward the ceiling.

"Prisoner L. Gates, report to the entrance immediately," a monotone voice said.

The announcement repeated, and Lee sat up. He looked at her. "Your number is up. Time for you to go."

23

LAUREN STOOD up and walked toward the entrance. There was only one door in the holding area. It seemed like everyone was watching her as she went.

She came to the steel door and stood there. It burst open with a clang, and a guard gestured for her to come out.

"Lift up your hands," the guard said and placed her wrists back in restraints.

"Where are you taking me?" Lauren asked.

"You have visitors."

She followed the guard and another one stayed behind her as they went. They led her through corridors that should've looked familiar but didn't. She'd been shocked by the events that had brought her here, and she could hear Isaac's voice in her mind, urging her to pay attention to her surroundings.

The guards brought her into a room similar to the room where she'd spoken with Investigator Demming.

A few minutes later, her parents entered. Her mother looked

relieved to see her, but her father looked ready to tear the whole place apart.

He glanced down at her wrists and slowly turned toward the guard. "Take those restraints off her at once."

The guard flinched a little and then straightened. "It's against regulations, sir."

Her father stared at him for a long moment, and the guard began to fidget. "How would you like this to happen?"

It was a simple question but carried with it a threat of absolute certainty. Her father's gaze was like molten fury, and it even surprised Lauren to see it. She knew about her father, what he'd done in service to the colony. Many people respected him, and there were some who feared him. But this was a side of her father she never really saw, and she suspected it was something he worked to keep her from seeing.

The guard blinked and glanced at his companion.

Her father glanced toward the other guard. "Go ahead. Reach for that shock stick." He paused for a few moments. "You don't have it in you. Now do yourselves a favor and remove those restraints."

The two guards seemed to wither under her father's powerful gaze, but they didn't dare take their eyes off him. He tilted his head toward her in one smooth motion.

Muttering, one of the guards went to Lauren and removed her wrist restraints.

"Good, now get out," her father said.

The guards left.

Her father's gaze softened as he looked at her, giving her a quick once-over. For a moment, she was reminded of being a little girl, basking in the protective presence of both her parents, but that feeling was gone in an instant and part of her missed the reassurance.

"Are you all right?" her mother asked.

Lauren nodded. "They're accusing me of murder. Murdering a family."

Both her parents' eyes widened.

"That's crazy," her father said. "Did you speak to anyone?"

"Yes, with a man named Demming. He's an investigator," she said and frowned. "I told them I wouldn't talk without a representative, but he...he got me to speak, anyway."

"It's okay," her father said. "We're going to get you out of here."

"How?"

"Do you think we'd allow you to be kept here?" he asked.

"Connor," her mother said.

They shared a glance. "That was before," he said.

They did this sometimes. They'd have a conversation that only the two of them could hear.

"I will not run away," Lauren said, and they both looked at her.

"No one is suggesting that," her mother said.

Lauren looked at her father. He didn't say anything else.

"We've brought Miles Duncan with us. He's a legal expert who was helping create the constitution for the Earth Alliance," her mother said.

Lauren only remembered him from a few advisory meetings they'd had before setting up the medical clinics in the cities.

"Where is Isaac?" her mother asked.

"He's probably searching for answers," her father said.

Lauren nodded. "They blocked my comlink."

Someone knocked on the door, and they heard a muffled conversation coming from outside. Frowning, her father palmed the door controls.

"I told you my client is inside that room, you brute," said a short woman with blonde hair and big blue eyes. She looked inside and smiled at Lauren. "There, you see, my client."

The guard at the door looked at Lauren.

"Who are you?" her father asked, blocking her from entering.

She looked up at him. "I'm Kay Garrick, General Gates, and I'm the best hope you have of saving your daughter from being charged with multiple murders. Now are you going to be a dear and let me in?"

Her father blinked in surprise for a second, then shook his head. "I don't know who you are. You're not with the envoy, so you have no business here."

Kay rolled her eyes and chuckled. "Yes, I saw your man over there." She frowned for a second. "Miles, is it? Miles Denkin... Dunkin." She shrugged. "It doesn't matter," she said, locking gazes with Lauren. "I'm the one you need."

Her father looked at the guard. "We have no idea who this is, and she's not representing our daughter."

Another guard stepped over and began shooing Kay away, and she gave an exasperated sigh.

Keeping her eyes on Lauren, she said, "Do you know what you're being charged with? The implications? Multiple murders, if you're found guilty, always carries the death penalty." She glanced up at her father. "Unless you're planning to remove her by force—which I suggest you don't, not unless you want to permanently damage future alliances between New Earth and this old planet here." She looked at Lauren. "You've done a lot of good for us. I've been keeping an eye on you in particular, considering what happened to your brother."

The skin around Kay's eyes darkened a little and her eye color changed from bright blue to green.

Lauren's eyebrows raced up her forehead, and she nearly gasped. "Dad, wait," Lauren said. Both her parents turned toward her, but the guard kept ushering Kay away from the room. "Stop!" Lauren called. "She's with me. Let her in." They hesitated. "I said, let her in!"

Kay pulled her arm away from the guard, scowling up at him. "See! Now go do something useful and leave us alone."

The guard's mouth hung open and Kay hastened into the room.

"Shut the door, General Gates," Kay said. When it was done, she gestured for them to come closer, and she peered at Lauren. "Thank you."

"Don't thank me yet," Lauren replied. "I'll listen to what you've got to say, but I'm not agreeing to anything."

Kay smiled. She was small with narrow shoulders, looking almost fragile but so full of life. She glanced at Lauren's parents. "Okay family, this is the deal. You're all in it. You all have a role to play, and every action you take will affect the outcome of this trial."

"There isn't going to be a trial," her father said.

Kay glanced at him for a second and then focused on Lauren. "Listen to me, Doctor Gates. There will be a trial, a highly publicized spectacle that is going to have long-term repercussions if we don't win this case."

The door opened and Miles Duncan entered the room. He frowned at Kay. "You! You've got no business here."

Kay grinned. "You're pretty smart. I can use your help, but if you annoy me, I'll make you leave."

Miles blinked, his eyes darting to the others. "There is going to be a hearing on this in less than two hours. They've already assigned a case."

"Not a surprise. They want to get the spectacle going as quickly as possible," Kay said.

Miles ignored her and looked at Lauren. "We haven't

officially met, but I do recognize you, Doctor Gates. You're facing multiple murder charges, and given the high-profile nature of this case, it's going to put a huge spotlight on a lot of other issues."

Kay snorted. "You have no idea."

Miles scowled. "Does she need to be here? I think it's time for you to leave."

He walked toward the door.

"You haven't asked her the most important question," Kay said.

Lauren frowned and looked at Miles. His back was to her, and he paused before the door, hand hovering over the controls, but he lowered his hand and turned around.

He cleared his throat and looked at Lauren. "Are you guilty of what they're accusing you of doing? Did you do it?"

"Certainly not!" Lauren nearly spat. "What kind of question is that?"

"Not the toughest question you'll answer before all this is done," Kay said, regarding her thoughtfully.

"What do you mean?"

Kay gave her a sympathetic look and sat down across from her. "I told you I've kept an eye on you. Not just me, but a lot of us have been."

"Who is us?" her father asked.

Kay arched an eyebrow and didn't take her eyes off Lauren. "Do you want to tell them?"

Lauren blinked and glanced at her parents for a moment. "She's a hybrid."

Kay smiled, and a giggle bubbled out of her chest. "I'm sorry, it's just that you made it sound so dramatic." Lauren stared at her, and Kay made a dismissive gesture. "It's just how my mind works. You say you didn't murder anyone. That's a good start.

How about unintentionally?" she asked. Everyone in the room became still.

"Unintentionally?" Lauren repeated and shook her head. "Of course not. How would I unintentionally murder someone?"

Kay smiled. "Very good, Doctor Gates. You put the burden of proof on the questioner. It really helps when you don't make the prosecution's case for them."

Miles sighed. "Doctor Gates, I must advise you to stop taking advice from this woman."

Kay spun toward him, full lips pursed. "Tall, dark, and handsome...I thought you were smarter than this. If you wish to win this case, you'll listen very carefully to me because you won't succeed without me."

Miles shook his head and palmed the door controls.

Kay turned toward Lauren. "It's your choice. No one else in this room can make this decision. Not your parents, even ones as powerful and resourceful as them," she said, and then, nearly rolling her eyes, "and not Miles Derking." She shrugged. "He means well, but you need me because I know the local laws they're going to throw at you. It'll take tall, dark, and handsome too much time to get brought up to speed. No amount of AI assistants will bridge the gap of firsthand knowledge." She tipped her head to the side. "Plus, no one from the envoy will have my perspective. You see, Doctor Gates, there is a lot riding on this trial, the implications of which will be far-reaching for the people here, even after the envoy has left. We'll be the ones who must live with it. What I'm after, aside from proving your innocence, is a better state of affairs for everyone exposed to this."

Lauren's gaze sank to the table while she considered it. Everything Kay Garrick had said implied so much more. There was a growing mistrust among the people of Earth, and the spacers returning only made those tensions worse. A period of adjustment was to be expected, but Kay was right. There was a trend of attitudes and events.

Miles cleared his throat and sat next to Kay. He tried to give her a reassuring look. "Doctor Gates, I agree with my colleague that there is more riding on this. Proving a murder is actually quite difficult. What is less difficult is proving negligence, and the end result is the accidental murder of the victims."

He glanced at Kay with raised eyebrows.

She looked at Lauren. "He's right. They'll obfuscate the facts and paint all your efforts, conversations, and actions in the most suspicious light. It's no secret that you seek to reverse the effects of hybridization."

"Don't answer that," Miles said and looked at Kay. "Aren't you getting ahead of yourself?"

Kay blew out a breath. "Why waste time? If she wanted me to leave, she would've said so by now." Miles looked at Lauren and then back at Kay. "Come on, Derkin, you're sitting in a room with three of the most formidable women you'll ever encounter."

Miles's mouth hung open for a moment, and then he shook his head. "My name is Miles Duncan."

The edges of Kay's lips trembled a little in mirth. "I apologize. You can address me as Ms. Garrick."

Lauren snorted a little, and Kay smiled at her. She liked her, but should she trust her fate to a woman she hardly knew?

She inhaled a breath and held it for a few seconds, considering. "You'll co-represent me. I want you to work together as a team."

Kay smiled, and she glanced wickedly at Miles, eyes gleaming.

Miles tipped his head to the side. "It will be as you say, Doctor Gates."

Her father cleared his throat and locked gazes with Kay. "You're bound by client privilege, correct?"

"Yes, General Gates. Anything that is discussed here, I'm bound to keep between myself and my client."

Her father nodded a little. "Okay, then. I'll make whatever resources you need available to you. However, if I get the sense that this trial has become a sham, make no mistake," he said and looked at Lauren, "I *will* take you away from here."

Her mother nodded, making it known to her that she completely supported her father in this decision.

The others waited for her to respond, and she knew she needed to address this.

"No," Lauren said and paused for a moment. "I know you can do this. I know you want to do this, but it would be wrong, and you know it." She held up her hand as both her parents began to speak. "Please," she said, and they stopped. "I'm not going to run from this. I didn't do anything wrong, not even accidentally so. I know what's going on here, and I know what's at stake. I know someone has put this together to undermine what the envoy has been working toward. Those same people want divisions, and they're trying to use me as a means to get to both of you. I've made my decision."

Her parents shared a look for a few moments and then her father looked back at her. Seeing her like this couldn't be easy for him.

"Dad, they expect you to take me out of here. Let's show them who we really are. Let's show them that we're not afraid of them. They can't push us around. These are desperate actions that require a specific timetable. I aim not to cooperate with that."

Her father chuckled. "Where did you get that from?"

Lauren eyed them. "My future husband is an intelligence agent. We talk...a lot."

"Where *is* Isaac?" her mother asked.

"My guess is that he's conducting an investigation of his own," her father said and looked at her lawyers. "Can you get her released?" Miles nodded while Kay shook her head. "Which is it?"

"They're not going to release her," Kay said. "Public pressure. I can push for better accommodations."

Lauren thought about the people she'd seen in the holding area and shook her head. "Don't do that."

"Lauren, you don't know what you're asking for," her mother said. "If they can get you a better place to stay, you should do it."

"I don't want to be accused of having special treatment. I'm not going to give them any more ammunition than what they already have."

Kay regarded her for a few moments and gave an approving nod. Then she looked up. "General Gates, Doctor Bishop, would you mind giving us a few minutes alone? Just a few minutes, I promise," she said and looked at Miles for support.

Miles nodded. "Please, it'll just be ten or fifteen minutes, tops."

Reluctantly, her parents left the room.

Kay regarded her for a long moment. "That can't have been easy for you."

Lauren frowned, her shoulders tight. "What do you mean?"

Kay smiled. "Doctor Gates, I've sat in the same chair you're sitting in right now. Trust me, none of this is easy. I know you're putting on a brave face to ease your parents' worry, but you can be honest with us." She tipped her head toward Miles.

Miles looked a little surprised for a moment, but he nodded toward Lauren.

Lauren looked away for a moment, gritting her teeth.

"Honestly, it makes me angry. Whoever did this, they hurt that poor family."

Kay pursed her lips thoughtfully. "You've seen the images?"

Lauren nodded. "Inspector Demming showed them to me."

Kay nodded. "To get a response from you."

"It's manipulative."

Kay shrugged. "It is, but he's doing his job."

"Is he part of this?"

"I don't think so."

Miles shook his head. "We'll need to do better than that."

Kay rolled her eyes. "Fine. No, it is my heartfelt conviction that Inspector Hal Demming is not corrupt and is, in fact, trying to solve a murder."

Miles eyed her for a moment. "You know him."

"Correction, I know *of* him. He's…good at his job. He'll go wherever the evidence takes him." Kay looked at Lauren. "Do you mind if I call you Lauren?"

She nodded.

Kay smiled. "Thank God, I was getting tired of being so formal. Please call me Kay when we're working together. Out there, we'll need to be formal. No helping that." She paused for a moment. "I know you don't want any special treatment—"

"I don't need it," Lauren said quickly, then frowned a little. "There's more going on here than this."

"What do you mean?" Miles asked.

"Some of the things the people I met in the holding area said. They implied that they're being held wrongfully. I'm not sure what the right term for it is. I'm not even sure if it's illegal, but some of them felt like they'd been targeted."

Miles considered it for a moment and sighed. "Lauren," he said, then paused for a second. "I know you want to help, but there is a time for that, and then there is a time to look out for yourself. You're in considerable danger. The longer you're here, the more exposed you'll be for even more pressure on the others."

Kay stared at him and then slowly clapped her hands. "Nicely done, Miles. First you tell her to look out for herself, and then you tell her that the situation she's in, which is beyond her control, I might add, is going to put extra pressure on her powerful parents. Your people skills need a little work."

"So does your tact."

Kay narrowed her gaze playfully.

Lauren cleared her throat. "Do you know what I'm talking about, Kay?"

Kay's expression sobered, and she nodded a little.

"Would someone please fill *me* in on what you're talking about?" Miles asked.

"It's a gray area," Kay said. "Kinda like diplomacy, I would imagine. Easy to make accusations and sweeping gestures, but not a lot of substance…Except for those involved."

"I still don't understand."

"It's the hybrids," Lauren said. "There are a lot of them in the holding area. Some other people, too, but they seem to be connected to other hybrids. Not sure why they're being held, but one woman told me she'd been there for eight days."

Miles pressed his lips together for a moment and looked at Kay. Her eyebrows flicked. "Local laws are different here. Back home, a person could only be held for up to forty-eight hours."

"Well, you're not at New Earth anymore, and until that new constitution you're advocating for is approved, we're still under our current, if fragmented, system. Meaning that here in the city of New Hope, a person can be held for two weeks without being charged."

"Does that happen often?" Lauren asked.

Kay sighed. "It's happening more now than it did six months ago, and is a symptom of the current problems we're facing."

"We're doing our best," Miles said.

"Stop taking things so personally. This isn't about you, Miles, or the envoy—at least not entirely. We need to stay focused on Lauren and proving her innocence. That is our highest priority."

Lauren leaned back against the chair and blew out a long breath. "Okay, what do we do now?"

Kay smiled and then looked at Miles. "Hey, would you mind using that diplomatic gravitas you were waving around earlier and get all of us some lunch? I'm starving, and I think Lauren could use something to eat as well."

Miles's shoulders slumped a little. "I'm not your valet."

Kay pursed her lips toward him, almost blowing him a kiss. The edges of his lips lifted despite him trying to keep his face straight.

"Fine, for Lauren," he said.

"Woo-hoo, touché. We're going to get along great!"

Miles left the room, and Kay looked at Lauren.

"It's just us girls here. I'm willing to let you go back into holding. You should be fine, but it could get a little rough, too. Miles is right about the risk, but don't tell him I said that. He'll get full of himself, and I've got him right where I want him."

Lauren's eyebrows pulled together. "Why are you helping me?"

"Because you're one of the good ones. I question some of your motivations, particularly in regard to developing a cure. I know you don't want to call it a cure, but that's what it is, and that's how it will be perceived. There's a long history of other such efforts being forced on people. It's never a good thing." Kay paused for a few seconds. "The cure you were working on. Have you tested it out on anyone?"

Lauren shook her head. "No, not yet."

"But you were ready to test it."

"I was ready for some peer review of my findings. Then I was planning to seek approval for testing."

Kay nodded. "Did anyone have access to your research?"

Lauren shrugged. "I followed security protocols. Isaac had access."

Kay shook her head. "Yeah, I'll rule your future husband off my list of suspects, unless you feel like he should be there."

"Never. He'd never do that to me."

Kay nodded slowly. "Okay, I still want to speak to him, which, based on what you said before, might be a little difficult. What's the best way to get in contact with him? You know, the kind of comlink he'll be sure to answer."

Lauren chuckled. She had no idea where Kay had come from, but she was sure glad she'd shown up when she did. "I can help you out with that."

"I thought you'd be able to."

24

ETHAN STOOD over the partial remains of a dead person. Scavengers had devoured parts of the legs and midsection. The area stank of putrid death, and he covered his nose and mouth.

Jared Andrews squatted over the remains. He wore a mask and extended a palm scanner toward the body.

Ethan backed up a few steps to a spot where the stench wasn't quite as potent.

Jared stood and walked over to him. "Looks like they've been dead for about four days. No idea what could've caused the injuries."

Ethan frowned. He wasn't accustomed to being near a dead body. "How can you tell anything about what happened?"

"The scavengers did a number on them, but the severed leg, and left shoulder and arm were completely torn off," Jared said, gesturing toward the body. "That skin is stretched, and there aren't any indications of bite marks like what you'd see with smaller scavengers. See the area near the right knee?"

The skin looked shredded, and the sight made Ethan's

stomach flip-flop. He inhaled a few breaths and then sighed. "So, something killed him. It's gotta be male, right?"

Jared nodded. "Definitely a male."

"Okay, so something killed him and then just left him here. Then the scavengers came along after that. You're saying he died about four days ago?"

"That's correct, judging by the decomposition of the skin."

Ethan glanced around the area. The body looked as if it had been dragged. He spotted an area of dried blood on the ground. They followed it about thirty meters and found the location where the person had been killed.

"Looks like there was a fight," Jared said.

There were crushed saplings and shrubs around them.

Jared walked over to a dark patch of earth and took a sample. "It's human blood. Matches the body we found."

Ethan frowned in thought for a moment. "Hybrid?"

"I can't tell. I don't have a way to determine that." Jared eyed him for a second. "Can you tell?"

Ethan blinked. "Me? Why would I be able to tell?"

"Because you're a hybrid."

Ethan shook his head. "Maybe if he was alive, I could tell."

He heard some of the others arriving, and he and Jared returned.

Ethan saw Clip bending over the body, peering at it.

He stood, lifting his chin toward them. "What did you find out?"

Ethan told him. "We're not sure if he was a hybrid."

Clip frowned at him. "What do you mean? Of course he was a hybrid."

"How do you know?"

"I can smell it."

Ethan blinked and glanced at the remains.

"Can't you smell it?" Clip asked.

His stomach threatened to slither up into his mouth and he swallowed hard. "That's disgusting. No, I didn't smell it."

Jared stared at Clip, looking unsure whether he believed him.

"The clothing is of a kind spacers wear," Clip continued. "I'm not sure why he'd be out here all alone."

"Maybe he wasn't alone," Ethan suggested.

Jared held up his hand. "I still don't understand how you can determine that he was a hybrid."

Clip regarded him for a few moments. "See that patch of skin on the upper thigh?" Ethan looked and saw that it was dark with dried blood. "That's not blood."

Ethan peered at the wound and saw it. The other areas of the body, which he'd thought was blood from his wounds, were discoloration caused by being a hybrid.

The body had no head, and his clothing was shredded. There were no wrist computers or implants, which did narrow things a bit. Most people didn't have implants. There were some spacers that had them, but certainly not everyone. Ethan knew they hadn't been a colonist, so they had to be an Earther or a spacer.

"Okay," Jared said. "But that doesn't explain what he was doing out here."

Ethan looked at the body for a moment and then at the others. "He could be like the others we found. The feral hybrids. But that would mean that he's relatively new to it. We'll need to bring the body back with us for analysis."

"We'll mark the site," Clip said. "I'm not bringing that on the ship. We don't have the proper equipment to transport it."

Jared nodded. "He's right. We need a quarantine team to safely retrieve the body."

"Did you get a recording of the area?" Ethan asked.

Jared frowned, looking confused.

"When you scanned the body. Can you send me the recording? I know someone I can send it to."

Jared regarded him for a long moment. "I'm not authorized to do that. Make that data available, I mean."

Clip glanced at Ethan.

"This isn't confidential," Ethan said.

"I understand that, but there are protocols to follow, and I will not deviate from them," Jared replied.

He quickened his pace in the direction of the camp, and Ethan stared after him.

Clip cleared his throat. "No use pursuing it."

"I don't get it, Clip. Sometimes everything is fine, and other times it's like Jared puts a bunch of stumbling blocks in the way. I thought we were cooperating."

They'd been traveling together for days, following the trail of feral hybrids, which was strange enough on its own, but there were things that Jared and Sergeant Handler were doing that were making him suspicious of them. He didn't like it, but it irritated him like an itch in the middle of his back that he couldn't quite reach.

"I can't advise you on that," Clip said. Ethan looked at him and he shrugged. "I don't like making assumptions either."

Ethan regarded him for a few seconds. "I feel like you were going to say more about it."

Clip shook his head. "It's better if I don't. For now, we all need each other. Every team has its quirks."

Ethan sighed. "We're not a team. It's very much us and them."

"And you're caught in the middle."

Ethan arched an eyebrow. "It's almost like you planned it like that."

He shook his head. "No, I didn't. I just like being prepared for certain eventualities. I had no idea we'd encounter anyone from the CDF, but it wasn't outside the realm of possibilities."

They walked toward the camp in silence. Ethan hadn't checked in with the CDF since they'd left. Technically, he wasn't in any trouble just yet, but he knew he was treading on thin ice. At some point, he'd have to check in and face the strong possibility of being recalled.

They reached the camp and Corporal Linette Nance came over to them. "Do you have a minute, Lieutenant Gates?"

They were on the outskirts of the camp.

Clip tossed a wave over his shoulders. "I'll see you there."

Nance glanced at him, waiting for a few moments until they were alone. "There's something going on, sir."

"What is it?"

Ethan was outside her chain of command, but he knew there was some friction between her and Sergeant Handler.

She stared at him for a moment. "Permission to speak off the record, sir."

"Nance, I'm not even in your chain of command."

"I know that, but you are my superior."

"Okay, whatever you say to me now will stay between us."

She bobbed her head, looking relieved. "Sir, I don't think Andrews and Handler are reporting in to COMCENT."

Ethan frowned. "What do you mean?"

"I mean, since the destruction of our Hellcat."

"Why wouldn't they?"

"I don't know, sir, but when I went to forward my report to COMCENT, Sergeant Handler nearly bit my head off. He said my report was supposed to be routed through him."

"He's not wrong."

"No, but I don't think he's sent them through. Usually, I'll get confirmation through our squad status channels, and there hasn't been anything. I know communication here is spotty, but I did initiate a check-in while we were en route here. Our squad still has a deployment status."

Ethan's eyes widened a little in surprise.

Nance nodded. "Our loss of transportation and a retrieval team for the Hellcat wreckage should be noted." She sighed. "Burk would never have done that. I think Andrews and Handler are hiding something."

Ethan considered that for a few moments. "Is everything else Jared said true?"

"Our reasons for being out here, you mean? Yes, that's true. We were investigating reports of strange hybrid activity, but it was being driven by Andrews. I think there's more to it than that."

He nodded, glad Jared was at least telling him that much of the truth.

Nance narrowed her gaze curiously for a second. "Why are *you* out here, sir?"

He considered putting her off and dodging the question. "Searching for the feral hybrids, too, but I'm also looking for the source of the transmission that was received at the research lab on Mars."

She frowned. "The place you found before you picked us up?" Ethan nodded. "The Vemus origins. I remember you saying something about that."

"Yeah, I have something pulling data off the old communication satellites in orbit, hoping to narrow the search down."

Nance looked as if she was about to speak when Sergeant Handler called out for her.

She stepped back.

"What were you going to say?" Ethan asked.

Nance stopped and looked at him over her shoulder. "You're not the only one searching for old transmissions, sir."

She hastened away and Ethan waited a minute before following her. Jared Andrews was pursuing the transmission that indicated the origin of the Vemus had been found? Why would he?

Ethan tried to remember what Jared's reaction had been during that mission on Mars but couldn't. There'd been too much going on between the danger to the CDF soldiers and the aftermath when the mining facility and the research base had been destroyed.

Ethan walked into camp and looked over to where Jared was speaking with Sergeant Handler. They tolerated Clip and the others, but Ethan knew Jared had some deep-seated issues that he blamed the hybrids for. The attitude had affected most people in the CDF platoon that this squad had come from—but not all of them, Ethan thought as he glanced at Nance. She was speaking to Handler.

Ethan looked at Jared. His fiancé had been killed on a salvage mission that encountered a Vemus nest. For some reason, they suspected that the joint mission, which included hybrids, had somehow been responsible for the mission going bad. Lives were lost, and suspicion had peaked afterward. The CDF platoon had been taken out of service rotation while they went through psychological evaluation. But none of this really answered the question at the forefront of his mind. When Ethan had asked Jared how the CDF had found out about the strange encounters with feral hybrids, he'd only gotten vague responses. Maybe he should've pressed for more information, but Ethan was trying to keep his whereabouts on the down-low for the time being.

They both had something to hide.

Cynergy walked up behind him. He knew it was her without having to turn around.

"You're getting better at that," she said.

He smiled a little. "You'll just have to work that much harder to sneak up on me."

She shrugged. "Wouldn't work. We're part of each other now, so you're stuck with me."

He chuckled. "I think you've got that reversed."

The connection with her had been strange at first. It was almost like she was an extension of himself, but that diminished what he felt. He'd tried to describe it to Lauren, but he was sure he'd botched it. Lauren had used readings from his biochip and an external sensor that Cynergy held to try to measure it. The response was physiological, with patterns that were similar to people who had been married for a very long time.

Cynergy looked up at him. "So, are you going to tell me?"

They could sense each other's moods as if they were sensitive to them. It was like having data from a biochip sent right into his brain. She had it for him as well.

Ethan sighed. "I'm not the only one interested in finding the link to the Vemus origins."

Cynergy frowned and then looked at where Jared was speaking to Handler. "Are you sure?"

Ethan nodded and told her about what Nance had said.

"What are you going to do?"

"I thought about going over there and just asking Jared about it."

"Do you really think he'd tell you?"

He closed his eyes for a moment, then looked at her. "It's not supposed to be like this, Cyn. It's not us and them. It's just us," he said, gesturing toward the others. "If we persist in this us-and-them mentality, we're never going to make it."

Cyn regarded him sympathetically for a long moment. "It's how they view us."

"Maybe some of them do, but that's not how it is for everyone."

She narrowed her gaze a little. "What do you suggest I do? Ignore the sidelong glances as I walk by. Disregard the lack of trust and hostility that comes from some people?"

"People are going to wonder. We'd do better by taking the mystery away," he said, and she looked unconvinced. "Hostility should be dealt with. No one should have to put up with that, but more hostility isn't the answer."

"Okay, if that's how you feel, you should have no problem going right up to Andrews and asking him what he's really doing out here."

Ethan was about to reply but stopped.

"There is how we want things to be and how they actually are, Ethan."

She wasn't wrong, but that didn't mean she was entirely right, either. If he went over to Jared and confronted him about the lack of data sharing, this uneasy alliance could suffer for it. Perhaps the direct approach wasn't the best way forward, but if he tried to bring it up out of nowhere, Jared would be immediately suspicious, and Handler would probably glower through the entire conversation.

He looked at Cynergy. "What do you suggest?" he asked and then held up his hand. "Something that doesn't involve leaving them behind."

Cynergy grinned a little and shrugged. Then she became serious and hesitated.

"See, it's not so easy, is it?" Ethan said.

She exhaled a long breath, tipping her head to the side.

"You're right, it's not." Her eyes brightened. "Maybe Hash could help us."

"How?"

"He's quite resourceful. He just needs a little direction."

"All right, let's go talk to him."

They walked to the ship and found Hash sitting at a workstation. He was staring intently at several data streams on the holoscreen.

"Hash!" Ethan said, causing him to nearly jump out of his seat, and several metallic things bounced on the floor.

Chuckling, Ethan picked up some things that had been dropped and handed them back to Hash, who was glowering at him.

"I told you I hate it when you sneak up on me."

"I'm sorry about that."

Hash narrowed his gaze, tossing the pieces of the communications module onto the workbench nearby. "No, you're not. I know, I know. I brought this on myself. I snuck up on you *one* time and it became open season."

Ethan gave him an innocent look. "Truce?" he asked, sticking out his hand.

Hash looked at the proffered hand for a second before deciding to shake it. "Truce."

He glanced at Cyn and frowned.

"Go ahead, Hash. Show him," Cynergy said.

Hash's eyes widened. "Are you sure?"

She nodded.

"I've been monitoring comms chatter and I noticed something being pulled down by our friends," Hash said.

Ethan arched an eyebrow. "Hash, you're really good, but there's no way you can decrypt CDF comms."

He smiled. "You're right, I can't do that. I can just note that the communication has taken place. But what makes this so interesting is that the data dump didn't come from any CDF protocols. It came from one of the old satellites in orbit."

"Okay, did you intercept the data dump or something?"

Hash shook his head. "I didn't need to. I just resubmitted the data request and told the satellite to resend the dump here."

Ethan pursed his lips, impressed. "Great, what did you find?"

Hash smiled and glanced at Cynergy. "Not so much as a 'what' but a 'where.'"

Ethan waited for him to continue. "We'll go back to open season if you're going to make me drag it out of you."

"All right, all right. I tracked the original broadcast as it bounced around a number of old satellites still in orbit, but I managed to isolate the location. Here, I'll show you on the map," Hash said.

He brought up a regional map of the area. "It was sent up from a place near this lake here."

Ethan peered at the location and frowned. "There's nothing there."

Hash frowned. "What do you mean? The data clearly shows the source was coming from there."

Ethan shook his head. "I understand that, but there was never any kind of research facility at that location."

"And how do you know that? Did you go there without telling anyone?"

"No, but research facilities were located near major cities or old military bases. None of that applies there."

Hash shrugged. "So it's a secret research base that no one knows about. This was before Earth was quarantined. Wars had already broken out. The transmission could've come from anywhere."

Ethan considered that for a few moments. "It's landlocked.

Doesn't fit the profile we created for finding the location. We expect it to be along the coast west of here. That's where major research centers were located."

Cyn shrugged. "It's a lead, and it's one that they know about as well."

Ethan thought for a few seconds and then nodded. "Looks like I've got my in. Let's go see if they're willing to go along with it."

Hash's eyes widened. "You're just going to tell them?"

"You're welcome to come with us if you want," Ethan said.

Hash shook his head. "That's all right, I'll skip it and monitor from here just in case."

"Suit yourself," Ethan replied.

They left the ship.

"Are you going to tell Clip?" Cyn asked.

"Why don't you do that? I'm going to talk to the others. Bring Clip along."

They separated, and Ethan walked over to the CDF squad.

Handler saw him approach and lifted his chin a little.

Jared turned around, eyes coming right to Ethan.

"I thought I'd lay my cards on the table," Ethan said.

Jared frowned, and Handler's gaze narrowed.

"I know about the transmission you received," Ethan said. "We're looking for the same thing. The origins of the Vemus."

Jared regarded Ethan for a few seconds, then said. "I've been pushing the request along after you left us."

"I was ordered to come back here for reevaluation. It's not like I didn't want to be part of this."

Jared shrugged. "So what? I figured you'd be happy about this. If it's being investigated, that is."

Ethan arched an eyebrow. "Happy that you tried to keep it a secret from me? No, I'm not happy about that."

"Well, it's not like you were exactly forthcoming to me about it."

Ethan blew out a breath and nodded. "Okay, I acknowledge that. It's going to take both of us to scout out this place."

Jared glanced at Handler for a second and something unspoken seemed to pass between the two. Then he looked at Ethan. "Do you think Clip will take us all there?"

Ethan nodded. "Yes. He's a good man, Jared. These are good people."

Jared looked as if he were on the verge of saying something, but then the walls went up.

Handler was as stone-faced as always.

"Let's work together by sharing our data. Come up with a real plan," Ethan said.

Jared looked away for a few moments with a thoughtful frown. "You might not like where this leads." He thought Jared meant whatever they discovered would affect hybrids. "The feral hybrids we've been tracking seem to follow a trail of their own, as if something is luring them."

"How?" Ethan asked. "It's not like there's a ryklar control signal."

"I thought of that. You're right, there is no control signal, but they're moving in a south-west direction, which puts them on a path to the location where the transmission was sent."

Ethan considered. He knew what it could be but was hesitant to share it with Jared.

"All right, let's talk to Clip and then go check out this other site."

25

ETHAN SCANNED the area ahead of them as he flew the carrier toward their destination. The cockpit was quiet, and he started thinking about the 7th A-Wing. They'd been deployed somewhere in the star system, flying support missions for known Vemus remnants in salvageable locations. He missed them. Flying the Talon V Stinger was for elite pilots of the CDF. Many pilots petitioned to fly them, but few qualified. He'd thought it was to be the pinnacle of his military career, and now it seemed like it was a lifetime ago. Aspirations to command the A-Wings, and perhaps mixed fighting groups, were things he'd seriously considered. He'd been well on his way to achieving those goals, but now he felt as far away as he'd ever been. Cyn was right. He wouldn't be able to return to his old life. He hadn't wanted to admit it, but he was beginning to acknowledge that the path his life was on had forever changed. All he had to do was decide what he would do from here on out.

Ethan glanced up at the holoscreen that showed a video feed of the cargo area. The CDF soldiers were checking their combat suits and other equipment. Seeing them reminded him of home. He glanced at Cynergy as she stood talking with Clip. She gave a small shake of her head as she spoke, her long blonde ponytail swaying a little.

He opened a broadcast comlink to the others. "Heads-up, we've reached the search grid."

The others gathered around a couple of holoscreen workstations, and Cynergy entered the cockpit. Jared followed her.

Jared peered at the main holoscreen. "Looks like it matches up with what's on record, except for that lake."

The lake had tall ridges surrounding it, and the water was ocean blue.

"It might be the top of an old volcano, or this is a crater," Cyn said.

Ethan opened a sub-window and zoomed in to the lake. There was a small island on the far side away from them, but there was an even smaller island barely cone-shaped near the eastern walls.

The walls were covered with trees, but the rocky ridges poked above them. The lake itself was ten kilometers across by seven kilometers.

"Looks like there's some kind of monitoring station on the southern ridge. I'll set us down there," Ethan said.

He flew the carrier toward the waypoint and landed.

Jared stared at the video feed on the main holoscreen. "The area is kinda remote, don't you think?"

Ethan nodded. "Probably by design."

Jared slowly nodded. "I don't see any of those feral hybrids."

Ethan glanced at the video feed for a second and then stood. "So, no welcoming committee."

They walked into the cargo area. The loading ramp was

already down, and Sergeant Handler descended with the CDF squad to scout the area.

Will and Coreen spoke with Clip and then also left the ship.

Ethan retrieved his weapon and field kit. He walked past Hash, who was sitting at a workstation in the cargo area.

"Good luck," Hash said. "I'm going to monitor things from here."

"Boring," Ethan replied, drawing out the word.

Hash shrugged and turned back to his holoscreens.

Cynergy leaned toward Ethan as they walked down the loading ramp. "Clip doesn't want to leave the ship unguarded."

He nodded.

The tension between the two groups had settled into a watchful regard. While it wasn't openly hostile, it wasn't exactly harmonious either.

The monitoring station was a mobile HAB unit that looked more like a metallic camper than something permanent. It had large windows facing the lake, which was about three hundred meters away from them. The metallic gray walls looked weatherworn and the windows had been broken, exposing the inside to the elements.

Private Braxton climbed through the side window and opened the door for the rest of them to enter.

Specialist Gutierrez went around to the back of the station, examining the mobile power unit. Ethan glanced at it and doubted that it had any power left.

"That's not going to work," Cyn said to him.

Ethan nodded. "He's got a portable power unit, and it should give us minimal power to access the computer system inside."

They walked up a long ramp that went around to the side of the building and entered through the door.

Jared and Sergeant Handler were already inside. Clip was there, along with Emma.

"It's clear that the lake was the focal point of this monitoring station," Clip said.

Ethan glanced around the room. There were several workstations and three offices in the back. The workstations were covered with a gritty substance that came from decades of exposure. He was pretty sure that even if Gutierrez could get the power on, the computer systems linked here would never operate again.

Clip looked at him. "You don't look hopeful."

Jared and Handler glanced over at him.

"Not for anything out here. Check the offices," Ethan replied.

They headed toward the back and Ethan spotted stairs leading down. "I'm going to check the lower level."

He walked down the stairs and Cynergy followed him.

A sliver of daylight came in on the far side of the room. They must've been on ground level. There were storage containers along the wall.

They walked over to the light.

"A storage shed," Cynergy said.

Ethan pushed on the doors, but they didn't move at all. Crouching a little lower, he pushed harder, and the door grudgingly moved outward. More light came in, revealing an old rover that could only seat two people. The small tires looked decayed, and the rover tilted to the side.

Ethan circled around the vehicle and saw huge gouge marks along the side. The rear wheel had been torn off.

Cynergy stared at it. "What could've done that?"

"Something big. Look at the spacing between the rend marks. If this is a claw, its palm is almost the size of my chest."

Jared and Handler came down the stairs.

"We're heading down there now," Handler said. "Where?"

"Should be a panel on the wall." Gutierrez's voice came from the comlink.

Clip and Emma went down the stairs.

"Nothing works upstairs," Clip said.

They found a panel on the wall, and Handler followed Gutierrez's instructions. There were blinking lights inside, but when Handler tried to restore power, there was a loud pop, and a thread of smoke came from inside the panel.

Sighing, Handler turned toward Jared and shook his head. "The place is dead."

Ethan walked over to a workbench where it looked like several items had been covered. He lifted the coverings but there was nothing underneath.

"This is another dead end. We should scout the surrounding area," Handler said to Jared.

Ethan walked to the rover and opened the door. It looked clean inside and remarkably well preserved. He climbed in and tried to power the rover's systems, but they were dead.

He found an auxiliary port in the center of the dashboard and connected his portable power supply to it, then brought up his wrist computer and used a power regulator application that probed the rover's systems. Detecting that some of the systems were still accessible, the power output increased, and the rover's systems came online.

A partial holoscreen came to prominence. Ethan routed the data feed to his wrist computer and projected it outside the vehicle.

Cynergy smiled at him, impressed.

"What's this?" Clip asked.

Jared and Handler stopped speaking and came over to them.

"It's the nav system on the rover," Ethan replied and brought up a regional map of the area. "Looks like there are other monitoring stations nearby."

There were three other stations scattered like the points of a compass.

"They're all centered around the lake. There might be something hidden in its depths," Jared said.

Clip blew out a breath. "I don't have equipment to get us there, but we can split up and check the other monitoring stations."

"We'll check the lake," Jared said.

Cynergy frowned. "How? Do you have a submersible that we don't know about?"

Sergeant Handler grinned. "No, darling, we've got something better," he said and walked toward the partially opened door.

He enabled the helmet to his combat suit and easily forced the door open the rest of the way.

Jared enabled his helmet and followed Handler outside.

Cynergy scowled after them and then looked at Ethan. "That's just great. What if they find something down there?"

Ethan walked toward the door. "It's fine," he said.

The others followed him outside.

"What do you have in mind?" Clip asked.

Ethan enabled his MPS, and it changed to form one continuous piece of nanorobotic armor. It was nearly as protective as the combat suits the CDF soldiers had, but it was better than what the others had.

"I'm going to follow them into the lake," Ethan said.

Clip frowned. "You don't have an oxygen supply. Their combat suits do."

Ethan smiled. "I don't need one. I can hold my breath for almost ninety minutes if I need to."

Cynergy's eyebrows pulled together in concern. "Ethan," she began.

"I can show you, Cyn."

Emma's eyes widened a little. "What's he talking about, Cyn?"

Cynergy wore an MPS as well. It could seal them up inside and protect them from the cold lake water. But she'd never done what he'd been able to do. He didn't just hold his breath. Part of his physiology adapted to increase his body's capacity for storing oxygen in his blood, similar to what seafaring mammals did, but it required him remembering to breathe. The first time Cynergy had found him practicing, it had startled her because of the connection they shared. She didn't like it at all and advised him not to do it anymore. They could only handle so much adaptation from being a hybrid. Ethan didn't agree. He'd learned to control it.

"Ethan," Clip said, "are you sure about this?"

"Well, I'm not going to stay on shore and watch the others go down without me. This is the place, Clip. The last transmission came from here. It's remote, so it's easily hidden."

Clip pressed his lips together and glanced at the lake. Jared and Handler were speaking to the other soldiers. "I don't like this. Can you show me how you do it so I can go down there with you?"

He frowned. "I don't know about that. It would take too long. Maybe if we had more time. And you're not wearing an MPS."

"I've got this, Clip," Cynergy said. "I'll go with Ethan. You check those other monitoring stations."

Clip regarded her for a moment and then nodded.

They walked over to the CDF squad.

Cynergy leaned toward Ethan. "I hate the water."

Ethan blinked and then stared at her. "Seriously?"

She nodded, and then scowled at him. "But I'm not letting you go in there without me."

"Do you know how to swim?"

She rolled her eyes. "Of course I do. What kind of question is that?"

He frowned. "It's just that, well, you spent most of your life on space stations."

"We did bathe, and there were large water reclaimers. Of course I know how to swim," she said, looking at the lake.

Ethan finally understood. "Oh, I see. You've never swum in something like this."

She shook her head. "No."

"We'll need to split up," Clip said to Jared. "We'll leave the ship here and take the motorcycles to the other monitoring stations. We can do all three, but I thought you might like to check out some of them as well."

Jared looked at Handler. "What do you think?"

"We should," Handler said. "Corporal Nance, take Logan and scout the location of the monitoring station." He paused, looking at Clip.

"I'll send you the coordinates, Corporal Nance," Clip said.

They walked away, leaving Jared there with Handler, Braxton, and Murrey.

Ethan watched as Cynergy spoke quietly to Emma and then came over to him.

Jared peered at Ethan and lifted his chin a little. "What are you doing?"

"I'm going to show Cyn how to swim in the lake," Ethan replied. Jared turned to Cynergy for a second, looking doubtful. "Don't worry about it. We're coming with you."

Jared raised his eyebrows. "How?"

Ethan tilted his head to the side and gestured toward the lake. "Because we're going to follow you into the lake. We've got MPS suits. Add both me and Cyn to the team channel."

Sergeant Handler looked at him, considering. "Are you sure you'll be able to keep up with us? Recon drone might've detected several large animals under the surface."

"We'll be right behind you," Ethan assured.

Cynergy came to stand in front of him. Ethan retracted the MPS from his hands and held both of Cynergy's hands in his own.

There was a definite switch that happened when he embraced his hybrid nature. He was sure Lauren could spout the scientific terminology that better explained what happened, but Ethan preferred to simplify things. He stared at Cynergy. Her skin was black with a purplish sheen to it, and her eyes became bright green. Completely embracing his hybrid nature changed the sensitivity of all his senses. It was only through control that he didn't become overwhelmed by the new stimuli. He stared at Cynergy and they each anchored the other. He heard Handler speaking quietly to Jared. Ethan's back was to them, but he somehow sensed that Handler was gesturing toward them, and he was scowling while he did it. He could hear the faint whir of the combat suit's power core. He could also hear with startling clarity the subtle breeze that swept over the water, causing small ripples as it went.

Clasping hands with Cynergy gave her keen insight into the changes his body had gone through to change his nervous system. Ethan inhaled several deep breaths and held the last one. Then his heart rate slowed. Maybe a biosensor could detect the changes that were occurring on the inside, but to the casual observer, they were just standing there. Once he felt that

Cynergy had a firm grasp on what he'd done, he let go of her hands.

Jared and the others strode into the lake.

Ethan looked at Cynergy and she gave him a firm nod. His MPS covered his entire body, sealing him in.

They walked toward the water and dove into the lake.

26

THE LAKE WAS a lot deeper than it appeared on the surface. They'd only swum about thirty meters before encountering a steep drop-off to the dark depths below.

Ethan heard Jared grunt through the open comlink.

"Watch your footing, sir," Handler said.

"I'm fine. Just descending faster than I thought we were," Jared replied.

Lacking the heavy weight of the CDF combat suits, Ethan and Cynergy swam toward the bottom of the lake. They'd attached headlamps to their helmets, which penetrated the swirling depths only a short distance.

"What's your status, Ethan?" Jared asked.

He brought up his wrist computer and entered a quick reply.

We're making our way to you. Won't be long.

There was a long pause, and Ethan thought he could see a dim glow in the distance.

"What's with the text reply?" Jared asked.

Can't talk like this.

"Is something wrong?" Handler asked, sounding irritated.

"I don't think so," Jared replied.

Nothing is wrong. Go on ahead and we'll be right behind you.

"He can't speak right now. Told us to go on ahead without them," Jared said.

The changes that both his and Cynergy's bodies had undergone to be able to do this limited their vocal ranges. They could make sounds, but to Jared and the others, it would sound like clicks and long moans, similar to that of whales.

A few minutes later, they finally reached the bottom of the lake. The MPS had adapted to a deep-water environment and added weight to their waists and feet, enabling them to walk with ease.

A waypoint appeared on his HUD, which showed the location of the CDF squad ahead of them.

Cynergy swam ahead with a burst of speed, then whirled around in front of him, giving him a wave. She'd updated the configuration of her MPS so they could swim. It elongated the material around their feet and hands, enabling them to move the water and propel them forward. The MPS suit assisted the wearer, augmenting their movements.

Ethan pushed off the ground while pulling his hands back in a powerful stroke. He moved through the water as if he'd been born to it. They soon caught up to the CDF squad. Lights from their combat suits penetrated deep into the darkness, and out of the murky depths appeared an underwater facility that stretched off in both directions.

Ethan saw the extensive communications equipment on top of it. The closer they got to the building, the more the temperature of the water increased. The building was a pale white color and had some kind of recessed lighting on it that lit an area near the ground.

The area was covered with trees that had somehow settled at this location near the facility. Ethan could feel a gentle current drawing him toward the building.

He swam toward it, both he and Cynergy easily outpacing Jared and the others. Several areas near the building seemed to come online, and the light around the facility brightened as many more light sources became active. A pool of light appeared underneath the building, revealing the earthy bottom.

Ethan led Cynergy closer. The building was situated above the bottom of the lake, with metallic pillars going into the ground, anchoring it in place.

He swam to the underwater access area and headed for a metallic staircase. Grabbing onto a railing, he pulled himself up out of the water. They were in a pressurized receiving area. Cynergy was right behind him, and he helped her out of the water and onto the deck.

It was a wide-open rectangular area. The access looked large enough to accommodate a small submersible, but there weren't any docked.

Ethan brought up his wrist computer and checked the atmospheric readings. The air was definitely within breathable range, if a little cool. He spotted several air ducts where warm air was being blown into the room.

He nodded toward Cynergy and then retracted his helmet. Changing back to normal was akin to putting on old, comfortable clothing. He exhaled the breath he'd been holding and let go of his hybrid nature. He heard Cynergy gasp next to him. She struggled for a few seconds and then calmed herself, taking several slow, steadying breaths and nodding that she was okay.

Handler and Braxton burst up from the water, using their combat suit jets to hover in the air, looking as if they were showing off. Then they landed on the deck. Jared and Murrey climbed up the stairs.

Handler and Braxton readied their rifles and looked around the area as if they were expecting to be attacked.

Jared walked over to Ethan. "We saw something move through the area out there. Did you see anything?"

"No," Ethan replied.

"More than one for sure," Braxton said.

Handler walked toward a door that led out of the room and palmed the controls. There was the sound of a mechanism retracting into the door and then it popped open. Handler pulled it back and secured it open using a latch designed for that purpose.

Braxton hastened over to him and poked his head out into a well-lit corridor. "Clear, Sergeant."

Handler nodded and looked at Jared. "I suggest we get a quick layout of the place to see what kind of shape we're in."

"Let's go," Jared said.

Ethan followed the CDF squad, and Cynergy walked next to him.

"How does this place still have power?" Braxton asked.

Not only did they have power, but the facility was extremely well preserved.

"Anyone know?" Braxton said.

Jared looked over his shoulder at Ethan. "This place has to be at least over two hundred and fifty years old."

"If it's where the transmission came from," Ethan said, "someone sealed the place up and left. There were no vehicles in the access area."

"The facility has to be purpose-built, so putting it on standby isn't outside the realm of possibility," Cynergy said. "We found old space stations that still had plenty of power reserves."

Ethan nodded. "We should find out the system status so we know how much time we've got."

Braxton looked back at him with a concerned frown. "Why? What happens if we lose power?"

Jared looked at him, and even Handler peered at him after a moment.

"It'll be flooded. We could get trapped in here."

Braxton scowled in disgust.

"Secure that, Private," Handler bellowed. "If we lose power, your combat suit will protect you. We'll wait for the pressure to equalize and then get through an exterior wall or back through the underwater access area."

They followed the maps on the wall, which led them to the command center. It was centrally located, and the facility was much larger than Ethan thought. It was curved, like they were walking in a giant circle. There were no windows in any of the corridors, but its bulkhead doors were all open.

They reached the command center and Braxton opened the doors.

Ethan stood just inside and felt like he'd stepped back in time. Amber recessed lighting along the ceiling became brighter, as if systems were still coming online. The workstations reminded him of the systems used on the Ark that had been preserved as museum pieces. The holoscreens flickered to life, showing a basic startup sequence.

Cynergy looked up at him. "What's the matter?"

"Nothing, it just reminds me of the Ark."

Jared turned toward him, and his eyebrows raised. "At the colonial museum in Sierra? That's why it looked so familiar."

Cynergy shook her head and frowned. "You put perfectly good computer systems in a museum? Any of these systems would've secured food and water for years."

"It's outdated," Ethan replied.

"But it works."

He couldn't argue with that.

Handler stood by a workstation. "Gutierrez, are you getting my video feed?"

The tech specialist replied that he was.

Ethan walked over to another workstation and initiated systems access using his security tool. A map of the facility appeared on his holoscreen. The structure was about half a kilometer in diameter. There were other control centers, but he'd been right about the corridors. They connected to other observation centers, and he was willing to bet that they lined up with the monitoring stations on the crater's ridges.

He initiated a data dump to a storage module in his MPS and then explored the computer system and found a subsystem. "Main observation. I wonder what they were observing," he said and selected the option.

An error message came to prominence, and Ethan frowned. He traced the source of the error and found it linked to another part of the facility.

"Where is that place located?" Jared asked.

Ethan brought up a sub-window, which showed him the location. "We'll go take a look."

Jared frowned, and Ethan noticed that the others became still, which made him suspicious.

"You can come with me if you want," Ethan said, backing toward the door.

"I don't think splitting up is such a good idea," Handler said.

"Well, then you can all come with me, but this is the command center of the entire facility. Once I get the other site online, you'll have direct control from here," Ethan said. Again, there were a few hesitant glances, as if they were having some kind of unspoken conversation. He sighed and walked toward the door. "Do what you want. I'm going."

He gestured for Cynergy to lead the way. Once they were far enough down the corridor from the command center, she gave him a sidelong glance. "Was it me, or did things get really tense in there?"

"It wasn't you."

"Oh, that's good. I'm so reassured—"

She suddenly stopped speaking. Something big whooshed outside the corridor, and the floor vibrated enough to notice.

Without another word, they started running. The others said they thought they'd detected something big, and now whatever it was seemed to be following them.

The door ahead of them was closed, and the sign above it showed that it was called Observation Two.

He palmed the door controls and sounds came from the mechanism inside as the door retracted. The interior of Observation Two was dark, with the only light coming from the corridor.

Ethan activated the team comlink. "We're here, but it looks like the systems haven't come back online."

"Look for a manual reset," Jared said.

The room was circular, with only a couple of central workstations positioned to face toward the middle of the facility itself.

Ethan found a control panel on the wall and opened it. He frowned. Someone had manually disabled the systems there.

"That's it. Just turn it back on," Cynergy said.

He pressed his lips together thoughtfully. "Someone turned it off for a reason. I'm just trying to think of why that might have been."

Cynergy frowned in thought and then shook her head. "It

could be anything—faulty equipment that wasn't safe to leave on for long periods of time, or some kind of maintenance cycle and they had to evacuate for some reason."

She was right. It could've been any of those reasons, but it was the ones he couldn't think of that made him pause.

"Did you find it?" Jared asked. "Gutierrez says you just need to turn it on to restore power."

Ethan looked around the circular room, searching for some kind of clue as to why someone had left it like this. There had to be a reason. This wasn't an automated shutoff that had been initialized remotely. Someone had to have been there, which meant that there had to have been a good reason for it.

He looked at Cynergy. "Would you go wait out in the corridor?"

She glanced at the control panel and then shook her head. "I'm not leaving you."

He should've known better than to ask. He sighed. "All right then, here we go."

He reached inside the panel and pulled the lever to restore power to the section.

A warbling sound came from nearby and the lights came back on. A pair of holoscreens flickered to life. Ethan glanced around the room, almost expecting an alarm to begin sounding at any moment.

Nothing happened.

They went to the workstations and sat down.

"Looks like the facility is connected to those observation stations outside the lake," Cynergy said.

Metallic panels in front of them began to slowly retract, revealing windows to a darkened underwater exterior. Then, huge spotlights illuminated a central area. He watched as four other light sources came on. The one to his left was the command center.

In the middle of the central area was a dark, somewhat obelisk-shaped stone. It was surrounded by what seemed to be a containment energy field. The obelisk gave off a purplish glow, and the surface appeared as if it was in motion. It wasn't very large, only about three meters. It expanded toward the bottom, and he thought he saw rounded cones near the base.

Ethan stared at it, unable to look away. There was a thick cable that fed into the containment field. Another set of cables went beyond the field and were attached to the bottom.

"Are you seeing this?" Ethan asked.

"Yes, we are," Jared replied.

"What is it?" Cynergy asked.

"This is what the transmission was referring to. It has to be the source of the Vemus."

She frowned in disbelief. "It looks kind of small, doesn't it?"

Ethan looked down at the holoscreen, and a data window appeared. His eyes widened as he read it. "Vemus star probe... Probe! They thought it was alien."

A small ripple spread across the dark surface, as if they'd just disturbed something that had been sleeping.

Cynergy was looking at him. "It's words on a screen. It's just someone's opinion. It looks like a rock."

Several large shapes swam around the probe, cutting off his view of it. They had a dome-shaped heads akin to that of a dolphin, but their bodies were more humanoid shaped. Ethan felt as if something had slithered down to his stomach, and Cynergy gasped.

Ethan brought up his comlink. "Did you see it?"

"Yes, but I don't know what it is," Jared said and stopped.

Ethan thought he heard Handler speaking, but he couldn't hear what he was saying.

"The research, are you sure?" Jared asked.

Another comlink registered to both Ethan and Cynergy. It was Clip.

"What's your status?" Clip asked.

"You're not going to believe what we found—" Ethan began.

"Are you still with the others?" Clip asked.

Ethan frowned and glanced at Cynergy.

"No, Clip, we're away from the others," Cynergy said.

"Good. That's good," Clip said, sounding relieved. "Ethan, do you remember what we talked about concerning the origin of hybrids?"

Ethan blinked. "Yeah, that they were created, the result of experimentation..."

He looked at the obelisk, eyes widening, and inhaled a sharp breath. "This is where it happened? This is where they created them."

A purplish flash came from the obelisk, but the energy field seemed to contain it. Several more flashes came, but they were isolated in certain areas, and the cables connecting to it began to thrash from side to side.

"Ethan," Jared said, his voice sounding detached, "we've got a problem."

Cynergy went to the holoscreen and brought up a couple of data windows. "Ethan, the probe was brought here. They retrieved it from the Pacific Ocean within a thousand kilometers of the coastal waters of the Asian Alliance."

Both Clip and Jared began speaking at once, and he couldn't hear what they were saying. The Asian Alliance had gotten hit the hardest in the earliest part of the rise of the Vemus. They'd thought it was an NA Alliance biological weapon. Global war had erupted, and that was when the Vemus spread across the globe. It had spread among seafaring mammalian life and then invaded the land. Where nation states had once battled for dominance, they banded together to fight the Vemus.

Ethan looked at Cynergy's holoscreen. There were records of the obelisk changing hands as various powerful organizations sought to control it.

The door to the observation center closed and he heard the security mechanism lock into place.

"I'm sorry, Ethan," Jared said. "I'm really sorry."

Ethan ran to the door and tried to override the controls, but he was locked out. "Jared, don't do this."

"This is war, Ethan. The probe is a first-strike weapon, and both you and the others have been caught up in it."

Cynergy pulled the access panel off under the door control systems.

"Jared, you need to stop this. You don't know what you're doing."

"You're wrong. I know exactly what I'm doing. This is what should've been done when they first discovered this damn probe. I'm going to destroy it."

"If you destroy it, we learn nothing. Nothing! Nothing about who sent it or why they sent it in the first place."

"You've been compromised. The probe can affect you. It's all here in the reports."

Ethan looked at Cynergy and she shook her head. She couldn't get the door open.

"So, you're just going to murder us? That's your plan?" he asked.

Jared let out a long sigh. "I'm sorry."

The comlink severed, which somehow included the one to Clip.

"I can't reach anyone. They've got to be using a suppressor," Cynergy said.

Ethan stared at the obelisk, his mind racing. More of those strange creatures swam into view, circling around the obelisk as if they were drawn to it.

27

"WE CAN'T STAY HERE," Cynergy said, walking to the other door.

Ethan turned toward the holoscreens and then moved to the observation windows beyond.

Cynergy let out a frustrated snarl, then gave up on trying to open the door and joined him.

"What if he's right?" she asked. "What if we're just some lab experiment?"

Ethan shook his head. "No, we're not." She stared up at him, looking as uncertain as he'd ever seen her. "Maybe it started out that way. I don't know. But we're not them; we're not Vemus."

"How do you know, Ethan?"

"Look at the records," he said, gesturing toward the holoscreen. "Look at all those experiments. They were trying to find a way to stop the Vemus. Some of the organizations were seeking a way to make a weapon out of them, while others were searching for a way to interact with them. They were trying to make contact."

Cynergy looked at the probe. It stood among the swirling depths, looking both like it belonged at the bottom of the ocean and like any number of rocks flying through space.

Ethan pulled his rifle off his back.

Cynergy looked at it, eyes widening a little. "What are you going to do?"

"We can't stay here, and it'll be easier to get through the windows than it will the door."

"But what about those things out there?" she asked and then gestured toward the probe. "What about that?"

"We need to stop them from destroying it. We also need to warn Clip and the others."

"Nance is up there. She wouldn't hurt him."

Ethan thought about it for a moment. "Handler could order her to take Clip and the others into custody, and then he could do whatever he wanted once they got out of here. If they manage to convince her that we've been compromised, then..." he left the rest go unsaid.

"Jared thinks he's doing the right thing. He thinks he's helping us," Cynergy said.

Ethan nodded a little. "I know. He'll take the data recovered here and use it to convince everyone that hybrids need to be quarantined. He'll destroy the probe and we'll lose any chance of learning more about the Vemus origins."

He looked out the window and saw the others making their way toward the probe. There must've been an access hatch to the lake nearby. The lights on their helmets sent shafts of light toward the probe. Several of the large creatures swam toward them but faltered as the soldiers fired their weapons.

"How are they able to do that?" Cynergy asked.

"They configured the ammunition to use elongated darts. It

increases their density and the shape is conducive to the water," he said.

They enabled their MPS suits, but Cynergy was having trouble changing her physiology. He uncovered his hands, and she clasped them. Then she could mimic what he could do.

Ethan brought up his weapon. Using explosive rounds, he fired several shots across the center windows. There was a brief flash and the windows shattered. Shards burst toward them with an onrush of water. They hurried to the side and waited for the room to fill.

Ethan swam out of the room first, heading toward the soldiers. Cynergy was right behind him.

A dark shape moved in front of him, and Ethan changed direction, using the creature to cover his approach to the soldiers.

He only needed to stop them from destroying the probe. The humanoid creature was three meters long and looked more than triple Ethan's weight. He kept his distance at first, but they seemed to ignore him.

The creature let out a high-pitched moan, and Ethan felt something bounce off his MPS. He looked down and saw that several large holes had been blown through the suit at its chest.

With a sudden burst of speed, he darted around the probe. Someone was at the containment field generator. It had to be Jared. Handler, Braxton, and Murrey had taken up positions nearby, firing their weapons at any of the creatures that swam near them.

Ethan swooped toward the ground and darted toward them. Jared jerked back from what he'd been doing, and Ethan shoved him away from the generator. Jared grasped one of the thick cables, and the generator dragged behind him. The field shifted to the side, and the top of the probe breached the field.

A powerful surge bounced from the tip of the probe to the ground and back up. A wave of purple burst from the tip, spreading so fast that the water seemed drawn to it before pushing them all away, scattering them. Ethan tumbled, trying to get himself situated. He saw Jared tangled in the cables connected to the containment field generator.

Ethan's back slammed into the facility, and rushing water surged past him. He saw Cynergy at the feet of one of the CDF soldiers. The soldier looked as if he were trying to step back, but he couldn't be sure. Dirt billowed from beneath them, swallowing them up, but not before he saw the soldier lift his weapon.

Ethan pushed himself away from the facility wall, and with a burst of speed, swam right into the cloudy mess, blindly searching.

Another burst came from the probe and the energy swept away the dirt and debris. Ethan swam just above the ground and was spared most of the energy the probe gave off.

He spotted Handler. He was struggling with Cynergy, each trying to wrestle for control of his weapon. It was no contest. There was no way Cynergy was strong enough to withstand the augmentation that the combat suit gave the wearer. Handler shoved Cynergy away, sending her careening toward the probe.

Handler brought up his weapon just as Ethan slammed into him. He hit him with so much force that he dragged him to the side, and they toppled over.

Ethan pushed away from him, and someone else grabbed him from behind. He bucked against them, and someone else grabbed his legs, pinning them together.

Handler pushed himself off the ground and came over to him, weapon raised.

"Wait!" Jared said.

He'd come out of nowhere.

"We can't wait. You saw the data. He's one of them," Handler said.

Ethan struggled against the other soldiers. Braxton muttered an apology, but he wouldn't let go.

He spotted Cynergy moving off to the side, making her way toward them.

"Watch out!" Jared cried, and Cynergy barreled into Braxton.

Ethan slipped out of the MPS, and the cold lake water seemed to seize hold of him, but within seconds he couldn't feel it anymore. He glanced at his skin. It was dark, and the purplish sheen matched that of the Vemus space probe.

The two CDF soldiers were left holding his MPS. One of them had grabbed onto Cynergy's leg and flung her toward the probe. Ethan watched as she pierced the containment field. Tendrils shot out of the probe and latched onto her.

Ethan tried to scream, but it sounded strange, like a mournful wail. He swam toward her, and several projectiles darted past him. The tendrils began pulling Cynergy toward the probe, but he was able to grab her waist. Ethan banged his fists against one of the tendrils and it let her go.

The probe was knocked back and it swayed for a long moment before falling. The tendrils detached from Cynergy, and Ethan pulled her away from the probe. She was unresponsive, and he started to panic.

Several large creatures swooped past them, but Ethan didn't stop swimming. They soon reached the surface, and Ethan dragged her to a small island. He disabled her helmet and saw she was unconscious. Her skin was back to normal, but she wasn't breathing. He lifted her chin and exhaled forcefully into her mouth. He did this two more times and she began to cough.

A bright flash came from the depths below and Ethan looked

down at Cynergy. She was still disoriented. He kissed her forehead and then dove back into the lake.

Ethan embraced his hybrid nature, quickly adapting to the water, and darted toward the bottom.

His MPS was gone, and he'd dropped his rifle, but he could see. His eyes adapted to the underwater environment.

Bright flashes came from the probe.

He closed in on it and saw that the creatures had pinned the three soldiers to the ground. He spotted another figure farther away. He was retreating, and his combat suit was damaged.

Ethan swam over and saw that it was Jared, and he was moving with awkward jerks. The combat suit had large gouges taken out of it. The life support systems were failing, and the suit was malfunctioning. If Ethan didn't do something, Jared would die.

The command center was a short distance away. Ethan grabbed Jared and swam to the access hatch of the control center. He closed it and the water drained from the room. Ethan removed Jared's helmet.

Jared coughed and spat out water, then heaved several breaths.

Ethan stared at him.

The floor began to rise, and he suddenly realized they were in an elevator. It stopped and a door opened to the control center.

Jared sputtered, stumbling away from him, flinching as if he were about to be attacked.

"Damn it, Jared, I'm not the enemy!"

Jared looked over to the holoscreens nearby and then out some observation windows. "But the data, the reports. The hybrids succumbed to the probe."

Ethan looked over at one of the holoscreens. There were multiple sub-windows active. They showed recordings of people reacting to the probe and the burst of energy that came from it. The images were time-lapsed and showed hybrids changing into Vemus.

Ethan swallowed hard. The people didn't look like volunteers. They'd been forced to endure it.

He shook his head. "I don't know how to explain it." A shifting of the light and shadows drew his attention to the window.

Jared gasped. "The others."

"The creatures have them," Ethan said, trying to peer through the cloudy water billowing throughout the area.

"We have to get out of here!"

Ethan snarled. "I'm not leaving them behind."

"You can't help them!"

Ethan gritted his teeth as he tried to think of something he could do, but he didn't like any of the ideas he kept coming up with.

"They're already dead," Jared said. "As soon as they're brought to the probe, they'll be gone."

The cloudy water swirled, and he glimpsed the CDF soldiers fighting the creatures, but there were too many of them.

"Ethan, we have to get out of here."

He spun on him. "What happened to you, Jared? First you try to kill me and Cynergy, and now you're willing to leave them behind to save your own skin? Is this the kind of man you are? You were going to be a doctor. You're supposed to save lives, not abandon them. Is this the person your fiancé loved? What would she think if she could see you now?"

Snarling, Jared stomped toward him, bringing up his sidearm. "Don't you dare judge me!"

"Shooting me isn't going to bring her back. Murdering all the hybrids isn't going to bring her back. *Nothing* is going to bring her back!"

Jared clenched his teeth and jabbed the pistol toward him.

Ethan glared at him for a few seconds with a half-formed snarl, then looked away. All his anger and frustration melted away, and for a moment he felt exhausted, as if all the pressure of the things he'd been coping with had become too much. He lifted his gaze to Jared. "This is what happened before. This is what it did to everyone here."

"What are you talking about?"

"The Vemus," he sighed. "They nearly wiped us out. We tried to control it, and it divided us. It's been hundreds of years and here we are doing the same thing all over again. We should know better than this." He pointed at Jared and then at himself. "We're better than this."

Jared swallowed hard and shook his head, ashamed. Then he lowered his weapon. "I'm sorry," he said and blew out a long breath. "You're right, Ethan. I don't know what's wrong with me. I just miss her so much. I wish I could have had more time. I'd give anything for it, but you're right. She would've hated what I've done."

Ethan turned toward the window and Jared came to stand next to him.

"How are we supposed to go against that?"

Ethan glanced at him, taking in the state of Jared's combat suit. "We destroy the probe."

Jared's eyes widened. "What!"

He nodded. "It's the only way this ends."

"But you said we needed to study it to learn more about where it came from."

"Come out of the combat suit," he said, moving behind him.

Jared initiated the shutdown and stepped out of the suit.

"Take the helmet, though," Ethan said as he opened the power core.

"What good is this going to do me?" Jared asked after he grabbed the helmet.

"It'll protect your head, for one. It has emergency life support, which you'll need to get out of here."

"What are you going to do?"

Ethan hefted the suit's power core in his hand. It was a small containment unit, but it was very powerful. "Would you be surprised to learn that each of these suits has a self-destruct built in? It's part of the power core, and it's meant to prevent the suit from falling into enemy hands. But if I can get close enough to the probe, it just might be enough to shatter it."

"Those creatures are never going to let you get close enough to do that."

Ethan smiled and embraced his hybrid nature. The change was so quick that it almost felt normal to him now. "Not if I look like one of them."

Jared frowned. "Maybe I could distract them," he said and went to one of the workstations.

"Okay, but as soon as you see me reach the probe, you need to get out of here."

"How am I going to swim to the surface with just a helmet on?"

Ethan shook his head and detached one of the suit-jets on the back. "This has backup power, and it should get you most of the way up. Emergency life support will be enough for you to reach the surface."

Jared bit his lip and then nodded.

"You've got this. I'm going to help the others."

Jared pressed his lips together. "Handler would've done it, you know. He would've killed you."

Ethan nodded. "I know. He thought he was doing the right thing."

He went back to the elevator and headed back down. Jared sat at the workstation, navigating through the interface.

Water flooded the elevator and the doors to the access hatch opened. The skin between his feet and palms expanded, enabling him to swim with powerful strokes.

The creatures swam in a wide circle around the space probe, kicking up dirt and material from the lakebed. Ethan swam toward them and then was among them. He could detect subtle vibrations coming from each of them—a chorus of clicking sounds followed by high-pitched whines. He started to mimic the sound, and it seemed to focus his mind on a purpose that wasn't his own. He felt himself begin to slip and turned toward the Vemus probe. He angled toward it, working his way through the hybrids. They'd once been people, subjected to horrible experiments, but somehow they'd been preserved for hundreds of years.

Tendrils coming from the probe had lashed onto the CDF soldiers. They must've been powerful enough to overwhelm the combat suits. There would be no way Ethan could pull them off.

The containment field generator had toppled over, and the cables powering it had been ripped out. Ethan swam around the probe, trying to find the best opportunity to rescue the others and destroy the probe.

He looked down at the base of the probe and saw that thick tendrils had burrowed into the ground. A jolt of panic surged through his mind, and the compulsion he'd been feeling was pushed back. The probe was getting more powerful by the second. It emitted some kind of energy. He could sense it. It wanted to do what it was designed to do—convert, manipulate, and dominate. A surge of denial raged through him, and he faltered, falling out of harmony with the hybrids. They banged into him, and he felt something sharp lash across his back. The pain spread like hot lightning, as if his skin had been scourged.

Ethan pushed off one of the creatures and sped toward the probe. Black tendrils burst from the sides of it and Ethan dodged to the side, evading them. He grabbed hold of one as it retracted into the probe, and pulling out the combat suit power core, he slammed it onto the thick tendril as another one grabbed his leg.

Ethan watched as the power core disappeared from view, seemingly to be absorbed by the probe. He slammed his hands onto the tendrils that had ahold of him, but another grabbed his hands and brought him next to the CDF soldiers.

He struggled against their hold but couldn't break free. Then he did something that went against everything in him. Every instinct demanded that he fight, but he knew it was a fight he couldn't win. The Vemus space probe was much too strong for him to overcome. He thought about his father and everything he'd done for the colony—how he'd helped prepare the colony for the Vemus invasion and then fought the Krake in a war unlike any other that had ever been fought. Both times he'd managed to snatch victory from the certainty of defeat, and both times it wasn't because the CDF had been stronger than the enemy. His father and the rest of the CDF won those wars through cunning and sacrifice, by doing the things that the enemy least expected. Ethan couldn't overpower the Vemus probe, but he understood it more now than he ever had before. The probe was a programed biological intelligence. It was designed for a purpose, and it had rules.

He saw the CDF soldiers look toward him, and he stopped struggling, surrendering to the probe. Even though the tendrils squeezed him, he didn't resist, and his body became completely limp. He denied the part of him that demanded he fight with everything he had and focused on his memories of Cynergy. The moment she'd changed him into a hybrid was imprinted on his mind, and he could recall it with stunning clarity. He'd used that moment to help him focus his mind whenever new adaptations presented themselves as a result of being a hybrid. It was a function of the Vemus that was now a part of who he was.

The probe loosened its hold on him just as he hoped it would. It was a machine, a biological machine designed for a specific purpose, and it believed it had achieved it in him. He was just another in a long line of converts, but he shielded himself from truly yielding to the Vemus. He was different from all those who'd come before because his hybrid nature had been introduced generations after they'd been created. That was the only explanation he could come up with and one he hoped he'd find evidence for if he managed to escape.

The tendrils withdrew from him, and Ethan floated toward the nearest soldier. Spotting the AR-74 pressed to Braxton's side, he grabbed the weapon and fired it at the tendrils holding onto Braxton. High density darts tore through the tendrils, and Ethan opened the maintenance panel near Braxton's hip. He activated the ejection sequence, and Braxton jettisoned from his suit. Emergency thrusters pushed him toward the surface.

Dodging Vemus tendrils, Ethan did the same for Murrey. He wasn't sure if Murrey was even conscious. Handler was a short distance away. His combat suit was half torn off him, including the helmet. A tendril was in his mouth, and the skin around his face was becoming dark.

Ethan fired his weapon, severing the tendril. Then he reached for the stump and yanked it out of Handler's mouth. He looked as if he was already dead.

Across the way, a bright flash came from one of the

observation stations, followed by another. Each flash sent the creatures into disarray, causing a chaotic disruption.

Ethan grabbed Handler's arm and activated his wrist computer. Warning messages appeared from Handler's biochip, and Ethan activated the emergency override.

Dark shapes swooped toward him, and they reached Handler's combat suit just as the self-destruct mechanism engaged. A red flash shoved the water away, creating a pocket of expanding force.

Handler's combat suit opened, but not entirely. Thrusters fired, dragging them away from the probe, but only for a short distance. Ethan swam around and heaved him out of the suit, and Murrey's combat suit exploded with such force that it diverted the creatures into the probe. The fallen hybrids clustered around the probe, following an instinctual imperative to preserve it.

Ethan grabbed Handler by his waist and swam upward, pumping his legs with all his strength.

A bright flash came from beneath him, the biggest one yet, and a burst of current pushed Ethan and Handler violently toward the surface. It took everything Ethan had to hold onto the fallen soldier, refusing to leave him in a watery grave.

They broke through the surface, and Ethan was finally able to inhale a breath. Waves crashed nearby and Handler's body suddenly jerked. The blackness had spread across his face and neck. Ethan swam toward shore, dragging Handler's body with him.

Cynergy and Clip were there and pulled them both out of the water.

"Get away from him," Clip said. "He's becoming one of them."

Ethan stared at the CDF soldier, watching the change take place. Snarling, Ethan grabbed Handler's arm.

"No," he growled.

"Ethan!" Cynergy cried.

He looked at her. "Help me."

She blinked. "I can't do that for him."

He'd hoped that she could somehow prevent him from becoming fully Vemus. Not wanting to give up, he grabbed Handler's hand, and just as he'd trained Cynergy to alter her physiology for functioning in deep under water like him, he showed Handler how to be a hybrid. The Vemus inside Handler halted as if it had encountered a barrier, and for a few moments, Ethan thought it was going to work.

Handler opened his eyes and stared at Ethan.

"Fight it," Ethan said.

Handler's body convulsed in pain and Ethan watched as a wave of calmness overtook Handler. His whole body sagged as he blew out a breath.

"Not this time," Handler whispered.

Another convulsion overtook him, and then he became still.

Ethan blinked, peering intently at Handler, searching for some sign of life. "Wake up!"

He shook Handler, trying to rouse him, but it was futile. Handler was gone.

Ethan looked up at Cynergy. "I should've been able to save him. He was so close."

She squatted down, placing her hand on Ethan's shoulder. "Ethan, he's gone. There was nothing you could've done."

Clip squatted down across from him. "You did save him."

Ethan blinked, his mind refusing to understand.

Clip lowered his chin grimly toward Handler. "He's not one

of them. You stopped it from happening. One less soldier that the enemy can use against us."

Ethan's gaze sank toward Handler. The soldier's face looked oddly serene, as if he were in a deep sleep. He let go of Handler's hand, lowering it to the ground. Cynergy wrapped her arms around his shoulders, and he leaned into her.

"Clip's right, Ethan. You saved him. If it weren't for you, he would've been lost to the Vemus."

Ethan turned toward the lake. "The probe?"

Jared surfaced from under the water. Quickly removing his helmet, he gasped for breath. The others helped him onto land.

Jared looked at Handler's body with a pained expression for a few moments, and then he looked at Ethan. "It's all gone. The probe is destroyed."

"What about all the creatures?"

He shook his head. "Nothing was moving down there."

"How did you survive?" Ethan asked.

"Locked myself in the elevator. The facility protected me from the blast. Then I did what you told me to do. Emergency power doesn't last nearly long enough," Jared said.

Clip regarded Jared for a few seconds. "The data you recovered. I want it."

Jared glanced at Ethan for a moment, then brought up his wrist computer and made a passing motion to Clip. "There it is, but I do have a question."

Clip checked that data had transferred and then closed his holoscreen. "As long as this vendetta against hybrids is finished."

Jared looked away from him.

"You're not the first, and you certainly won't be the last," Clip said.

Jared sighed. "Yeah, but it's still wrong, and I'm sorry."

Clip glanced at Ethan.

"I might have explained a few things to him," Ethan said.

Jared nodded. "He did. What about the hybrids? The feral ones."

"It's not what we thought it was," Clip said. "The data we recovered from the observation stations had records from other research initiatives."

Jared frowned. "So, they're not other hybrids like you?"

Clip shook his head. "Evidently not. The Vemus have remarkable preservation capabilities that almost negate aging. It was this capability that the scientists were trying to exploit. These random encounters we've experienced are the results of those experiments. They're a certain type of hybrid, but not like us."

"And they've been roaming around for all this time?" Jared asked.

Clip nodded.

"I wonder if there is a way to help them. Reverse what's been done," Jared said.

"There might be," Ethan said, and the others looked at him. "Like it or not, this is going to be an issue we need to address but without going to extremes."

"I hope you're right."

Ethan looked at the others, his gaze lingering on Cynergy. "No one is going to force anything on you. It's not going to be that way. And if that becomes an issue, Earth isn't humanity's only home."

28

LAUREN STOOD outside the prisoner's entrance to the courtroom, and a pair of security guards waited with her. The corridor was extremely quiet. She'd been taken from the holding area and brought to the courthouse for her trial. Given the high-profile nature and colonial pressure, her case had been pushed to the front of the line. What normally would have taken several weeks or even months to put together had been accomplished in a little over a week.

Everything her primary defense attorney, Kay Garrick, had advised her about how fast this case would proceed had been correct. Kay and Miles Duncan had met with her more than a few times to strategize her defense and prepare her testimony. Miles had hoped to get the case dismissed without ever going to trial, but there was not enough evidence to support that. The compounds she'd been working with in her research to cure the hybrids had been found in each of the five victims. Lauren remembered their faces and wouldn't forget them or their names, but Kay had advised her at times to adopt a more forensic frame of mind, which would help her defense. Lauren struggled with that. She could attack problems that way, even complex problems, but the victims were people who'd come to her for medical care, and they'd been reduced to pawns in someone's twisted plan to implicate her in order to push forward their own political agenda.

The indicator light above the door turned green, and one of the security guards removed her restraints while the other opened the door. The courtroom was already filled with people. A wave of conversations echoed through the room, but as Lauren was escorted to the defense table, a momentary hush swept through the room and all eyes turned toward her.

Lauren straightened her spine, but the walk across the courtroom seemed to take much longer than it should've. She glanced behind where she would be seated and saw both her parents there. Her father wore his formal CDF uniform, which was an impressive sight. She saw that the rest of the envoy was there to show their support.

Both her parents stood and hugged her across the divider. There was an empty seat next to them for Isaac. She glanced at it and her mother leaned toward her.

"He sent word that he's running late but that he would be here."

Lauren nodded.

She'd noticed a few recon drones surveilling her location. Most people didn't know what to look for, but she did. They were small and easy to miss, but she'd been expecting them.

Kay gestured for Lauren to sit between her and Miles.

She eyed Lauren for a moment. "How do you do that?"

Lauren frowned. "Do what?"

"You walk into this room with a grace I wouldn't have on my best day. You have a commanding presence. Do you know that?"

Lauren felt a little embarrassed.

"What do you think, Miles?"

Miles blinked and quickly recovered. "It's going to take more than that to win this case."

Kay rolled her eyes and sighed. Then she leaned toward Lauren. "Sometimes he's a little uptight. Anyway," she said, moving on to the next thing on her considerable mental list, "you're prepared for this, Lauren. We've gone over everything. But it doesn't matter what I think; it only matters what I can prove and the holes I can poke in the prosecution's case. All that aside, how do you feel?"

Lauren considered for a few moments. "Like there are a few million people watching me." She wasn't sure how this trial would be perceived by the public or the jurors that had been selected.

Kay smiled. "You're not wrong about that. And it's actually —" she stopped speaking when an officer of the court stood up.

"All rise for the honorable Judge Alexander Stone."

Lauren stood, as did everyone else in the courtroom. Conversations stopped.

Alexander Stone strode into the room as if he'd done this many times. He was an imposing man—tall, broad-shouldered, and dark-skinned, with a strong face and a no-nonsense look in his eyes. His hairline receded to the top of his head, and his dark hair had more than a little gray in it.

He stepped up onto the elevated platform where his seat and desk were and sat down. The people sat in response.

Judge Stone brought up a holoscreen and glanced at it for a few seconds. Then he looked directly at Lauren for barely a second before starting.

Lauren had been advised as to how the trial would go, but she hadn't anticipated how convincing the prosecuting attorney,

Denton Lambert, could make his case. She tried not to look over at the jury as they listened to him make the case that Lauren had murdered an entire family. Kay had told her they might go for the accidental death charge, but that was not what happened. Lauren was being charged with murder, and as Denton Lambert gave his opening statements, Lauren felt as if everyone in the room was staring right at her, conviction and certain judgement in all of their gazes.

She watched as Denton Lambert turned his expressive, justice-seeking gray eyes toward the jury, promising them justice and punishment for Lauren's crime. It made her stomach clench, and she tried to be as stoic as possible. She was innocent, but could Kay and Miles convince the jury of that fact?

When Kay gave her opening statement, it was straight to the point, with a sprinkling of her sparkling personality peppering through. At one point, she saw Miles give a small nod of approval.

Lauren watched as the prosecution called up their expert witnesses to give testimony about her alleged crime. Watching the evidence being paraded in front of her and showing the murdered family made her throat constrict. She clenched her teeth and a few times had to look away, her eyes becoming misty. It felt like the murders were being thrust right into her face. What was irrefutable was that Lauren's experimental data and compounds had been used in the murders. Kay focused Lauren's defense on poking holes in how Lauren could've performed such an action.

The hours went by, and they had a recess for lunch. Isaac hadn't shown up, and Lauren was becoming agitated. She needed him there with her. She wanted him to stop what he was doing and be by her side. She knew he was trying to find a way to exonerate her, but she doubted he would find anything. If he hadn't by now, there was nothing for him to find.

When they returned to the courtroom, it would be Lauren's turn on the witness stand. She was expecting Kay to call her up, but she didn't.

"First witness is Mary Chang," Kay said.

Lauren frowned for a second, but then she finally recognized the name.

She turned as Mary Chang walked past and was sworn in. She sat in the chair and only glanced at Lauren for a brief moment.

"Mrs. Chang, do you recognize my client?"

"Yes, that's Doctor Lauren Gates. I met her in General Holding."

"Could you describe that first meeting?"

"I had no idea who she was. She was helping a man named Jankle. I tried to warn her away from him. He sometimes lashes out and he has challenges of his own. But Dr. Gates wouldn't listen," Mary said and shook her head, looking at Lauren for a moment. "We spoke for a bit and then she was summoned away by the guards. Considering that she was with the colonials, I didn't expect to see her again after that."

Kay nodded encouragingly to her, but Denton voiced an objection.

"Your Honor," Kay said, "Mrs. Chang is a character witness."

Judge Stone nodded. "Overruled," he said and looked at Mary. "Please continue, Mrs. Chang."

"She came back and began talking with a lot of people—told them how she was a doctor and could help them with their health problems."

"How did people react to that?"

"Most were suspicious of her," Mary said and looked at the

jury. "Most of the people in the holding area were hybrids or somehow connected to hybrids."

"Objection. The witness is offering conjecture as to the legality of the other prisoners. She has no expertise in this matter," Denton Lambert said.

"Mrs. Chang is giving her opinion of the situation as she saw it."

"I'll allow it," Judge Stone said.

"But your honor. This is—"

"Overruled, Mr. Lambert," Judge Stone said with a warning tone in his voice.

Mary Chang stared at Denton Lambert for a second, then looked at Kay. "As I was saying, most people were suspicious, but Dr. Gates is an extremely stubborn woman. She helped a lot of people in the holding area, giving them advice on treatments, things to take up with the medical clinics when they got out."

There was a loud buzz coming from outside the windows, and Lauren looked up at them. More than a few people did as well.

Kay cleared her throat. "Just one final question, Mrs. Chang. Would you go to Dr. Gates for your medical issues?"

"Absolutely."

Kay smiled. "Thank you," she said and looked at Denton. "Your witness."

Denton stood up. "Mrs. Chang, what were you being held for?"

"I was brought in for questioning."

"About what, specifically?"

"I was in the vicinity of a rally near the spacer ambassador offices, where they've been spreading lies about hybrids throughout the city."

"Don't you mean protestor?"

Mary grinned a little. "We still have the right to assembly. Besides, I was released, and no charges were filed against me. If you ask me, it was a waste of time, but it was also used as a tactic to intimidate us."

Denton smiled and looked at Judge Stone. "Your honor, I'd like that last stricken from the record."

Judge Stone nodded. "Sustained," he said and looked at Mary Chang. "Thank you. Please show her out."

Lauren watched as Kay brought up another three witnesses, all of whom had been in custody with her, and then brought another resident from the city.

"Objection," Denton Lambert said.

"We haven't even started yet," Kay replied, and several of the jurors chuckled.

Denton looked at Judge Stone.

"Counselors, approach the bench."

Lauren watched them walk up. Kay was such a short woman that Denton was over a foot taller than she was. Lauren used her implants to increase her auditory sensitivity. No alarms had been raised, and she wondered whether they could be detected.

"How many of these character witnesses are we to listen to?" Denton asked.

"As many as it takes for the jury to understand that my client isn't guilty of the crime of which she's being accused."

"This is a waste of time," Denton said.

"No, it's not. Dr. Gates has had a profound impact on not only the community here but everywhere she goes. The testimonies are the same."

The buzz outside the windows increased, and with her increased hearing she finally figured out what it was. There were people outside the courthouse, and it sounded like thousands of them.

"Do you hear that?" Kay said, gesturing toward the window. "There are tens of thousands of people out there to support Dr. Gates. All of them will say that she is incapable of murder."

Lauren watched as Judge Stone regarded them both for a moment and then sent them back.

He turned toward the jury. "It has been brought to my attention that the defense has an extensive list of people offering to be a character witness for Dr. Gates. However, after the first three witnesses, it is my ruling that unless there is something new to be learned or revealed, we do not need to hear from any more of them."

"Understood, Your Honor," Kay said. She made a show of checking her holoscreen while glancing behind her for a fraction of a second. Then she turned back to her screen.

Denton stared at her with a smirk.

"Next witness," Judge Stone said.

Kay stood, looking apologetic.

Denton cleared his throat. "What's the problem here? Your Honor?"

Judge Stone arched a thick eyebrow. "Call your next witness, Counselor."

"Your Honor," Kay began and the door to the courtroom opened. Kay spun toward it and smiled. "Yes, Your Honor. The Defense calls Isaac Diaz."

Lauren's eyes widened, and she turned to see Isaac striding toward the divider.

One of Denton's colleagues whispered something to him, and he nodded.

"Objection, Your Honor. Isaac Diaz is the accused's fiancé, and as such, not exactly an unbiased witness."

Judge Stone's gaze swooped toward Kay.

"Yes, Your Honor, this is true. However, Isaac Diaz is my

expert witness with a unique background that will lend considerable credence to the defense."

Judge Stone looked at Isaac for a long moment. "What is his background?"

"He's a medical doctor, but he's also an investigator for the Colonial Intelligence Bureau. I have his dossier here for review."

"Send it," Judge Stone said.

Both Judge Stone and Denton reviewed what Kay had sent them.

Judge Stone looked at Isaac. "Dr. Diaz, it seems that you're a man of many talents."

"I am, Your Honor."

"How are we to trust your testimony?"

"Your honor, I've been a CIB Agent for over a decade and have worked criminal cases for scenarios that are broad afield, usually beyond what local law enforcement is capable of investigating. What Ms. Garrick is doing with me is consolidating two expert witnesses into one." Isaac's gaze slid toward Denton and his team. "I was under the impression that there is a need to move the trial along to its fair and just conclusion, Your Honor."

Judge Stone regarded Isaac for a few moments. Lauren thought he could make a boulder give away all its secrets if he kept staring at it. "I will allow this witness."

"Your Honor," Denton said. "We'd like to bring in our expert witness to refute the testimony that will be given."

"That is your right, Counselor," Judge Stone said.

"Your Honor," Kay said. "I would like to add that Dr. Diaz consulted with Captain Mitchel from New Hope Security. I'm prepared to call him up after this witness."

Lauren saw the slightest of twitches on the edges of Judge Stone's lips as he nodded.

"Understood and noted, Counselor."

Kay looked at Isaac. "Do you prefer to be called Dr. Diaz or Agent Diaz?"

"Dr. Diaz seems the most appropriate."

Kay nodded. "Very well, Dr. Diaz. You've conducted your own investigation into these murders. Would you please share your findings?"

"Thank you. During my investigation, I noticed that the lab security records had been sabotaged within a twelve-hour window from when the accused is thought to have committed the crime."

"Twelve hours. What happened after that?"

"The security protocols began recording as normal, which indicates that the system itself had been compromised using sophisticated time exploitation that was scheduled beforehand. However, the exploitation worked in such a way as to erase its footprint from the system," Isaac said and turned toward the jurors. "This isn't unheard of with security breaches. The evidence that couldn't be altered was the lack of logs for the period during which the system itself recorded these events as an error. I have pulled this data for you to review."

A large holoscreen came on, displaying multiple sub-windows showing what Isaac had found. Kay asked Isaac to take them through the evidence, which he did.

Kay looked at the jurors. "So, we have evidence of a security breach in the lab where my client was known to do her research." She turned to Isaac. "What else did your investigation reveal?"

"The security breach shows that anyone could've accessed the lab and all the research stored there. I reviewed the medical examiner's records for the victims. The compounds Dr. Gates was testing for her hybrid research proposal were found in all of them, but they'd been altered."

"Objection, Your Honor. We've presented the medical examiner's records, and the compounds are the same."

"Your honor, Dr. Diaz has access to more sophisticated technology for this kind of analysis and has performed his own testing with the cooperation of the medical examiner's office."

Judge Stone frowned and looked at Isaac for a moment, then looked at Denton. "I'll allow this line of questioning. I want to know what was found."

Denton seemed to deflate as he sat.

"Thank you, Your Honor," Kay replied. "Please continue, Dr. Diaz."

"First, it should be clear that Dr. Gates was researching the extent of Vemus hybridization in humans, measuring its influence as it exhibits a wide range of symptoms to include those of remarkable capabilities."

"What was the extent of your involvement in this research?" Kay asked.

"I helped her. We work closely together, so I'm very familiar with what she was doing. She was working on a peer review proposal so other experts could validate her findings. This included reversing hybridization altogether, which I know is a controversial subject."

"Yes, that has been making the rounds in town halls and in recent demonstrations. Please continue."

"The compounds used on the victims contain the same compounds taken from Dr. Gates's lab storage kit. However, there were also additional compounds that, when combined, poisoned the victims. The CDF has encountered this before and has found records for its use on Magnus Station."

Many of the jurors looked at one another, and there was a sweep of hushed conversations across the courtroom.

"I have records of this as well, and they're part of what I provided to you. These are well documented and authentic."

The holoscreen updated with the new data.

"Why wouldn't the medical examiner here in New Hope be able to detect this during his analysis?" Kay asked.

"They don't know what they're looking for and it's designed to evade detection. It's likely that the relationship among hybrids and humans on Earth is more harmonious than it was proven to be on Magnus Station."

Lauren knew all too well what the political elite from Magnus Station had done to hybrids and to anyone who didn't fit their ideals for citizenship. Some were exiled off station, but many were coerced into a plot to breach the Earth's quarantine zone. And this was before an all-out attack on hybrids that Magnus Station Security knew lived in remote stations throughout the star system. The attempted genocide almost worked but for the heroic efforts of the CDF and Ethan in particular. She wondered where her brother was. She hadn't seen him. He'd never come to visit her while she'd been captive, which was strange.

"Thank you, Dr. Diaz," Kay said and looked at Denton. "Your witness."

Denton stood and looked at Isaac for a few moments. "No questions."

Isaac stepped down and winked at Lauren as he walked past her, then took the open seat next to her parents.

Lauren glanced at Denton, wondering why he hadn't seized the opportunity to question Isaac. She then glanced at Kay and thought she was wondering the same thing.

"Next witness, Counselor," Judge Stone said.

Kay nodded. "Yes, my next witness is Dr. Lauren Gates."

Lauren stood and walked to the witness stand. Miles had

advised against this, and even Kay expressed some doubts, but Lauren wanted to do it. She knew the prosecution would seize the opportunity to assert their case against her.

She was sworn in and then sat down.

"Dr. Gates, what was the nature of your relationship with the victims?"

"They came to the clinic, the mobile clinic. They were concerned about going to the hospital in their district because of the anti-hybrid demonstrations going on. They were such a nice family. Tally, their daughter, was eight years old, and their son, Alex Jr. was ten and a half," she said with a sad smile. "Alex Sr. and Nora were concerned about the recent symptoms presenting in both their children. I examined them and found that their symptoms were similar to what I've seen in other children with hybrid parents." She looked at the jurors, some she suspected were hybrids. "Vemus hybridization presents itself in the form of accelerated adaptations that can occur suddenly. It can put a very difficult strain on the person. Sometimes the strain is too much, and the risk of death becomes probable."

"That must've been hard for the family to hear."

"It is. Doesn't matter who it is. Parents love their children and never want to see them in pain. Treatment options are somewhat limited, given what is currently available. I recommended a treatment of medical nanites with protocols that would essentially train the adaptation to lessen its onset. This, coupled with behavioral focus-type practices, can help reduce the pain associated with the symptoms. I also informed them of the research I was doing and wanted permission to contact them in the future."

"How did they react to that?"

"It's experimental, so caution is always advisable. I informed them of the status of my research initiative and how it was to undergo peer review. I'd wanted to bring them back in for a consultation, especially with the persistent symptoms in Tally and Alex."

"What is the success rate of your recommended treatment for them?"

Lauren considered for a second. "It's in the thirty- to forty-percent range of success in reducing the symptoms, but that's based on a small data set of just a few hundred patients."

"And the research you were doing, assuming that the peer review confirms your findings, what would the success rate of that be, also assuming it was the appropriate treatment?"

"I'm glad you asked it like that. I can't assign a value to the range. At this point, it would be irresponsible of me to do that. My hope is that reversing hybridization or significantly reducing its effects is a real possibility."

Kay nodded and glanced at the jurors for a moment. "And controversial."

"Yes, there are significant concerns that should my research be successful, it would be forced on hybrids. That is not my intent, and the risks of that ever happening are quite low."

"Thank you, Dr. Gates," Kay said and returned to her seat.

Denton stood up. "You're obviously very dedicated to helping others. Would that be an accurate statement?"

"Yes."

"It has been noted that your brother has recently been forced to become a hybrid. This was over four months ago."

"Ethan was dying, and him becoming a hybrid was the only thing that saved him."

"But it was against his will. So, it was forced on him."

Lauren sniffed. "Mr. Lambert, my brother is one of my patients, which was his request. Trust me that he has made his peace with becoming a hybrid."

"All right," Denton said and pursed his lips for a moment. "We have several statements of conversations overheard where you've stated your concerns about your brother being a hybrid and the risk he was in because of it."

"Objection," Kay said. "This line of questioning has nothing to do with the crime of which my client has been accused."

"Your Honor, I'm establishing a precedent for motivation."

Judge Stone considered for a moment. "Overruled."

Kay looked disappointed as she sat.

"Dr. Gates. Would you please answer the question?"

"You're asking me whether I'm concerned for my brother because he's now a hybrid? Yes, I am concerned. He's my brother and I worry about him."

"So concerned that you'd force your experiments on an unsuspecting family to speed up the availability of your solution to the hybrid problem."

"Absolutely not! I would never compromise my ethics by doing that to anyone."

Denton arched an eyebrow. "Really? Not even to save your brother's life."

Lauren leveled her gaze at the man. "Never."

"The conversations in these depositions state—"

"That I love my brother. That what I've seen with how hybridization affects a person, especially at the early onset, which includes him, is cause for concern. But I would never compromise the safety of any patient in my care."

Kay stood up. "Your Honor, I object to this whole line of questioning. The prosecution is attempting to defame my client, and it's failing. On top of that, the defense has already established Dr. Gates's character. There are tens of thousands of people here to support her. In light of the evidence presented to the court that widens the window in which anyone could've accessed Dr. Gates's lab equipment and its contents, anyone could've stolen those compounds. That, along with the experimental compounds in combination with the known method of executing people of whom the Magnus Station's elite disapproves, the evidence points to an actual conspiracy for the murder of the victims that my client has zero connection with."

Denton's eyes widened and he turned toward the judge. "This is ridiculous. Your Honor, we've presented more than enough evidence to convict Dr. Gates. Shouldn't the jury weigh in on the evidence presented?"

Judge Stone was quiet for a long moment while he considered his response. He then shook his head. "Objection sustained. Sit down, Mr. Lambert."

Denton looked as if he was going to protest but thought better of it.

Judge Stone looked at Lauren. "You may return to your seat, Dr. Gates."

Judge Stone then ordered a thirty-minute recess while he considered the request to dismiss the case.

Lauren looked at Kay. "What's happening?"

Kay shared a knowing look with Miles and smiled at Lauren. "Something wonderful."

"Will he dismiss the case?"

"We've got a good shot at it."

"But what about the jury?" Lauren asked.

"Getting the case dismissed is better than allowing the jury to render a ruling," Miles said.

"He's right, Lauren. Your fiancé dropped a hell of a bombshell on the case against you."

Lauren frowned for a moment. "But what about the victims? What about justice for them?"

Kay reached out and placed her hand on Lauren's. "Another

time, Lauren. It's beyond the scope of this case. This is about proving *your* innocence."

Lauren thought about that. She wanted the people responsible for this caught as much as she wanted to prove her innocence. All Isaac's testimony did was point to a huge gap in security, putting the case against her in doubt. Doubt didn't mean she'd been entirely proven innocent. Someone had used her research to commit murder. One could believe that this didn't necessarily mean she didn't do it, but that there were other people who could've done it. This also assumed she didn't have the skills or the access to compromise the lab's security system, but Isaac did. Would this hunt expose him?

Lauren looked at Kay. "Could they try to pin this on Isaac?"

She frowned in thought for a few seconds. "They would need more evidence to leverage against him, and that's something they're lacking for *anyone* accused of this crime," she said and paused for a moment. "Plus, there's the political profile of this case."

"Because of the impact it would have on my parents and the envoy's mission."

Kay tipped her head to the side. "This is outside my area of expertise."

Miles rolled his head. "Please, don't pretend to be humble now."

"If I were to place a wager on it, I'd have to agree with you. However, my first priority is to ensure that you're not found guilty of a crime you didn't commit."

Judge Stone returned to the courtroom. He turned to the jury and then looked at Lauren. "Cases like these don't come along often. In my two decades of experience, I've never had to preside over one. However, we do keep extensive records so there is precedence that I can lean on to make a decision. It is my hope that cases like these and the implications they bring are not the start of a new trend. The implications are quite alarming." He paused for a moment. "Dr. Gates, I find that the prosecution has failed to make a compelling case against you. Based on the substantial evidence provided in your defense, it would be negligent on my part to allow this case to move forward. On a personal note, it is my heartfelt desire to implore you to keep doing the work you're doing. We need more doctors like you caring for us and trying to improve things. On top of that, we need people like you who have the courage to take on these highly controversial undertakings for the sake of giving people the option to improve their lives, even if your work could be used by others toward their own questionable agenda. Jurors, you are dismissed. This case is dismissed."

The courtroom erupted into hundreds of conversations all at once, but Lauren couldn't pay attention to any of that. Her throat became thick, and her eyes tightened. She felt as if a huge weight had been lifted off her shoulders, but her heart ached for the victims and the lack of justice for them. Isaac leaped over the divider and hugged her fiercely. She held on to him so tightly that it surprised even her.

"I've got you," he whispered.

She couldn't bring herself to speak, but there was so much she wanted to say.

"Let's get out of here," he said.

She nodded. She was free to go.

"We have transport waiting out the side entrance," her father said.

Lauren frowned, glancing at the others. Kay watched her intently.

Lauren shook her head. "No, I'm not going out that way. I'm going out through the main entrance."

Isaac raised his eyebrows. "There's a lot of people out there."

"I know," Lauren said and began walking.

The others followed her, and Kay walked next to her. She heard her father order his protective detail to lead the way, but he insisted on making her wait a few minutes while they assessed the main entrance to the courthouse.

Kay smiled at her.

Lauren returned the smile. "Thank you so much for all your help."

"Thanks for trusting me to help you," she said and gave Miles an appraising look. "Even if I had to endure Mr. Duncan."

Miles grinned. "Couldn't have been so bad. You did accept my invitation to dinner."

Kay grinned and rolled her eyes a little. "Yeah, well, what can I say? You tick a lot of boxes."

The CDF security detail returned and gave the all-clear.

Lauren walked out the doors first and stopped at the top of the wide staircase. Thousands of people waited outside. They began to cheer when they saw her.

She wanted to speak to them and spotted someone with the local news association. "Can they hear me if I used your setup?"

He blinked for a second, surprised that he was even being spoken to. He nodded and handed her a microphone.

Lauren took it and waited for him to give her the go-ahead before beginning to speak.

"Hello, I'm Dr. Lauren Gates. I think I recognize some of you." She paused while they cheered. "Thank you so much for coming here and showing your support. Since I'm standing here, it's safe to say that the case against me has been dismissed."

More cheering. She waited for it to subside before continuing. "This news is bittersweet for me. While I'm happy not to be found guilty of a crime I didn't commit, the real perpetrators are still out there. Alex Sr., Nora, Tally, and Alex Jr. deserve justice. I will be sharing the details of the case in the hope that someone will step forward to assist New Hope Security with finding the real perpetrators. This is a terrible ordeal, but I get to go home tonight. Today, I'm the lucky one, but my heart weeps for the family that was murdered. And murdered for what? To create divisions among us? To seize power? My work is controversial, but so is all important work. Life is going to change for us all, and that bothers some people. I can't control that, but what I can do is propose some solutions. The world that was is gone and it's time for us to move forward. We can no longer be divided, with each city standing apart. It was necessary before but not any longer. The alliance with the New Earth Colony isn't going anywhere. This is why I urge the ratification of the Earth Alliance, which is more of a necessity now. However, I want to move forward with my research by selecting members of a governance committee with representatives across the spectrums. The key here is to get consensus and address concerns. This will allow us to have an open line of communication, which will prevent the misinformation that's currently being fed to you from gaining the traction that it has. All my research initiatives concerning hybrids will be made public, as well as my goals for it. I have nothing to hide. But I do have a message for those responsible. You should do the right thing and turn yourselves in because I have it on good authority that your crimes will not be kept secret. All of you will be brought to justice. I just pray that it's before anyone else gets hurt."

Lauren handed the microphone back to the news representative. Screaming cheers followed Lauren as she walked toward the CDF escort vehicles waiting for her.

She climbed inside, followed by the others.

Kay grinned at her. "I have to admit I didn't see that coming. You were on fire. Are you sure you're not going to run for some kind of office?"

Lauren shook her head. "No, I have plenty of work to do without adding that to it."

"How long have you been planning on talking to the people out there?" Kay asked.

Her father snorted, and she looked at him. He smiled at her, then looked at Kay. "She spoke from the heart."

Kay's eyes widened. "Seriously? That wasn't prepared at all?"

Lauren shook her head. "It needed to be said, and I wanted to deliver a powerful message to the people who are really responsible for this."

"You did good," her father said.

"You did amazing," Kay said. "I've never seen a judge react that way. I think you've made a fan of him."

Isaac held her hand, and she looked at him. "So, no time off now?"

Lauren shook her head and Isaac gave her a pained expression. "Oh, all right, maybe a day or two at the most, but that's it."

"I'll take it!"

29

AFTER THE DESTRUCTION of the Vemus probe, Ethan insisted that the CDF be brought in to salvage what was left of the facility. They needed support, and some of them needed medical attention. A team was dispatched, and they'd set up a temporary quarantine to examine everyone who'd been exposed to the probe. None of them were in any danger. Salvage of the site was ongoing, and Ethan and the others were brought to the city of New Hope. Clip and Cynergy were asked to participate in a debrief session, while Ethan and the other CDF soldiers had no choice. They were in an old warehouse that the CDF had converted into a temporary work area.

Jared Andrews, and the rest of the squad were escorted from the lounge area, leaving Ethan, Cynergy, and Clip.

Clip eyed Ethan. "I'm surprised they didn't make you go with the others."

He shrugged. "They're not going to forget about me."

"What's going to happen to them?" Cynergy asked.

"I'm not sure. Their actions will be reviewed by their

superiors, which will be kicked up the chain for a full investigation. They will be held accountable for their actions."

"They tried to kill us."

"They did. Their reasons were obviously flawed, but given the data that was uncovered about the Vemus probe, they might be given some leniency. I don't know."

Cynergy blew out a breath. "Leniency? Are you serious?"

"What do you want to see happen to them? They've experienced loss like you have, and they're under tremendous pressure like all of us are. I'm not condoning what they did, but we're not in a position to render judgement."

Cynergy contemplated Ethan's words, and after a few moments Clip cleared his throat. "I think Ethan is right to trust his superiors. Overall, the CDF has been more than fair in their dealings with all of us. I trust that this will not be any different."

She nodded a little. "I guess we'll see. I don't know what the appropriate response would be, but it should be more than a mere slap on the wrists."

"Agreed," Ethan replied.

A soldier came into the lounge, and Ethan thought he was being collected for his debrief session, but instead he was taken to a medical examination area.

Ethan waited there for a few minutes and a doctor arrived.

"Lieutenant Gates, I'm Major Phillip Watters. I've been asked to review your medical history."

He was a few inches shorter than Ethan and had a bit of a paunch near his middle. His graying beard was neatly trimmed, and his head looked recently shaved.

"I've already been cleared, Major Watters."

The major arched an eyebrow, and his aged brown eyes held the aura of experience and surety that he already knew how this conversation was going to go.

"You've stopped your biochip from reporting in. You were sent here for re-examination based on your unique condition. Is this correct?"

"I *was* sent back for re-evaluation, and I *did* stop my biochip from reporting in."

"Well then, I'd like you to grant me access."

Ethan regarded him for a long moment. "No."

Major Watters blinked. "What?"

"I said, no, sir."

"So, you will not cooperate?"

"I didn't say that, sir. I said I'm no longer going to transfer the data from my biochip. I pose no danger to myself or anyone else; therefore, it is within my right to renege on this requirement. I can quote you the regulation that grants me this right if you want me to."

Major Watters' lips pursed thoughtfully for a moment, and then he sighed. "You're leaving me with very little choice but to note this in my report, and the likelihood of you returning to duty will be virtually nonexistent."

Ethan knew that taking this stand could mean being discharged from the CDF, but he'd made up his mind. He'd live with whatever the consequences of his actions were going to be.

"You do what you need to do, sir. I'm not going to change my mind about this."

"Very well," Major Watters said and left the exam room.

Ethan sat there alone for almost twenty minutes before someone came and brought him to an empty office where he was told to wait. He'd assumed his debriefing would begin, but instead he took a seat and waited. Hurry up and wait seemed to be the theme of the day.

He soon became restless, sitting around, and stood. He walked over to the window and peered outside, watching as several troop carrier transport ships departed. There were soldiers going about their days, performing their assigned tasks. It reminded him of his days with the 7th A-Wing. He'd spent a lot of time on the hangar deck and in the cockpit, both flying missions and leading others.

The door to the office opened and the last person he expected to see walked in.

Ethan straightened and saluted his father.

"At ease, Lieutenant," his father said and closed the door.

Ethan relaxed his stance and waited for his father to speak. There were military protocols that must be observed, and right now he was addressing the second most powerful man in all the CDF.

His father regarded him for a long moment. "You don't make things easy on yourself, do you?"

"I was taught that important things are rarely easy, sir."

His father chuckled as he blew out a breath. "Major Watters just informed me of your reluctance to cooperate with your eval."

"I've been cooperative," Ethan began to say and then paused for a moment. "Permission to speak freely, sir?"

His father's gaze narrowed a little. "Ethan, it's just us here. I know this can be complicated, but I want to hear it from you straight."

Ethan relaxed a little. "No amount of time is going to change what's on my biochip. I'm a hybrid and that's never going to change, no matter how much data they gather."

"I see, so the question is, what happens now?"

Ethan sighed. "I'm never going back to the 7th, am I?"

"Is that what you really want?"

Ethan blinked and considered it. "I thought I did, but things have changed. I really don't know what would be best— trying to go back to the way things were before or pushing for something new in the CDF—but maybe it's time for me to move on."

His father's eyebrows rose a little, which was tantamount to a display of shock from a man who had seen so much in his life. "I know what you've been doing…what we've both been doing."

Ethan frowned. "I'm not sure what you mean."

His father gave him a knowing smile. "Sure you do. This thing we've been doing ever since you joined the CDF. I don't like that we've allowed it to form a wedge between us, son."

"I don't want any special treatment, and I didn't want to put you in any position that could be used against you."

His father smiled. "Ethan, I've been at this for a very long time. Someone is always going to find a way to twist things if they're determined to do so. I appreciate that you're trying to protect me, I really do, but it's not necessary. My expectation of you as a soldier is to act with the professionalism commensurate with your rank. I don't give special treatment to anyone. You could even say that my reputation regarding this is quite notorious."

Ethan pressed his lips together. "Maybe it's my own temptation that I'm struggling with then. It's unspoken by other soldiers, but it's there. The implication I mean. I've learned to deal with it, and I stand by my record."

"That's exactly as it should be." His father regarded him for a moment. "What will stop, is this wedge between us. Your mother is caught in the middle, and that's not fair to her. I'm your father. You should always be able to come to me for guidance, especially with matters of the CDF. You've never abused our relationship, and you never will. It's not in you, and none of your commanding officers ever had anything remotely like that in their evaluations of you."

Ethan had wondered about that. Some of them had hinted

that they thought he was leaning on the family name, which entitled him to some kind of privilege.

"All right, Dad. I won't hold back from you anymore."

"Good."

"So, do you want to hear about it?"

He arched an eyebrow. "About what, exactly?"

"The Vemus Space Probe. Earth was attacked. Someone sent that probe here for a purpose."

"I've read your preliminary debrief about what happened. I've also been apprised of what happened leading up to it."

"So, what happens now?"

"The probe was believed to have arrived hundreds of years before it ever became active. According to the records you recovered, the scientists believe it used that time to evaluate the Earth before releasing what we know as the Vemus contagion. Then it changed hands as different alliances tried to control and manipulate it."

The probe was gone and, with it, anything they could've learned from it.

"I had to destroy it. The containment field was failing, and it was being used to create hybrids. I was worried that the containment field failure would've kicked off another Vemus uprising."

His father nodded. "It's never easy, and there will be no shortage of people questioning the decisions made after the fact. For the record, I think you did the right thing."

"I wish I could've found a way to preserve the probe so we could learn more about it. Maybe it would've given us information about who sent it."

Connor shrugged. "We'll never know for sure, but we know a lot more than we did before, and that's thanks to you."

"It was more than just me."

"I know that, but you were the driver. You were the one who pushed for this. It's obvious to us that you tried to go through proper channels and met with some resistance."

"You mean the research base on Mars?"

His father nodded. "We already knew that the Syndicate was experimenting with controlling the Vemus."

Ethan had been frustrated when the mining facility and the surrounding area was destroyed, but the data he'd managed to get from it led to him finding the probe.

"So now we come back to the beginning. What is it you want to do? Either in the CDF or beyond?"

Ethan had so many questions. Should he leave the CDF? How would his father react to that? Would it hurt him? Was leaving the CDF what he wanted?

His father cleared his throat. "I'm open to suggestions, so don't just tell me what you think I want to hear."

"Couple of things, really. I was thinking that a joint cooperative task force should be created that includes the CDF and hybrids, and probably the new Earth Alliance I keep hearing about, but definitely hybrids—you know, similar to what was done to bring the Ovarrow into the colony."

"What else?"

"We should search for the source of the Vemus. Earth was attacked."

"How do you suggest we go about searching for them?"

Ethan looked away for a moment as he thought about it. "We start exploring more but be systematic about it. I feel like we're still vulnerable."

"We always will be to one degree or another. All we can do is mitigate the risk as best we can."

Ethan nodded. "And that should include getting back out there and exploring other star systems. If a probe was sent here, perhaps more were sent elsewhere as well. What worries me is whether someone will come to check on the probe they sent here." Ethan paused and regarded his father for a second. "This must've been what it was like when you were searching for the Krake."

His father nodded. "It's similar, but I have a question for you. Do you think you can accomplish everything you just proposed by staying in the 7th?"

Ethan shook his head, finally admitting to himself that he no longer belonged with the elite space fighter attack wing. "No."

His father smiled in approval. "I'm glad you can see that. You've demonstrated exceptional leadership skills, and I couldn't be prouder of you. I also think you're ready for what comes next."

Ethan frowned. "What do you mean?"

"Well, a promotion to captain for one. You'll need the rank for the new task force you're going to put together."

His eyes widened. "Me?"

He'd only been making suggestions and had never considered that his father would put him on the spot like that.

"Who else could it be? Who else is better suited? You're a hybrid, and no matter what happens, you insist that you'll remain a hybrid."

"I know I said that. I think it's what's needed to find the Vemus. I think it'll take all of us, including the Ovarrow."

"And that's exactly the attitude that's needed," his father replied. "I've also spoken with Clip about it."

Ethan smiled. "What did he say?"

"He told me that your talents shouldn't be wasted. So, what do you think?"

Ethan eyed his father. "Do I get to pick my own team?"

"Of course. They'll be subject to approval. I'm not just going to turn you loose. We'll start out small, maybe a couple of platoons to start with and expand from there."

Ethan blinked. "A couple of platoons to start?"

"Yes, try to keep up. This task force will be a mobile unit, which will require a wide range of skillsets. You'll need some time for training, and eventually you'll be put into the rotation."

"Rotation?"

"Yes, there might be more sites to investigate like the one you found on Mars. I'm going to send them all to you. Break time is over, son."

Ethan's thoughts raced. This was all coming so fast, and for a moment he felt overwhelmed. Then he took firm control of his thoughts.

"Good, no need to reinvent the wheel. I just don't want sites destroyed out of turn, at least until we've had time to learn what we can," Ethan said and frowned. "This is going to take more than just one task force."

His father gave him a lopsided smile. "You bet it will, but this is how it starts. It's how the CDF was started."

"I'm not trying to form a new military."

"No, just the next step. There are things that are going to change, and the role of the CDF is among them."

Ethan frowned. "What do you mean?"

"Something Nathan mentioned to me about the creation of an exploratory division among the CDF, but with the Earth Alliance, we'll need to expand that to something more like what you're proposing, which is a joint task force. Don't need all the details, but this is the groundwork." His father paused and arched an eyebrow. "It's a good foundation on which to build a career."

Ethan inhaled a deep breath and chuckled.

His father smiled. "You didn't really think you were going to walk away from the CDF?"

"I don't know what to say."

"Well then, allow me to say it. Keep following your instincts. They're good. Push the limits and be methodical at the same time. This is just another step in a long line of many people who came before you."

Ethan had been feeling a little lost before, but he didn't feel like that anymore. "Who will I be reporting to?"

"You'll be within my purview."

Ethan started to question that but stopped.

"We're a small military, and as long as that is the case, there will be overlap. Do you have any concerns about that, Captain Gates?"

"Negative, General Gates."

"Good, now let's get out of here. Time to shake things up."

His father went to the door and Ethan hastened to follow, feeling that maybe he wasn't the only one who'd been feeling restless lately.

AUTHOR NOTE

Thank you so much for reading. *Fallen Earth* is the 15th book in the First Colony series. This series has been home to my imagination for a long time. Helping me to stay motivated to write these stories has been the enthusiasm of the readers who've reached out to me and the people who took the time to review my books. I sincerely hope you enjoyed this latest book in the First Colony series. Almost inevitably, I get the question about whether this will be the last book in the First Colony series. No, it won't. I think there are a lot more stories to tell in this series and more characters to explore.

One of the things I've enjoyed about writing this series is that it allows me to imagine a future with hope. There are hardships as well, but I like writing stories that contain glimmers of hope even when things are bleak.

One of the questions I often get asked is whether I'd planned out the entire series, which at this time is 15 books long. No, I didn't. This series was developed in chunks, based on ideas that

I've had and reader reactions to the story. It's been a great ride, and I look forward to writing more in this series.

I hope you enjoyed getting to know Ethan and Lauren, and the continued appearance of the enduring characters in the series. I couldn't wait for Connor's children to grow up and take their place among the cast of characters, making their contribution to this series.

I continue to write stories in the First Colony series because I enjoy it and because people keep reading the books. The best way for me to gauge whether people want more First Colony stories is by people reading the books and perhaps leaving a review, or recommending it to a friend or a group. Word of mouth is crucial. I take a lot of pride in my work because I think the quality of the story matters, as well as your experience reading it.

Thanks again for reading my books. Please consider leaving a review for *Fallen Earth*.

If you're looking for another series to read consider reading the Federation Chronicles. Learn more by visiting:

https://kenlozito.com/federation-chronicles/

ABOUT THE AUTHOR

I've written multiple science fiction and fantasy series. Books have been my way to escape everyday life since I was a teenager to my current ripe old(?) age. What started out as a love of stories has turned into a full-blown passion for writing them.

Overall, I'm just a fan of really good stories regardless of genre. I love the heroic tales, redemption stories, the last stand, or just a good old fashion adventure. Those are the types of stories I like to write. Stories with rich and interesting characters and then I put them into dangerous and sometimes morally gray situations.

My ultimate intent for writing stories is to provide fun escapism for readers. I write stories that I would like to read, and I hope you enjoy them as well.

If you have questions or comments about any of my works I would love to hear from you, even if it's only to drop by to say hello at KenLozito.com

Thanks again for reading *First Colony - Fallen Earth*

Don't be shy about emails, I love getting them, and try to respond to everyone.

ALSO BY KEN LOZITO

FIRST COLONY SERIES

GENESIS

NEMESIS

LEGACY

SANCTUARY

DISCOVERY

EMERGENCE

VIGILANCE

FRACTURE

HARBINGER

INSURGENT

INVASION

IMPULSE

INFINITY

EXPEDITION EARTH

FALLEN EARTH

SPACE RAIDERS SERIES

SPACE RAIDERS

SPACE RAIDERS - FORGOTTEN EMPIRE

SPACE RAIDERS - DARK MENACE

FEDERATION CHRONICLES

Acheron Inheritance

Acheron Salvation

Acheron Redemption

Acheron Rising (Prequel Novella)

Ascension Series

Star Shroud

Star Divide

Star Alliance

Infinity's Edge

Rising Force

Ascension

Safanarion Order Series

Road to Shandara

Echoes of a Gloried Past

Amidst the Rising Shadows

Heir of Shandara

If you would like to be notified when my next book is released visit kenlozito.com

Made in the USA
Columbia, SC
07 January 2024

29979777R10212